CW01202770

Get Ted Dead

Ross Young

Sulk Media

Family

Contents

☠ <u>DEAD FOLK</u> ☠

Nothing flashed before his eyes when he slipped. Oblivion beckoned to him from the waters beneath and again, just like last time, and the time before, there was nothing in the split second before he nearly plummeted into its inky depths. He caught himself on all fours like an animal, scrabbling for purchase on the slippery surface at the top of the wall. "What are you holding on for?" He asked himself.

Not all dead people are evil bastards, some of them are just bastards, others are just dead. Augustan Blunt lurched towards evil like a man with too much alcohol and not enough good sense. Skirting the edges of rage ever closer to falling into darkness. Which, by coincidence, is exactly what he was doing as he stood up and walked along the top of a wall over a perilous precipice. In one hand he carried a bottle. Its contents were alcoholic, or whatever passes for alcohol amongst the dead. He knew that it wasn't alcohol in the mortal sense, but they used the same name for the sake of simplicity. The bottle had little remaining in it.

"Do this Blunt, investigate that Blunt, stop annoying everyone Blunt. Make your sodding minds up," he muttered to himself.

The wall was not a well-constructed barrier against the elements. It was more of a nod towards common sense. A courtesy offered to those who complained about health and safety. In Gloomwood, those who cared about such things were a vocal minority. Who cares about minor injury, or major, when you're already dead? The occasional stone would clatter down to the road a meter and a half below or tumble the other way where it would spin into an abyss. The churn of the waters below too furious for a mere rock to cause any kind of noticeable disruption.

He slipped and stumbled, catching himself with his hands and knees on the wall once more. His trousers ripped across one knee exposing his skin to the abrasive surface of the wall and he let out a storm of expletives before pulling himself into a sitting position facing out into the nothingness of the Styx seas. "Pretty," he said.

The waters below, if they were even waters, gave up their churn less than a hundred feet from the base of the wall. From there the waters appeared calm, a silk ocean of purple beneath the darker sky that disappeared into the horizon. "Horizon?" He said to nobody but himself, "no sun, no other land, not a horizon is it? Is the afterlife round?"

There was a cough from behind him and he turned. The movement was too quick, and he dropped the bottle as he caught his balance. The unlabeled green glass bottle bounced once on the road and then smashed. What dregs remained inside, vanishing in the puddles that filled potholes in the ground.

"Look what you did!" Blunt shouted at a shadowy figure.

"I-I'm sorry. Was it my fault? Oh, it was... everything is," the voice was mournful.

"Bleeding idiot. Now what am I going to drink?" Blunt said.

The figure came forward, stepping into the low glow that emanated from a streetlight. The pallid light it offered did little other than cause shadows from innocuous objects seem ominous and malevolent. "I have this," said a man dressed in a tweed suit with a homburg hat balanced upon his head at an awkward angle. He proffered a silver flask.

"Oh," Blunt said, "What is it?"

"Um, whiskey, I believe."

"Doesn't matter. Give it, apology accepted."

The man held it up to Blunt, who snatched it out of his hand and took a swig. It gave a reassuring burn as it hit his stomach. "Nice. Thanks," Blunt twisted the cap back on to the flask and handed it back considerably lighter than it had been a moment ago.

"Want some company?"

Blunt shook his head and released a belch. "No."

"Ah, yes, well, me neither."

"Great. Suppose you can hang around then."

"Actually. I was just wondering if you'd hold this for me." The man removed the hat and waved it in Blunt's direction.

Blunt took it with suspicion. "Why?"

"I won't need it. There's a note inside it to anyone who cares."

Blunt nodded. "You're going to jump?"

The man let out a sigh. "Yes. I think so."

"Oh well, this is just bloody typical."

"Oh, how so?"

"I was going to jump. Now you're here and it's bloody awkward."

"Ah... I see."

The silence dragged on.

The man let out a cough. "Well. I suppose you were here first-"

"-yeah but now you've given me your hat."

"Oh no, I couldn't possibly. I'll just walk up a little further."

Blunt looked up at the wall in the direction the man pointed. "What up there?"

The man followed Blunt's gaze. "It's as good a place as any."

"No, you can't jump from there. You'll get mugged before you jump in."

"Oh, that's fine. I have nothing of value on me."

"That's even worse. They'll just cut you up. Body parts are valuable, you know?"

The man nodded. "Yes... I suppose."

"And then you won't be able to jump because you'll have no sodding legs."

"Right."

They fell into a sullen silence once again. The man took a drink from his flask and then placed it back within his suit jacket before looking up and down the length of the wall. "It seems this is the ideal spot."

"I know," Blunt said scowling, "I've been planning this for a little while now. I'm not just some Johnny-come lately to the whole jumping into the Styx thing." He swung his feet over the top of the wall, so he was sitting facing towards the city. The urban sprawl at night did nothing to lift his spirits. It was a dark and foreboding mishmash of narrow alleyways and flickering lights. A blend of gas-lit streetlights and abrasive neon that refused to accept any kind of aesthetic link. The wind howled through those narrow streets of the dead, adding to the crescendo from the waves below. The corridors of the city were homes to the furtive, the threatening and the naïve, in equal measure.

"I had done little planning really," the man said, interrupting Blunt's brooding once more. He wore gloves and a scarf as if he had prepared for the elements. Blunt by comparison wore only his battered trench coat and a shirt that was missing the top button. It was cold.

"You dressed sensibly though," Blunt said, nodding his approval. "Suit like that means you won't be able to change your mind."

"Oh? Well, yes, I hadn't really thought of it."

"No? It's good for sinking. You should wear that. Tough to swim when you're weighed down with all of that wool, is it?"

"Ah, yes."

"Is wool expensive? I mean it's not really wool because there's no sheep but, whatever wool is, it must be expensive, right?"

"Oh, well, I suppose it is, yes. It's not new though."

"Well, it would be silly to jump in new clothes. Not like they're going to be able to get them back. Bit of a waste."

The man nodded. "Are you going to convince me not to jump?" He asked.

Blunt frowned. "Hadn't planned on it. Are you going to talk me out of it?"

"I... I'm not particularly good at that sort of thing. Can I ask why you're... um... is it... is it you know…"

"Suicide?" Blunt asked.

"Yes, is it?"

"Nah," Blunt waved a hand, "can't be, can it? I mean it's not murder, so it can't be suicide, probably call it self-Ableforth... no that doesn't work because it should be the opposite of Ableforth shouldn't it."

"Ableforth is just the death of a dead person, isn't it?"

Blunt let out a noise that sounded like he was trying to whistle, but he just sprayed saliva in the man's direction. "Death of a dead person. That's impossible, no it's so much worse."

"Worse?"

"Yeah, definitely. You can't kill someone who's dead already. You send them into nothingness, a void where they don't exist at all. Emptiness where not even the old Grim Reaper dares to go. Scary stuff."

The man nodded.

"That's where you want to go, is it?" Blunt asked.

"To a place of eternal emptiness? Well, it's got to be better than here, hasn't it?"

Blunt looked around once again at the city. In the distance he could make out the rectangular block, the tallest building in the city, the Office of the Dead. "I don't know. I just don't want to do it anymore."

"Yes. I'm the same. We could...we could jump together."

"What?"

The man looked down at his feet, embarrassed. "Sorry. I'm just quite nervous. I don't mean to."

"Yeah. You seem like a nice enough guy and all, but I think that might be a bit... weird. I mean we've just met."

"Yes. I suppose."

"Oh look," Blunt said with a sigh, "let's go get a drink and think about this. We can't do it now. I'm not jumping knowing that it will be on your conscience and I'm not having you jump so I can feel guilty about it. Tell you what. How about I promise not to be here next Wednesday, and you promise not to be here next Tuesday?"

"Oh, I have my support group next Wednesday. Can't miss that."

"No, suppose not. Well, you have Tuesday then."

"But people might hang around here after I jump."

"Well, this is a right bloody mess isn't it."

REAPERS

Janice 'Twist' Lenworth had stood in the aisle at her own funeral and found herself touched by the numbers that turned up to pay her their last respects, even if a large proportion of people were there because they wanted to make absolutely sure she was dead. Nobody paid her any notice because she was dead and dead people on the wrong side of the mortal veil don't draw much attention unless they're quite disturbed.

'In life,' whoever the man with the priest's collar was saying, 'Janice Lenworth was many things,' she'd laughed. She'd laughed so much that it had felt as though she'd been crying. She'd been many things but what choice was there. A grifter, a queen of the long con who had graduated to the big game after being a street urchin pick pocket. So well known by the long arm of the law that they'd grown fond of her. Like people get fond of the cat that only hangs around to tear up your furniture and eat your food. The walks of life who attended her funeral were not just disparate, they were from every stratum imaginable.

She was content, which was frustrating. A content spirit left floundering in the mortal realm can do nothing but wait and hope that one day something will change. Then they wait some more and, the dead who are calmer and more collected, realise something is amiss.

Her non-corporeal form gave her back her youth, though it was of no use to her. As she was dead, it was nothing more than an image in which her form was held. While she felt mostly corporeal, the living world appeared mist-like, as if everything was made of fog. It was nice though, for a while, not to feel the aches and pains of age. She found her mind as sharp as ever, a razor blade she had used to bend the perceptions of others for a lifetime. To shave at their confidence and trust until she had what she needed.

Then one day, some long time after she was dead, there came a figure. It wasn't the first she'd seen of the dead. Others had waved goodbye as they were escorted away by figures in black, surprised to see this vibrant woman watching wistfully as they complained they weren't ready to go yet. This time she had been waiting for the figure in black.

Standing by the bed of someone near death wasn't what she had wanted to do. Technically lingering around the spirit of another person waiting for them to die was what a ghoul would do, but Twist knew nothing about ghouls. Fortunately for her, they had little attraction to the dead, but to the nearly dead and the living, so they kept out of her way. All the wraiths, ghouls, ghosts, and other creatures on the wrong side of the veil avoided her as only the dead can truly harm the dead.

She had a plan. When the figure in the black gown arrived, with their hood shrouding their features, Twist stepped forward.

"It's time," the figure said.

"I see," Twist replied.

"You see what?" Barry Buck said. He had awoken to find two figures standing by his bed and was perturbed to find himself separated from his own body.

"Ah," the figure in black said, "this is awkward. I'm here for Barry Buck?"

"Yes, that's me," Twist answered quickly, "dead, am I?"

"What?" Said Barry Buck, "hang on, who's she? I'm Barry Buck, does she look like Barry Buck to you?"

"What?" Twist said, "Why do I look like this? Who are you? I just went to sleep. Never mind," she waved a hand, "weird dream, I guess. Come on Barry, wake up," she said to herself and then she carefully attempted to climb into the space where the now empty vessel, which had once held Barry Buck's soul, remained.

"Um, this is very irregular," the black figure said. "I'm afraid that you, um, or you maybe? Have died."

"I've what?" Barry Buck said from where he stood at the side of his own bed.

"I've what?" Twist said sitting bolt upright so that her lower half was within the body of Barry Buck.

The reaper, which is the name given to a person who collects souls, had never been in a situation like this one, but he had once become a reaper and this, or situations like it, is how reapers are born. It was how Janice 'Twist' Lenworth became a reaper because the easiest option for the figure in black was to take both Barry Bucks through the mortal realm and make it someone else's problem. This being a classic example of passing the buck.

Training of a reaper is a laborious process, but someone who is forgotten, missed, or slips between the cracks is a reaper with or without training. Without training, a reaper turns bad and a dark reaper does not bear consideration.

She trained, and she learned. Of the many things she learned, some of them were about why she, of all people, had ended up in this situation. Was it her life choices? The build-up of so many years of minor miseries heaped upon others for her own benefit. The time she had allowed a young orphan girl to take the blame for a crime she committed. Perhaps it was a reward for those she had helped. The donations she had made to those who needed it without ever saying where it came from. The women and children she had smuggled away from danger and the fury of otherwise impotent men thrust into the roles of father or husband they couldn't cope with? The men she had seen crushed beneath the heels of vindictive and selfish women who she had helped coax back into the world? No. It was none of those things.

They had abandoned Twist in the nothingness between worlds to exist as only a mild chill in the air because of timing. She had died on a busy day and because reapers work from handwritten lists, with sand timers and measurements from the stars and planets, by people who have been doing it too long, they make mistakes. The reapers called them happy mistakes. Without these mistakes there would be no reapers and with no reapers there would be nobody to guide lost souls to their correct destination, and there are many destinations including the ones the reapers should have gone to. There would be nobody to do the job except Him, and he was exhausted, and terribly busy.

Every reaper was a happy mistake. Which reaper was the first mistake it's impossible to tell, but everyone knows which reaper made the first mistake. His name is Grim, the Grim Reaper himself. Death may be infallible, but the Grim Reaper is not. His mistakes litter space and time like pinholes in the fabric of reality but, as with so many things, his mistakes are often his greatest work. Even if they're terrible, they still look pretty.

What a reaper does is collect time, saving it up one nanosecond after another. What they do with it is their choice. Most save it, working for age upon age, but time has no meaning to them when they can't use it, until one day they have enough to live, and, more importantly, die again. Twist had been saving for a long, long time.

TV DINNER

Power comes in many forms. As Crispin Neat stood in front of the microwave oven, in the modest house he owned in the suburbs of the city of Gloomwood, he depended on the little bell to tell him he could eat his food. The microwave bell held considerable power. In fact, at that moment in time, because it held Crispin Neat's attention as the dish of what we might call 'food' turned on its tiny little revolving dancefloor, it held almost immeasurable power. Though of course, as with all power, those obeying it have a will of their own, not that it is a will that is always put into practice.

Neat watched the food turn and, as any outsider would have declared he was statuesque in his patience, he fumed. A miscalculation has interrupted what had been close to the perfect day. One small misstep in an otherwise spectacularly mundane Wednesday. Hump day, some call it, not for Neat. Wednesday was a day of peak performance. Given any day of the week to live out for all eternity, he would choose Wednesday without hesitation. It lies at the zenith of the working week. While the rest of the working world sees it as the crest to their miserable nine-to-five wave Crispin Neat raced towards it, desperate to ride the wave of genuine unadulterated total and complete work mode saturation.

A miscalculation, and now he would have to rush. To change minute details to ensure the continued success of the day. He had removed his shoes without unlacing them, risking breaking the stiff heels by kicking them off like a slovenly beast. He had pierced the top of the microwaveable tray with a fork with nary a care for positioning. It would do no good to look now as there was at least one row of four poked holes that were not in line with the others, non-parallel punctures, sacrilege. He had loosened the tie around his neck, the top button undone, and now, if he could manage it, he would eat his meal in front of the television. This, he realised, might well be the end for him.

It would be his secret. One he would hold on to for eternity. His hidden shame. This, he knew, wouldn't be the last time. There was no use shutting the gate when the horse had already bolted. He placed the microwave tray onto a larger tray, so as not to burn his hands. On the tray he had already placed his cutlery and a single glass of Viognier. At least, that's what the label said. There are no grapes in Gloomwood so they can call it whatever they feel like, and apparently somebody decided they were going to label this Viognier. Neat was fine with this because he ignored the obvious fallacy and it wasn't as if he could compare the drink on his tray to the actual thing in the mortal realm. He resented paying extra, but that resentment was part of the reason he paid it. The increase in price is how you gain that resentment, it's part of the package.

He stepped into the living room, glanced over at the dining room table and looked away, shame. Then he took his seat in the chair beneath the reading light and looked at the picture on the wall. It was a landscape that people told him looked like a Monet. According to people from the mortal realm, Monet had been quite the artist in his day, but Neat had never seen an original work. The tray rested on his lap. The heat from the food made it a little uncomfortable but bearable. He opened a hidden compartment in the chair's arm and withdrew a remote control. With the click of a button, the picture frame on the wall slid to one side revealing the television.

Time was especially important to Crispin Neat. He was early to work, late to leave, punctual to all meetings, dismissive of those who were tardy, uncaring for those who stayed in work only for appearance's sake, furious if his schedule became disordered.

The voice over spoke while the camera panned over an image of the city. The near perfect circle of the canal, the cliff edge where the city met the ocean, and the edges of the midnight purple sands of the desert that surrounded the fringes of the sprawling city of the dead. In its centre was the Office of the Dead. The image was an artist's interpretation of it all, though it was quite a good one, there were imperfections. Though the image was only on the screen long enough for the voice, in an unnecessarily accented voice, to say, "..and now we take you to Gangrene Close, has Anna finally pushed Steve too far this time? Will Tan have an answer for Ash?" The map faded to black and the familiar theme tune, instantly recognisable by everyone in the city, whether or not they watched, began.

To call Neat fastidious would be like calling a collapsing star a bit 'grabby'. While on the surface he watched Gloomwood's longest running, and most popular, soap opera with a routine that far surpassed religious zeal, Neat was in fact filing, sorting, organising the day's thoughts and actions. This was his time to pause and recuperate. A release.

As the credits rolled up the screen he allowed himself a moment's reflection. Miss Scot had burned down the car dealership for the insurance money, but of course she had no way of knowing that Mario, her lover, was trapped inside. Worse still, Anya, owner of the local pub, was Mario's wife, and she had just discovered the affair. Oh, what a wicked web we weave, thought Neat, when we're desperately trying to keep our soap operas interesting. Of course, Neat realised, there was no way that Eric could be dead. That would be too simple. It would involve the police. A police force Neat recognised as significantly more useful than the real Gloomwood police.

He carried the tray into the kitchen. Dropped it into the bin. Poured a glass of water and returned to the single armchair in the living room. As he had walked by a water dispenser this morning, he had heard talk of the next show on the schedule and it intrigued him. He hadn't engaged in conversation, nor had he eavesdropped, that was beneath him, he had just overheard.

"What have we here?" He muttered to himself.

THE BEAR NECESSITIES

"Ladies and gentlemen, norms, gods, dreams, hopes, whatever your origin, however you died, here's the fella who wears a teddy bear hide. Our ursine guide to the other side. The bear who truly does care. He's furry and friendly but don't be fooled. Get on his wrong side and you will be schooled. Let's give it up for Teddington Rex!" The announcer's voice rose just above the crowd noise, and as he said 'Rex' the studio lights kicked in, flooding the stage with a glow while feverish applause from the audience, who by now had endured three warm up acts and the master of ceremonies, was loud enough to be painful.

Teddington Rex strode on to the stage. He did a little skit about the microphone being too high, which he hated, but the audience expected. A set of stairs on wheels were rolled on to the stage and he leapt up them just as they rolled past the microphone stand which he hung on to. He dangled from the top of the stand. Then pulled the microphone out of its holder and slid down the length of the stand like it was a firefighter's pole. "Well," he said into the mic, his voice sonorous, thick, rich, and low. Not what anyone expected, "one day that joke's going to get old, but not today," the audience laughed. They always did.

"Have I got a show for you today, folks. We've got music," he pointed over to the musician's stage to his right where the Lord Levi and the band played five seconds of something people recognised, "including a performance by the one and only Team Magill." The crowd exploded into more applause. Their hands slapping together like seal flippers begging for fish. Ted didn't know who Team Magill were, and he didn't care.

"I'll also be speaking to Blue Walters about his upcoming film, Tea for Two, and Chloe Quest, about her role on hit series, The Coffin-makers Apprentice. Plus, we have a surprise guest. Of course, the show wouldn't be complete with our man on the street. What are we talking about this week, Malcolm?"

Ted pointed towards a big screen set to the left of the stage. The lights dimmed, and he raced across the stage to leap into the chair behind the desk, ready to present the rest of the show.

Blue Walters was at least someone Ted knew. He'd interviewed him before. The man was a pain in the backside, but at least he would talk. If Ted didn't keep a handle on things, he'd dominate the entire show, which is why he'd argued against having him as the first person on stage. Chloe Quest seemed like a nice enough person, but she'd need to find a lot more personality if she had any hope of being noticed next to Blue.

Someone Ted didn't recognise wearing headphones and a beard that looked like he had grown it in a lab started counting down, "Five, four, three…" two and one were silent but the man waved his fingers. Fingers that were clearly custom made for the job, larger than the rest of his hand and, on the surface of them, tattooed with the numbers one and two, that, Ted admitted, was dedication. The camera light flashed red and Ted turned himself up to eleven.

He was funny and witty. His monologue to camera was equal parts heartfelt, hilarious, and scathing. He had learned that skimping on the scathing was a mistake. The easiest target was the Grim Reaper, the Office of the Dead, or some local politician. It had to be fresh, a divisive opinion, with a dislikable public face. That part of the monologue was easy. There are a lot more people to dislike than to like.

This week's target was a popular favourite, or rather a favourite target of abuse. One of the most despised people in the city; Augustan Blunt.

"So, Blunt used to be a big shot. For what? One case he kind of, almost, maybe, perhaps, sort of, stumbled over? Seriously? I sing along to songs sometimes in the car, which does not mean I'm responsible for Infinite Overdrive being at number one this week. The man is a has-been. I can see what you're thinking. Why even bring him up? I'll tell you why. This week they have announced that finally, FINALLY, the Office of the Dead have shut down the Office of Investigations." The crowd gave a small cheer, led by Dan, the master of ceremonies, "I know, I know," Ted waved with one hand, "as if we didn't see that coming. That's fine, I mean good, great, we know things can take time and for the OD a few months is a quick schedule, I mean, don't get me started on potholes in the road. No, this almighty investigator, Blunt, doesn't even want to give a press conference, but they have clearly made him, did you see this? You must have seen this!"

An important part of being a talk show chat show host, especially in an immensely popular time slot, is to clarify that you know your audience is more intelligent than the average person. Does it matter simple statistics will show you that your audience is likely to be, at best, of average intelligence? No. Nobody is ever going to admit they didn't understand something on a television show being shown at eight o'clock in the evening presented by a talking teddy bear. They'll just laugh when everyone else does. People are stupid. It was Ted's personal mantra.

Ted was good at saying things like, "you must have seen this," or, "well I don't need to tell you about this," as if every member of the audience was that person who already knew what was coming and they were just waiting for everyone else to catch up. Stupid? Maybe. But that was the art of the Bear Necessities, Gloomwood's number one live, prime time, television show, and it was why Ted was getting rich, fast.

The clip the production team rolled showed Augustan Blunt, former Chief Investigator of Gloomwood, the city of the dead, standing behind a podium. He was red faced with a five o'clock shadow and wore a hat he kept touching with one hand. The clip was short, but to the point.

Blunt looked slightly to the left of the camera that was recording.

"Chief Investigator-"

"What?"

"Um, how do you feel about the OD closing the Office of Investigations?"

"Honestly? I'm over the bloody moon. This city is a nightmare. I'd given up hope of ever sorting this mess out. Who in God's name thought this was a good idea? I mean, Jesus wept! I can finally get my life back."

The clip ended on a freeze frame of Blunt's face, grimacing as if he had just swallowed a wasp.

"Spectacular!" Ted roared. His voice disproportionate to his diminutive form. "I mean, is there a segment of society he didn't offend? Just look at the face of the third assistant to the manager of the OD," the image on the large screen focused on the man to Augustan Blunt's right, Ralph Mortimer, wide-eyed, open-mouthed, and filled with horror.

"Maybe I'm being unfair," Ted said in the studio, "I mean, we can all accidentally make a faux pas. Even if I have been guilty of misusing the word life, it's a hard habit to break free of, but you have to ask, is this man that much of an idiot or did he, with his last moment in the spotlight, deliberately attack every person he could? We've got blasphemy, we've got life, we've got hopes, we've got dreams, nightmares... The best bit, this isn't even the first time. So, I've got a message for you former Chief Investigator Blunt, come on the show. Let us know what you're really all about! This bear has got a few choice words he'd love to tell you in person!" The crowd cheered, as Ted knew they would, as the writers had predicted.

The rest of the show was the same. Dangle the bait, play the hero, mock the easy targets. The guests had their anecdotes ready, even the pointless, 'isn't this embarrassing' segment where mystery guest, it was Paul Sparks, revealed that he had once auditioned for the same role as Blue Walters but didn't get the part.

It was a good show, not his best show ever, but a good solid show. The show that would leave people talking about it until next week. A show that walked the fine neutral line and only mocked specific, and obviously at fault, people. No alienating the vast majority. Warm, fuzzy, devoid of any kind of actual content. It was mindless, blissful, entertainment, and Ted was the new king.

A BAD MORNING

It was rare for Ralph Mortimer to complain. He believed complaints were for writing on pieces of paper and posting to the relevant agency to deal with. Complaints were for problems that needed fixing. Everything else was whining and Ralph Mortimer was a lot of things, but he wasn't a whiner. So he didn't complain, but he didn't pretend he was happy either.

"What the hell is this about? You lot fired me only yesterday. Why am I even here?" Blunt said from the passenger seat of Mortimer's comfortable, ageing, black hearse.

Mortimer put the handbrake on and nodded. "I know you don't want to be here, but this is a big deal and Mister Neat said if you come and look you would do the city a service."

"I've been doing the city a service."

"And then he said if you argue about it I'm to remind you we could audit the Office of Investigations, take your office and home from you, and begin the long and laborious process of ensuring that you reimburse the city for anything you owe."

Blunt slammed his hand down on the dashboard causing the glove department to pop open revealing a pair of red and pink striped wool gloves. "I don't owe the city anything."

"It's not about that, it's about having to go through the whole thing... in public."

"This is blackmail. You humiliate me in public, then drag me out here to work for you anyway, after I'm fired. Who the hell has gloves in the glove compartment of their car?"

Mortimer frowned, furrowing his brow as his moustache twitched. "I do, and that's what a glove compartment is for."

The noise that Blunt made was neither an answer, not a curse, but something in between. He yanked at the car door and climbed out like a teenager throwing an awkward tantrum.

"Did I mention we'll pay you?" Mortimer said.

Blunt's head appeared at eye level, his hat catching on the top edge of the doorframe. "A fair rate?"

"Yes," Mortimer said, "a fair rate."

"Fine. Come on then," the detective snapped. Blunt threw the door open and stepped out. The harsh, cold air outside the vehicle seemed to suck any warmth from the interior along with the detective.

Mortimer winced as Blunt slammed the car door, then took a moment to breathe. Less than twenty-four hours since the Office of Investigations had shut down, and he was with Augustan Blunt. He sighed, grabbed his gloves from the glove box, and left the car.

They stood side-by-side outside the Deathport. A facility that very few people visited more than once. The final terminal on the journey to the afterlife for residents of Gloomwood.

"I remember it being bigger," Blunt muttered.

"I don't remember it at all," Mortimer said, "it's so long ago... but it didn't look like this."

"How do you know if you don't remember it?"

"Because electric sliding doors didn't exist when I died," Mortimer replied as they walked towards the entrance, "it was more like a train station. Apparently, for a while, that was quite a theme. The old boneshaker was a train that flew through the station every day without fail, but it never stopped. I suppose it was just part of the mystery. It's not as charming now," Mortimer said.

"Charming?" Blunt snapped as he waved towards the top of the doors, waiting for them to open. "There's nothing charming about this place. It's got the same charm as a dentist's waiting room. Everyone who comes here is worried, nobody knows what to expect, but they're sure they will not like it. It's a good analogy. Except everyone who gets here is dead. Tell me again what the genius in security thinks happened."

The doors still hadn't opened as Mortimer explained, "He said he just left the building for a second, to check the perimeter."

"Which is bollocks because there's sod all to check here, so probably went for a cigarette like he does every ten minutes, or he was late to work,"

"Do you want to hear what he said?"

"Yeah, yeah, carry on."

"When he returned the immigration officer-"

"Immigration officer? Give me a break. It's some clown who they pay to sit at a desk and make the recently deceased even more worried than they were in the first place."

Mortimer sighed. "If you say so. The immigration officer's head was split in two, down the middle."

"Ouch, is he alright? Is that something you can recover from?"

"No," Mortimer shook his head, "that's Ableforth, and it was a lady. The security guard is pretty shaken up."

"Christ," Blunt said, causing Mortimer to wince, "that's pretty terrible. Who dies and then chops a person's head in half?"

"That's why you're here. Sometimes Blunt..."

"What? Go on, Captain Mild-mannered, sometimes you what?"

"Sometimes I wonder if you do it on purpose, just to annoy people."

"Of course, I do Mortimer. Haven't you learnt anything? Always pretend to be stupider than you are. How else are people going to underestimate you? Now, we both know these doors only open from the inside, right?"

It took a few more minutes before a police officer stood on the other side of the automatic doors to allow them to open. The officer waved in Blunt and Mortimer but didn't spare the detective a look of distaste. Music was playing in the background. The tune was familiar to Blunt, but he couldn't place it. He shrugged, "probably on a loop anyway," he muttered.

Mortimer hurried by, hoping to avoid another confrontation.

"Is that look for me or did someone take a piss in your cornflakes?" Blunt said. The constable had the good sense to walk away rather than engage Blunt.

Standing in front of a desk were several more officers and Chief Sowercat, head of the Gloomwood police, and one of the few people in the city who had a temper and attitude to match Blunt's.

"Oh, look lads. They've scraped the 'detective' up from the floor. I know I'm only a lowly copper, but I recall something about you being removed from your position. You don't work here anymore," Sowercat snarled.

"Well, that's modern policing for you," Blunt said, "I've never worked here, this is the Deathport, the person who you're staring at is the person who worked here. Not even one minute has passed and I'm doing your job for you, doesn't it get a little tiresome?" Blunt said.

"I meant… you know what I meant. Why are you here?" Sowercat asked as he waved away the constables standing with him. "Just so we're clear, I'm happy if you're planning on trying to walk back through the veil. Nobody's going to stop you."

"Can you do that?" Blunt asked.

"No," Mortimer said, "I'm afraid it's a one-way trip."

"Then how does anyone leave?"

"You don't leave," Sowercat said with a grin, "it's a permanent residency."

"Hotel California," Blunt said.

Sowercat frowned, "What's it got to do with California?"

"It's… forget it. Who's the victim?" Blunt asked.

"June Willows," the Chief replied, "deceased for seventeen years, worked here for all of them. She was probably the one who you met on your way in Blunt. Nothing about her that says this was personal."

"Just going to close off that entire line of investigation, are you?" Blunt asked.

"Oh, here we go, the big-shot detective telling everyone how to do their jobs. Thought you'd fired this useless doughnut, Mortimer? Why's he even here?"

Mortimer straightened his tie and cleared his throat, "we thought we'd ask him to consult-"

"That's not true, you know Blunt," Sowercat cut off the bureaucrat, "I got called to this by Neat and he didn't mention you once."

"What?" Blunt asked. "What's he talking about Mortimer?"

"Go on Mister Mortimer, tell us all how you brought your pet detective along out of pity because of the train wreck that was his press conference," Sowercat said. The constables around the room had all fallen silent as they watched the Chief of police finally say some things they'd been thinking for months. The demolition of Blunt's bravado a more interesting spectacle than the crime scene they were standing around. "Tell everyone here how for months the Office of the Dead has been trying to prove the Chief Investigator's office wasn't just some plan to cover your own arses when things went wrong. You got lucky Blunt, but it's all run out now, and we're not playing nice anymore. Sorry Mister Mortimer, but you can shove off."

Blunt pursed his lips. His hands curled into fists. Then he nodded. "Sorry to have bothered you, Chief," the Detective said, "someone misinformed me." He turned and walked back towards the doors, Mortimer following already beginning a line of apologies.

"Blunt," Sowercat shouted, "the Gloomwood police has got nothing against you personally, but if you get in our way again, we will show you what we're all about."

MORGARTH THE DESTROYER

Morgath the destroyer was... well, she was a destroyer of things. That was her sole purpose. Among the boiling cauldrons of Hell, between the screams of eternal anguish, and the horror of never-ending torture, she was known to all. Well, all the other demons anyway. Mortals sent to Hell didn't really know much about anything, as it usually only took a matter of minutes before they were gibbering wrecks who didn't understand what was going on.

She didn't dwell on that often. For demons, thinking too long about the fate of mortals was a slippery slope. Everyone knew endless torment was a waste of time. If you apply the correct level of torment for it feels endless anyway. Every soul has a breaking point and once it's broken... well, it's a case of job done. You're flogging a dead horse.

Only this morning she had been tightening a vice on a mortal's personal effects and realised it was pointless. It wasn't that the victim was enjoying the process but that any form of attention, particularly at this level of intimacy, was worth the pain. "Right, I'm going to go now," she had said.

"Oh no, don't go, I deserve this. I was a terrible person."

"Then you should spend some time thinking about that."

"I really think I should probably be punished. Maybe boil my head for a while? Oh, we could do the rack, it's been a while since we did the rack?"

"No. You're having alone time."

"Hah, well, you've fallen for it again. No more torture for me."

She sighed. "You don't really think that after millennia of doing this I haven't realised that some people are more terrified of being left for an interminable length of time in the abyss than they are of torture?"

"Well, yes," the man said, "I imagine they are. Pathetic, isn't it?"

"Yes," she said.

Under normal circumstances, she might have given a few extra lashings just for fun. Perhaps the old cauldron on the stomach with rats in trick. It was lazy torture, but terrifying. Plus, they could place bets on which rat would eat its way through first. Today, however, was different.

Beelzebub was trending. He was always trending. That's part of ruling over Hell and being in control of Hell's own social media. Bitter, where everyone was limited to a set number of characters and could post whatever rant they wanted, was the central driving force of all communication between demons. It comprised millions of messages, almost all of which were pictures of mortal pets. It's an inexplicable fact of Bitter that nobody could quite explain. The compulsion to post pictures of pets had reached a level where Beelzebub had ordered that the algorithm, 'all hail the algorithm', would temporarily ban anyone who posted a picture of any mammal unless it was dead. It made no difference.

The reason #Beelzebub was trending was probably because of the second most popular thing today on Bitter #Whereishe? 'He' was Beelzebub, and they had not seen him for several days. This wasn't unusual, but it caused rumblings of discontent amongst certain factions of demon-kind. Those factions being the union reps who insisted Beelzebub should lead by example. They insisted this quietly and behind the Lord of Hell's back, but insist they did. Statutory holidays were a hot topic.

None of this mattered to Morgarth the destroyer. What mattered is that she knew where Beelzebub was, and the bites on bitter were annoying her. She'd drafted several answers to those people using the opportunity to badmouth their eternal ruler. Unfortunately, having only 333 characters (666 seemed too obvious and quite lengthy) prevented her from delivering the full text of a demonic curse. Not only did she know where he was. She expected to be joining him there, along with several of his most elite demons.

Elite did not mean the same as intelligent, capable, or trustworthy as anyone who has ever met someone who experienced an 'elite' private education will tell you. Elite was code for demons who believed they were more important than others and verified this by climbing the slippery pole to fall into Beelzebub's favour.

Her phone buzzed in her pocket as she twisted the nut on... well, you get the idea. She paused, read the message, then slid the device back into her armour. Morgath called it armour because that's what other people called it, but being a female demon in a male demon's Hell meant her protective equipment was as capable of protecting her from harm as a feather boa would have been. In fact, a feather boa on its own might have provided more coverage. Tying the paltry pieces of leather on was almost more effort than it was worth. They left nothing to the imagination. Demonic armourers were pigs. Some of them literally.

The message had been simple, six minutes and sixty-six seconds, be ready. Of course, this was in fact seven minutes and six seconds, but it didn't have the same ring to it.

As she walked away from this mortal's chamber of isolation, his sobs faded to nothing but a low, consistent moan. She counted down the time. Timekeeping was important to her. Knowing how long to make someone hold a particular position, or how long to replay a particular memory, was vital. Checking the time to get it right ruined the experience.

She passed through the halls of terror. The seventh level of Hell staff room. The vending machine that only sold energy drinks and one chocolate bar that would forever remain trapped just above the draw for collection. Then she stepped into her own chamber.

A demon's personal chamber is a sanctuary within Hell. Their personal penetralia in the depths of eternal damnation. Hers contained a dressing table, a single bed, and a bookshelf. The top of the shelf displayed a row of shiny gold and silver trophies upon it for achievements in torture or inventiveness in fields of temptation and contract negotiation. She'd adorned the walls with posters of some of her favourite demon bands. Demons are often associated with rock music, but they have more versatility than they're given credit for, and she enjoyed electronica and synth-pop.

She unclipped the single clasp that tied together the thin strap of 'armour' she wore and let it fall to the ground. She closed her eyes and whispered, "three, two, one."

BREAKFAST

There's a coffee shop across the street from the former Office of Investigations. It's Helga's coffee shop. Helga is a cephalopod who changes gender depending on the weather. Today Helga is she, there are days when she isn't she but nobody knows that because she doesn't tell them, why would she?

People know Helga's coffee shop for two things. The first is coffee that is good considering how cheap it is, but that isn't actually that good compared to most places. The second is as a mecca for players of 'Battle Live'. A board game of obscure complexity that masquerades as a simple card game.

Blunt had little interest in either Helga or the intricacies of Battle Live. In fact, the only time he ever had a passing interest in the game was to provoke the occasional argument when he asked if it was Battle Live, as in we'll live again, or battle live as in a live performance. It was a more than a considerable bone of contention between players of the game and one that the game designers, and manufacturers, deliberately refused to resolve. It was too good a marketing opportunity to pass up. Blunt visited Helga's for the coffee.

In his opinion, it was the best coffee money could buy that was close to his home and work. It didn't sound like a rousing vote of confidence, but then nobody had ever asked him where the best place to get coffee was that was within twenty-five meters of the building. To be fair to Blunt, if someone took a map and drew a twenty-five-meter radius around the building, they would find that there was a second coffee shop within the circle. They called it O'Flanagan's, and the coffee was terrible, but they did good cheesecake.

This morning Blunt was sitting at a table on his own. In the background, he could hear the sounds of focused gameplay. The shuffling of cards blended in with the familiar music, which burrowed into his consciousness like an earworm but never surfaced enough for him to repeat it. He was sitting staring into the newspaper, which bore a picture of his own face. It was not a face he was used to seeing. The photographer had caught an impressive shot a split second before Blunt had expelled a large gasp of air. His cheeks puffed up, his eyes narrowed, the lines in his forehead even more deep-seated than usual. It was an unfortunate time for a camera to capture his image, or fortunate, depending on your perspective.

The headline was, in Blunt's opinion, too large and needlessly brutal. "The worst person in Gloomwood?"

Blunt had met many people in Gloomwood, and he could comfortably say that several of them were terrible people. Blunt knew he was no angel, but to compare him to people who chopped off people's body parts when they were drunk and then sold them back to the same people when they sobered up was harsh. There was a woman who made it a condition of employment that she took one of your eyes so she could trust you wouldn't steal from her. She kept them in a jar and, in the middle of the night, would shine a light on them so they'd wake up when they were at home in their own beds. No, Blunt was not the worst person in Gloomwood, but he was pretty sure the newspaper was being deliberately sensationalist in its headline.

The coffee was black, strong, and getting cold. He'd read the article beneath the headline three times. The first time he was furious. The second time had been upsetting. The third time he had felt numb. He was stupid. There was no getting around it. The Office of the Dead had been too slow to let him slink off into the corner somewhere and had insisted on trying to make the Chief Investigator job stick. A job he hadn't asked for, hadn't applied for, and Blunt was quite sure he'd never agreed to do.

Everything was about public perception. Months ago, something bad had happened, and they'd needed someone to either fix the problem or take the fall when it all went wrong. Blunt had fixed the problem, but he was quite sure that had been beyond all expectations. A fall guy. What do you say about a guy who dies and then, in the afterlife no less, gets immediately turned into a patsy?

Being dead was a car crash and the shitshow of a press conference announcing his own unemployment was just the ambulance taking a wrong turn on its way to the scene.

"Blunt," Helga said. Her eyes were on the ends of tentacles that burst out of the collar of her shirt. Helga might have had a head, but where it was located was not something worth considering. Her voice emanated from something that could pass for a priest's cassock. Blunt didn't know if it was a work uniform or just what Helga wore.

"Helga?" He said.

"You've been staring at that newspaper for nearly an hour."

"I'm okay, I just-"

"I don't care if you're okay. I care that you've been here for bloody ages and only bought one cup of coffee. If you want to hang around, that's fine, but I've got paying customers who would love you to leave. You're not exactly mister popular around here... or anywhere else really."

Blunt looked up and gave a thin-lipped smile. The smile you give to someone who has told you they only accept exact change when you know you haven't got it. Not all of Helga's eyes were watching him. Some of them were looking around the room, one of them was watching the television, but the majority were looking right back at Blunt. People say the soul of a person is in the eyes. If that's true, then Helga is probably not okay. "Can I have another coffee please," Blunt said.

Helga placed her hands on her hips and continued to watch Blunt with some of her eyes.

He let out a sigh. "And a piece of apple pie."

"Sir. Is there anything else I can get you today?" Helga asked.

"I don't know. Is there?"

"We sell those newspapers. I know you might not realise that as you often pick them up and then drop them back in the pile like this is special newspaper library."

"Fine. I would also like to purchase this newspaper. The man on the front page is extremely handsome. How could I possibly resist?"

Four of Helga's eyes narrowed. "Hey. It's not that I don't feel sorry for you but the things you said-"

"For crying out loud, Helga. It was just after they fired me and I was drunk. All those things are just sayings."

"It doesn't really matter if they're just sayings, does it?"

Blunt shook his head. "No. It doesn't. I know I need to think about what I'm saying, but there's just so much of it to remember."

"You've been dead a few months-"

"Oh, that's how it is? Don't most people get a settling-in period?"

"That's what I'm saying. You've only been dead a few months, but nobody ever mentions that. Everyone treats you like you've been here a while because of your position. Sorry. Your former position. We give most fresh meat a lot more time to settle. People will forget."

"Thanks Helga-"

"That's twelve nails."

"Twelve? That's a bit steep."

"It's five nails for advice, wisdom, or general uplifting."

"That's ridiculous-"

Helga pointed to the blackboard that hung on the wall behind the counter. The third column along had 'pearls of wisdom, nuggets of advice, vague recommendations, general uplifting, all available for five nails,' scrawled on it in chalk.

"Where's my vague recommendation then?" Blunt asked.

"As a general rule, be careful not to ask for things you're not prepared to pay for."

"That's the recommendation... clever."

"Isn't it just? Oh, you've also got company, so I put a coffee for her on the bill."

"You charged me for an invisible person's coffee?" Blunt asked.

All but one of Helga's eyes swivelled around to face the door.

Blunt turned around to see a woman in a long black coat making a beeline for him. She negotiated the tables filled with customers who were engaged in their arcane gameplay. There was little doubt she was heading for where Blunt was sitting alone with his newspaper and coffee.

"Mr Blunt," the woman said in a voice that was quiet but confident, as if she didn't want anyone else to hear her.

"Who wants to know?"

"It wasn't a question. It was a statement of fact," she said as she pulled out the chair opposite him and took a seat. "I am in need of your services.

THE PAST

He stared down into the foam of his latte. "It is lonely at times."

His companion, a man over-dressed for the faded Formica tables and vinyl floored coffee shop, shrugged. "You don't have to be alone. You could always try to put yourself out there. Make some new friends. Meet some people."

"I meet people every day," The Grim Reaper said. His skeletal hands wrapped around his steaming cup of coffee.

"Stripping people from their mortal coil is hardly speed dating."

"Yes, well, they're rarely happy to see me. I, well... it's embarrassing really. I'd just like to know some of them."

"I thought you knew everything about them?"

"Well academically I do. It's like knowing everything about a television show. I could answer all the questions on a quiz about them, but it's not the same as 'knowing' them."

"Do you mean that... sexually?"

"What? No. I mean really. You are quite base at times."

"I'm supposed to be. That's part of the whole prince of darkness routine. You know, Satan, the Devil, it's all carnal."

"I suppose so. Still, don't you get lonely?"

"Lonely? That's a laugh. I've all my-"

The Grim Reaper waved a skeletal hand, his dark robes adding a menace to the action that was unintentional. "Yes, you've got all the demonic minion hordes, but they're not exactly friends, are they?"

Beelzebub looked down at his own cup of coffee.

"I'm sorry, that was mean. I'm sure some of them are-"

"No, you're right, of course. They exist in a state of fear that heightens to a point of mindless stupefied terror every time I so much as sigh. It is... isolating. Which is why I appreciate our Tuesday morning catch ups."

It is difficult to drink coffee when you have no flesh. Opening his jaw, he poured the liquid into his cowl. An observer may have expected a pool of coffee around the Grim

Reaper's seat, but they would leave disappointed and confused. Wherever the coffee went, the foam from it still contrived to create a moustache where one would have been. "Are we... friends?" The Grim Reaper asked.

Beelzebub looked up. His horns curled back over his head like a ram. Without them, his height, or the lack thereof, often surprised people. It was the legs and hooves. A satyr's form isn't meant for towering over others, it was for speed and stealth, being bright red took away from the stealth element somewhat. "I ...it's very hard to tell when you're being serious. What with the skull face and everything."

"Ah-ha, yes, friends, silly really. Death incarnate having coffee with his old friend Beelzebub, as if." With the sleeve of his robes he wiped away the frothy moustache making a sound that may have been a sniff. "No, anyway, where were we?"

Beelzebub leaned forward. Straightened his tie, which was already perfectly straight, and spread out his hands. The talons on his fingers clicked against the yellowing table surface. "Business is good at the moment. I just wanted to check on the quotas. We seem to have quite an influx of professional types and our royalty figures... it's as if they aren't really trying."

"Ah yes. Royalty is becoming less of a thing now. The whole dynamic is shifting. There are still royals but they don't wield as much power."

"Oh...shame. They were a given with all of that hereditary power over others. Didn't really need to bother tempting them at all."

"Yes. You lucked out with the power-corruption thing for quite a while. Not to worry though, if anything the pool of souls is opening up even wider and they just keep reproducing." The Grim Reaper paused, reached into his robes, and withdrew a long black document tube. He gave a flick of his wrist, and with the speed and dexterity mortal magicians call magic, assembled a presentation board with multiple charts upon it. "You can expect an enormous increase in politicians over at least the next century, as you can see here. Should keep you quite busy."

Beelzebub grinned. "More fuel for the fire."

"I can only imagine you mean that literally."

TED

Being famous had its perks, but it was difficult to remain anonymous in public. It was even more difficult if you were two feet tall and covered in brown fur. Teddy bears, as a rule, are not considered a suitable vessel for a soul. Gloomwood had its fair share of the unusual, but even by the city of the dead's standards Ted was odd.

He'd used his differences to his advantage to force his way into the limelight, but he hated this form. He had spent the first two months of his time in the city trying to change things. The options were limited, risky, and all of them depended upon him keeping the teddy bear head. The soul resided there, and that was all anyone really was. The problem was that his soul didn't belong here.

"So, Miss Hughes. Let me get this straight," Ted said from where he was sitting on top of a booster seat at a table in Mario's diner. A high-end establishment that wouldn't open until much later in the day for the evening rush. Every other table was empty.

Across from him the reporter, Leighton Hughes, was scribbling notes in a little book. She wore a long coat and a hat that screamed, 'I'm an important and serious reporter', though the feathers on the end of the pen she was using did tone it down a little.

"You're doing a series of interviews highlighting successful minority groups?" Ted finished.

"That's right, Mr Rex. Under-representation of parts of Gloomwood society in the media is a growing concern, and I want to show people that there are people like you, people who have bucked the trend."

"I see. So, these questions are about wanting to promote better representation in the media?"

"I'm just trying to get more of a feel for your story. It must have been tough arriving here and realising you were different."

"Yes. Of course, it was."

"Can I ask, I mean you're known for being quiet about your, uh, life-"

"No. It is rude to talk about our lives. Everyone who is dead is the same, and I believe we should treat everyone equally."

"Yes, but-"

Ted held up his right paw. "Am I a hope, a broken promise, a dead god... that's what you want to know, isn't it?"

Leighton put down the feather topped pen she had been taking notes with on top of the notepad and rested her hands on her lap. "Mr Rex, I completely understand that you don't believe this is the information that needs sharing. I hope you know that the reason I want to share this is that there are so many people who you could help-"

Ted shook his head. "No. Revealing this information would alienate others and open myself up to being a representative of only one part of society. It's personal and I enjoy protecting my personal life. Not only that but, by suggesting this is something the public has a right to know, you're using the public as a weapon. The public doesn't have a right to know what I was, or who I was, before I died. This is where the divide in society comes from. If you know someone is a hope, a dream, a broken promise, a dead god, or whatever else they might have been, then you see them in that light. Take the police officer, for example?"

"Do you mean Constable Johnson?"

"A good police officer, an excellent one, something of a rarity, but look what happened."

Leighton sighed. "Some people say you were responsible for that."

Ted shook his head. "Are you really going to spout those old conspiracy theories? The poor constable had a breakdown because of the bullying he suffered because of institutionalised hopeophobia. What you're doing is only making it worse for everyone."

She gave the bear an icy smile. "I know what you're saying but don't you have a duty to support that part of society by-"

"I don't have a duty to do anything."

Leighton reached into her coat. A shadow moved behind her and a large man appeared with his hands outstretched to grab the reporter. Ted held up a paw and the man's grasping fingers stopped, lingering with no small amount of menace above her shoulders.

"It's just a piece of paper," Leighton said as she pulled it out of her pocket. "I wonder if you would look at this Mr Rex." She placed the paper on the table and slid it towards the bear. "It seems you don't exist."

Ted struggled to slide the paper towards himself. His furry paws didn't have the grip needed. He scowled toward his assistant, a worried-looking man in a green cardigan, with huge hands, who had been standing precisely two meters from the table and out of Ted's eyeline. The man reached forward, picked up the paper and held it in front of Ted's face. The bear reached up and tugged the paper towards himself with both hands.

"And this is?"

"A search for anyone with your name."

"It's a stage name. I hardly think that's surprising."

"A stage name?" Leighton said. "That's interesting because it seems all your property, contracts, and your registrations with the Office of the Dead are in this name."

Ted let out a bark of laughter. "Well, of course they are. I had my name changed with the Office of the Dead."

"There's no record of that."

"No? I suggest you look a little harder."

"There's no record of you before six months ago."

"This," Ted said, "is clearly not an interview for some fluff piece about minorities in the public eye. If it is, then you're doing it wrong. It seems you're looking for something else."

Leighton folded her arms and narrowed her eyes. "Who are you, Teddington Rex?"

"Well. That's a big question, isn't it? Who are any of us?"

"You know exactly what I mean."

Ted stood up on the chair and placed his paws on the table. "Miss Hughes, if that is your actual name," the bear said with a smirk, "it appears you have come here under false pretences. I don't appreciate that. I will make sure you never have this opportunity again. Don't worry though, I may well mention you in my show this week."

Leighton smiled. "Thank you. I was worried I was wasting my time looking into you, but clearly there is something to hide. You're looking a little... ruffled."

NOT HOME

One-hundred and eighty-five Pale Avenue was once the home of the Office of Investigations. It was not anymore. However, apartment 4b was still where Augustan Blunt could hang his hat. His brand-new hat that he had found on his head when he had awoken this morning, on the floor of his office, underneath his desk.

Ralph Mortimer had hammered upon his door incessantly for the best part of half an hour before Blunt had peeled his face off the floor where it had stuck, thanks to a pool of drool Blunt hoped he had produced himself.

Unkempt was a kind description of Blunt's accommodations. If it had been tidy one might have called it spartan. Possessions were not something he was big on. It was far from tidy. Had tidy been on a map, then Blunt's office would have been on a different map in another part of the universe. The room looked like someone had picked it up, shaken it around, and dropped it from a height. What meagre possessions he owned were strewn around the two rooms as if someone had taken the time to spread them out for an impromptu inspection. When Blunt had been told they were finally going to close his department he had considered packing, moving somewhere new, gaining a fresh perspective. By the time he had reached the bottom of the mystery bottle he had stashed in the drawer of his desk, his addled mind had insisted he do the opposite and so he had 'unpacked' everything.

Knowing what was waiting inside, he had asked Twist Lenworth, the woman who had approached him in the cafe, to give him a minute to tidy up. She had looked him up and down with eyes that did nothing to veil her growing disdain. "I'm on a tight schedule," she said, "make it a minute," a few days might have been more useful.

He opened the door and slid through the smallest gap he could make into the office. Then he began shoving everything that was out of place into the adjoining room, which housed a bunk and a wardrobe. Everyone has a junk drawer, the place where the used batteries and the brochures that were interesting six months ago live, Blunt has a room like that, for sleeping in. Kicking underwear and snatching up empty food wrappers he made quick work of making the office habitable and the bedroom something he might avoid ever opening the door to again. Then he opened the window and willed the foul odour to exit. It did nothing to help.

Things in Gloomwood break down. They decompose and rot. It didn't apply to everything, but anything that fueled the bodies they walked around in would rot because it was made with 'magic'. Nobody used the word 'magic' because it didn't sound scientific. It was fine to believe they were all dead, and that this was the afterlife, that their souls had lifted from their bodies, shifted their mortal coils like a snake sheds skin and then ended up in this place, but magic, no, that was a bridge too far. It annoyed Blunt.

With one last look over the office, he grimaced and turned to face the door. The frosted glass revealed the outline of the woman who had accosted him in the coffee shop. It was an outline of the base parts that Blunt could appreciate. Did he want to do this? He'd only lost his job yesterday. Before then, he had chased away most of the people he cared about. This morning the police made him feel like an idiot, which is like being told you're ugly by a blobfish.

'Struggling with death,' Blunt scowled as he remembered the words of the woman from his support group. As if being a little morose about your own demise was a condition and not a perfectly reasonable state of mind. Nobody goes skipping happily into the afterlife singing, 'oh, happy day.' He thought to himself.

Then there'd been the clerk at the Office of the Dead who had explained why he was being 'let go'. Budget cuts, financial constraints, maximising workforce efficiency and being mindful of the fact that it was the taxpayers who were paying the bills. It wasn't the real reason. Ralph Mortimer had explained, in his stuttering long-winded fashion, that Blunt was causing problems and not solving any. People were finding he was more trouble than he was worth.

Everything was going downhill fast. That was what happened when you were riding a toboggan rattling at speed to the bottom of the pile. More and more got thrown into the toboggan until stopping it became impossible. Blunt had plenty of weight in his sled, not least of which were the stack of bills that had gone from annoying to worrying. Now he didn't even have a paycheck coming in, and the debts had climbed to the lofty heights of insurmountable. Money, Blunt thought to himself, even when you're dead it's all about money.

He wrapped a hand around the door handle and opened it.

"Ready now?" The woman asked.

Her name was Twist, and she was what Blunt would have termed, 'a bit of alright' if he was inclined to judge people on their appearance. Which he was. That was a large part of his job. Some might even call it a skill, if it wasn't being a judgemental prick for a living.

"Sorry about that. I wasn't really expecting a guest. How's the coffee?"

"Reasonable for the price," she said.

"Well, I paid so-"

"Exactly," Twist said, dropping the almost full paper coffee cup into the wastepaper bin by Blunt's desk. She took a seat in a chair that faced the desk and crossed her long legs. The look she gave the chair while she took a seat suggested she would rather have perched upon a pile of manure.

"Well, make yourself at home," Blunt said, closing the door and walking around the desk. It was too close to the wall, and he had to slide in sideways and awkwardly position himself so he could get into the chair. "So, you want to talk about a case?"

She sighed. "I will be honest with you, Mister Blunt-"

"Detective," Blunt said, "It's Detective Blunt."

"Is it? Isn't that a police thing?"

"I'm not a police officer. I'm a private investigator."

"I thought you worked for the city."

"You've not seen the news then?" Blunt said. There was no point in trying to hide it. "The Office of Investigations no longer exists. They have shut it down. I'm a private citizen as of yesterday." He had wondered if she might react to the news. "Do you think I came here to talk about you?" She asked.

Blunt pursed his lips and nodded. "Well, that's fair. So, you don't care about any of that stuff. Right then. My rate is…" His rate was not something he had considered, "five hundred nails a day if it's full time. That's for the first three days. After that we can either continue at that rate, or I can give you a discount for a set period, does that make sense?"

"Not really. I'll pay you five thousand for a week, but you're not to engage in any other cases."

"Exclusive contract?"

"If they fired you yesterday, I can't see you having any others to worry about yet."

"Well, you're more than a pretty face-"

"Don't do that. My face has no relevance to any of this. Nor does my physical appearance or gender." She said it while looking towards the window as if it was a passing comment but her tone didn't leave room for it to be mistaken as anything as mild as that.

"No. Right. Well, I'm going to need some information before I can get started on anything. Miss Lenworth, right?"

"Yes, you can call me Twist."

"Unusual name."

"It's a nickname, and it's irrelevant to our relationship. I'm looking for someone."

Blunt picked up a pen from his desk and held it over a blank piece of paper. The desk was littered with other scraps that he hadn't bothered to sweep into the bin before she arrived. "Okay, missing person?"

"Not missing. They're hiding here."

"Here? Where is here?"

"Gloomwood, Mister Blunt-"

"Detective Blunt."

"That remains to be seen. Detectives detect things. I'm quite sure that most people don't get to keep titles like that once they're dead."

"Well, if we're going to be working together, maybe it would be nice if we could be civil."

"Have I been rude?"

Blunt felt the hairs on the back of his neck rise and knew that his face would betray his emotions. It was as if the woman was trying to make him angry. "What can you tell me about this person?"

"They're alive."

☠ <u>TOYS</u> ☠

The walking stick was an affectation. It was a calling card. The click, clack, sound of it against the floor, or walls, or anything he hit with it, was useful for punctuating the things he said. It was a visual and auditory aid when he was giving instructions. He also really liked the way it felt in his grip. When one is used to holding something it can feel uncomfortable to be bereft of it. "Tell me again."

"There are not that many toys around. There are no children, well apart from people like me, you see."

"You're not a child."

"No sir, I am not a child."

"You look like a child."

"Yes. There's quite a few of us. Less than there used to be. It's our right, as people who came here as children. It's not a secret."

"I see."

"Are you new?"

He smiled. His grin stretched too wide. He knew it did. The pointed teeth made people nervous, but it was the width of his grin that set, ironically, their teeth on edge. "No, no, I have been around for a very, very, long time."

The boy wore a waistcoat and a flat cap. Cover him in soot and you would have an urchin straight out of a Dickensian novel, but an urchin he was not. "Well then, you probably know all about Pabies."

"Pabies? That's what you call yourselves?"

"Pre-adolescent bodied individuals, sir."

"Oh, it's a bit of a mouthful, isn't it, pabies," he enunciated the syllables, "Pay-bees... hm, I'm not sure I like that. It's... creepy."

The boy shrugged. "We wanted something new, that's what we came up with. Some nasty stuff happened a while ago. We used to have the Youth Order, that was better-"

"Oh? That sounds like some sinister organisation run by children."

"Actually... never mind. We got what we could." The boy said.

They were walking down an alleyway towards a doorway on the side of a large brick building. It was a disused warehouse near the city's sea wall. The barrier at the edge of Gloomwood that met the Styx. It wasn't much of a wall, but the cliff drop on the other side of it made people nervous. It didn't stretch the length of the city and in many places was just a rickety fence, but the sea-fence didn't have the same ring to it.

When they reached the door, the boy rapped his knuckles against it in a complicated rhythm.

"A password?" The man with the cane in his hand asked.

"What? Ah, no, that's just an annoying song that's stuck in my head."

"I see. So, no password?"

"What for?"

"Security."

The boy blinked, then shook his head. "There's a lock on the door. Who's going to steal this crap?"

"Crap?"

"Sorry. I know you like this stuff, but nobody else wanted any of it. The norms don't like it, reminds them of things that will never be, we don't like it either... for the same reasons."

"What about the others?"

"Nobody likes it."

"And yet it exists?"

"Few people like creepy porcelain clowns either, but they still get made."

"I see."

The door opened inwards, and a woman who wore her hair in a tight bun and had only one eye, it was in the centre of her forehead entered. "Winnie," the woman said before looking at the man with the cane, "Sir."

"Nice to see you, Beth," the boy said, pushing his way past her.

"Yes, hello Beth. How's the tunnel vision?"

She shook her head at the man, "still getting the headaches."

"You really should wear glasses."

"Are you trying to be funny?"

"No. If I wish to be funny you will laugh," the man said. He wore a suit that was purple and mauve, it was embroidered with flames.

Inside the warehouse, along with the boy and Beth, were a few other people. They were unloading boxes from the back of a large hearse and stacking them in the room's corner.

"What are these boxes?" The man asked.

"They're what you asked for," the boy replied.

"I see. Remove them from the boxes and place them appropriately."

"Appropriately?"

"Yes, as if they're an audience."

The boy looked at Beth, who offered nothing in return.

"Right, of course."

It took them nearly two hours. By the end, the boxes were empty and stacked so that one side of the warehouse looked like the side of a stadium. Atop the boxes were toys. Soft toys of myriad shape and form looked towards the centre of the room. The bare lightbulbs that hung from the ceiling cast them in an orange glow that threw shadows against the brick walls in monstrous patterns.

"I think that's it, sir."

"Well done."

Beth and the boy looked at each other behind the man's back as he took his time considering the audience before him. "What time is it?" He asked.

"Uh, it's just gone five o'clock."

"Five? Hm, you can all go now."

The boy and Beth looked at each other. A discussion took place with no words being spoken. The boy raised his arms. The woman clenched her fists. They took it in turns to point at the man, then at each other. They shook their heads. They glared.

"Stop it," the man said, "you're irritating me. If you wish you can wait until after seven o'clock then I will settle your bill, or you can come back tomorrow."

"We'll wait," the boy said, and he took a seat on the floor, crossing his legs.

"You can wait," Beth said, "I'm going home. See you tomorrow."

"Actually," the man turned and pointed the cane in her direction, "perhaps it's better if you both wait. I might need your help with something else."

Beth sighed. Rolling your eyes when you only have one in the centre of your head is a strange look, but it still works.

"I will pay you double for the next two hours," the man in the suit said with a wink.

ARGYLE

Argyle was the name she had given to her personal research station. The city of the dead thaumaturgic communications network was a small closed system not open to the public. The unit that Leighton Hughes was using to tap into the library information store was one she didn't legally have any right to. She kept it in the back room of a small haberdashery, which she rented off the owner as an office. It used to be a changing room and barely fit one tiny desk and chair.

The skull vibrated within its housing as the typewriter platen juddered from one side to the other. The ribbon took a hammering from the type bars at a speed unfathomable from any but the speediest typists as the white letters appeared on black paper. The skull's empty eye sockets glowed with an ominous red while the machine revealed its search results.

Skulls like this one were scarce. The Gloomwood library was the central depository for all those who had desiccated, calcified, and let their bodies and minds crumble to dust. Only skulls remained, housing a soul that had turned in on itself. Some people said it was a choice, others said it just happened when they were left alone for long enough. This skull, Argyle, had been a little different. A petty thief who had offended one too many people over time and found himself interred in the library. That was its other purpose. A prison, although this prison is more of a shelf that sometimes gets dusted. The university had borrowed Argyle; he was zero risk of escape because nobody cared about him. Leighton had slipped a few nails to a friend to borrow him. It had turned into more of a rental agreement.

Cutting edge technology in Gloomwood had reached a peak with the automobile. There is little money in improving efficiency to make things happen quicker when everyone has an overabundance of time. Life is a battle against time that everyone loses. Death, on the other hand, is much more sedate.

The desk the machine was sitting upon wasn't as sturdy as it could have been, and as it shook, her pen rolled off the edge onto the floor. As she bent down to pick it up, she felt a presence behind her.

"Don't mind me," a voice said.

She turned and felt her mouth drop open as if somebody had released a latch that held it in place. Standing behind her chair, looming, because that is what he does, was the Grim Reaper.

"You...ah, okay then," Leighton Hughes said, turning back to watch the report as it spooled out of the machine. At least on the surface, that is what she attempted to give the impression of doing. Beneath the surface, concealed in the same way that an axe murderer might conceal their purpose by holding the axe behind their back, was panic.

The phrase, 'don't mind me,' is as ineffective a statement as one could imagine. It sits alongside, 'don't mention it,' which is only ever said after the 'it' in question has already been mentioned. Though it is not as bad as 'thanks in advance' but that's for another time. Here 'don't mind me' said by the most powerful, and terrifying, person in the city of Gloomwood was akin to asking someone to ignore the giant squid that had just chewed and swallowed them. It would not happen.

The Grim Reaper, Grim to his friends of which he had very few, if any, was the ruler of Gloomwood. As Leighton Hughes, reporter extraordinaire, waited on a report that she knew would return nothing of interest, her internal monologue turned all dials up to maximum and screamed at the engine room for more power.

Death did not always exist, because death cannot exist without life any more than light can exist without darkness or shopping trolleys can exist without one wheel that refuses to comply with the other three. Then, much to the disappointment of many inanimate objects, plasmoids, barren rocks, and quite happy but uninvolved amino acids, along came life.

Life came with a lot of baggage. Like that friend, who you invite for a weekend but turns up with several suitcases and a tactical plan to avoid any discussion of the end of their stay. It brought with it a world of potential, joy, happiness, love, and to be frank, it was all just a little too bloody perfect. Reproduction was also a big problem. An endless orgy of a problem. Then they killed him or her. Nobody likes to pry.

It was unpleasant. The details are a little hazy, which isn't really that surprising as it was a long time ago. Then there was the void. Darkness, endless oblivion for eternity, or so it seemed. The only thing that remained was a will. The will of the one they killed. Death was unleashed upon the world, and those who died needed a place to go. Belief took care of that. Belief by the living that there was something beyond. Which was all well and good for everyone who died next, but what about the first one?

The Grim Reaper let out a cough, breaking Leighton's chain of thought. It wasn't an actual cough. That requires lungs, and moisture, lungs without moisture, and air aren't much use at all. It was the sound of a cough.

Leighton turned once more in her chair. The machine had stopped some time ago.

"I think it's finished," the Grim Reaper said. He who existed through sheer force of will. He who had created Gloomwood. The embodiment of everything that life hurtles towards with unstoppable force, the dark knight, the angel at the start of the tunnel of light, Death.

"I'm sorry?" Leighton said.

"The glowy skull thing has stopped glowing. I think it's finished."

"Oh, right. Thank you," she said.

"What does it say?"

She turned back to the machine and snatched the piece of paper out of the top of it, tearing the paper in her rush. "Um, well, it's not very interesting, really."

"Oh."

"Just work stuff."

The Grim Reaper nodded, ominously. He didn't mean to be ominous it's hard to avoid when you're him. "You're a reporter, a famous one, that must be difficult."

"Oh, well...you know who I am?"

"Leighton Hughes, reporter extraordinaire."

"Yes...that's me." She squeaked.

"You dropped this," the Grim Reaper reached within his robes and withdrew a pink sparkling purse in sequins on the surface of it was the word, 'Badass'. "It has your business card in it. You write for the Gloomwood Independent." He thrust the purse in his skeletal hand towards her.

"Well I did," Leighton pinched the end of the purse working hard to avoid coming into contact with the Grim Reaper's fingers, "it doesn't exist anymore," she said.

"No? Shame. I quite liked it. Needed more cartoons, though. I draw cartoons."

"Do you?" Leighton said in a voice reserved for speaking to children or those who we are quite sure don't have a firm grasp on reality, "I bet they're wonderful."

"No. I'm terrible at faces," the Grim Reaper gestured to where his face would be, if he had one, with his free hand.

She tugged at the purse, but the Grim Reaper didn't release it.

"What are you looking at?" He asked.

"Ah, well, it's confidential."

The Grim Reaper cannot blink. He can't glare, frown, squint, raise an eyebrow, or smirk. Regardless of this, people will project what they imagine he would do onto the 'canvas' of his skull. While he remained still Leighton imagined a raised eyebrow and a disapproving scowl. Had he been able to express emotion visibly, she would in fact have seen embarrassment that he had been nosey, but you can't be nosey without a nose.

"Sorry, sir, I'm investigating a celebrity who I believe has an alternative agenda."

"Ooh, who is it? Is it Mavis Cuthelridge there's something suspicious about her?"

"Mavis...you mean the celebrity chef?"

"If that's what she calls herself. She's vulgar, lots of innuendo I'm told."

"She's... no, it isn't her. It's Teddington Rex."

The Grim Reaper, who was still holding the purse, nodded. "Right, and he's?"

"Oh. He's a presenter on a talk show. He's quite famous. He's actually a teddy bear."

"A puppet?"

"No, an actual teddy bear."

The Grim Reaper let go of the purse and Leighton jerked backwards, only then realising how hard she had been tugging at it.

"That sounds unusual."

"It is very unusual."

The Grim Reaper nodded again. "This is quite awkward."

"It is?"

"Yes, I was hoping to try on a robe, and this is the only dressing room."

"Oh."

THE SUPERMARKET

A mere kilometre from where Augustan Blunt was being laughed at is a supermarket. There are few in the city as there is little space to cram large retail buildings in amongst the narrow alleyways and terraced houses. What spaces there are gets filled by developers with eye-watering speed. They produce industrial style office buildings that make post-war architecture look glamorous, but the buildings are quick to build. It's no minor factor in the design of these buildings that labour is cheap and safety is of absolutely no concern. Rumour has it that in many of the office blocks there are people trapped between the walls where they may remain for eternity. Rumour is correct.

Supermarkets are on the outskirts of the city. A distance far enough to make almost anyone visiting them to be on a mission for a 'big shop'. There are no baskets at the supermarkets. This would be pointless. Instead, there are large shopping trolleys, or carts. They are cumbersome and oversized to make the journey around the shop more awkward. They are also exceedingly difficult to manoeuvre, which is intentional. A member of staff has the job of 'sticking' one wheel on every trolley. So large are the trolleys that even the most fervent of shoppers often feels the need to 'bulk up' for the trolley to seem full.

In the mortal realm, these supermarkets would come under scrutiny for having trolleys so large the contents would not decant into any average sized vehicle. In Gloomwood they build vehicles on the hearse premise, there's plenty of room.

"What would you have us look for?" A two-foot blue cuddly dinosaur asked in a voice that was born from the depths of Hell. Were it on screen, it would have needed subtitles.

In a suit so perfectly tailored it might have grown around him, Beelzebub stood leaning against a lamppost. The lamp was on despite it being only the afternoon. The sky was bleak, cloudy, ominous, and consistent with the weather of Gloomwood. "Watch the trolleys."

"The trolleys?"

"Yes, Morgarth, watch the trolleys. Look for the people who don't return them."

"Why would anyone steal a trolley?"

Beelzebub was smoking. He took a long drag on the narrow cigarette and exhaled, blowing the smoke into the dinosaur's face. Morgarth was used to the attitude of the Lord of Hell. Where others would fawn or simper in his presence, she waited, unmoved and unfazed.

"If you see someone steal one even better, but you're not listening. The trolleys belong to the supermarket, over there," he pointed to a trolley bay, "they are all collected awaiting use by customers. People take one, they walk around collecting their pointless crap inside, then they come out here. They move the rubbish they've spent hours of their existence working for into the back of their cars and then they return the trolley to the little trolley area."

The dinosaur nodded. Its head was over-sized and the large 'googly' eyes were supposed to be endearing. Being inhabited by Morgarth, the destroyer had turned the eyes black and her red irises flitted around as she took in the information. She waggled one of her forearms. A T-Rex body was inconvenient, but when you are a blind incorporeal form, you take the body available to you. "Then who takes the trolleys back?"

Beelzebub tutted. "It is a contract between the customer and the supermarket. An unwritten commitment. You take a trolley and then you return it to the bay."

"Why?"

"Why indeed? That's an exceptionally good question. They return the trolley because that is expected. There is no punishment for not doing so and eventually somebody from the supermarket will collect them and return them anyway, nevertheless, people return the trolleys. In the mortal realm people realised this was unwise and began making people leave money for the trolleys, they haven't caught up here yet."

Morgarth's eyes narrowed until her eyes were a small red line. "The people who don't return the trolleys are not fulfilling the contract. So, we're to punish them?"

This time he laughed. "No. They're the ones who we are going to help. They're the ones who are our people."

"Why?"

"It's a simple litmus test. Returning the trolley is what good people automatically do. It's the nice, kind, and expected thing to do. Not returning the trolley is not nice. It is selfish, uncooperative, and usually it means the person is so self-absorbed they don't see why they would do it."

"So they're... arseholes?"

"Correct. I want arseholes."

Morgarth's enormous pink felt eyelids drew fully closed for a moment. "Did you mean-"

"No, I didn't mean to say it like that. You know what I meant."

"Right," Morgarth nodded, "I'll tell the others."

She hopped away and then attempted to walk. Still unused to the body she was in. Around the carpark, at intermittent intervals discreetly hidden behind bins, cardboard boxes, and anything that might provide sufficient cover were twelve other soft toys. The demons from Beelzebub's elite summoned from Hell itself to aid him on his mission. Beelzebub had selected Morgarth to lead them for one simple reason. She was not as stupid as the others. She spread the word and Beelzebub waited.

The cigarette never ended. His powers in Gloomwood were limited, and he had yet to discover why. It was a strange place to him. A new place, and that was rare. The souls walked around as if they were in the mortal world, almost oblivious to the fact they were dead. He had seen them do good and evil. He had seen them do nothing of interest and yet find satisfaction in that nothingness.

There was something he didn't like about the place, it irked him. He had visited hells of all descriptions, and all manner of heavenly places. There were some that flaunted the line between either, but this, this was unsettling. It was as if someone had hit pause on death and just let things carry on. Then there were the other things. Things that weren't supposed to be here at all.

A man and woman were arguing over something, and he allowed himself a smile. They got louder and louder, then there was screaming and shouting. They threw the things they had purchased into the back of the car with such force that a carton of something burst, exploding inside and splashing the windows. "You will do," he whispered, "just leave it behind." The woman finished emptying the trolley, and the man gripped the handle before stomping heavily, pushing it back to the trolley bay. He sighed. "Such petty, trivial things you mortals agree to do without ever even realising it."

The cigarette smoke froze in the air as he stared across the carpark, a thought striking him. "You mortals... except you're not any more, so why does this still apply?"

UNHAPPY TED

The headaches had been bothering him for weeks, but they were getting worse. He lay on his back on a bed that exceeded any reasonable standard measure, neither king nor emperor would ever give a label to the level of excess Ted had reached. It was empty save for the two-foot teddy bear. The sleep mask he wore covered his eyes, plunging him into darkness, but it did nothing to soothe the pounding.

Doctors exist in the city of Gloomwood. Many of them charlatans. Most of them trained to reattach a limb and little more. Headaches were a problem seldom discussed and never solved. The skull was the home of the soul. The cage that bound their ethereal essence and, as was written above the entrance to the Nightingale hospital, 'It's not like it's going to kill you'.

The doctor that had turned up to help Ted was not new to the city, but he was new to Ted. An experienced practitioner, Ted had been told, well respected. Well respected, Ted now knew, was a euphemism for being known not to screw up and being bloody expensive.

"The head," the doctor said, "is the vessel for the soul. It's just a box in which a soul is poured like a tankard full of soul ale."

"Soul ale?" Ted muttered, "that's a terrible analogy."

"Well, that may be, but I'm not really here for my chat, am I, Mister Rex?" The doctor said.

Ted hadn't even taken the eye mask off when the doctor arrived, so he did not understand that he was talking to a cephalopod. Tentacles lend themselves very well to medical matters, dexterity was important when most doctoring meant sewing things back on to people.

"No. Look, it's a headache. Can't you just give me some paracetamol or something?"

"Ah, so you were a norm once?" The doctor said.

"This isn't twenty questions. I would like some painkillers."

"I'm afraid that's not really a thing we have here, Mr Rex. Perhaps the headaches are causing you to forget. I wonder if this is a symptom of your unusual circumstances."

"Which circumstances are those?"

"Well, the body. If you were once a norm you should have been provided with a specific body type. My analogy, which you so enjoyed, was quite accurate. Whatever the head might look like, its only real purpose is to hold our soul. We're not unlike the genie in the lamp."

"Can we pour my soul into a different head that isn't pounding like someone shoved a gorilla with a hammer in there?"

"Hangovers."

"What?"

"Hangovers are just about the only time people really get headaches here. They're mainly psychosomatic, you see. We feel like we should have a hangover, so we do. The manufacturers of alcoholic beverages work very hard to ensure that a hangover is felt. I suppose if anyone were to know about hangovers it would be the breweries."

Ted rolled on to one side and drew his legs up to wrap his arms around them. "It's not a hangover. It's a headache."

"A migraine?" The doctor said it as mee-grine.

"Ugh, my head bloody hurts. How's that complicated? Do something about it."

"I believe your headache is caused by something other than an illness. Perhaps, stress? You have quite a lot of pressure on you to entertain everyone. There is a substantial number of people who depend upon your skills in order to maintain their own careers."

Ted rolled into a sitting position and pulled the eye mask off. He recoiled for a moment upon releasing that he had been talking to a six foot tall squid-like creature but regained his composure at a speed that would leave even the sharpest observer questioning if it had happened at all. "I don't care about any of them, though. I'm not stressed because I don't care about these people. Everyone is here for all eternity. If they lose their job, it isn't that big a deal, it's not like they're going to die. There is no bottom rung of the ladder. Oh, they'll be sad and stressed, and worry about paying their bills, but they've got all the time in the world and nothing to worry about. What happens if you don't eat Doctor Oct-"

"Please don't call me that," the Doctor interrupted with a sudden lifting of four tentacles, "it is offensive. I am older than any comic book character in existence and my name is Kovacs, Doctor Jared Kovacs, thank you."

Ted shrugged. "Okay, Doctor Kovacs. What happens if you don't eat?"

The Doctor reached towards his face. It was near the top of his large teardrop shaped centre, his tentacles surrounding the rest of his body where he wore something that could have been a many sleeved waistcoat. His face, far more disturbing than the rest of his body, was human. It looked like it had been stretched across his squid-like torso. He rubbed the slight bump that might have been a chin before answering. "Well, it depends on the motivations of the person. With no fuel at all, the body would stop functioning and it would atrophy. Nothing happens to the person, but the flesh is temporary. A person could end up as nothing more than a skull. The chances are if a person has gone that far, psychologically, they have shut down. Then they might end up in the library... or worse."

"Worse?" Ted asked.

"Well, if they haven't provided any legal reason for it not to happen, they might end up gridded."

"Gridded?"

"It's modern technology. Horrible machines linked for the library central database."

"Like a network?"

"I guess you could call it that."

"You're kidding. The internet exists. I've been asking about the internet for months."

"How is your head?"

"Absolutely terrible. It feels like it's about to explode, but you're going to do nothing about it, are you?"

The doctor offered a thin smile. "I wish I could, but I believe-"

"You believe it's caused by stress, but I'm not stressed. I'm not even close to stressed. I don't write any of the show. I literally read out what they give to me. I'm a talking teddy bear. The most stressful part of my day is worrying that I might get caught on a piece of Velcro and have to ask someone to remove me from it. The worst thing that happens to me is getting wet, then I have to sit on a sodding radiator like a pair of damp trainers. I'm filthy rich, successful, popular, for Christ's sake-"

The Doctor flinched at the profanity.

"-I could probably take over the whole damn city if I wanted to. People are eating out of my furry little paws. It's not stress. Something is wrong."

"Well, there is…"

"Yes."

"There is the fact that you're a teddy bear."

"Why didn't you start with that?"

"I didn't want to be ursinist, or um, what is the term for someone who doesn't like…toys?"

Ted put his head in his hands. "It hurts. It hurts, It HURTS!" He rolled off the bed and landed on his feet with his hands still on his head. "You're a doctor. Fix this."

"I can't. If it isn't stress or a hangover, or psychological ailment, then it's your head."

"I know it's my head. That's what hurts."

"Because it isn't meant to contain a soul!"

"What?"

"How are you in that body?"

SARAH'S LAUGHING

"Are you done?" Blunt asked. They were standing in a laboratory. Around them figures in white coats scurried around or peered into pristine mechanical objects, through lenses into petri dishes, or in one case poked at a lump of purple goo with what appeared to be a long plastic stick.

Sarah was trying to stop a fit of giggles that had taken hold of her, leaving her out of breath and red faced. "I'm sorry, it's just," she took a deep breath, "you can't be serious."

Blunt didn't look at her as she spoke. Instead, he cast an eye over the lab. People in white coats shuffled around. Most of them were also in gloves and plastic safety glasses. They moved around test-tubes, stared down microscopes, and operated equipment that was beyond Blunt's understanding. "I get that everyone in Gloomwood is dead, I get that, but what if someone wasn't?"

"That's like asking in the mortal realm, 'what if someone didn't breathe oxygen'" She said.

Blunt shrugged, "they'd be dead, right?"

"Exactly."

"So, it is one hundred percent impossible. Scientifically, with no doubt that any living thing can exist in Gloomwood."

"No. That's not how science works. We don't like absolutes. As for living 'things' well we're getting into semantics now. It's just ridiculous for a person. Someone who was alive here? How would they even get here in the first place?"

"I don't know, and it isn't important. What about that," Blunt pointed at the purple goo that had leapt on to the man who had been poking it. He was screaming and thrashing about wildly while others tried to pry it off him. "Is that alive?"

Sarah looked over. "No, but you make a good point. It's more alive than we are."

"It is?"

"The Styx, the ocean not the neighbourhood, is a spectrum. The nearer you get to the other side, and it's a vast, essentially immeasurable, distance, the more life is present.

Some things in the Styx at this end have a tiny vestige of life... well, it's not so much life as time."

Blunt nodded. "Still laughing at me?" He asked.

"Yes, but on the inside. That thing is alive in an analogous way to a cooked sausage being alive."

He narrowed his eyes. "Is this about the hotdogs again?"

"No, ugh, no, it isn't about the hotdogs. How can I explain this like I'm talking to an idiot?"

"Did you just call me an idiot?"

"Yes. It's more like there is a tiny part of life, or time left in it."

"You're really confusing me now."

"Einstein said if you can't explain something in terms that a four-year-old would understand then you don't understand it yourself."

"He did?"

"I don't know. I died before he was around. He clearly never met you, though. The point is, there are things which are almost alive, in a way, that sometimes crawl into the city. They're not alive, but they're a lot more alive than we are. They've got temporal significance... time."

"Great, how do you find them?"

"We don't. You've just walked into a state-of-the-art facility. We're laboratory scientists, you find things like that out in the street. Look around, do you think many of these people get out much?" She said, a man in horn-rimmed spectacles gave her a dirty look. "Oh, get a life, Henry, you know it's true," Sarah said before turning back to Blunt. "The things we're talking about are pests. We have a man for that."

"And this man is?"

"We call him the pest control man. He brought in that goo."

"Well, does he have a card or something?"

"Just wait a minute, this is going to sting."

"What is-"

A red light started flashing, and a siren blared far louder than necessary. The occupants of the room stopped what they were doing, and many of them braced themselves against objects. Sarah's head and hands vanished. Then came the steam and the burning. A bright light flashed across the room and when Blunt opened his eyes, he found himself on his knees holding his hat on to his head. Tears were streaming down his eyes and his skin felt raw.

He stood up and looked around to see everyone in the lab making murmuring sounds. One or two of them might have been speaking, but the siren had affected his hearing. It came back with a piercing ringing. When he turned, he found Sarah looking at him with a grin on her face.

"You enjoyed that," Blunt said.

She pointed at her ear and shrugged.

"I said you enjoyed that," Blunt bellowed just as his hearing returned. Several of the laboratory occupants gave him a look that questioned his sanity.

"The benefits of a humiliating accident that mean your body pops in and out of this plane of existence," she said.

"Where do they go?"

She blinked several times. "You've known me for months and never asked that."

"Seemed rude to ask."

"And now it isn't?"

"I'm fairly sure you're laughing that I've been steam boiled, and you knew it was going to happen. Asking seems reasonable now."

"I'm still here, but for some reason I'm not. It's like I'm out of phase with everything."

"You can control it now, though. Couldn't when I first met you."

"I can make it happen... but I can't stop it happening."

"Eh?"

"Eh? I'm so shocked they closed the Office of Investigations. That kind of insightful questioning was the exact reason you were so successful... oh wait."

Blunt sighed. His face was red, and his skin felt like someone had rubbed it with sandpaper. "I came here for help from someone who I thought was a friend."

Sarah stopped, her mouth half open in surprise. "You're getting sensitive? You are pulling the 'woe is me' card on me? Well, Augie-"

Blunt winced at the use of the name. Only his mother had ever called him Augie, even his wife, in the living world, had called him Stan.

"This is how it feels for the shoe to be on the other foot. Now, I'm going to be the bigger person. You can find the pest control man by looking in the phone book. That's how we found him."

"The phone book."

"That's right. Comprehensive book full of phone numbers, it's in the name."

He nodded. "God help me for wishing Gloomwood was keeping up with the mortal world on some things."

SUPERMARKET SWEEP

"Here they are," Morgarth said as she opened the door to the grey Luton van by leaping up and hanging on the door handle.

Inside on either side were people. They varied in shape and size, but people were what they were. Beelzebub peered into the vehicle and surveyed the occupants. "They look frightened," he said.

"They were attacked by thirteen soft toys with demonic voices, had their hands tied, were gagged, and then thrown into the back of a van, sir."

"Yes, and they look frightened."

Morgarth nodded her tyrannosaur head. "I think they found the experience frightening."

"But you're toys. I thought toys were endearing. Did you try asking them to come?"

"We did, but the first one we asked kicked Vellmar the Vicious into some kind of dead bush. It took a long time to pull him out as he's mainly fur."

"These people do not fear the right things Morgarth. We need to rectify that."

"You'd like me to scare them more?" Morgarth asked, the soft felt fangs somehow grew more exposed.

"No Morgarth, idiot, these people are scared," Beelzebub said, "pointing into the van, I'm talking about these people," he made an expansive wave with both hands.

"Oh. That might take longer."

"Time is not something we have a lot of. I have plans for these people. Especially," he pointed at the one-eyed woman and the boy who were sitting furthest into the van, "those two traitorous money grabbing urchins. Expecting me to pay for their services. Since when did the dead demand payment for their time. That's like water demanding payment for being wet, it's all it has! We're going to play a little game."

"I like games," Morgarth said, and her tail wagged. She turned to glare at it. "This body is having an adverse effect on me, my lord."

"I appreciate that, Morgarth. It wasn't ideal, but I needed you to have heads and they are in short supply."

"We could empty some."

"I considered it, but it's not so simple. Heads are very much for life, I mean death...you know what I mean. It's a strange place."

"Where are we?" She asked.

Beelzebub took a long drag on his cigarette, "The Devil knows."

Morgarth tapped a plastic clawed foot. "Is the Devil going to share?"

"No. He isn't."

"Is he going to speak about himself in the third person forever?"

"Morgarth. This body... it seems to influence your level of respect."

"Sorry, your lordship. Perhaps you could tell us what to do with these people."

Beelzebub exhaled, filling the interior of the van with smoke. When he finished he grinned, it was a slow process. Each pointed tooth appeared in a sinister choreographed presentation. "Do shut the door Morgarth, there's a good dinosaur."

She kicked the door shut as the coughing began. A green monkey and a two foot tall yeti slid the locks into place from the outside. A moment later the shaking began. Something violent was taking place within the confines of the van.

Beelzebub, resplendent in another tailored suit, mauve purple and black swirling patterns, circles within circles, that seemed to move if you looked directly at them, stepped to the side of the van and perched atop a fire hydrant. "Did you get the box Morgarth?"

"Yes, sir. One presentation box, Garglemier, Dysentrous, bring forth the box." A giant stuffed mouse and a parrot with a button in the centre of its chest carried a large box towards them. The box had pink sparkling wrapping paper and a large blue bow.

"Oh yes, that is perfect, did you pick it Morgarth?" Beelzebub asked.

"No, your lordship, I asked the salesperson to give me the most insipid cutesy box they had, and she revealed this."

"Interesting. They did the job willingly."

"There was an exchange of money."

"Yes, but still. Why do it? They're all dead. Don't they realise they're dead? Trapped in this perpetuation of life as if it is normal. What did they live for if death is just a continuation of before?"

Morgarth was spared the need to reply as the banging in the van grew louder for a moment before settling to silence.

"If the living world is what they choose to replicate, then they can do so. Who am I to judge?" Beelzebub said.

"Sir, you're the Devil."

"Ah, then I suppose I should judge. Well then," he grinned that slow purposeful grin once more, "you better get in the box then."

MOOCHING AROUND

"Bugg.... rit... and the... mffhmm... hey, hey, you what's happening? Hmm, well, shh... what? What was that?" The muffled words came from behind the battered gas mask of Artful Mooch. He walked stooped over, his worn trench coat hiding his hunched form. Black gloves that were too big, and heavy unlaced boots that seemed to spring out of the green rubber trousers, completed an ensemble that covered every inch of his body. The only thing that proved there was a man inside were his eyes, small, dark and always furtive, never fixing on any one thing for more than a split second.

"Said nothing, Mooch. Nobody said anything." The man behind the counter didn't much try to hide his distaste. Artful Mooch wasn't disgusting, he didn't smell and his clothes were clean if threadbare. There was just too much that wasn't right about the man people called Mooch. "What you always say, 's'what you always say." Mooch said, his breathing laboured.

"Yeah, I guess it never gets old." The man, Trevor Spencer, was sitting behind a counter. Paperwork arranged in three neat piles in front of him and a clear plastic screen with a circle of holes in it between him and Mooch. "Here," the man said as he slipped a piece of paper beneath the screen towards Mooch.A blue rubber gloved hand flapped down and grasped the paper awkwardly. "Wassit?"

"It's today's job, same as it was yesterday, you expecting something else?"

"Same, always the same."

"Maybe it is, maybe it isn't. You read it?"

"Can read, always been able to read, not ignorant, not like some. Artful by name, Artful by nature."

"'Course you are Mooch. Any problem with it?"

"'s'never a problem for me. Problem for you?"

The man just shook his head and looked away, trying to find something to help him appear busy as he willed Mooch to leave. He picked up a pen and turned to one side as he scribbled on a piece of paper. "Bye-bye Trevor, have a nice day, nice day, yes." Mooch said shuffling away towards the door.

"Yeah, you too Mooch." Trevor said, breathing a sigh of relief and crumpling the meaningless doodles into a ball as the door clattered into its ill-fitting frame.

When he was outside Mooch looked at the work order again and struggled to make sense of the document. It was the same format he'd seen thousands of times. A time and place where someone had seen something untoward, a purple ink stamp confirming the request for pest control, and then Trevor's neat handwriting assigning the job to Artful Mooch.

Mooch wasn't a fool, and he was good at his job, but he was odd. He wasn't like the people he worked with. He wasn't like many people at all. He tried not to hear what others said about him. It had almost been so long he'd stopped caring, almost. "Nosey sons o... Artful doesn't need 'em anyway," he muttered to himself.

He folded the piece of paper up and shoved it into the pocket of his trench coat. It was too big, and he struggled to reach the flap low on his thigh before sliding the piece of paper into the deep recesses within. The dim grey daylight of Gloomwood offered little to lighten his mood, but then his mood was well established and it would take something more than a ray of sunshine to brighten it. Spots of rain disturbed his vision through the round acrylic eyepieces of his mask, and he wiped at them absently. The mask didn't come off, ever. People, the few who considered Mooch for more than a moment, thought it was an affectation, or something to do with his work. Mooch didn't know where it had come from, just that he didn't take it off. He didn't know how. Even when he showered his skinny bruised and battered body the mask stayed on, Mooch had never seen his own face, didn't know if he had one. He knew some people didn't, that got a face when they died, dreams, hopes, even some deities were faceless until they died, but he didn't know if he was one of them either. Nobody knew what Mooch was, and nobody seemed inclined to help him find out. He'd given up finding out who he was, given up asking for help.

He climbed into the drivers' seat of a battleship grey box van. It had 'GPC' stencilled on the side of it in what Mooch thought of as the least artistic font he'd ever seen. He liked art, Artful, he was supposed to like art, but everyone forgot his first name, they called him Mooch.

He turned on the engine and reached into his pocket again to pull out the piece of paper. "Where was it? What's the job?" He muttered to himself again. There was no frustration he was used to it, forgetting, forgetting everything. "s'near the station, s'not good, people there." He started the engine and listened to the familiar rattling of the doors that didn't quite fit, the glove compartment clattering. It would fall open when he drove over the first pothole he came across. He put it into first and listened to the crunching of the gearbox. The passenger door swung open before he pulled away from the curb, and a man in a long coat and a pretentious-looking hat leapt into the cabin of the van.

"Are you Artful Mooch?" The man asked in a tone that Mooch couldn't help but thing was needlessly aggressive.

"Yes, Artful Mooch, that's...me," he said.

"I'm Augustan Blunt, you've probably heard of me."

Mooch shook his head.

"Really? I... Detective Blunt? The Chief Investigator?"

"Sorry. Mooch doesn't watch much television, is he a... pretender... actor?"

"What? No, he's me, I mean I'm me, I'm Detective Blunt."

Mooch nodded, "Mooch knows... you said that. Wassit about? Need to go, thing, scorporabbit to catch," he waved his paperwork at Blunt.

"Is it alive?"

Mooch shrugged, "sort of."

"Amazing, let's have a chat, mister Mooch."

END OF THE WORLD

It is difficult to dismiss an afterlife once you are ensconced within it. It is nigh on impossible to dismiss the idea that something exists after death if you're already in the afterlife. This is one of the fundamental principles of Mankind's Everlasting, Eternal Purgatory. The church of MEEP had grown from strength to strength based upon this simple concept. This in tandem with the concerted insistence that translations of ancient texts had at some point suffered from a simple typo. The Meep shall inherit the earth.

Molly Gormley was an ardent supporter of the church. Her support was so vigorous and complete that she unnerved those who had taken sacred vows. Most members of the clergy were quite happy to work on growing their flock. As in all walks of life, there were those who saw this as a work of great import, and those who saw it as work. There were very few who saw it as a single-minded reason for their continued existence.

As a frequent attendee of any, and all, occasions at the Cathedral of Greg she had become 'known'. Her sermons, often delivered unexpectedly and without request, had caught the pastor by surprise the first time. After the third he had suggested she try delivering them on the cathedral steps where more people might hear her. Shortly afterwards he suggested she tried using the park across the street so she could find new members of the church.

It took higher members of the church to convince her to go... elsewhere.

Molly was a believer. It was the strength and conviction of her belief that made people nervous. That, and that she was quite adamant that anyone who didn't meet the expectations of God's own dead people should deserve quick and severe punishment.

"The end is nigh. Did you repent? The lord has damned us all to this place but there is still time to save your souls. Only the church can protect you. You will suffer a never-ending hell, pain and suffering, agony-"

"I like your board," a voice interrupted her.

She stopped her shouting and turned. A man was standing within the space the divine had gifted her. The space that others kept clear so that more could hear her message. Those untouched by the grace of the divine would mysteriously walk around a radius of nearly three meters to avoid the zone. Even when she wasn't preaching, they still kept this berth and Molly knew it was God's will.

"Are you talking to me?" She asked.

"Yes. I like your board. The end is nigh. People don't nigh enough these days," the man said.

He smiled a grin that made her nervous. She felt the colour rise in her cheeks, the warmth of a blush, and then she felt fury. An instinctive impure thought had entered her head. What tiny morsel of blood she still possessed revealed her impurity. She had not yet freed herself completely from the sins of the mortal world. "Thank you. I'm busy-"

"I can see that. Yes, of course, you must tell the people of the word of the church. It is the word of the church, isn't it?"

"Yes, of course."

"So, the church says everybody in this city is damned and only the people who are followers of the word of the... what do you call the book?"

"The Mible."

"The... are you being serious?"

"Yes, it's part of the great typo."

"The great...you mean the Meep will inherit the Earth thing?"

"It is not a 'thing'. It is the truth we realised upon our Death!"

"So, in one case the k changed into a p and in the other case a 'b' turned into an 'm'?"

"... yes."

"I see... well, that would require divine intervention... You realise it turned back into a 'b', shouldn't it be the Mimle?"

She was used to this. Those who questioned the wisdom of the lord. "Exactly, for that to happen, there must have been divine intervention. I take it you are a believer sir?"

"Oh yes, I very much believe in the divine," Beelzebub said, "in fact I believe the Lord is already changing things."

"Oh?"

"I have witnessed a miracle, now none of those who disregarded us will ever be able to ignore us."

"A miracle?"

"Yes, I have seen the living dead."

"The... but how?"

"I can show you, I have it in the back of my van," said Beelzebub without a trace of irony.

THE PRESENTS OF DEATH

As the figurehead for a nation of the dead, the Grim Reaper would never class himself as 'hands-on'. He believed in a very loose form of leadership. Not so much an iron grip as a slippery oiled up open palm. This didn't stop the citizens of the city holding him in the highest regard.

Grim himself did not court their favour. He preferred to keep to himself. Politics confused him, and he lacked any ambition or thirst for power. It was a fact that only those in the upper echelons of the Office of the Dead paid attention to. His was a simple role that a skeleton in a robe could do, which sometimes happened.

Crispin Neat was the true arbiter of the goings on in governing Gloomwood, and his management of the city was careful, deliberate and balanced. The Manager of the OD was, in some sense, an enabler. He held no animosity towards the Grim Reaper, quite the opposite, he quite liked Death, the person. It was just a fact that the Grim Reaper was far more interested in snow globes, bad poetry, and though it was a closely guarded secret, karaoke.

None of this changed the fact that people liked to buy the Grim Reaper presents. At times as an act of gratitude, sometimes because it was politically appropriate, and sometimes just because people are nice. There was a fourth gift type, but the thought of them made the Grim Reaper uncomfortable. He had never quite come to terms with the fact that some might find the supposed power he held attractive, and they disconcerted him with some proposals and pictures he received. It didn't help that he had absolutely none of that form of desire himself. Of course, lacking any 'equipment' didn't help.

It wasn't as though people brought presents to his office by wheelbarrow and showered them upon him like some child emperor demanding toys. This is Gloomwood, there are people who need jobs, which doesn't mean there are jobs that need people. The economy of Gloomwood worked under the unfaltering principle that what is quick and efficient for one person is often a slow and painful task, for five or six people who don't like each other. This is why 'teams' exist in most office environments.

The working party who dealt with the Grim Reaper's mail comprised several individuals, most of whom had 'leadership roles' where they spent hours plotting unnecessary changes that ensured the system remained broken. It being broken allowed for new fixes, which kept them in jobs.

Actual work involved the arrivals team who worked in the post room. Here they sorted all post into different piles, most of their role was checking correspondence and sending it to the right people. It is much simpler to just address any letter to the Grim Reaper and hope that the embodiment of Death itself has time to deal with the problem with whatever was delaying the bin collections. They then send presents to Chris and Chris. Their job was to peek inside presents, shake them vigorously, and squirrel away any rude photos they could pass around the office or, as long as the other Chris wasn't looking, slip into the drawer from where things never return. Once they ensure they have smashed anything that may be fragile into a thousand pieces, they send the presents upstairs.

The Grim Reaper's security detail were not part of the Gloomwood Police. Having the Gloomwood Police provide security was like asking the lions to guard the audience at the circus. There is an organisation who deal with things in the dark. A small clandestine unit who solve problems that are best hidden from the eyes of the public, or the important, or... everyone. Led by a man who goes by the name of Tomb Mandrake, it might be his name, it might be a fanciful moniker. After an extremely embarrassing episode several months earlier, they took the responsibility of providing security for the Grim Reaper and the Manager of the Office of the Dead. Part of this included inspecting any packages sent to either man. Fortunately, they were all guarding, and covering up, a strange episode at the Gloomwood Deathport.

From inside her box, Morgarth didn't know she was being scanned with a device to detect dangerous substances. The device, and several others like it in the security personnel's arsenal, did nothing. Had they bothered to crack open the plastic coverings, they would have found a few pieces of broken telephones and some stones for weight. Still, they diligently waved the devices over the large wrapped box, and ticked the boxes on their forms, before sending it to the next person on the list.

The position of receptionist to the Grim Reaper is one of the highest achievable positions within the city. It is also one of the few positions of such status that ever becomes vacant. People train for decades, gathering experience and qualifications that outstrip the competition. Stepping on the heads of their friends and colleagues as they drive towards this golden opportunity. The last hurdle requires them to endure a meeting with Crispin Neat and the Grim Reaper. In this meeting, they insist the position is extremely dull and that they are over-qualified. This, every sensible person knows, is a test. It is not a test. The average time spent by a high-achiever in the role of receptionist to the Grim Reaper is three months. It may singularly be the dullest job in Gloomwood.

Hours of silence behind a counter with nothing but the ticking clock and the ominous short few steps into the Grim Reaper's office. To his credit, the Grim Reaper did attempt to greet his receptionist every day and pass pleasantries.

This morning the receptionist, Ursula Panderpenny, was inspecting the letters, gifts and presents while sitting at her desk. There was never any sign whether the Grim Reaper was in his office or out. There was never a need for any notification as her job was to sit at the desk. At no point had anybody provided her with a calendar or a list of appointments and engagements. The only person who ever visited the Grim Reaper was Crispin Neat, and he barely acknowledged her existence. This, she had decided, was still part of the test.

The large box intrigued her. When it started playing music, it intrigued her more and so she opened it. It didn't occur to her that this might be a test. It was far too trivial. She had a master's degree in business, a doctorate in diplomacy, and a bachelor in thaumatology that she had studied through distance learning. She had lectured about postmortal politics. Was she qualified to the nth degree? Literally, the nth degree was part of her postgraduate studies. She could use her initiative.

She pulled the bow and carefully unwrapped the paper and folded it neatly to use it again. Ursula Panderpenny was that kind of person. Then she pulled open the top of the disappointing brown cardboard box to reveal a dinosaur soft toy who was holding a strange rectangular object. The object was a little larger than her hand, and it was playing music.

As she reached towards it the dinosaur growled, "it's for the Grim Reaper."

Ursula collapsed in terror. A demon voice has that effect. Morgarth stood up inside the box, her head peering over the top of it. "Am I in the 'presents' of Death... do you get it? Hello?"

MORE MOOCH

"So how do you find them?" Blunt asked. He was sitting in the passenger seat of the grey pest control van. It felt like they had replaced the suspension with concrete blocks. The seat, Blunt had decided, must have engineered to ensure maximum discomfort.

"Mooch doesn't find them, devices find them."

"Right," Blunt said as he nodded. Speaking to Mooch was an uphill battle where the strange masked man evaded a simple answer to any question. Every time Blunt asked anything, he felt like he was herding responses into a corner until there was no choice but to answer. It didn't seem intentional so Blunt had to assume that Mooch wasn't being evasive but that the point of the questions eluded him.

"The little doo-dah on your belt?"

The large rubber gloves looked like they were barely gripping the wheel as the van lurched around the corner, connected with the curb, and lifted for a split second on to two wheels. The resultant landing of the vehicle caused Blunt to bang his head against the passenger window and his hat landed in his lap.

"Mhmf, thassit, this one," the little man wasn't even pretending to look at the road anymore as he looked down and pointed at the boxes on his waist. "For prox... proximity to things, this one's for big nasty things."

The detective rubbed the side of his head. "So you can find things that are alive?"

"S'not life... not alive, no, no, no, can't be alive. Has time."

"Time?"

"Mmf, time, s'like life."

"So what's in the box?"

"Mhm, trade secrets-"

"It's important and I'm not about to start pest control."

"Already doing my job, yes you are, already trying to find pests. Things that don't belong."

Blunt hesitated to respond. Was that what he was doing? Was he hired as pest control? Why come to him then? The woman, Twist, she could've found this strange little man herself, couldn't she? "I don't want your job," he said.

"Say so, but Mooch doesn't know. What's your job?"

"I'm…" Blunt hesitated. He was unemployed and as he had agreed to work for the mysterious Twist without finding out anything about her, it would be an exaggeration to say he was under any kind of contract, even if he felt he was. "I'm a private investigator."

"Oh. Chasing people down, what's it, dark alleyways, knife fights on rooftops? Mhm, don't want your job either," Mooch said.

"Well… there's none of that. Mostly I just drive around asking people for help," Blunt said.

Mooch swerved to the right, the van lifted on to the curb and he hit the brakes hard. "Asking for help?"

"Yes," Blunt said, one arm pushed against the passenger side window and the other on the dashboard of the van to brace himself even though they had come to a stop.

Mooch nodded. "Artful Mooch can help, Art likes to help people. Find life by using life, living things, mhm, gather, collect together."

"Like magnets?"

"No, magnets don't work like that, magnets pull or push on poles, life only pulls. Life is really time, so find some time, or something that wants time, find life," he tapped the box at his waist.

"I don't understand."

"Come," Mooch opened the door and stepped out of the van. The screeching of car tyres and loud verbal abuse suggested he hadn't checked before opening the door.

Blunt stepped out of the passenger door onto the pavement. As he slammed the door, the pest control man appeared from behind the van.

"What are we doing here?"

"My workshop."

"So, you made the device yourself?"

"Mooch bought it from display next to batteries on the way out of the shop."

"Sarcasm?"

"Correct, Mooch doesn't speak to people much, did it right?"

"Yeah, perfect."

"Inside," he pointed to the kind of building that in the land of the living people would talk about in hushed whispers. There'd be rumours about the seventeen children who disappeared after entering the house over the last fifty years. The inhabitants of Gloomwood were, in most cases, people who believe this kind of gruesome history adds 'character' to a home.

Blunt followed once Mooch had unlocked a heavily barricaded metal door. When the door creaked open the smell from inside was a near physical assault. He gagged and tried to hide the reflex. "I can see why you wear the mask," he said.

"What mask?" Mooch replied.

"The, uh... nevermind," Blunt said as he looked into the glassy eyes of the gas mask. "Actually... I've got a reputation for putting my foot in it, and it will not change today. So is that your face?" He waved a finger around his own face.

"Mhm, seems to be, yes, my face. Just a face."

Blunt nodded. "Yup, that was rude of me."

Mooch shrugged, the too big coat bunched up above the belt and refused to fall back down. It looked like he'd inflated his top half and then had a puncture.

Inside the building was dark and the smell, which Blunt was growing acclimated to, was fetid, dank and humid, like having your face buried in a pile of damp autumn leaves. "So this is your workshop?"

"Mhm, workshop s'one name. It's a place for things."

Something rustled in the darkness.

💀 <u>JIMMY "BIG HANDS"</u> 💀

Jimmy 'big-hands' turned up on their doorstep with a story to tell. They called him big hands because he had huge meaty palms. A professional clapper by trade his applause could carry even the worst sitcoms, his guffaw wasn't bad either, but he wasn't laughing now.

John Jacob Jeremiah Johnson, constable of the Gloomwood police opened the door and took a step back. Jimmy was tall and gangly and sometimes it looked like the effort of lifting those hands, the size of frying pans, took it out of him. He was panting.

"Johnson, I need your help."

Gloomwood society is fractured, broken, disparate, and for anyone who is different, it can be unwelcoming. Johnson knew it better than most. As a former member of the Gloomwood constabulary, he had found himself the focus of every ounce of hatred the police had towards someone different. The police, it seemed, had a lot of hate to spare.

Johnson shouldered it and carried on. He was indifferent to their banter, their dismissive tones, their practical jokes were closer to assault than humour. The constable had told himself he could take it. He polished his boots to a shine, wore the grey uniform with pride, and patrolled the streets. Determination and will were his shield, but every tactician will tell you the hardest enemy to fight is the one on your own team. They had won.

"I'm not a police officer anymore, Jimmy," Johnson said. He stood in the doorway while the rain hammered down on the clapper who was wearing a soaking wet green cardigan. It was pouring and rivulets dripped off the end of the tall man's nose, but Johnson could see his eyes were red. The rain was only masking tears. Johnson sighed. "You better come in."

The house was small and the ceilings low. Jimmy "Big Hands" had to duck through the doorway and then found he couldn't stand up straight once inside.

"Yeah," Johnson said, looking at the bedraggled professional audience as he bent forward, "Petal suggested just getting rid of the second floor completely, but then we'd have even less space."

"Is he...here?" Jimmy asked, looking around.

Johnson shook his head. If Petal had been, it wasn't as if he would have been able to hide behind an item of furniture. Johnson's death partner, Petal, stood almost eight feet tall and nobody would ever make the mistake of describing him as 'gangly'. The huge Demi-god also had a reputation that had followed him for a lot longer than most people's do. That's the problem with a reputation, people can try to change, but a reputation won't make the same effort. "No, he's out working."

"Dealing-"

"No. He doesn't do that anymore. If you're so scared of him what are you doing here?"

Jimmy pushed the front door shut and followed Johnson into the tiny living room. A small black and white tube style television flickered in the room's corner. "I'm more scared of what I saw today."

Johnson nodded, "I'm listening Jimmy, take a seat, calm down. Do you want a drink?"

Jimmy shook his head as he lowered himself onto the brown sofa. It was old, and the springs in it weren't what they used to be. It didn't matter where you tried to sit, it would roll you into the middle. "No, no, it's fine," he flapped his hands. "I'm telling you this because I think they're going to try to cover it up and I don't think it's the first time it's happened."

Johnson took a seat in a chair on the other side of the room. He tried to look relaxed, welcoming. He wasn't great at it. "Okay Jimmy, tell me what happened."

"He sneezed…"

"Well, that's not unusual, norms do that sometimes. It's a reflex. The Captain sneezes sometimes and with those fake noses he wears, it can be pretty scary."

"Yeah, the sneeze wasn't that weird but after he sneezed the doctor... he..." The man's hands were shaking and when they're as big as Jimmy's it's a frightening sight.

"It's okay, Jimmy. There's only the two of us here. Who was it that sneezed?"

"The bear, that bloody bear, Teddington Rex. I've been saying there's something weird about him, he keeps going on about headaches, and then this happens."

"Jimmy, I want nothing to do with the bear. Everyone knows that. There's nothing in the afterlife that would make me want to have anything to do with him."

"What about Ableforth? Well?"

Johnson put his hands together and rested his elbows on his knees. "I'm not following you. He sneezed and then..."

"And then the doctor's face exploded out of his head, well his body, he was a squid, or something. Just one little sneeze."

"Just take a breath. Why would the bear sneezing have anything to do with the doctor's face exploding? You can't go around saying that kind of thing, Jimmy. People will panic."

"The bear knew he'd done it. He started panicking, saying, 'oh god, on no, I've killed him, or whatever you call it, we've gotta cover this up,'"

"That...sounds pretty bad. What do you want to do?"

"Me? I'm telling you. You're used to this stuff, aren't you? I mean with Petal," he looked around as if just saying the Demi-god's name could make him appear, "and the stuff the police see."

Johnson nodded. This had happened before. People turning up on his doorstep asking for help because they had nowhere else to turn. Jimmy "Big Hands" had been in show business for a while, so maybe he was forgetting. "I was a police officer, Jimmy, but... this is Gloomwood. You're not a norm. If the doctor was a squid, then he wasn't a norm either."

"It was Ableforth, Jay-jay. It doesn't matter who we are. The police might turn a blind eye to a Hope getting a kicking round the back of a nightclub, or petty crime amongst the pabies, but they will not sweep Ableforth under the carpet... will they?"

"No, no, you're right..."

"I'm going to go to the station... I just don't want to go alone."

"Jimmy... turning up there with me probably isn't going to help you."

"You're one of them"

"I was Jimmy. Come on, you've heard the stories, right?"

"I know, but they'll listen to you, they have to, right?"

Johnson shook his head, then ran a hand through his hair. He'd let it grow longer after leaving the police.

"And you know the bear."

Johnson swallowed. "Yeah, Jimmy... I do. Why don't you go home, get some rest? I'll take care of this."

Jimmy's hands stopped shaking, and the man smiled. It was the smile of someone who had just grabbed the monkey off his back and thrown it on to someone else without the slightest hint of guilt or guile. "Thanks, Jay-jay. I knew I could trust you. You're one of the good guys, maybe the only one."

"Yeah, Jimmy. No problem. I just do what anyone else would do."

"No, Jay-jay, you do the opposite of what everyone else would do. If you didn't, I wouldn't be here."

MOOCH'S PETS

There was a growl. A low snarl that faded to a throaty rumble. "Uh, what's that?" Blunt asked.

"That's Spot, he's a good boy."

"Spot?"

"Mhm, good boy Spot," Mooch said.

"A dog? I thought there weren't any animals-"

"Spot's not a dog and there are animals, birds, Corvidae."

"Crows-"

"Ravens."

"Tomato, tomato."

The growl came again, this time from the opposite side of the dark room they were standing in. The ceiling above them held a single wire with a bulb attached to it that barely illuminated the room. Around the room where the remains of various cages, boxes, and on one wall there seemed to be a collection of nets and chains. "That doesn't sound like a raven."

"Didn't say Spot was a raven."

"What is it, he, then?"

"Like this," Mooch pointed to the table in the middle of the room. On top of it were several small glass rectangular boxes.

As Blunt stepped closer, he realised they were tanks. Each of them had something inside, something that moved. The growling was louder and more persistent now. "Look, I just want to know how to find something. Your dog-"

"Not a dog."

"It doesn't matter what it is. Why do people think it's enough to say, 'oh don't worry, he rarely rips people's faces off and swallows them as they scream in terror'? What the hell is it?"

"I don't know," Mooch said, his voice low and quiet, "don't shout, Spot doesn't like loud noises."

"What in a bucket full of hand-washed squirrel excrement are you talking about? What the hell keeps growling at me like it's about to jump out of the shadow and impale me on its claws before tearing me asunder? And what does it have to do with the little box on your waist?"

The gas mask was impossible to read, but if Blunt knew one thing, it was people. This strange character in the oversized clothes who spent his time catching beasts or locked in a creepy dark room with a growling creature was trying to help, but his patience was wearing thin.

"Spot's okay, he doesn't like the light, won't come near you if the light is on, even if he did, he's friendly. That is his friendly voice."

"Wouldn't want to hear him if he wasn't being friendly."

"Mhm, wouldn't hear him at all if Spot wanted to be unfriendly." Mooch said without the slightest threat to his words. "Take one box. Thing inside is almost alive, ish, maybe, Mooch thinks it's like life but it likes life."

"Uh, it's like life... but it likes life?"

"Mooch said that."

"I'm trying to work out what it means."

"Means thing in the box moves towards things like it."

"Wait a minute, have you got one of these in that box on your belt."

"Mhm, and some other things... looks like a mechanical thing, isn't though. Mooch is clever," he tapped the side of his head where, if not for the mask, his temple might have been, "keep people guessing."

Blunt nodded and rubbed the sleeve of his coat across his forehead. He was sweating. Technically, there was no need to sweat, he was dead, but he did anyway, all the time, but especially when it was hot. "It's like a sauna in here."

"Mooch has work to do. Take a box, watch it, use it like a dog smells things, don't let it out of the box."

"Yeah, don't feed it after midnight, and don't get it wet."

"Wassit? Why would you do that?"

"Just a joke. Don't open the box."

"Don't open the box."

Blunt looked down at the table where the boxes rested. There were nine of them. Each one had something inside it. To the right of it was a roll of plastic. "What's this?" Blunt asked.

"For Spot."

"Oh, right-"

"For faeces."

"Ugh, okay-"

"Mooch hates it, has to pick it up, always still warm but not okay to leave behind."

"That's... fascinating."

"You're leaving now."

"Oh."

"Take a box. Leave Artful Mooch alone."

Blunt grabbed a box. He peered in and discovered it was full of maggots, or something that looked very similar to maggots, but they made no movement, so he shrugged and turned around to leave.

"Doesn't work through these walls, mustn't tempt them, no."

"Ah lead-lined, are they?"

"No. Painted with Styx water."

"Is it water?"

Mooch shrugged, causing his oversized coat to bunch up at the waist. "Bye now."

"Right, well. Thanks?"

"Mhm. Probably won't be thankful later."

It was only when Mooch slammed the door, and Blunt heard the bolts being slid into position from the inside, that he realised his car was miles away.

BRAINS

Dennis Barrington hadn't been the nicest person in life. He knew that, and he had made peace with it. In fact, he'd made such good peace with it he had no intention of doing anything to change in the afterlife. Dying while in the middle of an energetic session with his mistress, while his wife struggled to look after their four children under ten, and then waking up in Gloomwood had told him he could do no wrong. Maybe he was blessed, or none of it made a difference to anything, Dennis, or Mr Barrington, as he preferred, didn't care.

Dennis was the person who made people's jobs more difficult out of boredom, and because he was Mister Barrington, and he was important, and wealthy. When he'd arrived in Gloomwood, he hadn't been rich. He'd been, in his own eyes, disgustingly poor. This was something easily rectified. Anybody who knows anything about anything understands you get rich by doing horrible things to insignificant people, by keeping secrets and making sure people owe you favours, and by demanding it of other people. So, he'd found the people who understood, "terribly embarrassing old boy, I seem to have mislaid my wealth when I died," he'd said.

There had been a test, of course. It was simple enough. Ruin a few people's deaths, ensuring there was no risk of a moral compass, or worse empathy and compassion, oh how they had laughed. Mister Barrington, to you, wouldn't belittle himself by returning a shopping trolley. It was embarrassing enough that he had to visit the supermarket himself, but times were tough. He'd almost considered buying 'own-brand' toilet paper, but his arse deserved better.

He had seethed while waiting hours in the back of a van with common folk. Trussed up, not too different from the way they'd found his corpse on the living side of things. Except of course that had been a bit of escapism gone wrong, or, in Mister Barrington's opinion, a bloody stupid dominatrix. He might have had more of a right to blame her if he hadn't put himself into the position alone, while he awaited her arrival so he didn't have to pay for the part he could do on his own.

'Stuffed animals,' he had thought to himself, 'and not even the real ones who somebody has to kill, horrible tacky plastic ones. Gone were the days where taxidermy and realism were authentic art forms.' While he considered, then dismissed, chafing his wrists, trying to free himself from the restraints, he observed the futile struggle of the others in the van.

If one of them freed themselves, they would free him, so there was no need to waste his energy. Whatever was going on, there would be a simple and logical explanation that he could probably buy his way out of. Arrogance can be easily mistaken for bravery and steel nerves in the face of danger. It's not bravery if you're too full of self-importance to believe anyone would dare harm you.

When the doors opened, and the man in the suit looked in, was the first time Mister Barrington had wondered if he was in trouble. It was a nice suit. An elegant suit. A suit that was too flamboyant for Mister Barrington but that he recognised as being of a certain, 'level'. A suit that people who stood on the heads of other people without finding out their names wore.

When the doors closed, it didn't matter what Mister Barrington thought. He could smell the smoke. It caught in his chest. The others started coughing. Then they started screaming and shouting through their gags. The sounds of choking, suffocating, took over, and he fell forward onto his knees as he gasped as if desperate for air. In his panicked state, he didn't have time to question why he would need air. The others were moving. With impossible ease, they ripped through restraints and gags.

Mister Barrington had one thought before everything went dark. "Don't they know who I am?"

DEATHPORT

It was quiet in a way that made her skin crawl. Gloomwood was macabre and dark at the best of times, but the Deathport seemed to embody those characteristics like nowhere else in the city, except maybe the library.

At least, Leighton thought to herself, the library makes no pretence about its home for lost souls. The rows of heads on the library shelves that slowly turned into skulls as the flesh from them turned to dust were terrifying. Those calcified containers which kept the souls within trapped as they turned in on themselves.

She reached into her pocket and pulled out a packet of Feelbetters. The tissues were a cheat she had held on to. Building into an addiction. Realising she was developing a problem she had researched their effects, and it turned out it was the same magical impact of a cup of tea handed to someone in a crisis followed by the words, "it'll be alright dear," said in that special tone that some individuals have mastered. She blew her nose despite not needing to and felt her courage grow a little.

Nobody returned to the Deathport. It was a one time visit. You arrived in that strange little room with the luggage carousel and the lonely desk, bewildered and afraid. This was the destination, the chequered flag before you were indisputably dead. There was a reason that the Deathport only had an arrivals section, and it was only after you passed through those glass doors that you realised there was no turning back.

She stood looking at her reflection in the glass. There was no sensor on this side of the door. It was an exit only. Her hat was perched atop her blond curls, the little piece of card she had poked into the band of the hat said the word PRESS on it in bold letters. Only once had someone been stupid, or cocky, enough to pat her on the head and say, "well what happens after I press it?" He wouldn't make the same mistake again. She was diminutive, but not someone who couldn't take care of herself. The sand coloured trench coat cinched at her waist, and boots sporting only an inch of heel, put together what she considered the perfect reporter's ensemble. Appearances for Leighton Hughes, reporter extraordinaire, mattered.

With both hands, she banged against the glass. "Open the door. I've got questions," she shouted.

As expected, there was no response. It had been half an hour since she had arrived. Her plan was to wait until somebody turned up but, she realised, not that many people walked through these doors.

"Hey lady," a voice behind her said, "you can't go back. It's one-way only."

She turned to find a man leaning out of the driver's side window of a Gloomwood black taxi cab. His face was out of focus, blurred and difficult to look at. "Oh, thanks," the man said as Leighton squinted in his direction.

"I'm sorry I didn't mean to be rude."

"Relax, I'm kidding, I'm out of focus. Can't do anything about it, just the way they made me."

"You're... a hope?"

"Nightmare actually, but it's all the same. I'm the recurring one people used to have before the world went digital about every photo you own being out of focus. Not," he said, "that it's anyone's business, but you look like a lady who gets answers. Now, have things really got so bad that you want to walk back through the veil? Maybe a reminder you're a far sight prettier on the eyes than I am might help?"

Leighton offered a smile. The man, blurriness aside, seemed friendly enough. "A little misogynistic to go straight for a woman's appearance to cheer her up."

"What can I say," the taxi driver said with a wave of his hand, "I can be a nightmare sometimes." Even out-of-focus Leighton could see the grin.

"Okay, Mister Nightmare. I'm here, following up a report of Ableforth. I was expecting a scene. Police, reporters, you know?"

"Oh, that. You're late. That was this morning, and there weren't any reporters. Whole thing was just a mix-up, apparently."

Leighton's right eyebrow twitched. "A mix-up? What about the police?"

"Well, between you and me, they packed up pretty quick when the Manager of the OD turned up. Apparently it was all a big misunderstanding."

"What about Ableforth? Where's the security?"

"You mean Barney? He barely ever turns up for work and when he does he just stands outside smoking."

"So you're telling me nothing happened?"

"That's right. Nothing to see here."

"You're one of them, aren't you?"

"I don't know who you mean, Miss Hughes."

"Idiot, I didn't tell you my name."

The taxi driver's face flickered like an old television losing reception. "Shove off Miss Hughes, that's your warning. We've got this in hand."

NO PHONES

The Grim Reaper pressed pause on the speaker in his room. It was a coveted object that he saved for his personal use. Technology from the land of the living. True, had anybody known he was hiding such technology, and using living world materials, they might have raised an arched eyebrow, but they wouldn't have said anything. Still, he preferred not to show such hypocrisy, if only so he could pretend he was as virtuous as so many he was. His music choice was also not something he cared to have bandied around.

Being the Grim Reaper is fraught with expectation. It was a drain on him. He understood it, of course he did, he wasn't an idiot. It was still unfair. Dark and brooding, mysterious and terrifying, never the life and soul of the party... it would be ironic. Sometimes he just wanted to wear pink and dance like nobody was watching. Sing like nothing else mattered. Stroke a beloved pet without it collapsing into a tangled heap of dust and bones. This was the lot they had given him. All the same, if he sang along to 'Now here's Power Ballads; volume 2', that was his own business.

He held his scythe in one hand. It had more use as a prop than as a tool of the master of the dead. Accidents happened, but sneaking a microphone stand into his office wasn't as simple as slipping a speaker into his ribcage. He had tried putting the blade end on the floor, but it had taken almost a week to find all the bones from his foot after stepping on it. The hopping didn't go entirely unnoticed. Now he just tried to keep the blade turned away from his skull.

He placed it back in the umbrella stand by the door. Then, in deference to eared people everywhere, pressed the side of his head against the thick doors. Yes, he decided, there was activity outside the office. Despite the muffled sound he heard a bang, some shuffling, shouting... 'peculiar,' the Grim Reaper thought.

He composed himself, ensured the robe covered him fully. It got caught between vertebrae when he danced and placed a skeletal hand on the door handle. He had been told it was important he maintained an air of absolute control. Not that hard to do. Having no face made it quite easy to disguise emotions most of the time, unless his jaw was hanging open. That could be a giveaway. The only other thing he was moving with deliberate control.

The door opened, and he looked down the short flight of four steps to the reception area. The staircase was pointless and frustrating. The only thing it did was make the ceiling lower in his own office.

There was a cardboard box on its side by the receptionist's desk. Standing next to it was a fluffy tyrannosaurus rex and the receptionist... or at least her head.

"Oh," said the Grim Reaper.

"This dinosaur says it has something for you," Ursula said from the marble floor of the reception area.

"You seem shorter than I remember."

The receptionist scowled. "You have a visitor who did not make an appointment."

"Do they make appointments?"

"Yes," she said, "are you going to do anything about the fact that I've been decapitated?"

The Grim Reaper nodded. "It is quite frustrating. I've experienced it myself but, if you concentrate you should still be able to move your body. It's about proximity, you see. The body is still yours," he said, still standing at the top step of the staircase.

"Or you could move my head for me."

"No. You might accuse me of inappropriate touching."

"It's entirely appropriate. I've had my head chopped off."

"How do I know you didn't do it on purpose just so I would touch you?"

Her chin touched the marble floor as her mouth fell open, "What? You think someone would chop their own head off so you would touch them?"

The Grim Reaper waved a skeletal hand in her direction. "There's no need to say it like that. It's not about the opinion I hold of myself, it's the opinion I hold of other people. I don't know if you're secretly infatuated with me and you have spent decades trying to reach a point where you could get to this position only to decapitate yourself so I would touch you. People are strange."

"People? People are strange-"

"You realise you're waving your hands right now?" The Grim Reaper interrupted the spluttering Ursula.

"I, oh... I see, brilliant," she said as her body stood up and walked towards her, "you distracted me so I could move my body. Oh sir, you are clever."

"I didn't mean, oh, yes, I am sometimes. Where is this person who doesn't have an appointment?"

"I'm right here," Morgarth the Destroyer said from where she stood next to the head of the receptionist.

"Did you decapitate the receptionist?"

"My name is Ursula." The receptionist said as she lifted her head and tried to balance it on top of what remained of her neck.

"I know that," said the Grim Reaper, "how did a fluffy talking toy decapitate you?"

"Slowly," the dinosaur said.

The Grim Reaper tilted his head to one side looking at the toy, "Do I know you from somewhere?"

"This is for you," in one tiny T-Rex hand the dinosaur waved an instantly recognisable device.

"No, it isn't. We don't have those here. The only ones we have are brass and have no screens. They are evil."

The ringtone on the phone started. It was a familiar tune. The Grim Reaper froze for a moment and then pointed at the dinosaur, "that song. Turn it off."

"I can't, it's locked."

The Grim Reaper shrugged, "Well, I have got no fingerprints, so I can't unlock it."

"Same here," the dinosaur waggled its fluffy fingers, "It's on facial recognition."

"Beezy..."

NIGHT STICK

"This," he gave a flick of the wrist and the extendable metal stick he held flicked out to its full length, "is a nightstick."

"Ooh," the three constables standing in a circle around Sergeant Phillips said.

"Yeah, I know," Phillips continued nodding as he waved it around, "brand new, designed for maximum efficiency."

"Is it?" Constable Daniels asked.

"Yeah," Phillips responded; he was a broad-shouldered, squat man.

Daniels, by comparison, was extremely long limbed, tall, and bald. He had once gained the nickname of 'the needle' but, thanks to a penchant for violence, he had put an end to the name before it got out of control. "Why's it more efficient than this?" He waved his truncheon.

Sergeant Phillips gave the other constables a look that made it clear he expected them all to be calling Daniels names by the end of the conversation. "Because it's a nightstick, that's just a truncheon, obviously."

"Right..." Daniels was oblivious to the looks because he was not as stupid as he appeared, which was idiotic, "why's it called a nightstick then?"

"Because it's a long stick..."

"And?"

"And what? It's not a ball is it, a nightball would be pretty bloody stupid."

"What's it got to do with 'night'? Have you got a different one that you use in the day? Does it glow in the dark?"

"No you sodding smartarse, it just sounds better."

"Right, so it's just a fancier version of this," he waved his truncheon.

"No, it isn't...it's much more... expensive," to this the other constables could only laugh.

A keen observer would have noticed that throughout the exchange all four of them, Daniels, Phillips, Taffet and Furnell, appeared to be ready for violence. That's because they were. The Gloomwood police can find violence in any encounter. This is because they are violent, untrustworthy, and just as likely to attack each other, as they are an innocent member of the public. A police officer is always on duty, because if you're not, then another police officer might just beat you to within an inch of your death.

The four of them were standing on the corner of Urn Drive and Ashes Road. It was a brief walk from the part of town known as media central where, for the last seventy years, radio and television had been king. It was also a good place to stop and harass people on their way to be part of an audience. They were in a hurry, but it was important that people felt protected, which is why there was a rota for who got to work on that corner.

"You, are you wearing green?" Phillips asked a man walking by to change the conversation from the subject of sticks designed for hitting people.

"Uh, yes, officer?"

"That contravenes order 47b, subset 2," Phillips shouted.

The man looked around. Nobody on the crowded street even looked in his direction. "It...it is? Lots of people are wearing green."

"Are you questioning me?" Phillips asked.

The man nodded, "Yes."

"What did you just say?" Daniels stepped forward.

"I said yes."

"Yes, what?"

"Yes, nothing, I just said yes. Is your hearing okay? I'm actually an audiologist if you'd like me to check."

The constables and the sergeant took a step back and a whispered conversation took place, "but how much?" Taffett said.

"I don't know, but it's not cheap," said Furnell

"What did you say?" Asked Daniels.

"Right," Sergeant Phillips stood up, "since you've been so kind to offer, would you mind giving us a quick check up? Obviously, we'd forget about the infraction of by law 67f,"

"You mean 47b, subset 2?"

"Oh yeah, that one."

"Right, well, do you have a chair?"

All four officers immediately reached behind them with military precision and retrieved their patented police issue folding chairs from the special pack on their back. They stood in a line of four to attention with the chairs in their folded position as Sergeant Phillips barked, "Tension,"

"You mean attention?" The audiologist said.

"Don't interrupt please sir, tension refers to the elastic clasp around the middle of this piece of highly sensitive equipment. Ahem, Tension," the four officers unclipped the clasps, the four bands around the chair legs flicked off in perfect harmony, "seat legs," three choreographed men, and Furnell who was female, in grey flicked their retractable seats forward so the legs extended, "step round, and rest," they collapsed into the seats in a line. "Right then, let's get this done."

Before the man in green could get to work, there came a scream from further down Ashes road. The audiologist looked up, shook his head, and took a step back, tripping over the curb. "What's going on?"

"None of that buddy, deal's a deal."

"Didn't you hear that scream?"

Sergeant Phillips sighed. "Of course, we did, but we're in the middle of something here."

"What is that?" The audiologist said before scrambling backwards, climbing to his feet and running away.

"Oi, you can't run off, we've got a deal," Daniels shouted from his chair.

The four officers shared a look and, with none of the precision they had displayed assembling the chairs, stood up to peer down the street in the direction people were running from.

"Leg it?" One constable said.

A woman ran towards them, "Help, police, Constable Daniels, help."

"Bloody hell Daniels, that one knows who you are!" Sergeant Phillips shouted. "Now we're going to have to do something, right, nightsticks at the ready."

"We've only got truncheons," Furnell said.

"They're the same bloody thing," Daniels replied, pulling his own truncheon from where it hung at his waist.

It took a moment for the crowd to disperse enough to make out what was happening.

"Ugh, right in the middle of the street. I mean, that's not okay, look at them going at it."

"I don't think they're…"

"No, they're not."

"Are they…"

"Don't say it."

"Zombies?"

"Oh, for f-"

IN THE BOX

Blunt took the canal boat. It wasn't fast, but it was a lot quicker than walking and he knew he'd parked somewhere near the station. The few nails he had in his pocket were jingling a merry tune that was sounding more and more like a solo rather than an orchestra. As he took a seat near the back, he pulled the box out of his coat pocket. The maggots inside wriggled and squirmed in a repulsive dance. They kept moving from one side to the other, and it occurred to Blunt that holding it above the canal might have been cruel.

They crawled across the inside of the box and Blunt wondered if he'd wasted his time until the canal boat, on its endless loop around the city, reached Port Sheol. The things in the box, normally inching from one place to another, began launching themselves at the right side of the box. Behind him a pair of pabies were listening to a small portable gramophone. They had the volume on too high and were giggling to each other. It set Blunt's teeth on edge and they made it worse because they played that same familiar song that he couldn't name.

Turning the box in his hands, it looked like they were trying to force their way towards something off the boat. If not, then the maggots were extremely interested in the woman in a tartan coat who had somehow got a shopping trolley on to the ferry. She made eye contact with Blunt and he winced.

There are very few people who dare to make eye contact with someone on public transport. Among the myriad rules that involve the use of mass transit one of the most important is, 'do not make eye contact'. It stands alongside, 'when nobody notices, tutting is acceptable,' and 'never sit next to anyone if there are any other empty seats'.

"What's that?" The woman asked in a deep voice that spoke of cigarettes and long nights.

Blunt looked over at her from beneath his hat. "It's a plastic box."

"What's in the box?"

"Who are you? Professional box warden? Do I need a licence to carry a box?" Blunt asked.

She lowered a pair of star-shaped sunglasses that had gone out of fashion around the same time as flared trousers. "You're that detective."

He sighed and turned to stare out of the window, hoping to avoid the conversation.

"I'm a Hope I'll have you know," the woman said, her voice getting louder.

Blunt heard the shuffling around the other seats on the boat. He was familiar with the situation, having witnessed it before. This was the beginning of a haranguing. A public verbal assault on somebody for a perceived personal attack. A dressing down. Staring out of the window, he knew, would not prevent it from taking place. Trying to ignore it provided fuel for the fire.

"Do you hear me? It's ignorance like yours that divides society, you disgust me," the woman had moved along her bench and had her legs behind the shopping trolley that was pointing out into the aisle. It was both a shield and a weapon, but it was going to make getting past her more difficult.

He shook his head. "Were you the Hope that you'd be allowed a moment's sodding peace?" He muttered.

"What was that you fascist!"

"What? Fascist? That's a bit of a stretch you crazy trolley pushing psycho. Who just starts attacking strangers on the boat? Well? I don't imagine anyone else here was thinking, 'oh look, there's that knobhead detective. I'm going to have a right shout at him.'"

Blunt turned to her and, with the box sitting on his lap, raised his hands. "Listen, sunglasses, I'm sorry, I really am sorry. I didn't mean to sound like so much of an arse. I wasn't doing well, I've struggled with dying, and in adjusting with being here. I've got a drinking problem. I've lost my job, and everyone hates me. Would you like me to suffer more for saying the wrong thing? That's what I did, I made a mistake. I don't have an issue with you, or anyone else who has a unique background. I just didn't think about what I was saying. Yes, I know there are people who might take what I said as some kind of call to arms against people like yourself, I do, but that isn't what I wanted or meant. I will stand on your side of the argument in any way I can, but it was a mistake and I am paying for it. Look at this, I'm on a boat minding my own business and I'm getting screamed at by a complete stranger. Being made an example of in front of all these people by some angry, shopping trolley thieving, avenging angel, who thinks everything is about her."

The woman was leaning over her shopping trolley ready to deliver another volley when Blunt said his piece. As he finished, she leaned back a little. "Wasn't expecting that."

"Yeah, well, I wasn't expecting it either. Maybe wind your sodding neck in next time instead of attacking people. Honestly, dead people, it doesn't matter what you were, most of you are absolute arses," Blunt said, as he stood up pressing the little button on the roof of the cabin. A bell rang as the canal boat slowed. This wasn't a major station, but he wanted to get off the boat before becoming embroiled in any more haranguing. He knew, even if he accepted all culpability, he needed to leave. Whatever he said or did, he was going to be the bad guy.

He stepped off the boat onto the shore, across a perilous gap that would probably claim some poor soul to the watery depths of the canal soon enough. Nobody enjoyed apologising but for Blunt it was like pulling teeth and he had made a genuine effort but, he knew, it was a wasted effort. Nobody on the boat would remember anything except for some uncomfortable moments while a woman shouted at a man who scurried away. He was certain the woman wouldn't tell anybody either. Unless she told everyone how that horrible detective off the telly had called her names. He sighed. That, he decided, was definitely going to happen. She'd probably get in the papers.

He pulled the box out of his pocket and watched the maggots hurl themselves against the side of the box. They flattened against one wall, defying gravity as they got thinner until they filled the side of the box Blunt was pointing away from him. "Lead on maggots, you creepy wriggly bastards," Blunt muttered as he strode out into the street.

Rain hammered down and he pulled his coat tighter, flicking the collar up and smirking as he saw his reflection in the windows of a shop. He looked like he'd walked straight off the cover of a cheap paperback novel. Well, a little wider around the middle than he'd have liked, but still. It was a look he'd never had the guts to attempt when he'd been alive. It wasn't appropriate. Real-world policing didn't involve fancy hats and coats that defined you as a detective. Fortunately, it also meant encounters with cackling villains with strange unnatural features and Tommy guns were rare. Blunt stopped in the middle of the street and looked back at the reflection, "Are you trying to be Dick Tracy?" He asked his reflection.

"You're half right," a woman muttered from behind him as she pushed by, "stopping in the middle of the street like a bloody lunatic. Honestly, people today-"

Blunt couldn't hear what else she was saying, but he could guess enough of it to feel stupid. "People are bloody hilarious."

"You're the weirdo staring into a box in the middle of the street!" The woman's voice screeched out of the fog in front.

He blinked and shook his head before continuing through the mist and rain. The walls of the inside of the plastic box were steaming up, but he could still see the grubs inside moving. He reached an intersection, and they crawled into a corner, taking him left. In the distance he could see bright lights and he let out a groan. Now he remembered why this area was familiar. In the distance, the facade of Gloomwood's only five-star hotel appeared as he grew closer. "Rich people," he muttered, "more money than sense and attitudes that match. Bloody wonderful."

ROOM SERVICE

"This is bad," Petal said, his voice as quiet as he could make it. One of the many problems he dealt with was a voice for booming prophetic messages from the heavens. The curse of a reformed god is that some things don't have an off switch.

"Oh well, that's just special isn't it. 'This is bad'," Ted made his voice as high-pitched and whiny as he could, which was remarkably high, and very whiny, "the room is splattered in bloody calamari and I still have a headache."

"I think you kil-"

"You can't kill dead people, Petal. So, don't even start with that."

"Why did you call me?"

"Because... because you're...you know...bad."

Petal was standing in the centre of the hotel room. Ted perched on the double bed he had first spoken to the doctor. Beyond the locked adjoining room door, the only people who remained were there to further their careers, not because they had any interest in the doctor's circumstances. His assistant had run screaming into the night. The big-handed freak had turned pale and started murmuring when he'd walked into the room so Ted had sent him away with a simple warning, 'make a fuss and those hands could easily belong to someone else.'

"I'm not bad. Jay says I'm misunderstood."

"Jay thinks that everyone has a soft gooey centre and that people give a shit about justice."

"They do, I was a god. Justice is important."

"No, it isn't. What people really want is justice for them and to feel like they aren't the person getting the raw end of the deal. People are terrible." Ted waved a hand in the doctor's direction, "Can you make this go away?"

"What happened?"

"Answer my question first."

Petal held his palms out and turned from side to side. "Place is a mess."

"Yeah, I'm more concerned with making out that I've done nothing wrong. Don't really need a bump to the ratings right now."

"Ratings?"

"Television Petal, have you been living under a rock?"

"That sounds uncomfortable."

"Can we just shovel him into a load of takeaway boxes and pretend it was food?"

"That's disgusting."

"Well, what is the food? I always thought it was some Soylent Green thing, anyway."

"What's that?"

The bear balled his paws into fists and let out a groan. "It's so frustrating you know nothing."

Petal stared at the bear for a moment and then a smile spread across his face. "You do this when you're frightened. Start throwing around things from the world of the living to make yourself feel better about being clueless. Petal might be big and scary, but he ain't stupid."

"Petal might be-"

"Stop that voice. I don't sound like that."

"Stop that-"

The big man put his thumb and forefinger on his right hand together and snapped them. What might have been a casual, or rude, gesture from most people, was the equivalent of a furious thunderclap from Petal. The windows rattled from the sound. "You called me up and asked for help. Don't be pretending you're some kind of genius now."

Ted punched the duvet on the bed without making a dent. "Fine."

"I can shove him into a bag and carry him outside, but he's not coming back from his head exploding. That's Ableforth. It's a crime."

"It was nothing to do with me."

Petal nodded. "So, you sneezed and his face went bang."

"Coincidence."

"But your headache has gone away."

"It's a dull throb, annoying but not that bad, it's so thoughtful of you to ask."

"I asked because it's related. You sneezed, headache went away," he pointed at the body, "head went away."

"It has nothing to do with me and there's no way to prove otherwise."

"Then why call me?"

The bear sighed. "I already explained this. I need to make this disappear. So, it's simple. Pick up the body and put it in someone else's room to find, let them worry about it."

"What about the people who saw?"

"I'll tell them the doctor left, and he was fine."

"Didn't they see what happened?"

The bear shook his head. "Petal, you were a god, surely you know something about belief? Faith? Stupidity?"

"Eh? Faith ain't the same as stupidity."

"Really? I'm going to go next door and tell everyone the doctor is fine. It was just a dizzy spell and everyone's going to believe me because it's me saying it. They are stupid enough to have faith in me. Even the floppy handed clapper will accept it because I'm saying it and they all want paying."

"But... there's stuff everywhere."

"Ink, his body sprays ink when he gets excited."

"Lumpy fleshy ink?"

"Yup, everyone knows squid spray ink."

"They will not believe you."

"Of course they are. I'm their meal ticket, so they'll believe I'm telling the truth because it's the best thing for them. Faith in me because they're greedy and stupid. Isn't that basically what you did before you died? Believe in me because if you don't terrible things will happen? Believe in me and I'll make the terrible things stop happening? It's exactly the same thing."

Petal clenched his fists, the size of bowling balls, and grimaced. "You ain't a god to these people."

"No, I can make a difference. I can stop them being paid. I'm far more important than a god. I talk to them through the screen. If they annoy me, I just have to say so and the entire city will hear about it and I will ruin their death. Their death, Petal, the rest of eternity because I chose to."

"There's something wrong with you."

"I have a headache."

Petal sighed and shook his head. "Right. So's you just want me to move it? Couldn't someone else have done that?"

"No, ugh, Petal, I need someone I trust who won't tell other people the doctor is dead."

"We're all dead."

"Stop correcting that. You all need to stop correcting that and get on with things. It's ridiculous."

"Why wouldn't I tell anyone?"

"Because, you're an ex-drug dealer with a terrible reputation, so I'll just say that you did it."

Petal's eyes bulged. "You what?"

"Well, come on, who are people going to believe? Me, the fluffy teddy bear and media darling, or you, the giant thug who could crush their skulls in one hand and who might have done that to this poor doctor who was only trying to help me. What motive could I possibly have for harming him? You well, we could bring up Jay again."

"You evil little bastard. We're supposed to be friends-"

"Are we? Petal, are we? Oh, have a wipe around the place, you can just leave the towels where you leave the body."

"I'm not doing this-"

"Uh, you burst into my hotel room threatening me and the good doctor then you decide to just... what's the word?"

"Ableforth-"

"Right, Ableforth him right in front of me. It's a wonder I survived."

Petal's right eye twitched, "It really is."

GRIM TIDINGS

In Gloomwood there is no mobile internet, wireless information superhighways haven't taken off, and they never will as long as it is the Grim Reaper's afterlife. Analog, so the saying goes, is for eternity, digital is temporary. That is the way the Grim Reaper liked it and, on the rare occasions he had to flex any kind of muscle to prove his importance, it was on this issue. Coincidentally, the talk of flexing of any muscles in his earshot is something he isn't appreciative of either, it's a skeleton thing.

There were computers, housed in yellowing plastic with green text on black backgrounds, good for making things difficult and answering questions so that people didn't have to decide for themselves, but nobody liked them. There were mobile phones, made of brass that looked more like horns and had no display at all. They were prohibitively expensive and so few people had them they were almost entirely pointless, a fashion accessory with such a poor connection that it was impossible to have a conversation on them. Thaumaturgic atmospheric phenomenon, the TAP, prevented any wireless signal and nobody had the desire to work a way around it.

He was sitting in his office staring down at his desk where the mobile telephone played music at him. He wore no expression, for obvious reasons, but onlookers may have imagined a glimmer of consternation. In the chair on the opposite side of the desk, standing because it was impossible to sit with the long T-Rex tail, was Morgarth the Destroyer.

"Your lordship, are you going to answer?"

"I don't think so. We don't really do mobile phones here."

Morgarth had the job of delivering the phone. That was all Beelzebub had said. At no point had he demanded she persuade the Grim Reaper to answer the call but, she realised, initiative was what they knew her for. "I'm not sure that's relevant sir."

"I remember you. It was Morgarth, wasn't it?"

"Um, yes, sir."

"You didn't look like that when we met," he didn't look up, still staring down at the screen. It stopped ringing and Death placed his hands either side of it, on the table, willing it to remain silent. The song started again.

"No," Morgarth said, "this vessel is temporary."

"Did he think this was funny?"

"I don't know."

"Why is he bothering me now?"

"I don't know."

"Why are you here?"

"I... I don't know."

"No. I would imagine not. Beezy-"

"Beezy?"

"Beelzebub. He has a habit of telling people why things are happening afterwards."

Morgarth dipped her head. "Not my place to say, sir, I do as his Highness commands."

"Highness? Highness? Shouldn't it be Lowness? Isn't it the depths of Hell? I'm not answering the phone."

"I understand."

Grim waved a hand towards the door, "well, off you go then, back to Hell."

Morgarth turned her head towards the door and back again to the Grim Reaper. The song ended, and the phone let out a groan. The Grim Reaper leant over it.

'Pick up the phone, Grim, it's Beezy' read the message that popped up on the screen. The background was a picture of Beelzebub, ruler of the darkest dominion, with his arm around Grim's shoulder. They each had a cup of coffee in their hands.

The Grim Reaper remembered the photo. The terrified barista had, for a moment, glimpsed their true appearance. She'd dropped dead a moment afterwards. A massive and sudden brain haemorrhage had snuffed out her mortal flame. Beelzebub had laughed, Grim had to take the poor confused woman beyond the veil where he explained the photo had been a coincidence, it had been her time. They stopped asking mortals to take pictures after that.

The phone was unlocked thanks to the facial recognition being set to Grim's skull. He suspected that the phone might have been the same one they had taken the picture on. The same phone he had carried around in his black robes for centuries. Filled with memories he had pushed to one side.

"I'm not answering it," Grim said, this time ignoring Morgarth.

The phone let out another groan. 'Don't be such a baby, Grim, just answer.'

"Can he hear me?"

"I don't know, sir," Morgarth said.

"Are you going to leave?"

"I... I don't know where I'm supposed to go. The instructions were just to bring you the phone. I guess he'll explain what's next when you answer it."

"I'm not answering it."

"No, of course not, sir."

"Right. Well, that's clear then."

The song started again. The damn song. "Why is he here?"

"I think he will tell you if you answer the phone."

"Do you know?"

"No. Sort of."

"What's he doing?"

Morgarth looked around for support from the walls. She took in the snow globes, the amateur, and quite terrible, needlepoint hanging on the walls, the photographs of people standing on their own. "Why do you have those?" She asked.

"You're trying to change the subject. Those are pictures of me with some people I have met."

"But they're alone."

"No, they aren't. You just can't see me. I'm Death, Morgarth. If they could capture me on mortal cameras, it would make things a little awkward. You need a divine camera to take my picture like the one on this phone."

"Well, how does anyone know if you've met them?"

"The photographs aren't for anyone else, they're for me. How strange. Do people usually take photos of themselves with other people for any other reason?"

Morgarth nodded, her tail wagging of its own accord. "Usually people take pictures, or selfies with celebrities, to show off."

"They're not celebrities."

"Yes, they are."

"No, they're just dead people who were interesting."

"Is that Elvis?"

"So?"

"And that looks like John Lennon."

"Stop looking at my photos. What is Beezy doing?" The phone started again. "Oh fine," the Grim Reaper snatched the phone off the desk and pressed it to the side of his head. "What do you want?"

"Ah, Grim, did you have it on silent?"

"No, I was ignoring you."

"Oh, I imagine you're terribly busy. How are you?"

"What do you want Beezy?"

"Ah, straight to work stuff, maybe we can grab coffee after?"

"Beezy, I am not very happy with you-"

"I know. The incident, listen let's focus on work and hopefully you'll let me apologise afterwards."

"Maybe. What do you want?"

"I'm going to have to destroy this place."

"Which place?"

"This place... what do you call it?"

"I don't know where you are?"

"I'm in a bar."

"What's wrong with the bar? Stop destroying things."

"No, no, Grim, I mean this whole place, this city, you call it Gloomwood."

"Oh," The Grim Reaper held his hand over the phone and looked over at Morgarth, "he says he's going to destroy Gloomwood, did you know that?"

Morgarth shrugged, though it was hard to tell with the oversized head and neck coupled with the tiny arms.

"Grim, you're a skeleton, remember. I can hear everything, even when you try to cover the phone. You can hear me, can't you?" Beelzebub's voice, much gentler than you might imagine, asked from the other side of the phone.

"Yes, still here. The signal isn't great."

"Yes, it is."

"Nope, you're breaking up... shhhhkkkzzzz-"

"Grim, it's a divine phone. Never mind, I just wanted to make a big splash to say, 'I'm here in your little afterlife about to destroy it all.'"

"You're always so petty. Why can't I have an afterlife like you do? I'm older than you. I'm divine too."

"Would you like Hell? You've been there enough times. Does it seem like your cup of tea? Anyway, it's got nothing to do with you. I didn't even know you were here. I'm glad I finally found you, but I'm here because there's life in this afterlife and it's going to corrupt everything."

"Oh... that."

"What do you mean that?"

"Well, I had a funny feeling."

"A funny feeling? Grim, this is catastrophic. I'm here to help."

"No Beezy. This is work. You're here for something much worse," The Grim Reaper said, and he hung up, dropping the phone into the bin.

"Morgarth."

The tyrannosaurus looked up as Death himself gathered his robes and stood, hitting his head on the ceiling and muttering.

"Morgarth," he started again, "why didn't you say he's here to destroy this afterlife?"

The fluffy dinosaur squirmed.

BIG HANDS YOU'RE NOT THE ONE

Johnson had left the house when he was sure that Jimmy 'Big Hands' wouldn't see him. He dressed in black trousers, a plain black jumper over a black t-shirt, and donned his long black coat. The black wasn't a statement, it was just his preference. As a man who had spent his days being visible in the Grey of the Gloomwood police, he appreciated being easily overlooked now that things had changed. Though there was no doubting that he looked good in black.

The rain was lighter now, drifting with the wind so it seemed to come sideways towards him rather than falling downwards. As a police constable, they had loaned him a car when on duty. One car was never clean, never maintained, and had a sticking clutch that caused the gears to grind between first and second. It had been only for Johnson's use. Another example of the preferential treatment his colleagues in grey had doled out to him daily.

He walked through the Styx neighbourhood, crossing the street to avoid walking past the doors of the buildings which the unpredictable, violent types inhabited. It wasn't a complicated place. Poverty caused people to get desperate, the more desperate they became the more inclined they were towards doing something they shouldn't, the line kept getting pushed until it was nothing but a memory, the distinction between what they should do, and could do, blurred. Needs must. It was Johnson's neighbourhood.

It was late, but people were milling around. A game involving dice was being played in front of a pub doorway and he walked around it. A hand lay on the floor in the centre of the circle of participants and a cheer went up as someone pulled out a vicious-looking machete.

"Right then Paul, what'll it be?"

"Ah come on, this is rigged. Fine, how about a foot?"

Johnson walked by. Paul was going to wake up and realise he'd lost a foot and a hand when he'd had too much to drink, but it was all legitimate, nothing to see here.

He rounded the corner and carried on towards the wall. The edge of the Styx neighbourhood meets the sea wall. It was the barrier between Gloomwood and the purple seas that turned from placid to tumultuous without rhyme, reason, or warning. He slipped into the steady gait of the beat cop doing the rounds. It was a force of habit, built in through time and training.

He walked along the seawall and stopped at the edge of the neighbourhood to turn into an alleyway. Underneath a sprawl of graffiti that read, "get lost hopes," was the car. He pulled off the tarpaulin that covered it and unveiled a machine that Petal had paid for and bought for him when Johnson had joined the police. It had been a proud moment, filled with joy, dashed within a day when someone had smashed in the windows and scratch 'hope dies' across the bonnet. Petal had been furious. Johnson had made the mistake of believing his fellow officers would help him find the perpetrators. Much later he'd realised that it was his colleagues who had caused the damage.

It was a police car. A police car unlike any other seen in the city of Gloomwood, black with the word police emblazoned on its side in stark white letters. A siren perched on its roof. Petal had explained it was a living world design, made by a wealthy norm who had decided he wanted to make a film but had run out of money. He called it a Morris Oxford S3, from 1957, not that its history meant much to Johnson. The car itself meant something to him. It represented everything he had hoped for when joining the force. The police they showed on television, in movies. The police he had read about in pulp novels as he had tried to pull himself out of the addiction he had lived under. The foggy cloud of Gloomwood's number one narcotic, Oblivion.

Cars not based on a hearse were a rarity, and this one stuck out like a rose against the grey of Gloomwood's never-ceasing drive towards morbidity. Something that people like him, hopes, dreams, even the gods, hated.

The siren was an actual bell, an almost joyous sound compared to the mournful howling of the Gloomwood police sirens. Sirens the police usually only used when bored to force traffic to get out of the way. He dragged the tarpaulin off the car and dumped it on the floor. He had hidden the car down this dark alleyway for long enough. Whatever happened from here forward, he was no longer a member of the constabulary. So, he might as well make the most of the car. They'd scratched 'Hope Dies' into the bonnet and he ran his fingers along the letters. "They're afraid of us, they're afraid of hope," he said to the car. He opened the driver's side door and slid into the seat, "they should be."

WAIT FOR ME

"Tentacles?" Blunt said, shaking his head. "Bit much isn't it?"

"Would sir kindly stop slapping the facilities?"

"They keep trying to touch me. Get off my hat, you thieving bloody... tentacle."

"Your hat and coat, sir," a man with a moustache and beard that was too long, too curly, and too mobile said from where he stood just inside the doorway of the hotel.

"Exactly," Blunt snarled, "my hat and my coat, get your sodding suckers off them."

The thin-lipped smile offered by the gentlemen standing in the doorway was not friendly. "Perhaps sir is at the wrong establishment."

The tentacles gave up and retreated around the edges of the doorway.

"I know where I am thanks," Blunt said, waving his box of maggots, "I've had directions."

The man's smile faltered for a moment, his moustache flicked up and the ends of it smoothed back the hair on his head, "I don't think you can bring that in here, sir."

"No? Why's that? You have tentacles hanging around your entrance grabbing people and their possessions, but I can't bring in my little friends in a box?"

"The 'tentacles' as you so politely term them are a luxury hat and coat removal system that our guests appreciate. It shouldn't be necessary for the best in society to remove their own items of clothing."

"Wait...do you have tentacles in the rooms here? That's... that's obscene."

"I assume sir is not a guest?"

"I'm here to visit someone."

"The tradesperson's entrance is around the side."

"Excuse me? Are you modelling our society of equality and partnership with his kind of attitude?"

"Gloomwood is not a society of equality and partnership, and if it were, that would end at this entrance. Good day, sir."

"Good day? Good bloody day, you don't get to 'good day' me. You jumped up hairy-faced, stick up the backside, pompous-"

A polite cough from behind Blunt interrupted the build up to what was going to be a moment of righteous indignation. A rebalancing of things after Blunt had been on the receiving end of a haranguing.

"Mister Blunt," her voice caught his attention, and he turned to see Twist Lenworth, his employer, standing behind him. She wore an expression of mild amusement. "So glad you could finally make it. I was just running some errands. Mister Weighman, if you would be so kind as to have the bags transferred to my room," she waved a hand at an extensive selection of shopping bags, the kind that looked handcrafted with the sole purpose of making any other bags feel inadequate.

"Of course, Miss Lenworth, is this gentleman with you?"

"Phrasing Mister Weighman, phrasing, he works for me and we have an appointment. It's not quite the same as being, 'with me,' is it?"

Weighman's moustache curled and bunched together until it looked like someone had glued two delicate swirls onto his face.

"Really Weighman, casting aspersions upon a lady," Blunt said, unable to resist putting the boot in.

"Shall we Mister Blunt?" Twist said as she walked through the entrance and passed the astonished mustachioed man.

Blunt smirked as he walked by.

"Blunt, now I remember your face," Weighman said, "you're that anti-altmortal bastard from the telly."

"Manners Weighman," Blunt said in his best impression of Twist.

They passed through the reception area of the hotel. Brass, marble, mirrors, and disdain for the poor, seemed to be the decor of choice. Twist ignored everyone, including Blunt, while they waited for the lift to arrive. It disappointed him not to see a velvet wearing bellhop hoping for a tip when they stepped in.

"Staying here?" Blunt asked.

"Yes, but I was also following you. It's embarrassing that you would end up on my own doorstep. Is he here?" She asked without turning to look at him.

"He, is it?" Blunt could see her reflection in the polished doors and the smirk on his own face when he caught her slip.

"I expect so," she said, "but you never know about these things."

"I think you do."

"The little box-"

"Maggots."

"Yes, the maggots. You got them from the strange masked man?"

"You really have been following me. I didn't even notice."

"Is it something you would have noticed normally? Do you expect people to follow you?" She asked.

"No, but-"

"Investigate, find things, work out what happened, those things you do. Battle crime? Spycraft? Avoid detection? I didn't hire you for your subtlety, did I?"

"I can do subtle things," Blunt said.

"Of course you can."

"Don't patronise me-"

"Why not?"

"Because...it's rude."

"Oh my. What do your little maggots say? Would it be easier if I just took them from you?"

"I think it's the top floor," Blunt turned the box around and the maggots clamoured to keep pointing in the same direction. "Did you just threaten me?"

"Maybe," she said.

"I'd like to see you try to take them."

"Ah, you're one of those."

"What?"

"You know, the type who likes to watch... or maybe you're the type who likes a little violence."

"I'm the type who doesn't hit a lady, but I would call no one who hit me a lady, get it?"

"Oh my, so big and strong. If you're right, and he's here, stay out of the way, Detective Blunt."

"Why?"

"Because, obviously, you being in the way would make things more difficult."

The bell in the elevator rang as it lurched to a stop and the doors opened to reveal a man with a blue complexion who filled the corridor as if folded into it. "Excuse me," the man said with a voice that rumbled like distant thunder, "just taking out the laundry," he waved bed sheets he held in one hand. They looked heavy.

As Blunt looked at the man, a tentacle unfurled and dangled free from the wrapped-up bed-linen. "Did they have that in the room?"

"Um…" The big man looked at the tentacle, back at Blunt and Twist, then at the tentacle once more, "it's not what it looks like."

"Oh, I don't blame you, bloody things tried to steal my hat and coat. Do I know you?"

"Yeah, now you mention it. I'm Petal."

"Blunt, nice to meet you… again."

"Blunt," Twist interrupted. She nodded at the box in his hands, "stay out of the way."

Blunt looked down. The maggots were up against the side of the glass case crowded towards the end pointed towards the big man. "Oh."

☠ <u>OUT OF THE BOX</u> ☠

The Grim Reaper strode through corridors in the Office of the Dead. His robes billowed around his ankles, kicking up dust reserved for the footprints of the Grim Reaper or Crispin Neat.

"Where are we going?" Morgarth asked from where she followed in his wake.

"You ask a lot of questions for a demon," Grim replied.

"I show initiative."

"Beelzebub used to frown upon that. Times have changed."

"His Highness doesn't seem to mind it from me, I don't know why."

"Interesting, when did this happen?"

Morgarth went quiet for a moment. "I think after you stopped having coffee together."

"Oh? Very interesting."

"Where are we going?"

The Grim Reaper halted, causing Morgarth to get tangled in the back of his robes. Grim turned and with the blunt end of his scythe pushed the fluffy dinosaur backwards. "We are going to test a theory."

"Torture?"

"No. A theory is not a person."

"But hopes and dreams are?"

The Grim Reaper cocked his head to one side. The corridor was dark and his silhouette was all that Morgarth could see. "No...ideas can also be people so theories can too...in this case it isn't a person...but we are going to see a person."

"That's confusing."

"Yes. It is. I need to test my theory because this may be my fault, but I don't think it is," Grim said. Then he turned once more.

The Office of the Dead is a building of industrial clarity that has been over-engineered to a point where it balances on the edge of causing more problems than it solves. Every night the clockwork mechanics in the lower basements of the building turn. They cause an intricate cascade of events that reshuffle the walls throughout the building. Floors move, rooms drop through multiple levels, doors vanish and reappear elsewhere. A map on the ground floor displays these movements. The idea, though nobody is sure who had it, was to reduce workplace complacency by changing the environment of the workplace every day. It almost worked.

In order for the mechanics to work the architects of the building had to provide access to the moving pieces, the cogs, gears, and pulleys, invisible to all apart from the architect, the Grim Reaper, and Crispin Neat, were in these corridors.

The Grim Reaper strode up a flight of stairs. He crossed over narrow beams and ducked through access portals, climbed ladders, and in one strange moment carried Morgarth in his arms as he leapt over a dangerous gap. They came to a circular vault-like door somewhere near the top of the building. Grim placed his hands on the handle wheel and grunted as he turned it.

"Can I help?" Morgarth asked.

"Not with those little arms," Grim replied, "I'm perfectly... capable... there we go."

"I thought you'd be stronger."

The Grim Reaper turned with one hand on the vault door. "Why?"

"Well... you're Death."

"I'm a skeleton. Is it not incredible enough that I can move? You also expect me to have superhuman strength?"

Morgarth stared back with her oversized eyes wide open. "It is incredible, sir."

"Bah, superhuman strength, waste of time. If I wanted to, I could snap my fingers and dissolve this entire reality."

"You could?" Morgarth asked.

"I... think so. I've never really tried anything quite that grandiose. I'd really rather not have any of it."

"Any of what?"

"All of this," he looked down at the black robes, "the embodiment of eternal rest, you'd think it would be easier with a name like that, but it's not what I would have chosen. Not what I want."

"What do you want?"

"I'm not sure... a pet would be nice, maybe some friends, ooh, one of those frozen yoghurt makers. We're here, Morgarth, don't tell anyone about this."

"But I'm a demon."

"One with initiative, let's see what you do. Don't speak when we're inside, demonic voice remember, still quite scary even with all," he waved a long skeletal finger in a circle, "the fluffiness."

Morgarth said nothing as the Grim Reaper pushed open the vault door and stepped through into a candlelit room.

There was a desk against the far wall of the room, which was small but tidy. Leather-bound books and strange concoctions in jars with labels in illegible writing lined the walls. There was a hexagonal raised table upon which glass round bottomed flasks bubbled as they hung from brass clamps over bunsen burners.

A hunched over figure stood by the desk in the far corner. "Heard you coming, swishing along like a woman in a long ball gown," the man said without turning.

"Thank you, it is quite an elegant robe, I just had it made," the Grim Reaper pinched the sides of the robe and lifted it, "I do like the swishiness."

"I'm ready for our rematch," the man said.

"Oh, I completely forgot about that."

"Four-thousand, three hundred and forty-seven games and you forgot we were yet to reach the end?"

"Well, you insist on a rematch every time."

"And you give it! You could just say no!"

"Then who would play?"

"I've been practising," the man said, turning on the stool. His skin was dry as paper and he glared at the Grim Reaper through a monocle. The other eye was missing or hidden beneath the wrinkled scowl.

"You have? Oh, good."

"The board is by the window."

"Chess? Again? Oh, I fancied dominoes."

"Dominoes? It's always chess!"

"It doesn't have to be."

"But I've been practising chess, learning every game, observing the greatest players through time. I've been playing games- uh, mentally."

"You've been playing against Crispin Neat."

"How did you know?"

"I'm Death. Anyway, does it really matter what we play."

"Yes, yes, it matters. It matters because Death plays chess, Death always plays chess."

The Grim Reaper shrugged, "fine, if it's so important to me."

"If it's... For thousands of years I've been trapped. Of course, it matters."

"You still can't leave then? Didn't find a magic spell or potion to let you escape? Stuck between the living and the dead."

"Because of you."

"You challenged me! Hardly my fault we keep reaching a stalemate!"

"You're doing it on purpose!" The man wailed.

The Grim Reaper walked around the table in the center of the room and pulled a stool from beneath it. He dragged it towards a small round coffee table by the window. Upon the table was a cheap chess set on a cardboard board. Morgarth followed Grim close at his heels.

"What's that?"

"Hm?" Grim asked.

"That?"

"Oh, this is a demon. If you lose today, I suppose she'll take you to Hell."

"That's a demon? It's not very scary."

"No, but neither am I once you get to know me."

"It's a fluffy dinosaur."

The Grim Reaper turned on his stool. "Could you introduce yourself?"

"I am Morgarth the destroyer, leader of the elite guard, servant of hell, ambassador for Lord Beelzebub and the deliverer of righteous suffering on all mortals who cannot meet the standard. I usually just go by Morgarth the destroyer, or Morgarth," her voice tore through the silence of the room as close to the physical manifestation of torture as is possible. Worse than a cartoon character in double time through a loudspeaker.

The man was unperturbed. He hopped down from his chair, removed his monocle, and began polishing it vigorously. "What is the standard?"

"It's-" Morgarth began, but Grim held up a hand.

"Morgarth is here only to escort you to your rightful place should you lose."

"You said you forgot."

"I must have remembered before I got here, then forgot while I was here, now I remember again."

"What?"

"Are you sure you want to play today? I could come back later, give you a chance to see if some new miraculous way to escape my clutches occurs to you."

"Really?"

"Yes, why not? You do a lot to help us here, it's the least I could do."

"Right, fine. Maybe another day."

The Grim Reaper stood up and made a show of swishing his robes as he did so, "right, well nice to see you again."

"You too!"

Morgarth followed Death through the vault door and watched as the Grim Reaper rolled the wheel, setting the locking mechanisms in place. The Grim Reaper gave the door a quick tug to check it and then walked back the way they had come.

"Was that it?"

"Yes."

"And?"

"Whatever is bothering Beezy is nothing to do with me. My guest is neither alive nor dead, but he also isn't in Gloomwood. It worried me he may have escaped. Must be something else."

CRASH, BANG, TEDDY

Blunt ducked for cover as a cloud of dust and pieces of plasterboard from the hotel walls showered over him. They had destroyed the hallway. Twist Lenworth had pulled a folding scythe from within her coat. When extended it stood at above head height with a blade that was, in Blunt's opinion, far too long to be practical.

She swung it at the big man carrying the laundry bag, but he ducked and she took out half a wall. Whatever the big man was, he wasn't slow. He swung an enormous fist in Twist's direction but she stepped out of its range, knocking Blunt backwards, with a smirk on her face.

"You don't belong here," she said as she took a fighting stance.

"Well alright, it's posh, but I was leaving anyway," Petal replied as he brushed dust and rubble off his shoulders. "Is that a scythe-thingy?"

"A scythe thingy? Wait, who are you?" Twist asked.

"I'm Petal. Most people know who I am. Who are you? Running around attacking people with scythes as if you're the Grim Reaper or something. It's just rude."

Twist frowned and grabbed the box from Blunt's hands. The maggots writhed away from her, but as she turned the box, they gathered in whichever point was far from her. "Try it again," she thrust it at Blunt, "the stupid thing is broken."

"It's not a thing," Blunt said, "they're maggots. There, see, straight at him."

"It's not him," she said, her voice approaching a snarl.

"What's that?" Petal asked.

Blunt ignored Petal as he turned the box in his hands. He looked up and watched as the big man in front of him scooped up the tentacles into the bag. One tentacle was wearing a wristwatch. "Why's it wearing a watch?"

"What?" Petal said.

"Why is that tentacle wearing a watch?" Blunt said, standing straight and slipping the box into the pocket of his coat.

Petal shrugged.

"What are you doing?" The detective asked.

"Told you before, laundry. Get out of the way."

Blunt shook his head. "Nope. What's in there?"

"It wasn't me. You're going to think it was me, but it wasn't me. The bear is going to tell you it was me, but it wasn't me. It was him. He said he sneezed, and it just happened. I didn't do nothing wrong."

"Blunt, we haven't got time for this," Twist said.

"I think we do," Blunt said without taking his eyes off Petal, "I remember you now. You're friends with that constable. The ex-constable... you were a good guy, but I've got a feeling that that weird liquid dripping from the bed sheets is something it shouldn't be."

"What should it be?" Twist asked.

"I... good point. Anyway," he turned back to Petal, "what wasn't you."

"You can get out of my way or I can go through you," Petal said.

Blunt gave a small smile, "you could definitely walk through me. I've just seen you plough through a wall like it wasn't even there but she," he flicked a thumb in Twist's direction, "she would give even you a hard time."

"I don't appreciate being dragged into your chat with this goon, Blunt, it's not our concern," Twist said. She was still holding her scythe in a tight double handed grip across the length of her body.

"Her... nah. I was just being gentle. I'm a gentle giant."

"You wouldn't last five minutes," Twist snapped.

"Five minutes?" Petal's grin was huge and genuine, "who takes five minutes to finish a fight? Both of you get out of my way."

"What's in the bag?"

Petal's smile vanished. "Just get out of the way. I don't want to be here... stupid bloody bear... move."

"Bear?" Blunt said, "you don't mean that little bastard from the telly?"

"Uh, maybe, you're not a fan?"

"You don't recognise me?"

"Yeah, but from that thing months ago with the pabies."

"Pabies?"

"Pre adolescent bodied individuals, you know, the kids."

It had been several months earlier when Blunt first arrived in the city. His first case as Chief Investigator had involved the children of Gloomwood, specifically a small section of their society who had been hellbent on bringing life to the city. They had failed, just. Blunt never felt he would recover from the mental scars of that case. "You and that police officer helped. Does that mean you're a good guy? Or that you hate the, uh, pabies."

"Bit of both, maybe?" Petal said.

Blunt nodded. "I still need to know what's in the bag."

"You've no right to be looking at what's in here. It's my business, mind your own. Like the lady said, it's none of your concern."

Twist sighed and looked back and forth from Petal to Blunt, "Fine." She moved with blinding speed. Blunt saw nothing but a blur. Petal was quicker, but he was caught by surprise. Twist leapt forward and cut the blankets the Demi-god was holding just below his hands.

The blankets thudded to the floor, and the body of the doctor tumbled out.

"It's not what it looks like," Petal said.

"Looks like a giant squid with a stethoscope and a hole where a face might have been."

"Yeah... well, it is that, but I didn't do it."

BEELZEBUB

Beelzebub took the phone out of his pocket. It was paper thin, flexible technology, with a bar at the top of it which housed a front and rear facing camera and whatever else it needed to work. He held it up a little above the height of his own head, tilted his head to one side and hit the red button on the screen.

"Hello, my pretties, this is your Lord and ruler just checking in while I'm busy at work, as usual. I hope you're all helping make sure our customers are suffering in extreme agonising torment and mental anguish. Demonfolk, don't forget, Beezy loves you, kisses." He stopped the recording and lowered the phone. Twice he watched the video back while muttering to himself, "filters, crop, just fix that, smoothing...oh, a few floating emoticons...hm, that'll have to do." He hit send and uploaded the video to Bitter, Hell's own social media construct. He waited a moment and the numbers beneath his message shot up. "Now, where were we?" He turned around to focus on Molly Gormley.

The woman's arms and legs hung from either side of the interior of the van. Her torso lay on the floor and her head was sitting on a cardboard box in the middle of the van. There was no blood. Blood, Beelzebub had learned, costs extra. You can also sell it if times are tough and Molly had been through tough times.

"Are you finished yet? This is really getting quite tiresome," Molly said.

"What?" Beelzebub's right eyebrow twitched, "that's my line. How dare you!"

"You can do what you like. The lord is my shepherd."

"Is he?"

"What?"

"Is he your shepherd? I mean that's Psalm 23 from the King James version of the bible," he pronounced it bibble, "does he 'maketh you lie down in green pastures'? Where does that happen? I thought it was the Mible here."

"It... it is-"

"And the Mible has that too, does it?"

"Yes."

Beelzebub nodded, "yes, well that makes perfect sense doesn't it? The one true word of your saviour has a book full of typos in the living world, that's just like a book you have here in the afterlife which he has never visited... I admire your ability to bend any semblance of logic into a form that fits the narrative. It's a uniquely mortal trait you know, human mortals that is, of course you're a dead human mortal but it applies."

"I don't understand."

"You don't seem to be in much pain."

Molly's eyes flitted around the van, spying her body parts on the wall.

"I mean, it's a delightful image, but you could have been screaming, or crying in horror, you just look gormless and uninterested. It doesn't look good, you understand. Optics are important, especially in this day and age of social media. I have an image to protect. Of course, people will probably think you're just a mortal in shock."

"I... I don't understand."

He sighed, reached into the inside of his jacket, and pulled out the silver cigarette case he carried. He clicked the case open and lifted a cigarette out, "on social media it's important to project the right image. I'm far too," he lit the cigarette by snapping his fingers and producing flame from thin air, or the absence of air. He was still unsure. "I'm far too important, and busy, to see everything that's going on in Hell. I'm not omnipresent, or even omniscient, in fact I'm not even an omnivore provided you don't include wine and coffee as fruit and vegetables. Anyway, my point is, these little videos and pictures I send out are important to people. It matters to them. So, when I dismember you, but can still talk, the least you could do is clarify that it's because I'm making you continue to suffer. There'll be questions you know?"

"I don't understand."

"Oh, stop saying that. This is more of a monologue thing anyway, so don't worry. You don't even have a phone, do you?"

"They have one at the shelter," she said.

"They.. Oh, never mind. Do you know who I am?"

"You said you're the Devil?"

"Yes."

"But you can't be because the Devil is inside all of us and he is evil, but we're all evil, which is why we repent."

He exhaled in perfect rings, which grew as they travelled away from him and surrounded Molly's head. "The Devil is in all of you? Well, I suppose I could be temporarily but that's a lot of people and to be honest I don't find you all that attractive. Also, even for me, I mean I have stamina, just ask Mother Earth, but still."

"I don't understand."

"Ugh, you are tedious. Either that or you're some kind of genius. If I didn't know better, I'd think you were trying to torture me. 'I don't understand, I don't understand.' Let's see if you get this. You are going to be a queen, finally it's here, and you are the chosen one."

"The Lord's light will shine upon me?"

"Yes, sort of, well this Lord's light will shine upon you and that isn't a euphemism for anything untoward. All your faith, your shouting in the street, your fervour is wonderful. I approve of you."

Molly's mouth twisted in disgust. "You dismembered me."

"That was just a test. To see if you were as true to your beliefs as you said."

"But it hurt."

"Most people would have said it bloody hurt, or it, pardon my language, fucking hurt. They would have screamed blasphemy at me, 'please God let it stop', you didn't! I mean you screamed-"

"It hurt a lot-"

"Yes, but you kept your senses, and you behaved impeccably. You refuse, after all of that, to believe I'm the

Devil because you are sure, without a shadow of the doubt, that the Devil is not a person. Quite remarkable."

"You did that to me as a test?"

Beelzebub smiled, the cigarette hanging from his lips. "Oh fine, you caught me. It was mainly for the background of my little video. I'm in the details after all."

"You're not... never mind... what are you going to do with me?"

"I already told you. I'm going to make you a queen."

"I don't understand."

"I know, isn't it wonderful?"

GRIM & MORGARTH

"What are you doing?"

"Hm, I keep forgetting you're here, Morgarth. It's vulgar of me, but I'm not accustomed to company. What did you say?"

"What are you doing?"

"Are you a spy for Beezy?" The Grim Reaper asked. He was sitting at his desk with his skeletal feet perched on its surface, his legs crossed, and a paperback novel in his hands.

"No."

"Are you lying?"

"No, I'm not," Morgarth said from the seat on the other side of the desk.

"That's a relief. I don't like the idea of somebody spying on me."

The tyrannosaurus rex tilted its head to one side. "I could still be lying."

"Oh? Why?"

"If I was a spy, would I tell you?"

"Well, not the first time I asked you, but I asked you twice, that's an interrogation," The Grim Reaper said, and he nodded before returning to his book.

"Are you just reading a book?" She asked.

The Grim Reaper looked up. Had he taken the time to draw eyebrows on to his shining skull, he would have raised them in surprise. "Oh, Morgarth, sorry, I completely forgot you were there for a moment."

"We've just had this conversation. It finished and then I said, 'are you just reading a book' and it started again. The same conversation. Are you okay?"

"Hm, I don't think so."

"What are you reading?"

"A book."

Morgarth's enormous eyes, that one might call 'googly', narrowed, cartoonish eyelids half closed. "Yes, I had guessed that. Is it a helpful book?"

"Helpful?" The Grim Reaper said, "I suppose reading is a meditative process. It's escapism, particularly important to balance the stresses of life with something pleasurable. This book is about people who have magical powers depending on the season they're born, it's quite dark, and the-"

Morgarth leapt from the chair on to the desk. "It's fiction?"

"Isn't everything fiction in a way? Memories are imperfect, the reporting of facts is imperfect, what's real only exists in the present. A narrow edge in space and time that is so fine it is impossible to define, the edge of the scythe. Narrower than the smallest imaginable particle, smaller still," Grim said with a sigh.

"That's all very interesting, but what about what's happening here, in your city."

"Oh, it's not mine, it's theirs," Grim said.

"You will do nothing?"

"It's not my fault. I would feel bad if it was, but it isn't," he picked the book up again.

Morgarth shook her head and started pacing backward and forward across the Grim Reaper's desk. "I thought you would be different. One of the good guys."

"Absolutely not!" The Grim Reaper leapt to his feet, the book flying across the room. "I am, and will always be, neutral in matters of good and evil. This place is neutral. Do you have any idea how hard it is to remain neutral? How I must stifle any emotion that would pull me in either direction? That's why I made this place. It is in balance, not good, not bad, not happy, not sad, not exciting, not dull, neither quiet, nor loud, neither peaceful, nor at war. A bureaucratic non-political government running a city with people who died in the grey."

"The grey?"

"The area where the balance was hard to find. You would be amazed by how easy it is to file people to the appropriate afterlife."

"Really? I thought everyone just came to Hell?"

"Pah, Hell, schmell."

"Schmell?"

"There are more afterlives than there are stars in the sky."

"In Hell, the sky is a raging fire that blinds you if you look at it."

"Oh, yes, I remember, sunglasses help. The point is, I will remain neutral in this matter as that's my job."

Morgarth sighed.

"Oh, what is it now?"

"It's boring. I thought you'd be more interesting. I thought Lord Beelzebub was making this personal."

"Personal?"

"Yes. You were friends, weren't you?"

"He doesn't have friends," The Grim Reaper said as he took a seat once more. The chair, a rocking chair, creaked beneath him.

"If it is personal... then it's kind of your fault."

Grim leaned forward and began tapping his fingers against the desk. Click, click, click, "Are you trying to manipulate me into taking action?"

"Yes."

"For some evil purpose?"

"No, just because I'm bored."

"Hm, seems reasonable."

BEHIND YOU

Petal stepped to one side as Blunt poked the squid with the end of a pencil.

Twist shoved the end of the handle of her scythe at the body. It made a squelching sound, and the tentacles twitched. "That's disgusting," she said.

"This is a person's remains," Blunt said, "have some respect."

"It's a squid."

"Actually, I think he was an octopus," Petal said.

"Hang on," Blunt stood up from where he had been crouching by the body, "you're not from here are you?" He asked, turning to look at Twist.

Twist scowled, "Use the box of maggots, I'm clearly dead."

"They don't like you."

"I can rub people the wrong way."

"I don't think they're that discerning. You thought this was a squid."

"Fine, it's an octopus, how is that relevant? Did I give you the impression I was a marine biologist? I'm your client, Detective, my knowledge of cephalopods is irrelevant."

"This was a person," Blunt pointed his pencil at the body, "you're fresh meat, or not from here, which is it?"

Petal interrupted, "Can I go?"

"No, this is Ableforth. It's a crime. We need to call the police."

Petal narrowed his eyes. "You think the police will investigate this or just try to lock me in the library, and Johnson too, just for being associated with me, if we're lucky maybe you as well. They're not exactly fans of yours, are they?"

"No, but it's the law."

"Yes, we believe you big blue man," Twist said, placing a hand on Blunt's shoulder directing him down the corridor while waving for Petal to move, "you can go. I'm looking for the person who did this. You said he was a bear. This will be interesting, a challenge."

"Um, a teddy bear, like-" Petal started.

"That little bastard did this? I don't care where you're from. That spite-fuelled cretin needs taking down a few pegs. Here," Blunt pulled the box from his pocket once more and waved it around. He pushed by Petal and the maggots kept pushing in the same direction. "Sorry about before Petal," Blunt said over his shoulder, "You'll need to make a statement and explain why you were carrying the body. Next time try not to stand in the line of sight. You confused my maggots."

"It's a straight corridor, there's nowhere else to stand," Petal said without expecting a response.

"Yes. Mistaken identity. You're quick, though. Impressive," Twist said as she walked around Petal, brushing against the unbroken corridor wall to his side, without taking her eyes off him.

Petal didn't move a muscle. Frozen as if a wild animal was approaching him. When she was beyond him, he asked, "What are you going to do to Ted?"

"Kill him, of course, that's the job."

"See," Blunt said, "you're new or not from here. You can't kill a dead person."

Twist let out a little chuckle. "Very good, Detective, and yet I will kill this bear."

Petal turned as the two walked away with his back to him. He looked down at the remains of the doctor who now lay in a sad, crumpled pile on the floor. "S'not right this," he mumbled before carefully wrapping the body once more in the sheets he had pulled from the bed. "I'm sorry about what happened to you," Petal said, "stupid, Petal, there's nobody there to be sorry to. Ableforth leaves nothing…"

Satisfied that he'd wrapped the body, he moved it to one side in the corridor and let out a sigh. "This is going to get messy. Petal hates messy."

He turned with his hands on his hips and looked back down the corridor. "It's none of your business…"

Somewhere further down the corridor he heard a bang and the sound of splintering wood followed by screams and Blunt bellowing, "You can't do that!"

"Out of the way detective, I've no quarrel with you," Twist's voice came from up ahead.

Petal started moving.

THE CAR

He wore driving gloves. They were soft leather, except they weren't, because there wasn't any authentic leather in the city. Johnson knew that. Petal turned maudlin sometimes with the way everything was 'near-genuine'.

"Near genuine don't mean nuthin," he'd moaned, "I'm a near genuine ballet dancer if I want to be. It's just fake. Stupid OD and its stupid labels on anything. It just spoils it. Reminds everyone that we don't know what real ever was. It's real to us, just take the stupid labels off." It was a rant that Johnson had heard plenty of times, and he didn't disagree, he just didn't feel that strongly about it.

In the near-genuine gloves, he gripped the wheel. Weaving through traffic in a car he knew shouldn't have driven this well. No power-steering, no assisted braking. The engine should have been rudimentary compared to the others on the road, but it drove like something magical. He put his foot down as he reached a curve in the road accelerating into it and told himself that he was rushing.

The streetlights and neon signs painted patterns on the road ahead that passed over the car for moments like slow strobe lighting. Nobody called the night illumination of Gloomwood pretty but they had a feeling, a glow, to them that painted the grey with a kind of mystique.

Rain hit the windscreen as if it was flying towards the car with intent. Droplets of near-genuine water hit the glass windshield and were swept away by the wipers that, even over the roar of the engine, squeaked.

Petal had taken the car to Downtown Tony. His actual name was Gary, and the garage wasn't in an area anyone would mistake for downtown, but the mechanic liked the name and people liked him enough to use it. Downtown Tony wasn't a norm, nobody was sure what he was, but it was rude to ask and it didn't matter, because he was a genius with cars. He'd owed Petal a favour and if you owe Petal a favour, it's for something big. Johnson had learned a long time ago that the big man didn't believe in exchanging favours unless it was for something big. The car had paid a debt and Downtown Tony had been proud of it. So proud that he'd stopped talking to Petal and Johnson when he'd discovered they'd hidden it away.

The interior vibrated with the low hum of the engine. He downshifted and hit the acceleration, feeling a surge of power as it shot forward. This, he'd decided, wasn't the car for a police officer. It was a getaway vehicle, a street-racer, a car driven by dangerous people in dangerous situations. It was the car Johnson wanted to drive.

He slowed the car as he hit traffic. This neighbourhood never went quiet. During the day, it bustled with the people who had money to spend on overpriced lattes and even more expensive designer clothes. When dusk came, the cafes closed down, but high-end nightclubs and bars opened their doors to eager customers desperate to be snapped by the throngs of paparazzi surrounding the entrances to the latest Gloomwood hotspot.

Johnson knew a good portion of the Gloomwood police moonlighted as security at the establishments in the area, and Petal occasionally took a stint there, though the big man distracted from the customers. You don't hire a Demi-god and expect him to skulk in the shadows. Petal hated being rolled out just for appearances, but sometimes money was tight. They had never offered Johnson the work, his reputation preceded him, and his former colleagues in grey wouldn't work alongside him if they didn't have to.

The car stood out, but the windows were tinted. Its unusual appearance drew attention from some, but there were plenty of others, many with celebrities hanging out the windows, who were crying out for more attention from the waiting photographers. Johnson, who had walked this beat in uniform, recognised the journalists and the fakes. There just weren't enough outlets to supply celebrity journalists for the number of people clamouring for their fifteen minutes of fame. To ensure that people felt like they might get their face in a newspaper or magazine, the club owners hired ringers. Fake paparazzi for nobodies and wannabes to make their evening by forcing a camera into their drunken faces or, for the great ringers, shouting their names as if anyone cared about what they were doing.

Things had gone so far that members of the press had, in a situation that nobody saw as ironic, become famous. Some photographers were more famous than the people they took pictures of. Johnson shook his head as he spotted the woman he had expected to see. Rita Swanson, belle of the paparazzi, stood outside Pallbearers on a raised platform with a camera hanging around her neck and another in her hands as she photographed people desperately strutting by her.

The standstill traffic was so slow that Johnson watched as people who had been queuing to get into the club left the line and started at the back for a second attempt at getting snapped in just the right pose for Swanson to put them in the morning papers. Johnson knew she'd received a significant fee from the owners of Pallbearers to appear. Everyone knew.

People crossed the road between the cars as if it were a carpark rather than one of the city's major thoroughfares. He resisted the urge to hammer the car horn in frustration. Somebody would abandon their vehicle at some point, which would only make matters worse. The hotel, The Light at the End of the Tunnel, was less than a kilometre away but the one-way system meant he had to sit in this traffic until he got close enough to turn off the road down a back street that would mean he could cut out the rest of the throngs of party-goers.

"Patience," he muttered, "Petal won't do anything stupid. Just get there, get Petal out, then keep our heads down until this whole thing has blown over."

DEFENESTRATED

There was blood.

When people with money get attacked there is always blood. The most frivolous of expenditures. High society types would have their thumbs pricked as they entered VIP areas as proof of their status. It was pointless, extravagant, a sign of the hubris of the wealthy. Blood was as unnecessary as the designer handbags and the wristwatches that glittered as they hung heavy on their owners' wrists.

Petal was standing on the edge of the doorway, leaning down with his head tilted to one side as he peered inside the hotel room. Blood did not mean severe injury. Blood was like salad dressing splashed over the carnage of torn vegetation. If the vegetation consisted of body parts and screaming dead people.

Detective Blunt had both hands on the woman's scythe. He was trying to wrestle it from her grip and failing.

"Hey," a voice shouted, "over here, don't just stand there, help us!"

Petal looked down to see a man lying on the floor. In his right hand; he was clutching his own severed arm. "Why?" Petal asked.

"Do you know who I am?" The man said.

Petal twisted his mouth and glared at the man, "did you really say that?"

"Do something, aren't you security? It's your job. I will ruin you."

The look of disgust on Petal's face changed to a grin. "You look pretty 'armless to me," he said. There were others trying to demand his assistance, but Petal ignored them as he strode into the room. "Why did you do this?" Petal said.

Twist didn't seem to be struggling against the detective's attempts to pull her scythe away. She was simply holding it. "They were in the way. I did ask them to move."

"She was going to attack Mister Rex," the man holding his own arm said.

"Mister Rex? Oh, you mean Ted," Petal said, "and you really care about him."

"Of course we do," a woman said from where she was hiding behind the arm of a sofa pushed up against the wall.

"Because he's your meal-ticket," Blunt growled. He was red faced with gritted teeth. His knuckles were white as he held onto the shaft of the scythe.

"Detective, let go or I will void our contract."

"Technically," Blunt began, "I... have... already... done... my... job."

Twist stood up straight, let one hand drop to her side, still easily matching Blunt's attempts to wrest it from her grip and sighed. "I suppose that's true," she reached inside her long coat and withdrew a small black bag. "Here you go," she dropped it on the floor below the scythe. "Take your money and scuttle back into a bottle if you would. You're not actually as interesting as I imagined."

"Where is Ted?" Petal asked, interrupting the conversation.

Blunt and Twist both looked over to a closed door that joined the two hotel rooms. Petal shrugged, "While you two play... uh... whatever it is youse are playing. Me and Ted are going for a walk."

"Ted and I," the woman by the sofa said.

"You're really going to draw attention to yourself to correct his grammar?" The man with one arm said.

"I'm a writer," the woman said.

"We know, you told us four times before I cut off his arm," Twist said.

Petal stepped over the one-armed man, well technically he had both arms but only one was attached, and kicked open the door. Then he was gone.

Twist spun the scythe with one hand sending Blunt sprawling across the floor and then she was gone after the big demi-god. Blunt scrambled to his feet, grabbed his hat, and ran after them.

"What about us?" The man on the floor asked.

"Oh, shut up Glenn."

"They left us because you're a pedant."

"Meh, meh, meh, meh, meh."

Blunt could hear them bickering as he stepped into the next room. Petal was standing in the centre of the room. Twist stood to one side, by the door from the corridor. Behind Petal, standing on an ornate upholstered chair, was Teddington Rex. The same bear who had made a laughing stock of Blunt multiple times on his chat show.

"Get out of the way," Twist said, "you're making this unnecessarily tedious."

Petal shook his head, "You don't get to go around chopping people up."

"He's not people," Twist widened her stance and glanced around the room taking in the dimensions of the space, the bed, the dressing table, coffee table, the unused trouser press, "he's a teddy bear."

"Don't let her get me Petal, she's a monster," Ted said.

Blunt caught the sudden flash of disgust across Twist's face as he watched the scene in front of him.

"You don't belong here. You're a thief, stealing time from those of us who worked for it, how dare you make others suffer?"

"What is she?" Ted said.

"I don't know Ted," Petal said as he planted his feet ready to block any attempt to get to the bear, "don't worry. I'm right here."

Twist shook her head, "Enough. You're good but you're not that good," she moved at a speed Blunt couldn't track but Petal seemed to know what was going to happen before it even began.

The demi-god caught the first three strikes from the scythe on his forearms, just below the blade. He kicked out with his right foot but Twist ducked and spun in the air delivering a blow across the big man's brow that would've cracked most people's skull. Petal blinked as Twist moved to get a better attacking position.

"Blunt, get Ted," Petal said, "she can't go Ableforthing people." Then the big man darted forward.

Twist deflected the fist that was aimed at her body and used the dressing table to aid her leap into the air. She spun the scythe but Petal moved his head just in time taking only a glancing blow across the shoulder from the shaft. The blade continued its arc through the bed cutting it clean in two.

"Now," Petal shouted.

Blunt leapt forward. As he passed Twist she brought down the scythe but Petal caught it in one huge hand. The detective grabbed the bear with both hands and hit the chair. It fell backwards and Blunt followed with the bear in his hands. He came to a stop pressed against the window. Petal, straining to hold on to the scythe, kicked Blunt in the backside, hard, and the detective, with the bear in his hands, hit the glass.

Detective Blunt felt his nose crumple as the glass shattered and then he was falling into the wet dark night as the pavement below raced up to meet him.

OUTSIDE

Morgarth hung back as the Grim Reaper walked out of the Office of the Dead. The building filled one side of Dead Square. The opposite side of the square led to a pedestrianised cobblestone road. On the two remaining sides of the square was a shop that sold office stationery, a patisserie which was really just a doughnut shop with a name written in italics, and a shop that sold neckties.

The Grim Reaper's robes billowed around him in the breeze as he strode down five wide steps that led down into the square. As he reached the bottom he turned around.

"I think it's him."

"It is, why's he here?"

"Well, he works in that building, it's not that weird really."

"I know but out in public. He never comes out in public."

"Do you think he can hear us?"

"Yes, he can," The Grim Reaper said.

Silence descended on the small crowd of people who had surrounded him. He didn't move from where he was standing staring upwards at the clock at the top of the building that housed the Office of the Dead. He had, up until only a few moments ago, been quite unaware of the small crowd that had gathered around him. This might have been because people were too afraid to stand closer than three meters to him. Molly would have said this was divine space.

The clock was moving.

"He can hear us," a voice said in a faux whisper.

"That's very rude," The Grim Reaper turned to look at the crowd. "Gloomwooders-"

"Oh? I thought we were Gloomwoodians," a man in a waistcoat and a bowler hat said.

"No. It's Gloomwoodarians," a woman wearing something resembling a circus tent said.

"Gloomwoodarians is quite a long word," the Grim Reaper said.

"He's right! Get her!" The crowd burst into angry cries and a scuffle broke out.

"What are you doing?" The Grim Reaper said. He didn't shout. There was no need for him to shout. The crowd froze. "Leave her alone. You can't kill people here. Have you people learned nothing? You're all dead."

"Oh yeah," the bowler hat man said. "You bunch of idiots."

"Yes. Very good hat wearing man. Now, as I was saying...citizens of Gloomwood-"

The bowler hat wearing man interrupted "So not Gloomwoodians?"

"Is it important?" The Grim Reaper asked.

"Well. It speaks to the identity of all of us doesn't it?"

"Ah. I see. Well then I suggest Gloomwooders, it's short."

"Why not Gloomwoodians?"

"He's arguing with the Grim Reaper!"

"Tear his arms off!" A child screamed.

Death shook his head and turned back to the clock. It intrigued him. He watched as the large hand, with a groan, moved.

The noise behind him began to die off to the point where it was little more than muttering but he could make out the conversations nearest to him.

"Why's he out here?"

"I don't know. We never see him. He's too important I guess."

"Well he is in charge."

"Do you want this arm? It got kind of twisted."

"We're honoured to be in his presence."

"Yes we are!"

"Why?"

"Who said that? He's the Grim Reaper."

"Yeah...but why-"

The Grim Reaper turned to look at them again. The man in the bowler hat still somehow had it on his head even though he was lying on the floor without any arms. "Does that hurt?"

"Yes, your, uh, Highness, quite a lot."

"Mhm. I will arrange for new arms for you. My apologies."

"What kind of arms?" The man asked.

"Well, whichever arms you want," Grim shrugged.

"Any arms I want, what about my legs."

"Why? You have legs."

"Yeah, but they won't match."

"Fine, arms and legs then."

"Any I want?"

"Yes, any you want."

A man stepped forward. He had a shopping bag in one hand. They all looked the same to the Grim Reaper. Flesh was not something he paid much attention to. "What about me?" The man asked.

"You appear to have the standard number of limbs I'm not sure how-"

"I think it should be Gloomwoodtarians," the shopping bag wielding man said.

"You can-"

"Get him!" Someone from the crowd screamed.

"Ah...I see. Everybody go home," The Grim Reaper said and then, as if compelled, they began to. The square cleared until the only movement was caused by discarded food wrappers, napkins, and a newspaper that flapped a picture of Augustan Blunt's face in the wind.

He walked back up the stairs to where Morgarth stood just outside the doors. "Interesting. The clock is working." Grim said looking down at the dinosaur.

"Well that's good, isn't it?"

The Grim Reaper shook his head. "It really isn't. It's not good at all."

Morgarth nodded, "I see."

"You don't do you?"

"Nope."

"It means Beezy is right. I do hate it when he's right."

"So… you're on his side?"

"Absolutely not. I am neutral-"

"Yes, you said that sorry…"

Death didn't move and Morgarth found herself twiddling her tiny fingers.

"What were we talking about?" The skeletal figure asked as he loomed over the fluffy dinosaur. Further in the building several low-level office dwellers tried hard to watch while not watching at all. Paper was shuffled with near reckless abandon, that's near reckless, not reckless enough for it to be disorganised, these were bureaucrats from the Office of the Dead, not amateurs. It was late though, these were the hangers on, the lingerers.

"You said the clock is working."

"What? That's terrible news Morgarth, why didn't you say something earlier, are you sure?"

"What is wrong with you?" Morgarth asked trying to keep her voice down which, given that she was a demon with a voice designed to instil instant bowel emptying fear into anyone that heard her, was difficult.

"Nothing…it's, time, time is a problem for me."

"But you're immortal."

"We're all immortal if time doesn't exist but we also don't live. Are you immortal if you've never lived at all?"

"I ask these kinds of questions when I'm torturing the arrogant."

"Who's he?"

"Them, there's lots of them, people who liked to pretend they had all the answers."

"Ah, and do they answer?"

"No, they no longer pretend to know."

"Interesting."

"Lord Death."

"Please call me Grim."

"I shan't if that's okay."

"No? Oh… we're not, um, friends?"

Morgarth shook her head. "Demons don't have friends."

"Ah, neither, it seems, do I."

GET IN THE CAR

There was no balcony. Nor was there a conveniently placed awning or outdoor swimming pool. In fact, outdoor swimming pools were banned anywhere in Gloomwood since people didn't need to breathe and spent too long in them. The problem was that the pools inevitably deteriorated until the liquid inside them changed into the same stuff the Styx and canal was filled with. The strange pinkish purple fluid would eat away at flesh. More than one poor soul ended up as little more than a skull and needed fishing out of the water by a net attached to a long pole. Let's not even mention what it did to the pool filters.

Blunt knew all of this. When Petal's foot thrust him through the glass hotel room window he could see, immediately, his final destination. There was a good chance it would be directly onto an inconveniently placed fire hydrant. When imagining being launched from a high rise building people expect to hit hard pavement. A resounding 'whack' or 'splat' but there's more chance of hitting something, or at least part of you hitting something, than people realise. Even in that last moment there are obstacles in the way. A bloody fire hydrant. Well, at least if he hit it dead on there was a chance he could impale himself headfirst on it guaranteeing Abelforth. The pavement was probably more risky, there was a chance of survival, well not survival as he was dead already but a slow Ableforth where his shattered skull released him to nothingness by increments.

When you are dead there's negligible risk of your life flashing before your eyes. If it did that would be a little unfair. You might have been dead for centuries and then instead of experiencing glimpses of all the time you had existed you would only get to see the first five percent of your experiences. It would be unreasonable, and nobody wants to be on the receiving end of that kind of complaint, especially from the dead. Dying leaves people with an abundance of supplementary complaining time.

As he hurtled towards the pavement he held on to the teddy bear in his arms. Squeezing it against him in instinctive panic. Reduced, in that instant, to a state of child-like helplessness he closed his eyes and waited for darkness. Everlasting Ableforth. The true big sleep. Blissful abrupt and sudden nothingness of the abyss. If anyone could have seen his face as he zipped by the windows of the Light at the End of the Tunnel hotel they may have seen the flicker of a smile for the briefest of moments.

Then it all stopped. He opened his eyes to see the pavement three feet below him. Time, it seemed, had frozen. "It's...magic," Blunt whispered.

"There's a tentacle wrapped around your legs," Ted said from where he was upside down and with his face half hidden in Blunt's crotch.

Blunt looked up. After fighting with his coat that was flapping around his head he managed to shove it to once side to see the tentacles, the same ones that had tried to take his hat and coat, holding him. "Uh, thank you?" Blunt said and the tentacles lowered him to the ground gently before unravelling themselves. He placed Ted on the ground and clambered to his feet dusting himself off. The tentacle returned and placed his hat, which had fluttered away in the fall, back upon his head. "Right... thank you again," Blunt said addressing the hotel. "Excellent customer service. Well done."

"Can it hear you?"

"I don't know but it did just save us."

"It saved you," Ted said, "I would have been okay. I'm foam."

"It still would've hurt," Blunt said, "I wouldn't have felt anything... I don't think."

Blunt looked up to see Petal's head poke out of the window, "RUN!" The big man shouted before disappearing back inside.

"We're safe," Ted waved a hand, "Petal will take care of that madwoman."

"No, he won't," Blunt said, "he was barely keeping up with her."

"Don't you know who Petal is?"

"Not really, a bloody big bastard?" Blunt said.

"He's a god-"

"Don't start with that," Blunt interrupted, "who is that woman?"

"I don't know."

Blunt turned on the bear who was standing on the pavement looking bored. "You're a liar. She knew you and she paid me to find you. Turns out she wants you dead, which doesn't make any sense because you're already dead- I'm not sure why I stopped her either as you're an Ableforther. What exactly happened to the squid?"

A horn interrupted Blunt and he looked up to see a police car unlike any he had seen in Gloomwood pull to a stop. The driver side window rolled down and a man Blunt recognised poked his head out.

"Constable Johnson, new car?" Blunt asked.

"Old car, not a constable anymore, and where's Petal?"

"Ah, are you checking up on your boyfriend? How sweet." Blunt said.

"Death partner," Johnson replied, "where is he?"

Blunt pointed upwards at the building. "He's in there fighting a woman with a scythe who wanted to 'kill'," he made quotation marks with his fingers, "the bear."

"The bear is Teddington Rex, Mister Rex to you," Ted said.

"The bear is about to get kicked into the street because he's an ungrateful shit. Your boyfriend, sorry, death partner, just kicked me out of a window several floors up to help the bear escape."

Petal's head poked back out of the window. "Jay, get them away from here. She's going to win."

"Win what?" Johnson asked as Petal's head disappeared.

"The fight I guess?" Ted shrugged.

Johnson's eyebrows shot up. "Get in the car Ted. You too Blunt."

"Why?"

"Get in the car," Johnson snapped.

A huge crash came from above and pieces of the hotel began to shower down upon them. A block of cement the size of Blunt's head hit the fire hydrant and it burst open. Water shot into the air as Blunt pulled open the rear passenger door. He grabbed Ted, who was heavier thanks to the water, and threw the bear into the car, hard. Ted slapped against the opposite window and fell into the seat as Blunt climbed in. He slammed the door behind him.

Johnson threw the car into first launching it forward.

"What about the big guy?" Blunt said as the sudden acceleration threw him backwards into the seat.

"He'll be fine. He's only buying time for us," Johnson said without turning to look at his passengers.

"He was losing," Ted's voice was difficult to hear over the roaring of the engine.

"She's not from around here," Blunt said, "so who the hell is she?"

"Your boss, apparently," Ted shouted.

"Hold on tight," Johnson shouted as he spun the wheel.

NO NEWS IS GOOD NEWS

She was good at running. It had been a habit from life that she had decided not to shake. Endorphins. They had told her about them at her support group. It wasn't really a support group, it was a running club, but it ticked the box that everyone needed to tick. Everyone was required, by law, to attend a support group. Most people attended several.

Her feet beat a steady rhythm against the pavement as she ran. In front of her was Florence, behind her was Dave. Holding up the rear were the stragglers, the ones who didn't really want to be there and spent half of the run wondering if they could take a short cut.

She watched Florence land in a puddle and smirked. Florence who never wanted to run side by side with anyone because then she wouldn't be winning. Leighton didn't care about that kind of thing. Running was her meditation and this once a week late run was the only time she didn't run solo so she was grateful for the company. It wasn't meant to be a race, but of course, that's all some of them wanted to do.

The puddle sailed beneath her as she adjusted her stride gaining a little on Florence. Winning, she reminded herself, wasn't the point. It was supposed to be fun. Which is why she would creep up on Florence and put a burst of speed on just before the run finished. Not because she wanted to win, but because she wanted Florence to lose. It was just a bit of fun.

Her investigation into the bear had proven fruitless. Which only served to make her more intrigued. Something didn't add up. No, she reminded herself, nothing added up. The bear didn't belong. That would be tomorrow's work...well maybe after the run, just for a bit. Then there was the Deathport. Her sources had said Ableforth, the taxi driver too, but there was no evidence. It had been buried.

Distracted for a moment she bumped into the back of Florence who had stopped and was standing still, staring at something further up the road.

"Are you okay?" Leighton asked.

"What's that?" Florence said, still catching her breath.

Leighton brushed a few hairs to one side that had escaped her ponytail as she looked. "Some kind of party?"

"That's not a party. They're...they're coming this way," Florence pushed Leighton to one side and sprinted off in the direction she had come from.

Leighton found herself rubbing her ribs where the small woman's fingers had dug in as she looked up the road. The rain and the poor lighting made it difficult to see the crowd ahead but they definitely didn't look like party goers. As she watched a figure in the grey of the Gloomwood police burst out of an alleyway followed closely by a man dressed in a pink cardigan and brown trousers.

Moments later two other policemen stumbled out of the same alleyway. They were almost swallowed by the crowd behind them but seemed unconcerned as they walked forwards. Their movements were sudden but uncoordinated. As if they were drunk but determined to march like soldiers.

As Leighton watched she realised Dave was standing behind her. "What did you do to Florence this time?" He asked.

"I didn't do anything, look."

"It's the police?" Dave said.

"I was more worried-"

"I hate the police."

"Everyone does Dave, more importantly-"

"My old man always said that innocent people should be the most afraid of the police."

"What? I mean in Gloomwood that makes sense but not in-"

"At least if you've done something wrong you can reconcile being treated like a criminal, but if you're innocent a run in with the police can shatter your world view, that's why my dad robbed banks."

"Dave there's-"

"So he could reconcile his world view. It was the police that made him do it, see?"

"For Christ's sake Dave. Look behind the police."

"Are they zombies?"

"What, don't be ridiculous. You can't have zombies-"

"Leighton, look at me," Dave said.

She turned around and looked at Dave. He was what would politely be termed hirsute. Less polite people called him a yeti, sasquatch, the abominable snowman, which technically he was. Dave's dad had been the last person to see a living bigfoot.

"I'm half yeti, you need a guy who can spot something that people aren't used to seeing, then I'm your man, those are bloody zombies. You can stay here and watch but I'm off," with that, Dave started running. His oversized feet slapped against the concrete pavement faster than Leighton had ever seen him run before.

Leighton didn't move. She wondered for a moment why Dave was so dull given how interesting his father sounded. Robbing banks and having children with bigfoot sounded like a life well lived. Sasquatchian lifestyle wasn't something she knew much about. Time was on her side and she would've happily considered the strange world of bigfoot for longer. It wasn't as though the crowd was roaring towards her at a terrifying speed. She waited for the two closest figures to get within earshot then waved them down. They were both panting for breath.

"Are they zombies?" Leighton asked.

"Yeah," the man said, "run away."

Leighton nodded, "Where did they come from?"

"Well the two behind us were in my shop. Well only one was but then he bit the other one-"

The constable next to him interrupted. She was in better shape than the shopkeeper, but she didn't look comfortable. "Ma'am, this is police business, I'm going to have to ask you to move along, as quickly as possible."

"As quickly as you?" Leighton asked.

The constable glanced around behind her. At some point the officer had lost her hat and her manner was far removed from calm, cool, and collected. "Sod you, I'm off," the constable said before running in the same direction as Dave the yeti.

"I... I better go with her. I mean she's the police after all," the shopkeeper said.

"Oh yes. Of course. I mean the police know best. I'll be along shortly. Just catching my breath," Leighton said.

"Right ...I'll be off then."

"Right behind you," Leighton said.

HEADS UP

"You could have put me back together," Molly whined.

"Yes, I could have, but optics, remember? Also, I'm in a rush," Beelzebub replied.

He had repurposed his walking stick as a pike. It wasn't ideal. Waving around a person's head on a stick is cumbersome at the best of times. A head is much heavier than it looks. The average head weighs five kilograms, stick that on the end of a walking stick and you've got a very cumbersome party trick. "People think I do a lot of planning, you know."

"Sign-" Molly shouted before her head hit a stop sign like a mallet hitting a gong.

"Oops," Beelzebub said, "I keep missing the signs."

"No, you don't."

The Devil let out a chuckle. "No, I suppose not. Can you see them yet?"

"I don't even know what I'm looking for," Molly said.

"Oh, you'll know, tell me what your marble says about the Meep resurrection again."

"It's not a marble, it's the Mible."

"I know that," he said, stopping as he fished his phone out of his pocket.

They were standing in front of a locksmith, 'Tartarus security'. A tall figure popped his head out of the window. "Help you?" He asked.

"No thank you," Beelzebub said.

"Don't I know you?" The figure asked.

Beelzebub, who was staring at his phone, flicked an annoyed glance at the figure, "Ugh, Cronus, I was wondering where you'd got to. Why are you here?"

The big man shrugged, "everyone has to be somewhere."

"That's very philosophical for the man who ate a rock thinking it was a baby. I'm busy."

"You've got a head on a stick."

"And?"

"Just thought it was weird."

"Mind your own business," Beelzebub snapped.

The big man stepped back inside his door and closed it behind him, muttering, "wouldn't have dared if mum and dad were still around."

He looked at his phone until it blinked into light then scrolled through his notifications. "Nothing. What's he playing at?"

"Who?" Molly asked.

"People are so rude. They think it's okay to leave people checking every ten minutes for a message when they're expecting a response."

"What is that?"

"A phone. Argh, this place. Everyone is in the dark ages. Actually, that would be an improvement. Nobody remembers the positive aspects of that period in time. Come on."

Behind Beelzebub, in a line of twelve, marched an assortment of stuffed animals. They shared the occasional look that was most commonly associated with the glance of schoolchildren who knew they were under a watchful eye but could only resist temptation and boredom for so long. Arazaiphiealomus reached forward and flicked the ear of Clive, who looked like a large humanoid cat.

"Oi, sir, Arazaiphiealomus just flicked me," Clive, guardian of misery, said.

"Be quiet, Clive. We're working," Beelzebub snapped as he shoved his phone back into his pocket.

"But-"

"I won't hear any more of it, I'm sure he's sorry." What Beelzebub, Lord of Hell, and representative of the dark side of all things, meant was, 'I can't pronounce his name, and he's got a nasty attitude. If I say it wrong, we'll be here all day trying to get it right, and he'll only end up sulking so just suck it up.' It was a little known fact that Beelzebub did in fact have qualified teacher status after completing a postgraduate certificate in education from Middlesex University. The only reason it was a little-known fact was because nobody cared to listen to him espouse the virtues of pedagogy. Well, that, and he was a terrible teacher and hated children.

He carried on walking. "I mean, it's a simple enough technology. All of this would be so much easier with phones. It's obtuse, evil even, and I should know!"

"Are you... are you talking to me?" Molly asked.

"Well, who else would I be talking to?"

"The toys?"

"They are not toys," he said, lighting a cigarette, "they are some of the brightest and best demons in my service. They are specimens of true darkness who could cause a person's soul to fold in on itself countless times through agonising horror at the lives they have led. A demon isn't just made, it's about natural inherent ability honed over millennia-"

"They're quite cute," Molly said.

"Cute! I can't help it if nobody makes things with heads. What's that about? I would've got mannequins instead, but none of them have heads. It's done on purpose, you know. Just another way of the Reaper keeping the man down. Look at resurrection. It's perfectly reasonable. Time doesn't even work here. You, Molly, are going to lead the resurrection."

"I am?" She asked.

"Of course. Viva la resurrection!"

☠ <u>BUMPY RIDE</u> ☠

"Where are we going?" Ted asked as he looked for a seatbelt that didn't exist.

"My maggots!" Blunt said, staring at the little glass box. "They're going crazy."

Johnson scowled into the rear-view mirror but said nothing. He pulled the wheel, and the car slalomed between vehicles.

"Where are we going?" Ted said again, "I have places to be. We're safe now, so thanks for the help. My people will pay you. Jayjay? Can you hear me?"

"I can hear you. I don't want any money from the likes of you. I was helping Petal out. I'll dump you wherever he says," he took one hand off the wheel and jerked a thumb over his shoulder toward Blunt.

"Wherever I say?" The detective asked, "well I don't bloody know, do I? I was working for her with the Scythe half an hour ago. Then she went all assassin-like and started chopping people up. Oh, and there's the massive matter of a dead squid doctor to deal with."

"We're all dead-"

"I know! I bloody know we're all dead. I don't need to be told every ten minutes. It's just easier than going through the dead but not dead thing, Ableforth, blah, blah, blah, death of a dead person is impossible so instead we say, who gives a flying-"

"I'm not dead," Ted said.

Blunt stopped shaking the box of maggots and turned to look at the bear. "Constable Johnson, please take us to the Office of the Dead."

"I'm not a constable anymore," Johnson said.

"Oh? Well, I'm so glad to hear that, but it isn't really relevant, is it?" Blunt said, his voice drowning out the sound of the car's engine.

"I said sorry, Jayjay." Ted said in a voice coated with more sympathy than a cheap Chinese take away is coated in sweet and sour sauce.

"I don't think he cares, and I definitely don't care. If you use that voice around me again I'll stick your head out of the window and wind it shut with the rest of you on the inside," Blunt said. "You keep saying you're alive. My maggots say there's something wrong with you and somehow you hollowed out the head of Doctor Squid."

"Octopus, he was an octopus."

"Really Doctor-"

"Don't say it."

"Why would you need a squid doctor, anyway?" Blunt asked, "You're not a squid in a bear costume, are you?"

"No! That doesn't even make sense. He was a normal doctor who was an octopus. Are there so many octopi-"

"That's not the plural," Johnson interrupted.

"Are there so many tentacled things around that there's a need for squid doctors?" Ted said without missing a beat.

"Why were you seeing a doctor?" Johnson asked.

The car fell silent, and Ted tried to look out of the window. He wasn't tall enough and instead stared at the interior of the door.

"Office of the Dead," Blunt said again.

"Right," Johnson said, and they fell into silence.

There was no need to drive at speed, so Johnson slowed the car and took the most obvious route. It was late, but there would still be people at the city's bureaucratic centre. The cogs of time-wasting paper work never stopped turning, at least, not until the clockwork inside the building did, and then there was half an hour of strange whirring and banging noises from the inside of the industrial tower before it started again.

Paperwork, Johnson had learned, was both pointless and important in equal measure. Layers upon layers of official red tape were produced, not by those who dealt with it, but by people who made it necessary after something had happened. Form 117b-4 was a formal request to paint the exterior of a building in the same colour it was in. This may seem quite specific, a colour change involves several more forms for multiple reasons, neighbours may not appreciate one house in the neighbourhood being painted neon pink while the others were grey. However, the request still had to be made to refresh the same paint, for the same reason. The Joneses at number fourteen would not appreciate a newly painted building next door to their own building, which had been painted only six months earlier but had not aged well. A nasty argument might ensue, but form 117b-4 avoided this, because people could brandish it angrily in the face of the Joneses, which is what paperwork is really for.

He took a left, then hit the brakes. "What is this?"

Blunt shuffled forward so he could squeeze his head between the two front seats and get a better look out of the window. "Some kind of crowd," he said, proving once more why he wasn't really cut out to be the city's number one detective.

Something banged against the passenger door. Johnson wound the window down and a police officer pushed her head through the window.

"Is this actually a police car? Oh, Johnson, it's you," she said.

"Constable Furnell," Johnson said, "no, this is not a police car. It's my car that has the word police on the side of it."

"Oh yeah, now I remember, we... someone scratched graffiti into it."

"What do you want?"

"I'm commandeering this vehicle in the name of the Gloomwood police," she said, tugging at the passenger door. It was locked, "open the door."

"You can't commandeer this vehicle. It's mine."

"This is police business."

"It's being used already."

"I'm -"

"I've already commandeered my own car, Furnell, have a nice evening."

"This is an emergency."

"I agree, this," he waved at Blunt and Ted in the back seat, "is an emergency. There has just been an attempt to Ableforth Mr Teddington Rex and I am moving him to protective custody along with his bodyguard."

"Hello," Blunt said, "fairly sure he's telling you to jog on… literally."

"This isn't some celebrity desperately trying to get attention by faking some kind of crisis. Wait, aren't you Augustan Blunt the knobhead who thinks he's better than the police?" Constable Furnell said.

"I… how am I supposed to answer that without denying who I am, or calling myself a knobhead?" Blunt said before sitting back once more, "and it's not exactly a scale when the police are the bottom of the bloody measure is it? That's like saying you're taller than the ground."

"Open the door. I have a civilian in danger," she said.

"Where?" Johnson asked, making a show of looking around. He was not, by nature, a vindictive person. He believed in karma, though. Being a pragmatic sort, he also believed that karma was not magic, spiritual comeuppance, instead he believed karma was best used as a simple scoring system. The old, 'do unto others as you would have them do unto you,' which, logically, would also mean, ' do to others what you know they would do to you.' For this reason, he was perfectly happy to watch Constable Furnell suffer.

"He's on his way. What are you playing at Johnson? This is police business, we're all on the same side."

"Are we?" He asked, "you're trying to steal my car."

"I'm commandeering it, it's perfectly legitimate."

"Susan," Johnson said, "are you just running away?"

The constable looked back up the street, then back to Johnson.

Ted, with difficulty, wound down the window. "What is that?"

"Zombies," she said.

"You can't have zombies in the afterlife," Ted replied, "everyone is already dead."

"What's a zombie? It's the living dead, right? Well, they say they're alive and they want to bite people and-"

Ted sneezed. Constable Susan Furnell of the Gloomwood police department exploded. Parts of Susan Furnell's head splattered against the car. A cheek slapped against Johnson's face and slid down it. Her body remained upright, one hand pointing towards the crowd which was approaching.

Ted, Blunt, and Johnson stared at the place where a face had been moments before.

"... bless you?" Blunt said.

INVESTIGATIVE JOURNALISM

Leighton Hughes, investigative journalist, and 'fun-runner' walked in front of the horde of ill-looking citizens, keeping well out of arm's reach while she shouted questions at the crowd.

"What are you doing?" She asked them as a whole.

There was a lot of moaning and one or two voices, "hungry, alive, eat, bite, ugh."

"Okay, you, gentleman in the coattails, are you marching for a particular purpose?" She asked.

"Urrr," the man in coattails and a waistcoat replied.

"Right... who can speak?"

"Some of us can, some of us can't, don't know why," a woman with her hair in an impressive beehive responded.

"I can," a figure to her right who was limping on a twisted ankle.

"Me too," another somewhere in the crowd's midst.

"I can't!" Someone further back said.

"Right, you," she pointed at one of two police officers near the front of the crowd, "you're a member of the police, why have you joined this movement?"

"Movement? It's not a movement. We're alive!"

"Right, so is that what everyone thinks?"

A chorus of affirmative sounding moans came from the crowd.

"So how did this happen?"

"He bit me," the uniformed officer said, pointing to his colleague who was staring at her with his mouth open wide.

Leighton nodded. "Interesting, interesting, so you bite people and they become alive?"

"Yeah, obviously," the constable said with encouragement from the crowd.

"Obviously? I see. Are you marching for living rights then? What exactly is it you're drawing attention to?"

"Um, well, I can only speak for myself," the constable started, "but I suppose living rights is a good reason to march.

I'm not sure. We're all just going the same way... to bite more people."

"Where are you marching to?"

The constable stopped, and the mob stopped with him. He looked around and shrugged. "Everyone keeps running away so we walk after them... then we try to bite them."

"So, it's not an organised thing."

"No."

"Are you catching many people?"

"At first... but then we became a bigger crowd and everyone can see us coming. We don't move as fast as we did when we were dead."

"Right. Interesting. So, you've got no purpose other than to bite people and you're moving so slowly it's easy to, well," she looked down at herself, "just walk away."

"I guess," the crowd around the constable looked around confused. Many of them making low moaning sounds that Leighton interpreted as confusion.

"You didn't really think this through, did you? I mean, you're alive, or at least you think you are, and the only thing you want to do is... bite people?"

"Well, you're oversimplifying it."

"Am I? Usually when people say that it's because complicating the explanation makes it easier for them to justify what they're doing."

"I don't need to justify anything to you," the moaning turned into the occasional grunted heckle. "You're dead," the constable said, "dead people don't get to order about the living, that's all part of it."

"Ah...so you believe you're better than me because one of your friends bit you?"

"We are better, we're alive, you're dead."

"Okay...so you're a fascist movement of mainly incomprehensible people with a range of physical issues? Angry at people who haven't been bitten... because they haven't been bitten."

"Yeah!" The crowd roared.

Leighton pulled a notepad out of a pouch that hung from the front of a belt. It was variously termed a fanny pack, a bum bag, or more reasonably, a belt bag. She began scribbling furiously. "Fascist-"

"Don't write that down," the constable said, "it sounds bad."

"So, you don't hate people none of you have taken a bite out of?"

"No! We just want to bite them."

"Right...so they become the same as you?"

"That's right, perfectly reasonable thing to urrg... I mean, it's urrg... urrgh... bollocks."

Leighton nodded, "I'm going to quote you on that Constable... does that say Daniels? Yes, Daniels 'perfectly reasonable bollocks,' lovely. Right, I'm going to run down this road now and I'll catch up with you all later. Thank you for your time," Leighton said. She placed the notepad back into the pouch and zipped it up. Gave a smile to the crowd, a wave, then jogged away from them.

The crowd didn't move as an argument began entirely in grunts. Further down the hill she could see a vintage police car and as she caught up with the shopkeeper they both slowed down.

The constable who Leighton had briefly met earlier was standing pointing at the crowd. She had no head.

"Hello Leighton, nice to see you," a voice from inside the car said.

"Blunt?" Leighton asked.

"How's my favourite investigative journalist?" Blunt asked, leaning out the window that Ted was staring out of.

"What happened here?" She asked.

"Well, we think the bear sneezed," Blunt said.

It was only then that she spotted Ted. "You! Now this all makes sense. You're alive, aren't you?"

HEAD OF THE GAME

"Just around this corner. I don't think I've walked this far in a long time. In Hell, I can just snap my fingers, you see."

"You're not from Hell," Molly said from atop the Devil's cane.

He let out a chuckle before taking another drag on his cigarette. "Yes, sorry, I forgot. I am just a person having a psychotic break while I walk through the afterlife with your head, which I took after dismembering you, and my team of twelve animated cuddly toys."

"That's right," Molly said, "the Mible tells us that the resurrection will happen when one steps forward who does not walk, they will lead the living from the dead."

"I know! I read that bit. Fascinating. So, are we all ready to step forward?" Beelzebub said.

"What do you mean?" Molly asked.

Beelzebub ignored her. His grin stretched wider, the cigarette hanging precariously from between his teeth, as he reached the corner of the street. Behind him the twelve stuffed toys, some of the most feared demons from the darkest depths of Hell, marched in perfect step.

"Behold..." He raised his arms as he turned the corner. Then dropped them to his sides. "Well, this is a little disappointing. Still, it's a start."

"What's wrong with those people?" Molly asked.

"Well, that's rich coming from someone who is nothing more than a head on a stick," Beelzebub said. He waved his free hand in the direction of the motley crowd before them.

Men, women, and others milled around grunting at each other. It looked like a miserable street party where every person who attended had somehow conspired to be that one person who has drunk far too much and is embarrassing themselves.

"This," Beelzebub said to Molly, "is your righteous flock, oh chosen one."

"I... I'm not the chosen one," Molly stammered.

"Of course you are. We," he spun Molly on the cane, "are your disciples, and this," he twirled Molly around to point at the crowd, some lurching figures had noticed them, "are the Meep, those who have risen to life once more."

"No, they're not. They look like... sick people."

"Well, they are the living dead," Beelzebub said, "you're going to have to change your expectations a little."

"I'm not the chosen one," Molly said as she tried to shake her head. The effect was disturbing.

"But you are! Someone so overwrought with belief in your story it possesses you completely, absolutely, your entire worldview is twisted through your lens of belief there is nothing that can dissuade you from the path of, so-called, righteousness. My poor dear Molly, you even make the people who profit from your infatuation with the teachings of your typo ridden manuscript nervous."

"I didn't stumble upon you by happenstance. You reek of faith, and I know that might sound unpleasant, but, for once, it's a wonderful thing. These people need your burning resolve, your furious indignation at the mere thought anyone would not want to know the truth, as you see it. You will lead them to the promised land... or back to it, I'm a little fuzzy on the details. I'm more of a big picture person. Quote your Mible at them, scream your doubt upon the heathens who stand in your way. Give them purpose and they will give you yours!" He held her aloft as he spoke, growing in volume with every word.

"Molly, the prophet will reveal the truth to us all and lead the dead back to the light of life! Down with Death, we march on the Office of the Dead, to freedom, to redemption, to the end of days! Viva la resurrection!" He shouted.

"Urrhh, urrh, URURURURUrr!" Came a chorus of voices.

"Yes, blessed ones, you are the children of the resurrection, follow Molly, the one true prophet as she speaks the truth," Beelzebub shouted. He pointed his free hand to the soft toys, "here stand the apostles."

The roar of the crowd dropped to a confused hubbub as the toys spread out around Beelzebub.

"Molly, this is where you spout nonsense from that ridiculous book," Beelzebub said in a whisper.

"It is not-"

"Decision time, Molly. Isn't this all you ever wanted? To be on the righteous path with true fervent believers following as you march towards everything you ever believed in. It's you Molly, think about it, all those metaphors, the careful interpretation doesn't it all point towards you? To this?" He held the cane she was on out towards the crowd and then placed it in the arms of a stuffed dog soft toy. "Tremor Veritas Loquere will carry you... we just call him Trevor."

"Where are you going?" She hissed.

"I don't exist, Molly. I am just the hand that pointed you here, a little nudge in the right direction," Beelzebub said before melting into the shadows.

Molly remained, hoisted upon the cane carried aloft by a stuffed dog called Trevor, facing a crowd of the confused living dead.

"I, ahem, I am Molly," she said.

"Ur?" A few of the more vocal members of the crowd responded.

"And you are alive."

"Ur."

"And so, it is said, when the dead once more live they will march forth and retake their place among the living, for now is the end of days," her voice gained strength with every word.

"Ur." The crowd responded with more enthusiasm.

"For we are the Meep and the Meep shall inherit the Earth."

"Ur!"

"Viva la resurrection!"

"Ur-ur Ur URURURURUrr!"

FINAL DESTINATION

"That seemed a little unfair," Leighton said, leaning around the front passenger seat as she spoke to Blunt.

"If he sneezes, one of us might end up with our head exploding. What would you have done?" Blunt asked.

"Not the bear. The shopkeeper, sending him to the police, bit mean," she said.

Johnson, a man of few words at the best of times, remained resolutely silent.

"Someone had to tell them, and they hate me and you. This is Johnson's car, and he's driving... plus they hate him even more. They'd eat us alive. At least the shopkeeper has a chance of walking away, he's only a witness." Blunt said.

"You have a shocking ability to say the worst things possible without realising."

"What did I say?"

"Eat him alive? There're zombies walking around-"

"Not zombies, that's not true-"

"There's living dead going around biting people and you say, 'eat him alive', you're an idiot."

"From a media hack like you?" Blunt said.

The car fell silent except from the sound of wailing from the roof of the vehicle.

"He's still going," Blunt said, looking at the roof. "Does sound like a siren though."

Leighton looked up at the roof and rolled her eyes before turning in her seat to face forward again, "Why didn't we put him in the boot?"

"We don't know how it works, do we?" Blunt said. "He might sneeze in there and then when someone opens it, boom, head gone. Better this way. We tied him on pretty tight."

Johnson rounded a corner and swerved around a taxi pouring overdressed, or barely dressed, party goers out into the front of a seedy-looking nightclub.

"Heeeeeeelllppp meeeeeee," Teddington Rex, darling of the television world, howled from where he was strapped to the roof of the car. The blue and red lights, dim as they were, added to the distraction. Nobody looked twice.

"How far?" Blunt asked.

"Five minutes then we must walk," Johnson said.

"Right," Blunt pulled himself forward in the middle of the backseat. "We're going to need a plan. You both seem to know him. Who is he?"

Leighton looked at Johnson. A frown flickered across her face, but Johnson seemed not to notice. "I've been investigating the bear. I got curious when I saw an interview with him. He avoided a lot of questions about his past," she said.

Blunt nodded. "You're chasing celebrities now, just like every other rag out there. You realise they're only celebrities because you chase them around. It's just a mindless loop, Knobhead McKnobersson is in the papers again for being famous, which makes them famous, bloody-"

Leighton held up a hand and nodded. "I'm not chasing celebrities, I'm chasing criminals. At first, I thought he was some kind of criminal, but the more I dig the less I uncover," she was facing Blunt.

"What does that mean? Stop being cryptic and get to the point. Don't hide the lead, that's what they say, right?" Blunt said with a smirk.

Leighton's false smile did nothing to cover her growing frustration. "I found nothing. No record of him arriving here. No death details. No record with the Office of the Dead he was a Gloomwood citizen. Then I started wondering about his body. Sure, we've got people, GHPDXers-"

"What's that?" Blunt asked.

Leighton stopped and looked to Johnson, who still displayed the emotion of a cardboard cut-out. She turned back to Blunt and hissed, "Are you... are you being serious?"

He shrugged.

"Gods, hopes, promises, dreams, and other exes. Blunt, how can you not know that?"

He let out something approaching a growl. "Someone could've told me?"

"Who? You don't have any friends and don't talk to anyone except to accuse them of something or just shout about whatever they're doing," she said.

"The bear," Johnson interrupted, "is alive. He stayed with Petal and I for a few nights when he first arrived. I didn't believe he was alive and... he was unpleasant. One day he just left. He sometimes contacts Petal when there's work, or he needs help."

"Not you?" Blunt asked.

"No. Petal thinks we're responsible for the bear, I don't."

"Why would you be?" Leighton asked.

"Because he came to us first."

"So, you just let a living thing loose in Gloomwood?" Blunt asked.

"No. A con-artist who thought we were soft touches realised we had nothing worth taking and left," Johnson slowed the car and came to a stop. He turned to look out the back window as he reverse parallel parked. "We walk from here."

Blunt put his hands on the tops of the seats in front of him. "Look, let's just get this clear. You both think that bear is alive. When he sneezes heads explode. There are some kind of walking dead-"

"We're all walking dead," Leighton said.

"You know exactly what I mean. Living dead, biting people, wandering the city. There's a crazy scythe woman hunting him down. What are we doing?"

Leighton looked at Johnson as he turned to look at her. "I think," she said, "we're following you."

Blunt slumped backwards. "I should've sodding jumped."

POLICE

It had taken seven officers to get Petal into the back of the truck, and only three of them would return to duty without some serious help from somebody with a sewing kit. In comparison, Twist had been almost polite, almost. She had decapitated the first constable to interfere in her fight with Petal, but that had been instinct. She'd even apologised.

Over twenty officers, and the Chief of police himself, had been at the Light at the End of the Tunnel hotel within minutes of a call from the maitre d'. They were all armed with some kind of bludgeon. Some more subtle than others, there were classic baseball bats with nails on the top of them, crow bars, old school wooden billy clubs, police issue batons, the more modern extendable night sticks, and a range of others. They wore the classic grey uniforms of the Gloomwood police, brass buttoned short capes, oversized hats, steel toe-capped boots, and their back-up pieces; a discreet blackjack that attached to the inside of the right ankle.

You can rely on the Gloomwood police for two things, violence, and pandering to anyone with money. Anyone without money was an arrest waiting to happen. Gloomwood society had existed with it for so long that they accepted it as reasonable. Well, anyone who mattered accepted it, and if you have money, then the police believe you matter.

As Gloomwood's most prestigious, and only licensed hotel, the Light at the End of the Tunnel was the client the Gloomwood Police put on a show for. They'd also needed a ridiculous show of force to deal with the situation.

Petal had put a fist through the reinforced steel door of the police van before they'd got him to the station. They didn't have a pair of handcuffs among them that were big enough to fit around the big man's wrists. Two constables had tried to daisy chain together several sets, but it didn't work and instead they found themselves tied to each other. In an outstanding level of incompetence, usually reserved for only the most elite of puppet leaders in mortal national governments, it turned out nobody had any keys for the cuffs. Not a single officer. Probably because they rarely uncuffed anyone they arrested.

The enormous man was now sitting in the Gloomwood Central Police Station. They could have called it something more exciting, but it took paperwork and that wasn't something anyone in the police wanted to bother with. Most people just called it the police station. It was a squat building with no sign of its purpose on the outside except for a small plaque on the otherwise bare concrete walls. Everything around it, even in the middle of the night, was quiet.

In any mortal city, one might expect the centre of all law enforcement to be a bustling melee of activity. Furious criminals arguing with law enforcement and suited lawyers pulling deals in closed interview rooms for their clients. Not in Gloomwood.

Petal and Twist were sitting side by side on a wooden bench that faced the reception desk of police headquarters. Behind the desk a constable was reading a dog-eared paperback book and ignoring a telephone that rang incessantly. Every few minutes a constable would open a door to the right of the desk. They would look around the corner, sigh, stomp over to the reception area and answer the phone. Every officer aimed a glower of frustration with precision at the paperback reading receptionist.

"You're very good," Twist said to Petal as she crossed her long legs.

Petal glanced at her. There was no hiding the deliberation that was taking place behind his eyes. "Yeah, you too," he eventually said, "scythe is a nice touch though. Intimidating, that is. Makes people think of him."

"Him?"

"The Grim Reaper himself, you know, big scythe, Death."

She gave a smile. "He's not the reaper anymore."

Petal's brow furrowed, and he shifted his weight, causing the bench to creak. The end that Twist was sitting on lifted off the floor for a moment and she gave the big man a smile but didn't flinch as he shuffled to make sure it settled on the floor once more. "You can't just stop being the Grim Reaper."

"That's not what I mean at all. He's the Grim Reaper, he's just not doing the job, I am."

"Oh. Yeah, that makes sense. Everyone's met a reaper at some point. You're like guides."

"Guides?" She blinked at him several times, the smile growing wider, "do I look like a girl guide to you, Mister Petal?"

Petal stopped himself from shrugging. "Well no, but that's-"

"You were a god, weren't you? I can tell you know."

This time Petal grinned. "Can't keep that a secret when you look like this," he said.

"Well yes, you're exceptionally large, and most would call you attractive, but I meant the way you fight. You're too strong to be a mortal. Even here they haven't tapped into the infinite potential. You see Reapers can do that, we're trained."

"The infinite-"

"Potential. Well, we're all dead, aren't we? So, everything is just willpower. That's why you're so strong. Gods, even dead ones, are self-actualizing, you can do what you believe you can. So you're very strong, and you believed you could defeat me in battle."

"I can. I was holding back."

She let out a laugh. "Oh, I'm not laughing because I don't believe you. I do. You could have crushed me and yet I held my own. In fact, I should have defeated you, and would have if they hadn't turned up. I wonder why that is."

This time he did shrug. It was automatic, but the bench beneath them squealed in protest and then something beneath them snapped. Twist leapt to her feet at the same moment as Petal did.

"Are we done fighting?" She asked.

Petal nodded. "Yeah, all done. Why did you attack Ted?"

"Ted isn't what he seems. He's a nasty little sh-"

"Yeah, but you don't go Ableforthing people because they're not nice. If you do that, then I'd be walking 'round crushing skulls with my bare hands all bleedin' day. Have you met... people?" Petal asked.

"Yes, take that receptionist, for example. He's irritating everyone around him. He's irritating me, and look, he's one of those people who folds the corner of a book to keep his page. It's disgusting."

"I can hear you," the receptionist said without looking up.

"The point is," she continued, "I will not kill him, sorry," she held up a hand, "Ableforth him. Ted needs to die. He doesn't belong here. That bear is alive."

Petal shook his head. "Still can't go around just killing people. You've no right. Even if he's alive, that'd be murder. You're a reaper. If you murdered him, you wouldn't be neutral. I'm not as thick as people think. Anyway, if you're a reaper, are you even dead yourself?"

She opened her mouth to continue, but a man stumbled into the building gasping for breath. Shortly after, a man in a tailored suit appeared. The suited man smiled. "Do excuse us, we have to report something quite startling," the suited man said, "don't we Mister Golepeski?"

"Zombies," the panting man said between breaths, "real living zombies."

"Oh yes. Seems there's a living bear bringing people to life," Beelzebub said with a grin, "ridiculous, I'm sure."

OUT OF ROAD

Johnson walked in front of Blunt and Leighton, with the bear a few paces in front of him. If Ted sneezed it would be forward, and they would all just run backwards. Johnson was the quickest, and he had demanded he be the one to walk behind Ted. He could have requested and neither Blunt nor Leighton would have argued, demanding just made it easier for them.

"So why didn't you take him to the police?" Leighton asked.

"Do you want a list?" Blunt said. They walked side by side along the cobbled streets. This close to the Office of the dead, the roads were for pedestrians only. They couldn't have come any closer in the car because of the bollards blocking access.

"Yes," Leighton said, "I do want the list. This seems reckless and ill-conceived."

"Don't you start with me. This is very healthily conceived."

"That's not... never mind, just explain the logic please."

"Fine. Reason one, every time the bear sneezes someone's head explodes, and it looks like instantaneous Ableforth. The police would take him to the police station, where many more people might be Ableforthed. Reason two, the police would not believe what was happening and would try to pin the Ableforth on Johnson's boyfriend Petal, because he looks like someone who Ableforths people. Reason three, it looks like that bear is alive, which is probably a terrible thing for all of us, and definitely isn't something those idiots at the police would know how to fix. Reason four, there is someone who knows how all this works and he's in the Office of the Dead. At the very least, he'll know what to do and decide."

Leighton fell into silence as she considered Blunt's reasoning. "Okay," she said, "there's some sense there, but why are you here?"

"Me? Oh, right, well, because I was the one who found the bear."

"Because some woman hired you?"

"A woman who wanted to kill the bear."

Leighton nodded again. "Wouldn't that be the logical thing to do? I mean. We're all dead. He's the odd one out and him being alive, and sneezing, is Ableforthing people. So isn't she doing the right thing?"

Blunt took his own time, considering Leighton's point. It wasn't as though he hadn't thought about it himself. "Right," he said, "I'm not okay with murdering the bear. I really don't like him and I mean more than I despise most people, but I'm fairly sure I'll get blamed for at least two Ableforths and probably the Bear's. Possibly three Ableforths if they throw in poor June if I let him die."

Leighton interrupted, "the Deathport? You know about that?"

Blunt nodded. "Ralph Mortimer tried to give me some kind of pity case. I didn't realise what he was doing until Sowercat made sure everyone knew how pathetic the whole thing was."

"At the scene?" Leighton asked, wincing.

"Yup, right in front of everyone. Mainly police, but you get the idea."

"That's... sorry, Blunt. That's rough. I went to look, but it's a coverup. I don't know if it's any consolation, but I think the secret police kicked Sowercat's men out. It involves Tomb Mandrake and his cronies. Do you think it's related?"

"Based on absolutely no evidence or information at all? Yeah, probably. This whole thing is a night-" he stopped himself, "a disaster. I mean, what even happens if someone living then dies in the afterlife? This is all some existentialist next level philosophy. I'm not clever enough to work this out, Leighton, so hopefully he is. I think my client might have Ableforthed a woman called June." He paused for a moment, his scowl permanently etched in place deepened for a moment before he turned to her, "Shall we go?" he nodded toward the Office of the Dead.

"I met him this morning."

"Oh yeah? I've met him before."

"I know, the headhunting thing."

"Mhm, he's... he's a character."

"Yes. We were in a changing room together."

"You... wait, what? Why?"

"It's a long story... I don't think he's normal."

Blunt let out a chuckle. "I should bloody well hope not. If he's like the rest of us we are well and truly -"

ALL GONE

Captain Sowercat and the Gloomwood police left the station in a hurry while Petal and Twist watched until it became quite apparent the only person who was going to stay was sitting at the desk in front of them.

"Are you not going with them?" Twist asked the receptionist.

"Going with who?" The receptionist asked, looking up briefly from his book, "and who are you again?"

"We're-"

"Concerned citizens," Petal interrupted, "but it looks like we should come back another time."

"Oh," the receptionist nodded, "okay then, bye."

Petal stood up, banged his head on the ceiling, then started towards the exit.

Twist looked from the receptionist and back to Petal, who was pushing open the doorway that would take him out into the street.

"Where is everyone going?" She asked the receptionist.

"How should I know?" The receptionist said.

"But...isn't that your job?"

"Wait a minute, I thought you were here to report something? Hang on, you aren't under arrest, are you?"

"Me?" Twist said, "Really, I mean," she gestured at herself, "how rude."

"I, oh, I'm sorry ma'am."

"Ma'am?"

"Uh, miss?"

"Better. I demand to know where those officers are going. It is my right as a citizen and a generous contributor to the police...um...the...you know."

"The police social and pension fund?"

"Yes, that's the one."

The receptionist nodded, poked his head through the door to his right, shouted something, then returned. "They are on their way to defend the Office of the Dead against a potential domestic terrorism threat."

"Do we have another kind of terrorism?"

"Sorry?"

"Have we ever had a terrorist attack from a non-domestic source?"

"No ma'am, because the Gloomwood police are keeping you safe," the receptionist, in his grey police officer in uniform, said without a hint of irony.

Twist put her elbows on the reception counter and leant down so she was face to face with the sitting receptionist. "It makes me feel so much safer knowing that the wonderful Gloomwood police are protecting me. You're all so... competent," she smiled.

"Yeah, we are," the constable said before swallowing.

"I wonder if anyone has handed in a scythe. That's why I first came in, you see. It's very sentimental to me and some terrible people stole it. I think they may have thought it was a weapon, but it's just for decoration, those horrible scoundrels. If only there had been someone there to stop them... like a big brave police officer... maybe one who likes books."

"I...hm, I'll go have a look for you," the constable said, getting to his feet and moving, for the first time in several hours, with intent.

When he was out of the room, she let out a sigh and looked over the top of the reception desk. There was nothing there except a telephone and a row of paperback books. There wasn't even a notepad or a pen. She shook her head, "what do they do here?"

The constable scuttled back through the door carrying the scythe which got caught on the top of the door causing the constable to flail helplessly for a moment before realising what was happening. "Found it," he said when he had regained his composure, "actually it's surprising how many scythes are in evidence but this was the most recent one, also looked the, uh, nicest."

"Thank you so much, you're my hero,"

"No problem, I just need your signature."

"Oh, I don't have a pen."

"Right, a pen, uh, and some paper, I'll be right back."

He vanished out the door once more. Twist leaned over the reception desk and picked up the book the man had been reading. She read the blurb as she walked out of the police station with the scythe in hand.

"Hm, time traveling immortal violinists, whatever next."

Petal was standing outside the entrance to the station facing away from the building and staring down the street in the same direction a line of police vehicles, of varying shape, size and description, were moving.

She looked at the scythe in her hands as she stood behind the dead god. "I could take your head clean off your shoulders."

"You could try," Petal said, his voice a mirth-filled rumble, "but that would mean you thought I didn't know you were there."

"Eyes in the back of your head?"

"Ears, you're quiet, but that door squeaks and the only person left in that building is the receptionist."

"What about people in the cells?"

"They rarely bother with the cells unless it's the weekend. That's why we were sitting in reception."

"They don't bother. What does that mean?"

"Jay-jay says nobody wants to clean the cells, so they only use them on weekends, and then they charge everyone who stays in them. Kick them out again morning after. If they can't pay well… costs an arm and a leg."

"Doesn't that depend who you are?"

"I don't think they ask. Just in they pop with the bone saw and," he mimed sawing.

"Oh, a literal arm and leg, I see. Doesn't seem very... lawful."

"Who decides that?"

"Judges, courts, the government."

"You really aren't from around here, are you?"

"Where are you going?"

"Was gonna go home."

"Okay, well, I enjoyed our scuffle."

Petal nodded, then turned to look at her. "Where are you going?"

"Oh, home for me too," She said, nodding.

"Okay, bye then," Petal started walking in the same direction the police cars were moving. A moment later Twist started walking behind him.

"Are you following me?"

"No. I'm going in the same direction."

"We've already said bye…"

"I know…it's awkward."

COLLISION

Blunt, Johnson, Leighton and Ted huddled together, Ted at the front, as they looked across to Dead square. Leighton had her hands on the corner of the wall to a café as they peered around into the empty, exposed square. The Office of the Dead building loomed over them, casting everything about it in an impossible three-hundred-and-sixty-degree shadow.

"It's quiet," Blunt said.

"What did we expect?" Leighton snapped.

"I don't know. I'm still waiting for that scythe-wielding supervillain to appear and now we've got the walking dead crawling up our backsides at the pace of an angry snail. Part of me expected to walk into some kind of disaster film."

"The horde is behind us," Johnson said.

"Don't start calling it a bloody horde," Blunt said, "that sounds ridiculous. It's just a bunch of sick people walking around in circles looking pathetic. It's hardly something from the pits of hell, is it?"

"Would you know what that looks like?" Ted said.

"You don't speak," Blunt snapped. "The next time you bloody speak, it better be to tell us everything that is going on. Otherwise I'm going to kick you as far as I bloody can, clear?"

Ted shrugged.

"Do we just walk in?" Leighton asked.

"We're not going to be magically beamed in by a teleporter or something," Blunt said.

"Wait," Johnson put out an arm, blocking the others from walking into the square. "There's someone there, coming out of the doors."

"They're going back in again," Leighton said.

"And again... are they stuck in the revolving door?" Blunt said, "is that... bloody hell. The Grim Reaper is stuck in the revolving door to his own fortress of solitude."

"That's a terrible name for it," Leighton said.

"It makes perfect sense, it's what superman called his fortress."

"Who's superman?" Johnson asked.

"I hate being dead sometimes."

COPS AND DEVILS

He hadn't intended to join the police on their mission to secure the Office of the Dead against an invading horde of the living dead, but, as someone who dealt in temptation, he wasn't immune to it himself. At some point, he was going to want to see what happened.

This meant he had lined up his forces neatly. The police, the living dead, his demons, and of course his trick card. By the time Grim worked out who was causing all the time issues, well, it would all be over before it began. All Beelzebub would have to do then was watch and wait as they all tore each other apart, completely oblivious to the impending doom that time was bringing their way.

A rumour, a little fabricated supporting evidence, a suggestion of ill-motives. People would lap it up and this entire afterlife would explode. It was a match waiting to be lit in the firework factory of buried angst that drifted over this horrible little afterlife like smog. Once people had gone deep enough down the rabbit hole, there would be no turning around. If you venture down the tunnel of conspiracy, don't take baggage, like unfounded beliefs or convictions, or you'll never be able to turn around.

"I don't believe we've had the pleasure before," the constable, driving the car, said.

"The pleasure is entirely yours, I'm sure. What is that smell?"

"That is probably my aftershave, do you like it?"

"No. Must we have a conversation?"

The constable shrugged as he drove the car. "Just being polite."

"Yes, well, politeness noted. Thank you," Beelzebub said as he pulled the cigarette case from his pocket.

"Oh, can't smoke in here," the constable said. He was a man who appeared to consist almost entirely of a moustache. It grew from beneath his nose in huge tufts that curled and swept across his face, meeting eyebrows, ears, and hair so there was extraordinarily little of the man beneath visible.

"What?"

"Yeah, you can't smoke in here, sorry, those are the rules."

"Oh, rules, no, they don't apply to me."

The constable frowned and risked a sideways glance at the suited man in the passenger seat. "That's hilarious. Rules don't apply in a police car. Seriously though, no smoking in here."

"Why? It's not bad for your health. Everyone's dead."

"No, it just stinks. Guv hates the cars stinking of smoke, then your uniform smells of it, plus then you get people who just sit in their cars all day smoking. Nah, Guv's right, no smoking in the cars."

Beelzebub placed a cigarette in his mouth and clicked his fingers. A flame sparked from his fingertips and he lit the cigarette, taking a long drag on it while winding down the window. He exhaled out of the window. "Will that suffice?"

"No. You're in the car and smoking. Opening the window does not suffice," the constable pulled over the car to the side of the road. "You're going to have to either throw the cigarette away or get out."

"Excuse me? Your commanding officer told you to drive me to the Office of the Dead. Are you defying a direct order?"

"Yes, I bloody am. Get out of the car you jumped up toffee nosed tosser."

Beelzebub's mouth dropped open, the cigarette hanging from his bottom lip. "What did you say to me?"

The constable turned off the engine and reached down to his side where his baton was resting against the door panel. "I'm Gloomwood Police, and the Gloomwood police don't take shit from anyone, now get out of the car or we're going to have a real problem."

GOING LIVE

"It's simple, Grim. We hold the phone up while we sing and it records it. Then we post it on Bitter."

"Why would we want to do that?"

"Because the angelic choir keep doing it, and they're really smug about all their followers."

"What if it's not popular?"

"Grim, Bitter was a hell invention. I'm the lord of hell, of course they'll like it."

"I still don't understand why we can't just enjoy karaoke as usual."

"It's fine, look we'll do it live, even better."

"Live?"

"Yes."

"There's irony for you. Okay, but what song?"

"How about…"

THE DEVIL WALKS ALONE

He checked his collar and pulled at the cuffs of his shirt before slamming the car door. The darkness of the night was lifting, and he glanced at the sky. "Oh Grim, you could have been so much more imaginative about things, but our worlds are reflections of ourselves. There are upsides, I suppose," he said as he looked down at his suit, "I'd be covered in blood by now if I'd been in the mortal realm. People here are much less messy."

"You won't get away with this," a voice shouted from within the car, loud enough for Beelzebub to hear it clearly.

He opened the door while shaking his head. "I don't have time to waste crushing your head to a point at which I know for sure that it can no longer hold a soul, and to be perfectly honest I've been trying to make a point of not doing that. It's bad for business and my image. It's easy to go the whole, 'absolute power' route. If we all went around doing that there'd be no fun in anything. The actual skill lies in doing the bare minimum yourself. So, let's just say I get away with it, and you can start shouting for help in an hour, okay?"

"How will I know an hour has gone by?"

"Let's say when people walk by you can start shouting. Deal?"

"Seems fair. Nobody's going to hear me before then, are they?"

"No, they're really not."

"Right then... could I... uh, could I have a cigarette? I mean, you've folded me up like a..."

"Like one of those folding bicycles that some people are so fond of despite their complete lack of actual practicality?"

"Uh, yeah," the man said from his position on the floor of the car. His head between his knees and pointing in the wrong direction, "so I can't go anywhere."

"If you'd let me have a cigarette in the first place, we wouldn't even be here."

"Yes, but there are rules."

"Yes, there are, and you're still in the car, so no."

"You're just going to sod off?"

"No, I'm not going to, 'sod off'. I am going to walk away with dignity, a skip in my step, and more than a little sex appeal. Have a… a day, just a day, I don't really care what it's like," Beelzebub said before slamming the door shut once more.

He walked away, not waiting to see if the constable shouted. It would take at least half an hour to work up the courage for the police officer to shout. Beelzebub knew without a doubt, just like he knew that a more intelligent person would take much longer before they started shouting, because they would imagine worse things happening. The police officer had not seen the warning signs, had not recognised the inherent violence that Beelzebub wore like a shroud, and had suffered for it.

"Definitely less satisfying than when they're alive," Beelzebub muttered to himself, "I should make a note of that," he looked around with the cigarette in one hand. "Demons, never one when you need one, and when you don't, they're all, feed me souls, I exist only to serve, that's minced organs not jam, tedious."

He stopped on the corner of a street where a figure, squat and covered from head to toe in clothing, including gloves, a hooded coat and a scarf covering their entire face except for their eyes, was putting out a sign. The figure had stopped midway through unfolding the double-sided board as it stared at Beelzebub, who had been muttering to himself.

"Can I help you?" Beelzebub asked before taking a long drag on the cigarette.

"No, can I help you? You seem troubled. It's early, or late depending on how you look at it, to be walking the streets. Are you okay?"

"Am I okay?" Beelzebub scoffed, "of course I'm okay. I'm the Devil."

The figure nodded. "Okay, well if you're cold I'm opening up shop," the figure waved to the half open corrugated metal shutter of a newsagent, "just putting out the sign but I can spare a cup of tea and a bacon butty. No charge, you look like you might want breakfast."

Beelzebub looked himself up and down. "I look like... what does that mean?"

"Either it was a long night, or something's happened to send a fella like you out into the street this early in the morning. This isn't a neighbourhood where people wander around talking to themselves while dressed like they bathe in money. Tea or coffee?"

"I... wait, is there a neighbourhood in this city where it would be acceptable for a man like me to do that?"

"Eh?"

"Is there somewhere they would leave me in peace to take a very early morning, or late evening, stroll while having a private conversation with myself?"

"Uh... so no to a drink then fella? Just trying to help."

"You would engage a perfect stranger in conversation, while it's still dark, with nobody else around while opening up your shop, alone? It's quite clear you're concerned that I may be some kind of madman, and yet, even after all of that, rather than scuttle back inside your shop and wait until I've gone, you actively engage in a conversation with me? Invite me in? That doesn't strike you as odd?" Beelzebub asked.

The pile of clothes, because to call it a person would be an unreasonable assumption in Gloomwood, held out the arms of the coat. "Maybe, that's just the way we are around here. Rob you blind one minute, make you a cuppa and get you a blanket the next. You must be fresh meat."

"Fresh. Meat. I assure you I am not."

"Oh, sorry, no offence meant. I'm going to get on with opening my shop. Hope you have a lovely day."

Beelzebub stood watching while the man finished putting up the sign. It was a newspaper headline, "Bear Necessities of Life." Beelzebub couldn't help but grin when he saw it. He reached into his jacket and pulled out the phone. "You won't be able to ignore me for much longer, Grim... they'll come to me, they'll come to you."

💀 <u>BUZZ OFF</u> 💀

It was his robe.

As they approached the Grim Reaper, Death himself, ruler of this afterlife and the being that mortals feared more than any other, was trying to fight a revolving door, and losing.

With Johnson's help Blunt stopped it spinning while Leighton pulled, and tore, the lower part of the Grim Reaper's robes out from beneath the door. When she finished the angel of death had his bony ankles on show.

"This is embarrassing," he said.

Blunt, Leighton, and Johnson stood back. Hiding behind Leighton's right running shoe was Ted. They stood out in the square and as they all tried to think of something to say to the being who was supposed to have all the answers. The door turned again. Out of it leapt a small blue, furry, dinosaur.

"I will destroy you," it roared.

Blunt and Leighton fell to their knees. Their instinctive reaction to the demon's voice caused a reflex action of subservience and panic.

Johnson didn't blink. "Why would you destroy me?" the ex-police officer asked.

"This is Morgarth," the Grim Reaper said, "she's a demon from Hell trapped in the body of a blue dinosaur. Morgarth, this is Mister Johnson, Detective Blunt, Leighton Hughes investigative reporter extraordinaire, and Teddington Rex, he's on the television and... oh... and he's alive. Now it all makes sense."

Johnson grabbed Leighton and Blunt by the elbows, lifting them to their feet. He looked at the dinosaur, "is that going to happen every time you speak?"

"No." Morgarth said more quietly, "I take it you weren't ever a mortal?"

Johnson gritted his teeth.

"It's a good thing," Morgarth said, "all mortals are weak. That's why they collapse just from a little shouting."

"Listen, you pointed tailed little-" Blunt began.

The Grim Reaper raised a hand. He didn't point it at anyone, but it stopped the conversation. "Detective Blunt, please don't be rude to Morgarth. She's done nothing to you other than speak. How was she to know you would collapse like a house of cards?"

Blunt shook his head, "She's literally just said that she knew that would happen."

"Oh, did you?" Grim asked, looking down at the dinosaur.

"Yes, I did."

"Oh... why did you do it then?"

The dinosaur looked away, its left leg pointing its toes, "I... I was defending you. I don't know why. It was a lapse in judgement. Please don't tell Lord Beelzebub."

"Oh, he won't care," Grim said, "but thank you. Now, shall we take this to my office and decide if we're going to kill this bear? Oh, you can't all come though... Mister Johnson," the Grim Reaper pulled a coin from his pocket, "catch."

The coin spun, and Johnson plucked it out of the air. It was heavy and glass-like. "Thanks, what's this?"

"That is a coin," the Grim Reaper said.

The silence that hung in the air was palpable.

"Ah, I see," Grim said when he realised they were waiting for further information, "that coin means you are now working directly for me. You need to stand guard."

"I'm a grunt?"

The Grim Reaper tilted his head to one side. Being ominous all the time makes being overtly ominous much easier. He flexed his ominousness.

"Which is fine."

"You're the most capable person here. The building is near empty."

"And the coin?"

The Grim Reaper let out a sigh. It was not a sigh because a sigh requires lungs, but it was a very good approximation. "You're really spoiling this for me. It's for dramatic effect."

"So, it's not magic?"

"It came in a box of cereal along with a decoder ring. Miss Hughes, stay with him."

"Me? I'm not a guard?"

"No, you're an intrepid reporter who will be on the scene when the living dead attack this building, along with the Devil, and his demons. How exciting for you!"

Blunt put up a hand like a child asking a question. "Can't they just leave? You're putting them in danger unnecessarily."

"Oh yes, you can leave if you'd prefer."

"I'd get out of here," Blunt said.

"And you?" Johnson said.

"I think I'm stuck with the bear."

AHEAD OF THINGS

"Miss, excuse me, miss?" The man on a bicycle shouted towards Molly as she was being waved around on the end of the Devil's walking stick by a stuffed soft toy lion.

"Yes?" Molly said.

"Have you heard about our lord and saviour?"

"Yes. That's... that's exactly why I'm doing this."

"Then you too follow Teddington Rex?"

"Teddington... what?"

"Rex, you know, the teddy bear from the television."

"Oh, I don't really watch TV," Molly said, having to raise her voice above the horde of people who stumbled, crawled, and dragged themselves in her direction.

"You don't watch TV?" The bicycle rider said, confused.

"No, I don't own one."

"Oh," the man on the bicycle said, recoiling as if he had just realised that an unpleasant boil had been uncovered inches from his face. "So you never watch television, like, ever?"

"No, I have the Mible, I know it from memory, and that's all the entertainment I need," she said.

The man on the bicycle twisted his face in a look of disgust and pushed his bicycle into motion, "Mible mashing weirdo! Teddington Rex is the future! You're being followed by a bunch of freaks. The city is under siege. Our voices are being silenced by those in power who don't want the truth to be known. Follow the bear. You're just a head on a stick."

Molly rolled her eyes. "A head on a stick that will bring around the end of this sinful place. Viva la resurrection!" She shouted.

Behind her, the horde burst into chorus. It was an unintelligible chorus, but a chorus all the same. Their numbers had grown as they had shambled through the streets. Incorporating those who didn't move fast enough, or who didn't believe what was happening, into the whole. They were pernicious, determined to indoctrinate everyone in the city to their worldview, a task made much easier by the simple addition of a bite to any exposed flesh. The newer members led the charge, a little faster, a little more coordinated in their movements, many of them still able to string a sentence together. "Molly leads us, Molly has the answers, the Meep shall inherit the Earth."

"Meep, Meep," Molly shouted.

"Meep, Meep," the crowd replied.

"Viva la resurrection," she shouted, and the crowd responded in kind, "Viva la- Hello?"

A man and a woman walked across the intersection the bicycle rider had disappeared down. He stood taller than anyone in the crowd, his skin tinged blue, wearing a duster pulled taut across broad shoulders. She too was tall by most standards, dark hair and skin, wrapped in a black coat that almost touched the floor, she held a scythe in one hand and tapped a finger of the hand that held it against its shaft.

"Is this normal?" the scythe wielding woman said, her voice conversational but carrying far further because of the sudden silence from the mob.

The big man next to her shrugged. "Not my place to judge what's normal. We could ask them?"

The woman twirled the scythe in her hand and nodded before placing the blunt end of it on the ground once more. "Stick lady," she said, "is this normal?"

"Normal?" Molly, voice of the crowd asked.

"Yes, is that a puzzling question? Does this kind of thing happen often?"

"This is the end of days," Molly said, "the penultimate moment before the end of all things. We will rise from the dead, take our rightful place among the living, and cast those who are unworthy to one side. We are the Meep, and we shall inherit the Earth!"

"Oh," the big man said nodding, "this is a church thing," he said to the woman standing at his side.

"Ah," she said, "religion always seems so tedious. Well, good luck on your march. Hope you raise some money for worthy causes."

"We're not raising money," Molly said.

"I genuinely don't care. Have fun awareness raising or whatever. Come on Petal, we've got a big fight to have over killing the bear, or not."

RAISE ME UP

Blunt stood in the lift. To his right was the Grim Reaper and a small dinosaur toy that wasn't speaking because it was embarrassed. To his left was Teddington Rex, who was a teddy bear, who was sentient, and could definitely speak but refused to in case Blunt kicked him.

"So," the Grim Reaper said, "have you sneezed at many people?"

Ted didn't answer, but Blunt wasn't covering for anyone. "Yes, he has, at least two people. One of them was a doctor who had the body of a squid, another one was a police constable. She was the one who told us about the zombies."

"Ah yes, an army of the living dead. Hm. Why was the doctor in possession of a squid?"

"Uh, he was the squid."

"Oh, so you mean his body was squid-like, a cephalopod?"

"That's right… sir," Blunt stood with his arms behind his back, his feet shoulder width apart, as he stared forward at the brass doors to the lift. His eyes flicking upwards to watch the dial move from one floor to the next.

"The elevator is moving slowly because time is not working properly," The Grim Reaper said, noticing Blunt's gaze. "By which I mean time is working properly. It's the clock, you see. Everything in the building revolves around the clock in a very literal sense."

Blunt nodded, "And the bear-"

"I have a name," Ted snapped.

"You do, but nobody knows if it's your actual name or one you made up," Blunt said.

"It's made up," Grim said, "Teddington, really? That's the best you could come up with?"

Ted didn't reply. Instead, he crossed his arms and stared through his single blue button eye at his blurred reflection in the door.

"So, he's alive?"

"He's a reaper," the Grim Reaper said, "or he was. Isn't that right, Ted?" Grim said. It is hard to convey tone when your voice sounds like a death knell at the best of times, all the same, the Grim Reaper managed it. "Reapers replaced me, my choice of course, I wanted some time to myself-"

Ted made a noise not dissimilar to a can of carbonated drink being opened. It signified disbelief.

"It was my choice," Grim said, "thank you very much. I won't bore you with the details, Detective, I have little doubt you could find them out if you dig, but this is all to do with time. When someone dies a reaper collects them, like me. The difference with reapers is that they turn up a fraction early."

"Early?" Blunt said, turning to face the Grim Reaper and immediately recoiling when faced with Death himself. His rage quickly replaced with a perfectly rational fear of the embodiment of life's finality.

"A fraction early, not even a second, not even a millisecond, but early, nevertheless. That tiny fraction of time is taken as payment by the reaper for guiding you to the other side. Do you remember your reaper?"

Blunt nodded. His reaper had been a lanky, barely post-adolescent who had tried to rush Blunt through the mortal veil as quickly as possible. Later Blunt had realised that he had, in fact, travelled to the other side at a near record pace. Blunt had been, well he'd been himself, acerbic, unfriendly, even rude and aggressive, but, in his defence, he had just been stabbed in the chest, murdered. "Yes," Blunt said, "his name was Kevin."

"Kevin, he's still working, friendly chap. Anyway, for escorting you from the moment of your death to the afterlife, he could gather an infinitesimally small amount of time. Imagine the time it takes to fire a single neuron that makes up a fraction of a thought, well that would be far more time than Kevin gathered for bringing you through that journey. I hope you thanked him."

"I... I honestly don't remember."

"It's quite a thankless task, trust me," the Grim Reaper said. "Anyway, the reapers collect time, and when they have enough time, they can use it."

"Use it? How?"

"Hm, oh, by returning to the land of the living. Some of them only want a few minutes, others an entire lifetime. Most of them want exactly enough time for them to die again so they can travel to an afterlife rather than being stuck as a reaper."

"That sounds terrible, cruel even."

"Doesn't it just," Ted said.

"Mhm, perhaps, but there is more to it than that. Also, they never remember being a reaper, so it wipes the slate clean, so to speak."

Ted turned around and pointed a paw at the Grim Reaper "And we wouldn't know if we'd been a reaper before so wouldn't know not to do it again either, would we?"

The Grim Reaper tilted his head to one side and pointed a finger on the hand holding his scythe at the bear, "Jeremy Tibbins, I should've guessed it. Well, you have changed, and not for the better-"

Blunt stepped in front of the bear, his arms spread palms to the ceiling. "Okay. Let's not get aggressive now."

"Aggressive?" The Grim Reaper said, "never Detective, it's not in my makeup to be aggressive. I won't harm Ted, or Jeremy, or whatever he'd like to be called. Unfortunately, what he has done, stolen time to resurrect himself, has caused us a few problems. First, we have an old colleague in town, he's a bit of a troublemaker, then we have this living dead thing... which doesn't really make sense, and finally we have the impending end of everything because time will make us all crumble to dust... all of you. I'll probably just go back to work."

"Crumble... to dust?"

"Yes. That's right... well, except for Ted née Jeremy. He'll remain here until he dies, but nobody will collect his soul because this place won't exist. He'll endure eternity in complete darkness."

"So, oblivion?" Ted said.

"Oh no, oblivion isn't good but you don't suffer there because you're no longer a consciousness, you're nothing, no, this furry little time thief will know eternity and the everlasting darkness of nothing, quite unpleasant. I wouldn't wish it even upon him. Then again, I'm not one to judge."

The elevator bell rang with an incongruous chirpy trill and the doors shuddered open. Blunt, Ted, and the silent Morgarth the Destroyer, demonic Hell spawn and fluffy dinosaur, stepped out and followed the Grim Reaper as he glided towards the steps up to his own office.

"Hello Ursula," the Grim Reaper said to a woman who was sitting with her back against a desk and her head in her hands. "Surprised you're still here, isn't it a little late?"

"I... it's still here. Get it away from me," Ursula said, as she stood up, lifting her head high above her shoulders where it had once sat proudly atop her now severed neck. "It decapitated me!"

"Now, now," Grim said, "accidents happen. I will be in my office should you need me."

Blunt stopped by the woman as the others carried on towards the steps. "Are you... are you okay?"

"Do I look okay to you?" Ursula Panderpenny snapped as she lowered her head on to her shoulders. "That bloody monster spoke and did something to me. The next thing I know, I'm on the floor and my body is behind the desk. What am I supposed to do now?"

"Uh... do you get medical?"

"Do I get... what are you talking about?"

"Like insurance, for accidents and stuff-"

"I know how to get my head reattached, thank you, I'm injured, not stupid. I know you, you're that fascist detective."

"What? I'm not a bloody fascist. Who the hell goes around calling people fascist-"

A cough came from behind him. It was Death, and when the Grim Reaper taps you on the shoulder, metaphorically or otherwise, you don't ignore him. Especially if he feigns a cough. "Detective, we have more pressing matters and I'm sure Ursula has work to be getting on with. It's quite unfair of you to take up her time like that."

"She just called me a fascist," Blunt said.

"That sounds like a personal conversation," the Grim Reaper flicked his free hand so that his robe sleeve slid down, revealing the bones of his wrist. He tapped a finger against the bones in his wrist, making a clicking sound, "time is wasting... well, time is the problem so that probably doesn't quite apply. Needless to say, we are in a hurry."

"Right... how does a little dinosaur soft toy decapitate someone, anyway?" Blunt said as he caught up to the Grim Reaper and jogged up the four steps to the office.

"Don't ask her to tell you."

Music started playing when they entered the office. On the surface of the desk, a black rectangular object vibrated.

"You've got a phone?" Blunt asked.

"Oh, that old thing, yes well I need to upgrade-"

"How do you have a phone? The only mobile phones I've ever seen are brass things that barely ever work as phones. That looks like a phone from the living realm."

"Ah... funny story about that."

LOBBYING

They designed the reception desk at the Office of the Dead to make waiting painful. The theory being that if someone won't wait several hours to get whatever it is they want, then it probably isn't that important. Johnson had taken a seat behind it and Leighton had joined him.

"We're staying then?" She said.

Johnson was spinning the coin on the counter in front of him. The desk was long and shielded from the lobby by a panel of thick glass with holes drilled into it. The panel was there for frustrated people to slam their hands against it in impotent rage. A small sign in the bottom right-hand corner of the panel of glass read, 'please do not bang us, we're not goldfish, and they don't like it either.' Someone, who presumably had plenty of time, had scrawled over it in marker pen, 'Wouldn't bang you if it brought me back to life, yer pricks.' Scrawled graffiti lacks a certain elegance sometimes.

"I don't think we've got much choice. Just stay behind here. If it gets dangerous, make sure you're hidden. There's a lock on the door over there," he nodded the way they had come in. The lock in question was a metal vault lock designed to withstand an attack by an angry deity with a final reminder for his television license.

"And you're okay with them killing the bear?"

Johnson looked over to Leighton who was doodling on a pad of paper with a pen she had pulled off its chain from the other side of the counter. "Does it matter?"

"If you're okay with it, or if they kill the bear?"

"Both, but mainly the second one. We're all dead. It hasn't done us any harm. If that's the solution to saving all of us then yes, kill the bear."

"You don't like him very much," Leighton said.

"He is the reason I'm no longer in the police. It wouldn't change things if I did like him though."

"What happened?"

"It's a long story, but basically he was trying to get famous. Jokes about a drug dealing Demi-god being shacked up with a hope who was a police officer were easy. He used it in his stage act. Word got out, people paid attention, and then people started asking questions. Questions like, 'How did he get to be a police officer in the first place?' It didn't matter that I did it by hard work, the doubt was there. Political pressure."

"Sowercat just gave you up?"

Johnson sighed. "The Chief isn't as bad as people make out. He tried, but there was nothing he could do. I understood."

"So, it was Ted's fault?"

Johnson shrugged. "I might have lost my temper. There was an incident."

THE LAST RESPITE (Before)

Twist Lenworth was resting with her legs up on the table in the Last Respite. It was a dive bar filled with the lost and forgotten dregs of humanity. That was what they called themselves, the reapers, the forgotten dregs of humanity. It was accurate.

A lit, hand-rolled cigarette hung from her lips as she listened to the two men opposite her discuss the usual. The score was seven to three to Baldwin, a man who fit the ideal reaper mould with eerie perfection. Tall and slender with skin like alabaster. "Okay, bet you have had no one killed by a dishwasher," he said.

"A dishwasher? Too easy, everyone's had a dishwasher death, they're a pound a penny," the man challenging him said. In stark contrast to Baldwin, he was a mass of coarse hair. His beard seemed to grow up and above its position as if it was clamouring to swallow the face that remained beneath his long shaggy locks. His name was Orn.

"No," Baldwin said, "I said by a dishwasher, most dishwasher deaths are from falling on top of them when they're open. The dishwasher did nothing. That's like saying that someone who falls on spikes died because of the floor the spikes are on."

"What are you asking then? I'm calling convoluted, it's too confusing. Twist, call it." Orn said.

She took her feet off the table. Picked up the bottle of open unlabeled alcohol in front of her and made a show of taking a long drink. She smacked her lips as she placed it on the table. "The call is... killed via the dishwasher and not its contents. Right, Baldwin?"

"That's it," the bald man said, slapping the top of the table with his hand. He turned to face Orn, "Well?"

"Okay... okay... let me think for a minute," he pursed his lips for a minute then grinned, "got one."

Baldwin sat back in his chair, shaking his head. "Course you have, let's hear it then."

"Omar Baraid died, August fourteenth, nineteen-ninety-four. Fella was a warehouse worker. Crushed underneath a dishwasher when it fell off the top of a forklift. Washer bounced off the edge of a shelf, he turned around and didn't even know what hit him." He planted his bottle on the table and looked at Baldwin.

"Right, fair enough, I had a drug dealer murdered. They used the door of the dishwasher, kept slamming it shut on his head. I'll tell you, he definitely knew what hit him. Okay, you go."

The game was old and, once the scores climbed, it always got boring as the drink slowed their desire to tell the more long-winded stories. Twist wasn't really listening. Baldwin and Orn were nice enough, but there were better storytellers. The best stories were told straight after a shift when the memory was fresh in the minds of the reapers.

"Call the game, lads. This could go on all night and I'm losing the will to drink." Twist said.

They called it a day while Orn could still walk to his bunk and Twist remained sitting at the table looking at the board. It had been a good shift. She's managed almost an entire second worth of gained time. It wasn't like she'd be getting her chance soon, but it would come.

As happened to every reaper her eyes drifted to the names above the bar. Those reapers who had gone before and had achieved the impossible task. Everything was about time. The seconds collected in increments so small they were imperceptible to the living and dead were unaware.

A dark thought flitted through her mind for a moment. She didn't feel guilty about it, everyone had it sometimes. Take all the time at once. Snatch it and have that chance. Get caught though… There was talk of where you would go if you got caught and that place, contrary to the belief of the living, was not a place many people went to.

"Here Twist," a voice shouted over from behind the bar, "you hear about Jeremy?"

Twist shook her head as she looked over to the bar, "what about him?"

"Gone missing, apparently."

"Missing?"

"Yeah... um... apparently he took some time with him."

Twist frowned. "He's not been here long enough."

The bartender shrugged, "well he's gone."

"No, you're mistaken."

"Whatever, I just thought you'd want to know."

JUST KILL HIM

Blunt watched while the Grim Reaper opened a cupboard and then, as if he couldn't imagine anyone would think it strange, dragged out a seven-foot tall skeleton. "This bit can be a little tricky, if you wouldn't mind," the Grim Reaper said, turning towards Blunt while holding the skeleton up.

"What would you like me to do? Is that person?"

"This? No! I wouldn't keep a person in a cupboard. That would be a strange thing to do," Grim said.

"Right," Blunt said, "that would be strange."

"We need to put a robe on him."

"Okay."

"His name is Eric," Grim said.

"I thought it wasn't a person."

"He isn't a person, he's a skeleton, you can see that. People aren't just skeletons. Eric is my body double."

"I… okay, where's the robe?"

"Hanging up on the door, just help me get the arms and head in," Grim said.

Blunt grabbed a robe that was on the door and turned around.

"Not that one, that's mine. I don't mean to be rude, Detective, but you are odd sometimes."

"Oh, sorry, um, this one?"

"Yes, obviously," Grim said, holding out the skeleton arms.

Together the Grim Reaper and Blunt manhandled the skeleton into position, and then the Grim Reaper placed him in the chair behind the desk. After some careful adjustments, the Grim Reaper stepped back and nodded. "Perfect. Now if anyone comes in, they'll think it's me sitting at my desk having fallen asleep with my head in a wonderful book. A small deception that will buy us a little more time."

"You do this often?" Blunt asked.

"Hm, occasionally, people get a little nervous when I'm gone for any length of time, but I can't be here all the time."

Ted, who had watched them dress the skeleton from where he was standing in a corner of the small office, gave out a cough.

Blunt dove to the floor, cowering behind the desk. "Don't sneeze," Blunt shouted.

"It was a cough, you lunatic," Ted said, "if I was going to sneeze I'd aim it at him," he pointed at the Grim Reaper.

"That's rude. It wouldn't do anything anyway," Grim said. "You're not some almighty sneezing being who can destroy the embodiment of death itself. You're just a silly little man trapped inside the body of a soft toy. Try not to get ahead of yourself. Now, if you were to sneeze at the detective, that would be a whole different story. If I were you, I would avoid that as Blunt here might be the only person who can save you."

"Save me? I'm standing in a room with Death and a demon dinosaur. What's a crap detective going to do."

"Crap?" Blunt said from behind the desk, "that's uncalled for. I've already saved you once."

"Everybody needs to calm down," Grim said, and because the Grim Reaper said it, they all did, a little. "We need to get a grip on the situation before it gets out of hand."

"I think we might be beyond that stage already," Blunt said, "what's your plan?"

"Well, we need to get life out of Gloomwood before it destroys everything."

"Okay, I was afraid you'd say that," Blunt stood up as he spoke, "you're going to kill Ted? I'm afraid I can't let you do that."

The Grim Reaper looked at Blunt, clicking his fingers against the scythe that had appeared once more in his hands. A long moment passed while the four occupants of the little office glared at one another. "The bear is correct. You're not a good detective. Let's pretend for a moment that I wished harm on this… man, you would serve as no obstacle. On a personal level it would disappoint me to dispatch of you, but it really wouldn't amount to anything in the grand scheme of things, except to you and those who care about you."

"That's a pretty small number of people," Ted said with a snort, "if you're not planning on killing me, what is happening?"

"I can't kill you," Grim said, "I've killed no one and, as far as I am aware, I don't think I can. Death can't kill someone. Who ever died of death?"

Blunt put his hat back on his head again. "Death can't kill anyone?"

"Of course not. It's simple logic, Detective."

"Wait… am I here because you want me to kill him?"

"No." The Grim Reaper shook his head, "mortals are so obsessed with me, I mean Death. You are dead, Detective, dead people can't kill living people. That doesn't happen. Even mortal Hollywood avoids playing that card too often. It's always people frightened into doing something stupid and then falling down a flight of stairs, or being killed by flying scaffolding."

"That's oddly specific," Ted muttered.

"I'll kill him," Morgarth said.

The Grim Reaper tapped his chin, click, click, click, "I don't think that would be wise either. That would mean that a demonic influence had killed a living being in a neutral afterlife. It would complicate things. I appreciate the offer though, Morgarth, very considerate of you."

"Welcome," Morgarth said.

"Living people die of things that kill living people. It's not rocket science," Grim said, "we need to remove Ted from the city before anyone kills him."

"That woman wants to kill him."

"What woman?" Grim asked.

"Twist Lenworth," Ted said.

"Twist," Grim tapped a finger against his chin, click, click, click, "is she dead?"

"Don't know," Ted said, "but she's pretty angry."

"Why is she angry?" Blunt asked.

Ted looked from the Grim Reaper and back to Blunt, "It might not have been my time I used to get here."

"I see," Grim said, "well that makes some sense."

"Who is Twist Lenworth?" Blunt asked.

The Grim Reaper took a moment before responding. He looked the bear up and down slowly, which is harder than it sounds on a two foot tall bear, "Well... that's an interesting story," the phone buzzing on the desk interrupted him.

"The Devil is going to destroy the afterlife, and he's calling you, but you're going to ignore it."

"Correct, Detective. Now, about Miss Lenworth."

BITTER

"Beezy, have you seen Bitter? I've gone viral," Grim said into the phone he held in one skeletal hand. He stood at the side of a table in a popular fast-food restaurant as people walked by. Not one of them glanced in his direction.

"Yes, Grim, I saw," the voice on the other side of the phone said.

"Isn't that good? Look at how many more followers I have. I am very popular."

"I'm aware, Grim."

"Almost as many as you. We should do more videos together."

"Maybe. But let's leave it for a bit."

"Ah, okay. How did the angels react? I bet they're jealous. Do they get jealous? I suppose not. Jealousy isn't very angelic."

"You'd be surprised, Grim. Angels can be very petty."

"Can they?"

"Yes… look, I have to go, I'm quite busy."

"Oh, of course, I am too. Souls to reap, work to do, people are always dying."

"Yes. Well, speak soon then Grim."

"Speak soon… oh, you've already gone. Right. Where was I? Ah, yes, you're dead," Death said as he placed the phone back into his robes.

"I am? Who were you on the phone to?" A man sitting on a chair in a fast-food restaurant said.

"Oh, you'll meet him soon enough."

"How did I die?"

"Brain embolism, very sudden, you didn't feel a thing."

"No? Well, that's good."

BORROWED TIME

"Borrowed time," Ted said.

"Borrowed?" Blunt shouted, "You are a thieving little bastard. You're going to give the time back, are you?"

"If I can," Ted said, "I don't know how it works, do I? It's all metaphysical weirdness. They only teach you the basics."

"I resent that statement," Death said, "we take pains to be abundantly clear on the system, there are stops and measures, rules clearly set out, you cannot borrow time."

"Says who?" Ted said, glaring at the Grim Reaper with his paws on his hips, or what approximated hips on a bear. They were more like woolly curves, but the action was the same.

The Grim Reaper stood up straight and put both hands around the Scythe, his head tilted forward so as not to collide with the ceiling. "I say."

Ted's paws dropped to his sides, and the bear went limp, falling onto his backside on the floor. "I didn't want to be a reaper. I just wanted to die like everybody else. Nobody asked me."

"I don't recall being asked if I wanted to come here either," Blunt said, waving a hand around the office. "You don't see me stealing time off people and ballsing up the entire sodding afterlife because I'm a selfish prick, do you, Jeremy?"

The bear flinched.

"Anyway," Blunt continued, "if it's going to destroy the afterlife- "

"Just this one."

"What now?" Blunt stopped his rant to look at the Grim Reaper, who was holding a finger in the air.

"It will only destroy this afterlife. Time will have its effect. Imagine fast-forwarding time in the mortal realm, everyone will die. Here time doesn't really exist, it's a dimension thing."

"Doesn't make Monday mornings any easier," Blunt muttered.

"Really? I like Monday mornings. It's when the post comes. Anyway, time will exist here, it will spread like a disease taking root in everyone and everything until it all decays to nothingness. We invite entropy into the afterlife. Nasty little thing entropy, but it's contained within this afterlife, thanks to the veils. Like how they build ships with compartments in the hull, a leak won't sink the ship. There are multitudinous afterlives, it's only this one that's at risk."

"Oh, well, that makes it much better. So now it's only me and everyone in this afterlife being cast into eternal oblivion."

"Exactly," Grim said, "look on the bright side."

"That's not what I was doing. For God's sake,"

"Oh, please don't bring God into it," the Grim Reaper said, "that never helps."

"Fine, I'll kill him," Blunt said with a snarl.

The Grim Reaper nodded. "Yes, that would make things easier, but there are a few metaphysical problems with that. First, it doesn't matter if we kill him, his soul doesn't belong here so we get that out, and, Miss Lenworth is here, which can't be a good thing as she shouldn't be here, and, Beelzebub is here with demons, and- "

"It gets worse?"

"Oh yes. Shall I continue?"

"No. Just tell me you have a plan."

"I do, Detective. You're going to save the afterlife."

"Me? That's your job."

"No, I am neutral. Besides, I could get involved, but I'm quite recognisable. I can't just go wandering off and... let's be frank here Detective, you have nothing to lose, do you?"

Blunt narrowed his eyes, glaring at the ruler of Gloomwood. He can't know, Blunt thought to himself, he's not omnipresent... is he?

POLICE BLOCKADE

Petal and Twist walked side by side towards the Office of the Dead. The night sky was turning into the purple grey of daylight. There is no sunrise in Gloomwood instead night turns its back, leaving day exposed. When night falls once more it is only to glare down on the dead in disappointment.

"Those people don't look right to me," Petal said.

"And?" Twist snapped.

"Just making conversation."

"You could have said it was going to take this long to walk. Don't you have taxis?"

"What's your problem, it's not like we could've beat anyone there."

"I'm on a schedule. Time isn't limitless, you know."

Petal let out a chuckle, a chuckle that would have had followers kneeling in awe, "Yeah it is, you get used to it after a while. Being dead means you have all the time in the world."

"You wouldn't understand," Twist said.

Petal shook his head.

As they turned the corner they could hear a crowd of voices. It sounded like a chorus of constant complaints.

"Is this normal?"

"You keep asking me that," Petal said, "there isn't anything 'normal', it's just what it is."

"What does that even mean?"

"Nothing's normal here. One minute it's calm, the next there's a teddy bear talking to you, or a crowd of people who look like they're falling apart, some mentalist is chopping people's heads off, the pabies call themselves something different every week, the police are criminals, everything's got tentacles, there's a head on a stick, and a woman with a scythe is trying to kill dead people."

She stopped walking and turned to Petal. "Is that crowd of police officers trying to form a line, and failing, normal? Are they doing it in order of height?"

Petal paused mid-stride and looked back at Twist, "Probably. I mean, you've got to have some kind of order or nobody knows where to stand."

In one hand she twirled the scythe like it was little more than a baton, a sharp, deadly, baton. "It looks like the police are expecting the stumbling army. The bear's in there, is he?"

Petal nodded, "Everyone seems to think he is," he said, as he walked up to the police cordon.

"'Ere, didn't I arrest you earlier today?" A constable wearing a hockey mask, and carrying a medieval mace, said.

"If you arrested me earlier, wouldn't that mean I was a criminal on the run? And, that you would need to arrest me?"

The hockey mask wearing constable looked up at Petal, then at the mace in his hands. He switched his grip, looked up once more, and back at the mace. "Nah, you must just have one of those faces."

"Yup, lots of people with this face," Petal said with a grin, "big blue Demi-gods are pretty common. Can we come through?"

"You're not going to just smash through like some kind of steamroller?"

"Nah. I'm a peaceful law-abiding citizen here to apply for planning permission on a new garden shed."

"Oh, what stage are you at? I just got my mid-decade update."

"Way ahead of me. I'm only in the first twelve months."

"Oh, little tip, don't punch the glass, they hate that, and you madam, are you here for a shed too? Or perhaps for a formal letter of complaint, that's a pretty common one."

"Oh…" Petal turned to Twist, "well, which one are you?"

"Complaints, obviously," she said.

The constable nodded, "Right, well, you're on the left, try to keep the language clean, or at least less blue than our big friend here. You complaining and applying for the shed?"

"No, I guess I'm on the shed only side," Petal said.

"Wonderful, well your side has a chair on it when you get inside. Just the one I'm afraid, but you can queue for that, which is fun. Everyone likes a nice long queue, don't they? Except nobody has turned up yet, so you'll be queuing alone, which is just standing still for no reason. Before you go, just so we're all clear, as a member of the Gloomwood police I have to inform you we will deal with the terrorist threat, and if we're not all completely knackered, probably give you all a good kicking regardless of the side you pick."

"Seems fair," Twist said.

"So," Petal started, "what about stopping people from going into the building? Is that why the police are here?"

"Oh no," the constable said, "you can go in."

Petal and Twist walked across the square towards the steps that led up to the Office of the Dead. On the bottom-most of the steps leading up to the three revolving doors, Chief Sowercat of the Gloomwood police was eating a doughnut.

"Don't look at me like that. The shop's right there and we've all been working all night," he said as Petal's shadow loomed over him. He looked up from the doughnut and his eyebrows climbed further up his forehead. "Oh, I know you, ah, and the woman with a scythe. Should've guessed Gilbert on reception wouldn't have kept you there long. Y'know Petal, your boy Johnson should be down here with the rest of us. What happened was a real shame. I expect you're involved in this somehow?"

"So, you remember me?" Petal said, his voice a low rumble.

"Remember you? We spent nearly a decade playing cat and mouse with your underground Oblivion dealing psychopath competitors when you walked away from it all."

"Playing cat and mouse?" Petal said.

"Well, brokering deals and sorting out the hush money. You left a big hole in the underground when you walked away. Was it because of Johnson?"

"None of your business."

"No? If it was, then he achieved more for fighting crime before he became a copper than this lot will ever do."

"Don't talk to me about Jay-Jay," Petal said. He clenched his fists at his sides.

Sowercat held up his hands. "It's not like I can pop around for a chat, is it? Whatever you might think I've been trying to protect the lad, he's a good copper, was a good copper," Sowercat looked around at the constables who were taking it in turns to hit each other with their custom weapons. "Which is why he would never fit in."

"I think he's already here."

"Really?" Sowercat asked.

"Just a feeling," Petal stepped around the Chief of police and towards the building.

"You're going in there?" Sowercat asked.

"Gonna be worse out here soon, people will come to work," Petal said.

Sowercat nodded. "Yeah, there's that and a horde of zombies headed this way."

"Nah, they're slow moving," Petal said, "just chop off their heads and they'll stop, easy."

Sowercat watched as Petal strode up the steps, followed by Twist, and disappeared through the revolving doors. The Chief looked down at the cricket bat he had brought along. "Chop off their heads? We only brought sodding bludgeons with us," his nose expanded. "Atten-shun," he bellowed, silencing the police. "Does anyone have a machete, sword, knife, axe, or other implement which might be useful for the decapitating of a horde of zombies?" Half the officers raised a hand, revealing illegal weapons they had squirreled away. "Untrustworthy bastards, outstanding work."

TIME TO GO

The phone continued to buzz on the desk table. Blunt stared at it. He'd died before getting his head around social media and camera phones. Part of the, 'what's the point in that?' generation. Still, mobile phones made life easier. "You're sure about this?" He asked the Grim Reaper.

"No, not in the slightest, but you said it's what you would do."

"It is what I would do."

"Well then, do it."

"Would you do what I would do?"

"I don't know what I'd do."

Blunt held his breath for a moment, pursed his lips, then grabbed the phone. He hit the green icon on the screen and put it to his ear, "Who's this?"

On the other side there was a moment's silence before a voice, male, well-spoken, with a crisp home-countries English accent, "This is Beelzebub Lord of Hell, corruptor of souls, champion of the dark side, and seventy-four times winner of Divine magazine's most eligible bachelor, who's this?"

"Uh, Detective Blunt, dead detective, former Chief Investigator of the City of Gloomwood, and holder of a twenty-five-meter swimming badge."

"Really?"

"Yes really, I had the fifty meter one, but I lost it... come to think of it, I don't have any badges anymore," Blunt rambled. His eyes wide as he stared at the Grim Reaper mouthing, 'the effing Devil is real?'

"Well," the voice on the other side of the phone continued, "that's very impressive, but I was calling the Grim Reaper, is he there?"

"Um, no," Blunt said, "he must have left this here, it's a phone, we don't have phones like this here."

"Didn't you hear me?"

"What?"

"I'm the Devil, Detective, the actual Devil. Lying to me rarely works out very well."

"Did you just call me a liar? You might be the Devil but you're going to end up with my size ten boot up your backside if you think you can just call someone a liar, you hear me -" Without warning his fingers tightened around the phone. Blunt started spasming and dropped to the floor while his body jerked, his arms and legs thrashed, until the phone fell from his grip and skittered across the floor of the office coming to a stop by the door.

He lay still, panting. The Grim Reaper stepped forward and looked down at Blunt. "I meet many people this way," he said.

"I'm not... more dead?"

"Just as dead as before."

"Was it magic?"

"Magic? Oh no, divine rage isn't magic, it's just... well it's just very, very, angry. I think he electrocuted you, or something similar. How do you feel?"

"Like someone just dropped a toaster into my bathtub."

"Why would anyone do that? We are in my office... no, wait, I get it now. You would also have been in the bathtub, presumably with water."

"Are you okay?" Blunt asked, despite being the person who was still twitching.

"No. We need to leave. Beelzebub didn't fall for it, which means we're exactly where he expects us to be. If I were him, I would amass a blockade outside the building. He's quite evil, so he'll probably use our own people to do it. Also, there's an army of the living dead on their way here. They're definitely Beelzebub's work. 'Army' suggests a lot of them, which seems strange. Oh, Twist Lenworth just chopped off a blue man's head in reception. She's in the lift headed our way," Grim said.

"How do you know?" Blunt asked.

"I'm Death."

"There's one of those tube things that deliver letters behind him and he just received one," Morgarth said.

"It's a pneumatic mail system... and I also know things." The Grim Reaper loomed in Ted's direction, "Fortunately, so does your friend Miss Hughes, who sent this message. Quite impressive of her. They'll lock down the building, all we have to do, is get out of it."

"What can I do?" Morgarth asked.

The Grim Reaper looked at the dinosaur. "Morgarth, I'm going to ask you to go down the elevator and join our friends in the reception area. I'm not sure if you're helping this city or Lord Beelzebub, and of course there's no hard feelings either way, but it might be for the best. We seem to be getting quite serious now."

"I... yes, your lordship," the blue dinosaur said, nodding.

"Get out of the building?"

"Yes. Before it is completely overrun!"

"Why didn't somebody just lock the doors?" Blunt asked as he stood up. His hands were still shaking from the effects of Beelzebub's call.

"Don't be a ridiculous Detective, this is the Office of the Dead, they do not lock those doors. We can abandon all hope, we might stand on the precipice of disaster, the end of all things might draw near-"

"Nobody thought to lock the doors, did they?" Ted said.

"The special security usually do it, but they're all at the Deathport."

"They're all at the Deathport? So there's no security?"

"None. It was an emergency."

💀 <u>GOD HEAD</u> 💀

Petal looked up from the ground at his own body as he tried to move to pick up his… well, himself. Coordinating your body without an attached head is a much more difficult skill to master than people realise. A skill that was so difficult that there was a growing industry in hand operatives. People who had their limbs severed and could still control them. Their hands can then go into places that would otherwise be out of reach. Rumour had it that Jake 'the one eyed' Cobra, who had the misfortune of forcing his moniker upon people before realising it was a euphemism, had two eyes. He strapped one eye to his wrist like a watch, so it worked like a camera when he sent his eye places.

None of that was on Petal's mind as he watched himself, well his body, stumble around the reception area of the Office of the Dead. She had caught him by surprise with the old classic, 'staying in the revolving door' trick. As Petal had stepped out expecting to see her, she had appeared behind him. Before he had even realised what had happened, he had felt a sharp pain and then his world was spinning and tumbling as his head fell from his shoulders and bounced off the faded carpet and tiles of the Office of the Dead floor.

When he came to a stop, she knelt to look him in the eyes, "It's nothing personal. This is work. If I see you when this is over can we have a rematch?" She said with a wink.

He scowled but didn't say a word as he watched her walk away. Shouting and cursing would have done him no favours. Rage was a tool and, well versed in how to use it, Petal knew when it was best saved for another time.

The problem at hand was simple. He needed to pick up his head and stop Twist from killing Ted. He had a moral obligation and morals were something he held a great deal of regard for. Some people collect those creepy porcelain dolls, others have comic book collections which are all sealed away in protective plastic, Petal collected morals, and things like honour, respect, loyalty. They were the things he had long ago abandoned as useless but had, as time went by, realised they were worth something. Like remembering you had toys as a child that would be worth thousands now.

He was coming to terms with the fact that his own body wouldn't follow simple instructions. It didn't help that it was almost out of his eyeline, which meant he was blind to his own movements.

"Say nothing," a voice whispered to him, a voice he recognised. He felt his head lifted off the floor and then he was being carried towards his own body. With concentration, he held out his own hands, waiting to grab his head.

RETREAT

"Viva la resurrection!" Molly screamed as her crowd of the living dead bore down on Dead Square.

"Hang on, love," a man holding a baseball bat in one hand and a serrated bread knife in the other, said, "Gloomwood police. You're going to have to take this lot somewhere else. We're defending this facility from a terrorist attack."

"I am doing the lord's work."

"Which lord?" The constable said, looking around at the officers who stood in a line, a pace behind him. "I mean, we have certain rules for important people so…"

"The Lord, our one true Lord, God himself," Molly said to a chorus of, "Ur," from her followers.

"You can't say that," the constable said, "for a start it's blasphemy to use the lord's name in vain."

"It's not in vain. I'm using it for its purpose."

The constable nodded. "Fair enough. I take that back. You can't just say you're doing things because God said so. Where'd we be then?"

"That's how it works." Molly said, "that's exactly what I can do."

"Nah, that makes little sense at all. People would start wars just by shouting, 'God said so,' it's lunacy," a tap on the shoulder interrupted the constable. Another officer leant forward to whisper in his ear. "No? Really? Oh…" He stood up straight and looked at the slow-moving mass of people behind the soft toy that was waving Molly's head aloft. "It turns out that's exactly what people do. What is it you're intending?"

"We are alive!" She shouted.

"UR." The horde behind her crowed.

"And we will march into life, to take back the mortal realm, Viva La Resurrection!"

"UR."

The constable looked back at his compatriots, then back again to Molly. She looked down on him from her position on the stick as the toy tried not to wobble her too much.

"How does that work then? I'm only asking because it might be fine and there's a lot of you," the constable said, "and there's not that many of us, and the Guv said we should never start a fight unless we know we're going to win."

"We will march on the office of the dead, helping those who haven't seen the light join our ranks, and then we will demand the Grim Reaper opens the gateway to the land of the living where we will take our rightful place, so says the Mible."

"The Mible says you force the Grim Reaper to do that? Doesn't seem very 'Meep'."

"It doesn't exactly say that. It says we will journey back to life when the time is right."

"And is the time right?"

"I'm not debating this. It's time."

"Time for," A sound seldom heard in the City of Gloomwood interrupted. It caught the attention of everyone standing in Dead Square. The police, and the followers of Molly, all looked up to the clock high atop the Office of the Dead building as its bell, somewhere behind its dark face, tolled.

"Bong, Bong… Bong, Bong… Bong, Bong…"

"That's weird," the constable said, "it is six."

"It's time," Molly said.

BAD DETECTIVE

"We need to make a move," Blunt said, "for the last few hours everything has been happening around me and I don't like it. Sir," he turned to the Grim Reaper, "I don't think we have an alternative plan, so I'm in."

In life, he'd given up smoking, but death had taken away any health concerns and, despite what he said to others trying to quit, he'd never really wanted to stop. The smell of stale tobacco and alcohol first thing in the morning was enough to turn his stomach, but it wasn't the first thing in the morning. If things we're going to get serious, he was having a smoke. He held the cigar in one hand and fished for a lighter in his pockets.

"Detective, I'd rather you didn't," the Grim Reaper said.

"Does that mean I can't? Because I appreciate you'd rather I didn't but I'm already dead and you're asking me to save the afterlife where I might have to tussle with the Devil. This," he looked at the Grim Reaper and waved the cigar in his face, "shouldn't be a big deal. So, do you mind if I have a smoke?" Blunt asked.

"I suppose not. Shall we go?"

Blunt shrugged and lit the cigar that had been hiding in his coat pocket for too long. It was disgusting, stale, and disappointing, but Blunt didn't care. In his lower coat pocket Ted's head hung out, the rest of his soft toy body forced into a space barely big enough to hold it. The bear had been furious, but Blunt had pointed out that it was better than the alternative. That being if the bear would survive having his head ripped off the rest of his body.

The Grim Reaper stood next to a black rucksack he had dragged out from a dusty cupboard. "This is quite embarrassing, Detective. I'd prefer it if it wasn't common knowledge."

"You're acting like this is the first time I've seen you without a body."

"Ah, well, I suppose there's something to be said about experience," Grim looked around the room once more.

Blunt couldn't read any emotion on the Grim Reaper's skull but he'd seen enough men look around their homes wondering if it was the last time they'd see them to understand what he was watching. "We'll be back."

The Grim Reaper stopped and fixed Blunt with a stare. "Do not presume too much, Detective. Only two things in life are certain, me and taxes, after life not even I am certain." Then Grim clicked his fingers, and the robe collapsed into a pool on the floor. It would have been more dramatic if the Grim Reaper hadn't said, "ouch, every time, stupid pelvis."

"I don't want to sound weird," Blunt said, "but you know I'm going to have to, um, touch you."

"Everything's in the robes, Detective, just gather me up, and put me in the bag."

Blunt did what as he was told. Folding the robes over the Grim Reaper's body left him with a compact bundle of cloth, which he placed inside the rucksack before zipping it shut. "Can you hear me?" Blunt asked.

"Yes," Grim said, the bag seemed to do nothing to muffle his voice, "don't speak to me unless it's safe for me to reply Detective, I can't see if anyone's nearby."

"Okay, shall we go?"

"Oh no, I love it in here, please take a little longer and if we're lucky, the Devil himself will turn up ruining any chance we have of rescuing this whole situation and when he gets here, I'll be in a bag, perfect," the Grim Reaper said.

Blunt didn't respond. Instead, he picked up the bag, and, holding it by the handles, slung it over his shoulder. It thumped against his back, but the Grim Reaper didn't make a sound. He yanked Ted out of the coat pocket.

"Don't be so rough," Ted said.

"Thief, Ableforther, Destroyer of Worlds... and you took the piss out of me on television. I don't see why I shouldn't just tear your head off and see if things just work out." Blunt stared into the single button eye on the stuffed teddy bear toy. "You're one smug little bastard, aren't you?"

"I resent that."

"In the bag," Blunt said, shoving the bear into the bag that held the Grim Reaper's body.

"Oh, wonderful," the Grim Reaper muttered.

The Detective took a drag on the cigar, blew out a plume of smoke, tapped his hat with the hand holding the cigar and muttered, "easy little job, just find someone, what's the worst that could happen? Bloody living dead, Grim Reaper, talking bears, and the actual, real-life... real-death Devil. Should've bloody jumped."

DINO STEPS

Morgarth stepped through the elevator doors as they opened. Standing in front of her was a tall woman in a dark coat carrying a scythe. For Morgarth, she couldn't help but admire the look. It was something she would have worn herself, given the choice. "Hello," Morgarth said.

"Good morning," Twist Lenworth said.

They walked by one another. The tall woman disappearing into the elevator. Morgarth turned as the doors shut behind her and the dial above the door moved, showing its ascent.

It didn't occur to Morgarth until later that the woman hadn't seemed surprised to see a small soft toy dinosaur walk out of the lift. Nor did it occur to her that she had not tried to hide her demonic voice, which should, at the very least, have caused the woman to cringe.

She walked from the elevator towards the reception area where Johnson was standing alongside a huge man trying to balance his own head on his neck. A tapping to her right caught Morgarth's attention, and she looked up at the windows shielding the reception desk to see Leighton Hughes tapping on the glass with a pen. Morgarth padded around to the door at the side of the reception counter, which Leighton opened.

"Come in, we're safer in here."

"Safe from what?" Morgarth asked.

"Well, that big blue one is Petal, that's Johnson's boyfriend, he's a Demi-god. Nobody really knows what god, someone ancient. The woman who just got in the lift chopped his head off with a scythe. She must be the one that Blunt was talking about before. If they're here, then I think we can expect some more pretty soon."

Morgarth leapt up on to the counter to look out into the reception area. "They didn't lock the door?"

"Oh, I don't think anyone thought of that," Leighton said, "should we lock it?"

"Hey," Morgarth shouted, causing Leighton to fall to her knees, holding her hands over her ears.

Johnson looked over. "How did you get in there?"

"The reporter woman let me in," Morgarth said.

"Leighton? What have you done to her?"

"Nothing, she's right here. Oh, but she's doing that thing where they collapse when I shout. You should lock the doors."

"I'm dealing with something right now."

"There's definitely a joke about what you're doing right now."

"That's… inappropriate," Johnson said, a rare flush of colour appearing in his cheeks.

The revolving door started to turn and Captain Sowercat of the Gloomwood police strode into the Office of the Dead. Morgarth, knowing nothing about who he was, jumped back down from the counter and used one leg to push at Leighton's quivering form. "Hey lady, sorry for shouting. I'm not that scary, look, just a little dinosaur, right, us girls have to stick together."

"You're… female?" Leighton asked.

"Uh, Morgarth, that's a girl's name."

"It is?"

The one advantage to having large googly eyes, even if they are black with red dots for irises, is that they're fantastic for eye rolling.

"Okay," Leighton said. She pushed herself up enough to peer over the counter, through the glass, and into the lobby area where she watched Johnson talking to the Chief of police. "That's Chief Sowercat," Leighton hissed, "he's the head of the police. I can't hear what they're saying, but he fired Johnson from the police. He seems quite animated. Oh, he's pulled a stapler from his pocket… and… he's helping to staple Petal's neck back together."

"You can just do that?" Morgarth asked.

Leighton shook her head, "I guess so. I mean normally you'd go to a hospital or something and they'd do it properly so it's not so obvious but… I suppose staples would work if you put plenty in."

"This place is weird," Morgarth said.

"Are you really from Hell?" Leighton turned from the window and put her back against the counter. "I mean, that Hell, the actual place?"

Morgarth nodded her head.

"It's weird that they'd have cuddly dinosaurs in Hell. I suppose they would, though. I mean, everyone's afraid of different things."

"I'm not a dinosaur in Hell. I'm an eight-foot tall woman. This," she waved at her body with her padded hands, "is temporary. Beelzebub brought us here, but bodies aren't so easy to get hold of."

"Bodies are really easy to get. It was probably the heads that were the problem. There are loads of rules about making heads here," Leighton said. "This is a little weird, but could I interview you? We've had no one from Hell here before, I'm sure it would fascinate people."

"It's not that interesting, really."

"I bet it is."

ELEVATOR MUSIC

Twist tapped her foot in time with the soft background music as the lift lurched. She tried not to think about how little people seemed to care about basic maintenance as the light above her head flickered.

This was not how she had imagined this would happen. She had lingered in the space between here and there for longer than she could care to remember. Eons spent standing in queues next to shocked, desperate people who were struggling to understand that their miserable insignificant lives were over. There was excitement, the thrill of ghoul raids, or shadows from the nether that needed to dealing with. Being a Reaper wasn't boring, it was just repetitive, but then everything is repetitive when you do it forever.

The lift lurched, but decades of the ground shifting beneath her feet meant she barely noticed. Her balance was always perfect.

Stairs might have been a better option, but she couldn't have known how slow the lift was. It would be faster this way if it didn't break down before she reached her destination. At least the music was pleasant. A familiar tune, she hummed along to the melody that was coming in through speakers that in the top corners of the rectangular box.

Gloomwood irked her. For so long she had deliberated over a simple decision. The choice between life and death isn't so simple when you've lived your life and some of your death. Your perspective can change from the simple, 'I want to live' mindset. There was no way of knowing where she would end up if she lived and died again. Would her account be reset? Would the balance of good and evil change?

Her eyes narrowed when she thought about checks and balances. Jeremy had reinvented himself as Ted, stolen time and then used it to come here of all places. It made little sense to her. Who would choose here? This place wasn't heaven, or anything like a heaven she might have imagined. It was closer to a purgatory where life just continues, but it's worse.

Miserable, dark, filled with people who still, after having entire lives, didn't know who they were or what they wanted to do. This, she thought, was what they deserved. These stupid, selfish grey people. Who, in their infinite wisdom, had decided they didn't need to pay the balance for the lives they had lived?

The lift stopped. With a crunching sound the doors separated, a sliver of light from what lay beyond slipped between the gap. The motor whined and dragged the doors apart fully.

"Oh," she said.

"Hello again," Blunt said with a sigh. The detective was carrying a bag over one shoulder.

"Are you going to make this difficult?" She asked.

Blunt shrugged, then nodded. "It's pretty much what I do."

MEET THE DEVIL

His head wobbled. Staples just didn't have the same staying power as a joined up spinal column. "This is stupid," the Demi-god rumbled.

"Yes," Johnson said, "it is, but it will do for now."

"Are you ready?" Sowercat asked.

Petal looked at Johnson, who glanced down at his shoes, then nodded. The ex-police officer wasn't the type to suffer from nervousness, but what might come through the doors worried him. It wasn't the horde of living dead that bothered him; it was his former colleagues. Those who had made his death miserable.

Chief Sowercat went out the central revolving door. Three of the brass framed glass doors led into the lobby of the Office of the Dead. The reflective coating on them made them impossible to see through, but Sowercat had made the situation clear.

On the other side of the doors were two groups of people, both of them sick in different ways The Chief's plan was to send in some police. If the horde reacted as expected they would follow the force into the building while the police who remained outside could flank them. The doors would be a bottleneck so the police would just take it in turns to let the zombies, the Chief's term, come in one at a time. Dealing with them was, apparently, just a matter of decapitating them.

All Johnson and Petal had to do was watch and wait. They looked at one another.

"We could," Petal said nodding at the doors

"We're not locking them all out there," Johnson said.

"No, that would be a terrible thing to do. Letting the police get eaten by a horde of really slow-moving people who will probably all just fall apart with no one having to do anything."

Johnson thought about it.

"I'm joking, Jayjay, starting to worry about you. You didn't mention the bear to Sowercat."

"Didn't seem relevant."

"He's in the building and the last time I saw you, you were with him."

"How did you know to come here?" Johnson asked.

Petal shrugged. "Didn't. Some bloke with a creepy smile said that there was an army of the living dead marching here," he said.

"An army?"

"I'm not even sure if there's fifty of them, hardly an army, most of them look like they'll collapse if you wink at them. Where did she go?"

"You're in no state to fight her again. She chopped your head off. That's not a minor scratch. You don't get to leap up ready for round two, Petal. How did she even manage it?"

Petal stood up, one hand on the top of his head, trying to stop it from moving more than it should. "She was behind me, caught me by surprise. We had a kind of truce going on. I guess she'd just been waiting for the right moment and then," he drew a finger across his neck.

"Literally."

"Yeah. So, she's going up the lift to kill Ted. Like she's got a chance against the Grim Reaper."

Johnson nodded. "Exactly."

The door turned. Johnson turned to the reception desk and waved to Leighton to duck out of sight. When her head disappeared under the counter again, he turned back to the door. Side by side, Petal and he waited.

"Well hello," the figure said as he strode in the door, "I'm looking for the Grim Reaper. He hasn't been answering my calls."

BAG MAN

He was on the floor before he knew what happened. The pain in his face an explosion of agony accompanied by the instant awareness that a tooth was in his mouth, but not where it should be. He spat it out onto the floor and looked up.

"Are we done? I don't really take pleasure in this," Twist Lenworth said as she rubbed her knuckles of her free hand against her coat, then inspected her nails. She'd punched him and he'd gone down like a marionette that had all its strings cut.

With a sleeve he wiped his mouth, there was no blood, but he didn't have much in his body, expensive stuff. He was just grateful she hadn't hit him in the nose. The way his finances stood, he'd end up with a Sowercat special. "I'm just warming up."

"There's nobody watching Blunt, feigning bravery in these circumstances is only going to end up with you in pieces, and me wasting what precious little time I have. Where's the little bastard?"

"Why are you so determined to get him?"

"He took something from me."

"Time?"

She flinched. "So you've spoken to Him."

"Him, or him?"

"The Grim Reaper. The only way that miserable little bear would have admitted to anything is if Death himself had been there, and even then he'd have lied. So, Death took care of the bear. I'm surprised I didn't feel something. I guess I must speak to Death about getting my time back. You could have just said, there would have been no need to hit you."

Blunt shrugged. "You didn't give me a chance to say anything."

She started walking towards the office but paused as she passed Blunt. "I'm not normally like this, Detective."

"Spare me the deep and meaningful," Blunt said as he got off the floor and dusted himself down. He picked up his hat, then the bag, and put it over his shoulder.

"Ahem," came a voice from the desk by the short staircase to the Grim Reaper's office, "do you have an appointment?" Ursula Panderpenny asked.

Twist frowned as she turned and walked towards the desk.

"Hold on, you're not about to hurt anyone, are you?" Blunt said.

Ursula Panderpenny raised her own head up, "spare me your false chivalry, Detective. I've worked too hard and too long to have any need to hide behind men like you."

Blunt rolled his eyes and couldn't stop a chuckle as he stepped into the lift. As the doors shut he looked down at the bag. "Well, that was easy."

"I believe that is only the first step Detective," the Grim Reaper said, "We should not underestimate Miss Panderpenny either. She is one of the most qualified people in this city."

"She might be, but qualifications aren't much of a defence against a violent scythe wielding reaper."

"Perhaps not, but Miss Panderpenny has made people quake in their boots in the past."

There was music playing in the lift. That tune again that had been haunting Blunt all day. He opened his mouth to ask if anyone knew what it was when the elevator lurched. Then stopped. Blunt looked up as the lights in the ceiling flickered and died, along with the music. "You've got to be taking the piss."

THE DEVIL YOU KNOW

Petal and Johnson looked at the man who had walked through the doors as Sowercat left. He was smoking a cigarette with the over the top actions that made it clear he knew it was a no smoking area.

"You're not allowed-" Petal stopped Johnson from finishing the sentence.

"Take one a lift over there. There's a label on the Grim Reaper's floor. It's the button nobody ever presses," Petal said, taking a step back. With one hand on Johnson's shoulder, he pulled the confused hope back with him.

The grin that spread across the newcomer's face was wide and sharp. "How very accommodating of you," Beelzebub said, "there's something familiar about you."

"Yeah, I get that a lot, I've one of those faces," Petal said.

"Well, no time to chat. I've an old friend to meet," the Devil said as he walked by the two men towards the bank of three elevators. They were on the other side of the huge lobby area, and on either side of them were stone archways that led into administrative areas.

Johnson and Petal watched as the man pressed the button and waited, his back turned to them.

"Where'd he come from?" Johnson said.

"Outside."

"Obviously."

"No, Jay... I mean outside, outside, as in, he's not from around here," Petal said, his voice low, his eyes locked on the back of the man.

Beelzebub turned, saw them watching, and gave them a wave with his free hand.

"Should we have stopped him?" Johnson asked.

Petal shook his head. "I don't think we could've."

"This is weird."

"Yeah, yeah it is."

BAG OF BONES

"Is there any point in you being in there if we're trapped in here?"

"Detective, at any moment the Devil may arrive, in fact… yes, I believe the Devil is in the building," the bag on the floor of the lift, said.

"I could come out," Ted's voice came out of the bag.

The Grim Reaper continued as if the bear wasn't there. "Our goal is to get to the docks while the Devil, and his minions, and the undead, and the public, believe we're still in this building. If anyone sees the bear or I, then getting to the boat will become more difficult."

Blunt sighed. "I still can't believe there's no security. Isn't that skinny creep Tomb Mandrake supposed to protect you?" He asked. "We entrust his team with defending this city from any serious security risks."

"This isn't serious. We have it under control."

Blunt couldn't stop his mouth from falling open. There were increasing signs that the Grim Reaper was not what everyone thought he was.

"People will arrive to work soon. While people come in and out of the building, it should be easy enough for you, Detective, to slip out. Then it's a simple walk to the wall and the docks."

Blunt shrugged, "If we're trapped in here, none of that matters," he said.

"That is a problem," Grim said in a stunning display of stating the obvious. "Particularly as I wasn't expecting Miss Lenworth to arrive so soon. No matter, I'd imagine we have at least thirty minutes."

Blunt let out a cough. The cigar smoke was filling the inside of the elevator and he was regretting having lit it. "You really think it will take her half an hour to realise the skeleton, isn't you?"

"How would she know?"

"It doesn't talk," Ted chimed in.

"I'm not chatty at the best of times." The Grim Reaper's voice, ever sonorous, didn't sound like it was coming from the bag but from every direction at once.

"So, you'd just ignore someone coming into your office?" Ted asked.

"I made it look like it was reading a book. It would be rude to interrupt," replied the Grim Reaper.

"I'm not sure manners are going to be that effective at fooling people. Can we just focus?" Blunt snapped at the bag.

"Don't underestimate basic respect, Detective," Grim said.

AWKWARD SILENCE

A waste of time, Twist thought to herself. There was no nicer way of putting it. The receptionist seemed determined to make life difficult. The way she kept picking her head up off the desk was irritating. Who doesn't have their head attached? It's disconcerting.

Twist had been to other afterlives. She had seen things. Admittedly, she had spent no time in those places, but few of them were welcoming to one with a body. Most of it was ethereal, abstract, glowing lights and orbs. Sometimes there was music or the feeling of music. There was little she could glean from them and she had known, without ever having to do more than observe from a distance, that these places wouldn't have harboured anyone like her.

There were others, though. Places where the dead clung on to corporeal form like a safety blanket. The halls of Valhalla, for example. Not that they'd let her in to look around, but the guards had bodies. That had been what brought her to Gloomwood. They've got bodies.

It wasn't as if she had given the other reapers a choice in the matter. She would go with or without their blessing. Siding with Twist at least meant they knew what was happening. Knew where she'd be going. They'd all agreed. A collective experience of time untold had led them all to a state of disappointment. For reapers, they had known little about the afterlife. Each one of them slowly and painfully concluded that they knew the routes, but not what lay beyond. Like people who had memorised the maps but had never seen a picture. "Gloomwood," the bartender had eventually said as they had gathered around a table in the only bar for reapers, "it's where the Grim Reaper went, he could hide there, nobody gives a shit in Gloomwood."

She grimaced as she glared at the receptionist. "I'm going to see him now, we're old friends, he'll be happy to see me."

"If you haven't got an appointment, you can't go in," the receptionist said. Her head was on the table while she shuffled what were noticeably blank pieces of paper she had taken from a drawer.

"If you attempt to stop me, I will hurt you... more," she added, realising that someone doesn't get decapitated by accident.

The receptionist let out a sigh. "To be honest with you, Miss... whatever your name is, I don't care anymore."

Twist arched an eyebrow. "A bold move, thank you." Then she strode towards the small staircase that led up to doors which would have been impressive if the ceiling hadn't been so close to the top of them. As it was, it looked more like the entrance to an attic that somebody had forgotten about during planning. She knocked, but there was no answer. So she waited because this was the Grim Reaper.

DOORWAY TO DEATH

When the doors opened with a rattle, he couldn't stop himself from shaking his head. Not that he tried. This was the culmination of the Grim Reaper's own afterlife. Poor craftmanship, slack maintenance, zero security, and, oh look, a receptionist who doesn't even have her head attached. He ignored the woman while she rolled her own head around on the desktop, muttering to herself.

As he stepped into the reception area, it disappointed him to realise the floor wasn't marble, as it appeared, but some kind of textured plastic. It covered the length of a needlessly long and vacuous space where only the receptionist's desk waited. At the other end of the room was a staircase, well some steps, which led up to a door that looked like it was hanging from the ceiling. A woman with a scythe stood in front of the door.

"Grim?" Beelzebub said, his voice loud enough to carry across the room and bounce back again.

The receptionist grabbed herself by the hair and lifted herself to look at him.

At the top step, the woman with the scythe turned to look back.

"Grim, is that you? You have changed."

"Are you talking to me?" The woman at the top step asked.

Beelzebub was finding the receptionist distracting. Having someone wave around their own head made it difficult for them to be subtle when listening in.

"Yes, you're not Death?"

"No, do I look like Death?" She asked.

Beelzebub waved his cigarette. "How would I know? You wouldn't tell me if it was you, anyway."

"What? Then why even ask? Who are you?"

"You people have no imagination," he pointed to the two small horns that sprouted from his head on command, "and the red complexion, have a guess?"

Twist arched an eyebrow, "are you a cheap Halloween costume wearing car sales attendant?"

Beelzebub grinned before answering, "Car sales attendant?"

"What's wrong with selling cars?" Twist asked.

The receptionist stood up at her desk. She tried to hold her head above her head with both hands, then seemed to think better of it, eventually settling for holding it under one arm, as if she were holding herself in a headlock. "You cannot just shout across this lobby. This is the hallowed hallway of the Grim Reaper himself."

"Or herself," Beelzebub said, nodding towards Twist.

"I'm not the Grim Reaper," Twist replied.

"Neither of you have an appointment. You both need to leave."

"Or you'll call security?" Twist asked.

"You mean that pair downstairs?" Beelzebub asked, "they're a little busy."

"I... no, security are the Gloomwood secret service."

"Well where are they?" Beelzebub said, "This is just getting ridiculous. Is secrecy more important to them than security? Perhaps they're so secret they don't exist."

"There was a serious emergency," the receptionist said, "not that it's any of your business, mister?"

"Stop talking," Beelzebub said.

"Strange name and you can't speak to me like that."

Beelzebub strode towards the reception desk and looked Ursula Panderpenny in the eye. "Is that woman over there the Grim Reaper?"

She moved her lips but didn't make a sound until she uttered a quiet, "No."

"Thank you," he said before exhaling a plume of smoke from his cigarette.

Miss Panderpenny's eyes rolled back and her body fell into her chair. Her head dropped from her hands, hit the floor with a thud, and disappeared beneath the desk.

"Right," Beelzebub turned to look at the woman on the stairs, "you're not Grim but you're carrying a scythe. Is that a coincidence? Are you his guard?"

"I'm not a guard."

"For crying out loud, is there no security here? It beggars belief! It's as if none of you realise I am a threat to your very existence. I am the Devil."

Twist shook her head. "Did you just knock out the receptionist with cigarette smoke?"

"It's a little more complicated but yes. Your turn next."

She held up a hand. "Hold your hellhounds there Satan."

"Oh, a believer now, are we?"

"I'd rather not end up unconscious. It looks like we both want to speak to the Grim Reaper about the impending collapse of this afterlife and the cause of it, correct?"

"No. I know the cause," the Devil said, "it seems we're not on level terms."

"Oh, I know the cause. I know exactly who that thieving swine is."

"You do?" Beelzebub said, "well who is he? Not Teddington Rex, that's a terrible name, his real name."

"Jeremy," Twist said.

"Jeremy? Well, that's no better."

☠ <u>ALL KNOWING</u> ☠

"I have a bad feeling, Detective."

"A bad feeling?" Blunt said, staring at the bag. He had ground the cigar out on the floor of the elevator. "The Grim Reaper has a bad feeling. I don't mean to be disrespectful, but isn't that like God saying, 'oops, maybe I should try that again?'"

"Let's not bring Him into this. Detective, if we don't get this man out of Gloomwood, the city will succumb to time. It will crumble and turn to dust."

"Would that be so bad?" Blunt asked. "We're all dead. Most people thought we were just going to nothingness, dust on the wind, right?"

"Your outlook differs from many of the people in this city. Are you so keen to never see them again? The likes of your friends down in the lobby? There are surely some people you care about, Detective, everyone has someone."

"Do you?" Blunt asked.

"I have everyone," Grim said, "I don't want anyone to die, but also, I'm not a person, I'm a personification."

"Semantics. Aren't hopes and dreams, personifications too?"

"Not quite, maybe, hm. Regardless, we must get the bear out of the city."

"Can't you just magic me out of here?" Ted asked.

"No," the Grim Reaper's voice boomed, the elevator rattled, and Blunt winced.

"No? Just no." The bear continued, "Don't care to elaborate on that at all?"

"Do you have any idea how complicated it is to create an afterlife and keep it in existence?"

Blunt was sitting in the lift's corner. His feet pointed to the opposite corner where the bag with Ted and the Grim Reaper was. "No," the detective said, interrupting the bickering that had been going on for some time between the Grim Reaper and the man who was possessing the body of a soft toy, "but you've removed people before."

"Yes. By taking them to the boat and travelling across the Styx."

Blunt took his hat off his head and looked inside it as if it might have an answer. "Can't we just go to the Deathport?"

"No. That is a one-way route. It comes in, and not out. Could you imagine if people could just arrange a trip to another afterlife? Do you think people would stay in Hell if they could move elsewhere? The Deathport is much more like the exit at a very, very, long drainpipe... but with valves and a serious u-bend. There's no going out that way. As Tedemy probably knows."

"Tedemy?" Ted said, "can't you just use Ted or Jeremy? Yes, I tried going back through, but it's just a brick wall behind the curtain. There isn't anywhere to walk through." "Wait, did you try this morning?" Blunt asked. "No. What kind of person waits that long? I've been here for months. Reapers all know about the Deathport; it's where we drop people off," Ted said. Blunt shrugged. "I don't want to think about what Hell is," the detective said, "this might be Hell."

"It isn't," the Grim Reaper said, "I have seen Hell. Gratitude is a fleeting, Detective. Maybe I can't click my fingers and send you all elsewhere, but it seems Beelzebub has found a way."

"So he's responsible for the woman at the Deathport?"

"Oh no," Grim said, "that's not his style. I imagine it was Twist Lenworth who Ableforthed poor June."

"You don't seem very angry."

"I'm livid, but the secret police are dealing with that."

"And?"

"And what, Detective? It's a secret, obviously."

"Beelzebub," Ted said, ending the discussion about the Deathport, "there was a reaper who once met him."

"I know the Devil quite well," Grim interrupted.

"This reaper," Ted continued, "he's… he just screams. He has no eyes, empty sockets like they burst into fire on their own and he just… he just screams, Blunt, and he never sleeps."

The detective stared into his hat. "Sleep isn't something the dead get a lot of. The big sleep is just a lie. I haven't slept in months. I just drink and then wake up. There's nothing in between."

"Detective. There's no peace in what might come if we don't get this man out. As for you, so-called Ted, it's going to be much worse. Even if this place crumbles. If my afterlife fails. Beelzebub will not leave without you."

"Blunt," Ted said, his voice unsteady, "I'm damned if you don't."

"Hah, you're damned if I don't, and I'm damned anyway," the lift lurched and started moving again. "Lucky," Blunt said, "I was in danger of being allowed to think for a minute there. Wonder why it started."

"The shifting."

"Shifting?"

"It's seven o'clock, the building has finished shifting. People will arrive for work. Every room has its new place."

Blunt nodded. "That weird thing where the walls all move?"

"Not all the walls. My floor and the ground floor stay the same."

"Who thought of that?"

"I don't know. The building was here when I arrived."

"What?"

"The building was here when Gloomwood began."

"I heard you. How is that possible?"

"You can't see me shrugging, but that's what I would be doing right now."

BEST LAID PLANS

"This is a disaster," Johnson yelled over the sounds of battle.

The plan had been for a coordinated movement of police officers, so that the living dead would follow through the revolving doors and they could deal with them one by one. Police would surround the doors and decapitate the living dead, making them safe until they found a cure, or otherwise.

Sowercat had thought it was a good plan. It would have been a perfect plan if executed quickly and efficiently. "Like herding bloody cats," Sowercat screamed at his officers.

"They wouldn't listen," a constable trying to stop the central rotating door from turning said with a grunt, "that mad head woman on a stick just keeps screaming."

"I'm not talking about the bloody biters. I'm talking about us, you, the police. Absolutely sodding useless. Now half of you are outside losing a fight with people who can barely move."

"But they don't stop. They don't even feel pain. It's like trying to fight… uh…"

"Zombies constable? Like trying to fight bloody zombies, is it?" Sowercat bellowed. His nose had inflated to a point where he had to push it to one side to see properly. It was moments away from bursting and everyone knew it. The question was whether the tightly stretched 'skin' would burst as because of internal pressure, or if it would be burst by an external force when Sowercat joined the fray.Organisation is not something associated with the Gloomwood police. Unless it's in the phrase, 'what a massively feckless organisation the police is.' Having long thrown out the adage, 'if you can't beat 'em, join 'em,' school of thought, Sowercat had fostered a strong 'disorganised' outlook on crime fighting. The more disorganised they were, the harder organised crime would find it to elude them… well, it had been a plan. An ill-conceived plan that ranked, in managerial terms, right alongside, 'it'll fix itself'. It had left the police in a perpetual state of disarray that seeped into their very souls.

What had finally happened was the ancient tactical retreat first practised by Beelzebub himself at the pearly gates in a game called, 'pitter, patter, Peter'. Beelzebub would ring the bell on the pearly gates and hide behind a cloud to laugh at St Peter. Gloomwooders call it ding, dong, dash. It gave birth to the fabled, 'Leggit,' manoeuvre. Gloomwoodian scholars from the university have sifted through centuries of documents attempting to identify who Leggit was, but the name remains a mystery.

With regimented precision, the only time they ever display it, the sergeants of the Gloomwood police shouted, "LEGGIT!" With the well-oiled practice of experienced street urchins, Sowercat's men jumped into action. As with all talented leaders, he led the charge directly through the centre door, while the others followed, shoving anyone too slow out of the way.

Molly, the prophet of the lord, emancipator of the living dead, deliverer of the new dawn, righteous head of the resurrection, and bearer of excessive titles, drove her forces forward at… a snail's pace. The decomposition taking place in the flesh of the living dead seemed to be worsening but, fortunately for Molly, there were only three doors into the Office of the Dead.

What Sowercat had planned worked in reverse. The doors prevented a rapid escape for the police. All the living dead had to do was lurch onwards following the cries of, "leggit," while bellowing, "Viva la resurrection." It confounded the police. The spinning doors slowed them to a point where escape turned into a queuing system as the police had to wait, one at a time, to jump into the spinning chambers of doom. Tutting began and next came exclamations of surprise as the biting began at the rear of the group and eventually bloomed into chaos and panic as it spread.

The officers who made it inside were slow to take up positions by the door, despite Sowercat's bellowing of orders. Not that they didn't follow orders. They just weren't very good at it. "Chop their heads off, one at a time, and move the bodies out of the way. It's not bloody difficult!"

Sowercat's nose grew larger as he watched his men try to determine if those entering were everyday dead, or living dead.

"Are you dead, Harris?" A constable, wielding a non-standard issue machete, asked.

"Yes," the man said.

The constable smiled with relief, "Oh, right, in you go then."

"Great," the constable called Harris said, "Some nutter bit me out there."

"Hang on, sorry. Need to chop your head off."

"But I'm so hungry... so hungry."

Sowercat's nose burst. The bang carried even over the clamouring voices and grunts in the reception area. Then the shouting started. "You're a useless bunch of self-centred, cockwombling, smurfgargling..."

The tirade was lengthy, filled with invective, and, to the greater connoisseurs of abusive language, quite creative. All eyes were on Sowercat. Well, all the eyes that could be as there was a growing mound of human heads in the middle of the reception area who couldn't choose where to look.

From behind the reception desk in the lobby, four pairs of eyes watched the carnage beyond. It was chaos, and none of them had any intention of getting involved. In Johnson's words, "I am not helping those bastards in grey, if they all get eaten we can take care of the mess that's left at the end."

The attention shifted back to the revolving doors as another surge of the living dead shoved their way in. Sowercat had spotted the four hiding behind the counter and, with surprising agility, side-stepped several attempted decapitations to make his way towards them. "You four."

"What?" Petal said.

"I know a back door from here," Sowercat looked behind him, a frown across his face, "I think it would be sensible to seal off the building from the outside."

"Now you think of that?" Leighton said.

"That was the plan in the first place... but there were extenuating circumstances."

"You mean because the Gloomwood police are incompetent?" Leighton said.

"I'm offering an olive branch here. How about a little friendliness instead of the third degree Little Miss Journalist?"

"Why are you bothering us?" Johnson asked, "take some constables and do it."

Sowercat, nose hanging off his face, sighed. "Johnson, you and I both know that they're useless. If I leave it to them it's going to get worse. You're a good copper, I know, you know, and this lot can't," he pointed to Leighton, Petal, and Morgarth, "is that a toy dinosaur?"

"Yes and no," Leighton answered before Morgarth could say anything.

"Anyway, this lot can't be any more incompetent. Plus, I know they've not bitten you. Are you coming?"

KNOCK, KNOCK.

"Open the door, Grim," Beelzebub said. The Devil was standing on the top step as Twist Lenworth stood a step beneath him. Beelzebub had insisted she step down in case anything terrible came through the door, and not at all because it bothered Beelzebub that she was taller than him.

"If he didn't answer your calls why would he answer the door?" Twist asked.

"Don't talk to me like I'm some commoner. I am the Devil."

"I know, you keep telling me. You're just not what I was expecting."

"Hm, you mean the fire and brimstone, boiling rivers of blood and ripping the hearts out of people, type of stuff."

"More the bare chested, cloven hooves, tail stuff."

Beelzebub turned to her. "If I expose my tail, or my hooves, that's my business, I'm the Devil, not some freak show for you to ogle."

"Ogle?"

"Yes ogle. I'm going to open the door."

"You can't just barge in."

"I can." The doors swung inwards revealing an office. Beelzebub's hand shot to his mouth in shock. "Oh."

"Oh?" Twist said stepping up behind the Devil.

"Ahem, let the Devil lead."

"Why the reaction?" Twist asked, "it's just an office."

"Ugh, it's barely even that. It's so humdrum. This is the seat of all power in this afterlife. The throne room of the ruler of this mediocre grey city and all within it. It's... it's not even a big office. Oh, oh, no."

"What is it?"

"There's a cat poster, that 'just hang in there' thing. This is the stuff of nightmares, and I should know!"

"You!" Twist said seeing the figure behind the desk. She strode past Beelzebub into the middle of the room and tried to plant her scythe forcefully on the floor. It caught against the ceiling and nearly slipped from her grip. "You abandoned us."

Beelzebub walked around her and took a seat opposite the skeleton. "You know Grim, even for you this is disappointing," he took the cigarette case out of his pocket and took his time selecting a smoke. "I mean, fine, the afterlife of the grey people. I suppose I can accept that. This though, this humdrummery, Grim, you're the angel of death, not some sheltered office dwelling nobody. It was only a video for crying out loud... Grim... Oh come on. It was one thing ignoring my calls, but this is just rude. I'm right here. If you continue to ignore me, I will destroy this whole place. It's an abomination."

The Devil lit the cigarette with a click of his fingers and turned to look back at Twist. "Well? Are you going to ignore her as well Grim?" He asked.

"Yes, are you?" Twist said.

The skeleton didn't move.

"Grim. You can't really expect us to believe you're reading that book. It's upside down..." the Devil paused but the skeleton didn't react, "that usually works. Grim. Grim? Are you okay?"

"Of course he's okay," Twist said, striding forward. She hit the desk with one fist, causing it to lurch to one side. The skeleton rocked. Then its head fell off.

"Oh, oh, oh, Grim?!" Beelzebub said. "What did you do? What did you do to him?"

"I didn't do anything, I just touched the table. I didn't.."

"I will destroy you," Beelzebub said, "I will make you suffer for eternity by my own hand," the Devil had his head down but Twist could feel the heat coming off him.

"Wait," she said, "please it was just... wait a minute. How do we know that's actually him?"

"What?" Beelzebub looked up, his eyes nothing but fire.

"Well... he wouldn't just put a skeleton."

"A skeleton... oh, Grim, well that's just hilarious. He's Ericed us."

"Ericed us?"

"The skeleton, it's called Eric. Your plan was to kill the bear and then what?"

"Take his soul, and all the time he has left, back to the in-between."

"Ah, happily never-nether."

"The netherworld."

"Always thought it was better called the Ebecanether myself, nobody wanted to listen. You're welcome to tag along, the bear is a nuisance. Oh, and don't mention the, ah, minor reaction I had here. Bit ah, un-Devilish, of me."

"But... where has he gone?"

"Probably trying to get out of the building so he can run to his boat."

TAKEAWAY

Ahmed stabbed with the blade, burying the knife to the hilt. Then he sawed through the dough until he could pull a hunk off before throwing it down to knead. He hated his job. It was the same thing for hours on end. Make the dough, knead the dough, twirl the dough around if there was a customer that could see him. Then slap it on the side of the clay oven and let it cook. He didn't even like flatbread.

When the door opened at the back of the kitchen, he kept his head down. He knew who it was, and it wasn't fear that made him duck away from engaging. It was the monotony of the conversation. Thirty years he had worked in the restaurant and for thirty years Death himself had been walking through the back door and making a show of, "our little secret," opining the benefits of whatever hobby the angel of death had taken to, 'please not tap dancing again.' That had been painful. Watching the Grim Reaper strap bottle caps on his skeletal feet only to prove that knowing theoretically how to do something does not equate to being able to do it.

Having his shoulder prodded by the firm chunky finger of Chief Sowercat was unexpected.

"'Ere, where's the exit?" The Chief asked.

"Who are you?" Ahmed said raising the indecently long and dangerous looking knife as he whirled to face the unexpected intruder. "Who are all of you?" He said as he stared at a group of intimidating looking people. Especially the blue one who looked like a drunk had tried to make his neck look like a Frankenstein's monster costume.

"We're…" Johnson began.

"Health inspectors," Sowercat said, "checking out restaurants in the area. We notice you've got a door that seems to lead directly into the office of the dead. Bit of hazard but we can overlook that provided there is a nearby exit to the street otherwise it's not just food standards we need to think about, it's also the fire hazard," Sowercat waggled his eyebrows in a move that corrupt officials throughout the mortal world had mastered.

"What happened to your nose?" Ahmed asked.

"How kind of you to show such concern about my nose when we might shut down this restaurant at any moment, but maybe you could wind your neck in and focus."

"I, oh, right," Ahmed said, "there's a lot of you for an inspection. It's normally just old Frank."

"Frank? Frank has got himself into a spot of bother. Turns out, and this is just between us, Frank might have been accepting bribes," Sowercat said, "That means big trouble, not just for Frank, but for anyone who might have been bribing Frank."

"Why would people who paid Frank get in trouble?" Ahmed asked.

"Well, that's attempted bribery of a government official."

"No, it's not," Ahmed said, "it's bribery. Only attempted bribery is illegal, successful bribery isn't against the law. I checked."

"You checked?" Leighton interrupted, "as in you went down to the library and looked up the law on bribery?"

Ahmed nodded as he dusted flour on to the worktop in front of him to prepare for another batch of bread. "Got to be thorough."

"I have to say," Petal interrupted, "this place is spotless, and the food smells amazing."

"You're right," Johnson said, "absolutely amazing."

"The exit. Or I'll break your legs for paying Frank bribes instead of the police, like everyone else does," Sowercat snapped.

Ahmed pointed to his right. Behind a bin, a mop, and an enormous bag of flour, was a door that led out into the street. Petal had to move the bag nobody else could manage.

With floury hands, Ahmed waved them out of the door and slammed it shut behind them.

"What now?" Johnson asked.

Sowercat turned to the ex-police officer with a scowl on his face. "I've just abandoned my men inside that lobby with a bunch of biting bastards calling themselves the living dead. You better have a bloody good idea."

"I've got one," Leighton said.

"Oh, this'll be good," Sowercat snapped, "let's all invite the free press along to the worst thing that's happened to the police in the last fifty years."

"Really?" Petal said, "What about when they uncovered your illegal arms deals."

"Nobody was using those arms anyway," Sowercat said, "they were all spares where people had bought the right arm but not the left."

"Not really the point," Leighton interrupted, "I think I should get someone who knows about science."

"Science?" Sowercat said, "that's your answer, science? Whoever believed in science?"

"That's like saying you don't believe in explaining things." Leighton said.

"No, it isn't."

"Yes, yes, it is. Science isn't a magical, mythical thing, it's what we can show, with evidence, it's the opposite of magic… except thaumaturgic science because that's the science of magic."

"Ugh, evidence again, it's always about evidence," Sowercat said.

Johnson let out a cough, a cough devoid of the attributes associated with coughing. It was a noise. "Why don't we go around the front and make sure it's safe for the people before they turn up for work. Like you said Chief. The living dead should all be moving inside."

"We shouldn't call them that," Petal said with a rumble.

"Whatever they're called," Johnson said, "are inside the building. We can barricade them into the building, keeping everyone safe."

Sowercat nodded. "Right," he said, "This is the plan. Miss Hughes is going to get some sciencey types,"

"Scientists."

"That's what I said. Petal and Johnson, you two seal off the front of the building. Okay, let's get to it."

"That is exactly what we said," Leighton said, "and what are you going to do?"

"Me?" Sowercat shaking his head, "I'm in charge, idiot."

TAXI

"And then I said, why get married at all? I mean, everyone only ends up getting divorced anyway, right? That's the problem with being dead. It goes on forever. There's no blessed relief of death at the end. Least, that's what I thought. I mean, there are exceptions to the rule, of course there is. I'm just saying that it's not always worth it. Of course, then she starts with the whole, 'why buy the cow when you can get the milk for free' stuff. I've never understood that because milk isn't free. Whoever heard of free milk? I mean, even when I was alive I never bought a cow, and I paid for milk. It's a poor analogy, a terrible analogy I tell you."

The taxi driver's name was Larry, his friends probably called him loquacious Larry, that might have given his friends too much credit, maybe Loose Lips Larry. Under normal circumstances, Leighton might have tried to direct the conversation towards something that might be useful. She was a snoop, a journalist with a nose for a story and an itch that she couldn't scratch for unearthing the truth. People like Larry knew a lot more than they thought they did about the goings on of the city, but a lot less than they thought they did about everything else.

"All's fair in love and war, Larry," she said as she scribbled notes down into the little notepad. This living dead story was going to be a big one. The problem was getting it printed. Her name was still good for getting the story. It was a little muddier working for any newspaper.

She'd started the Gloomwood Independent to subvert the big media companies, it had been a success, and success had meant she was no longer necessary. Who needs a maverick reporter with a nose for danger when you have perfectly reasonable reporters doing a good job and are selling plenty of newspapers? The answer, Leighton knew, was that people needed her stories. Newspapers didn't.

"Not true, sorry, I mean we all have our opinions but it's just not true, is it? There's no Geneva convention for love, but there is in war. Those swine will catch up to you they always do. Trust me, I should know."

Leighton caught Larry's eyes in the rear-view mirror. "War criminal, were you?"

"No, me, have you seen me?"

She had and, 'war criminal' would not have been an unfair assumption, but that wasn't the answer Larry was looking for.

"No, I was the hope that lives in the bottom of the ice-cream tub when you've finally, indisputably, ruined your relationship. Guess a lot of people have given me up, huh?"

"Uh, yeah. Listen, Larry, don't take this the wrong way, but I never really understand why some hopes are so bitter about people giving up on them."

She watched as Larry's eyebrows shot up. This was dangerous talk, but she pushed on. "Just between you and me, and please, don't take offence, I mean you brought up the hope thing really I would never…"

"No, no, go ahead. These are the kinds of things that we should be able to talk about, right?" Larry said.

"Well, you weren't an individual until you got here, right?"

"Right…"

"So, didn't people giving up on you… make you?"

Larry took a left and stopped the car at a set of traffic lights. Morning rush hour was descending upon the city. The myriad vehicles peppering the roads were growing in number. Hearses, carts pulled by bitter looking folks who still watched automobiles drive by like they were some kind of evil magic, bicycles, motorbikes, even a powered penny-farthing.

"It's complicated. I mean, are you happy you're dead?"

She pushed out her bottom lip, then blew out air. "Yeah, I suppose it's the same thing. I'm dead. Nobody is glad they're dead, but death isn't all that bad."

"You got it, lady. We're all dead, nobody wants to be dead, but death could be worse, right? So what's going on at the Office of the Dead?"

"What do you mean?"

"Listen to this," Larry turned up the radio, the speakers in the back of the taxi crackled, they were tinny but clear.

'… blocked from entering Dead Square by official barriers ordered by the Grim Reaper as a clear domestic terrorist threat is taking place. We're here with Ralph Mortimer, who is manning one of the two cordons. We could not speak to the Manager of the Office of the Dead who is managing the other cordon as he has instigated a queuing system and anyone who tries to jump it is being issued with a survey.'

'Mister Mortimer, is it true this attack is being carried out by resurrection fundamentalists?'

'I'm afraid we're not able to comment upon the threat.'

'Can you tell us anything about the situation?'

'The police have it in hand and we expect to be returning to normal in due course.'

'Mister Mortimer… wait… is that a… are those toys?'

A loud screech interrupted the radio signal.

Looks like we're experiencing technical difficulties, ladies and gentlemen, but we'll return to our man on the scene as soon as we can. In the meantime, here's Gareth Knowles with his cover of that classic, 'Dead Eyes you're the one.'

"Well," Larry asked, "you're a reporter, and you were down that way."

"No idea," Leighton said, wishing, not for the first time, that Morgarth had not stayed behind the reception desk.

UNEXPECTED

Crispin Neat removed his bicycle helmet. His hair remained perfectly set in place. A side parting of severe and accurate delineation. His movements were precise as he folded the bicycle down until it was the size of a briefcase. It was still as heavy as a bicycle, but now would hurt a lot more if dropped or bumped into somebody. Marketers of the bicycle praised its value as a hand held bludgeoning device but Neat had bought it because he didn't believe it safe to leave a bicycle lying around no matter how many locks you had. Gloomwood thieves are tenacious.

He removed the bicycle clips from around his ankles, ensuring that there was no trouser wrinkling. There was nothing he could do if there was wrinkling. It would force him to endure the humiliation of a wrinkled ankle until he was in his own office, unless it was a truly horrific wrinkle, in which case he would reassemble the bicycle and return home to change. There was no wrinkling.

With one hand he lifted the bicycle. It was heavy, but not a glimmer of a grimace graced his face. He strode towards the Office of the Dead. He could have ridden the bicycle closer, but the cobblestones were an unpleasant ride. Nobody needs that first thing in the morning.

As he rounded the corner he heard, in the distance, something resembling... no, definite screams. To the casual observer it would not have been apparent that anything changed, but Crispin Neat quickened his pace. Not enough to be visible. He wasn't doing anything as unseemly as rushing.

Around the next corner, there was a barrier. A line created by wrapping kitchen roll around two lampposts on either side of the cobbled street. A large blue man was running between the lampposts, wrapping more and more paper as it disintegrated in the rain.

"What's happening?" Neat asked a man and woman who were wearing the black suits customary for employees of the

Office of the Dead. The man had his bowler hat in place but, Neat noted, no umbrella.

"Oh, Mister Neat, sir, sorry we're late, sir," the woman, who had her umbrella, answered

"You continue to be late as we're standing out on the street. Charlotte Winks, isn't it?" Neat said, keeping his voice a semi-tone of disdain away from condescension.

"Yes, sir, Mister Neat, sir. Ah, this man says there is a domestic terror threat currently in progress and that this line is an official barricade as ordered by the Grim Reaper himself."

"As ordered by the Grim Reaper, I see, and has he shown you paperwork?" Neat asked.

"Paper... paperwork? No, sir."

"You call yourself a bureaucrat and you didn't even ask for paperwork? Disappointing," Neat said. He shook his head once then, pointedly, raised his umbrella. Clicking the button on the side, it burst into shape above him.

A bumbershoot was the term Neat preferred, there was something more elegant about a bumbershoot. "You sir," he said as he walked towards the barricade, "I need to see your paperwork."

"No, you don't." Petal said without pausing in his jog from one side of the street to the other, "You need to step back."

"As the manager of the..." Neat began.

"Mister Neat, we've met. Long time ago now," Petal said as he stopped running. He held a roll of kitchen roll in one hand as the rain hammered down on this perfectly clean-shaven blue head. "Do you remember?"

"Petal. Yes, I remember."

"Crispin," Petal said, "this is serious. The Devil is here, and the Grim Reaper is in trouble."

Neat nodded once. "Don't tell anyone else that, please. It makes cleaning up afterwards much more difficult. What about the other street?"

"Johnson is doing that."

"Johnson... you mean the ex-police officer?"

"He's more than that but, yes."

"Hm, Mister Mortimer comes via that street. I will take care of this, join your... is he your."

"Yes, he's my boyfriend. Why is this so difficult to comprehend? Two men,"

"Men?" Neat asked, "you think people are that closed minded? That kind of thinking has never existed here."

"Oh, so I suppose a deity shouldn't be with a Hope?"

"You're very full of prejudice. It's the idea of an infamous violent criminal being in a relationship with an equally well-known do-gooder that's strange."

"Oh... right. That makes more sense. I'm retired from the violence- Oi," Petal pointed over Neat's shoulder, "if you even touch this kitchen roll I will tear your arms off and make it so you can give yourself a high-five in your own stomach, am I clear?"

"You were saying about retiring from violence?" Neat said.

"Semi-retired then. So, I just leave you here to deal with this?"

"I run this city. Tell Mortimer that this is a code thirty-seven G."

"Thirty-seven G?"

"He'll know what it means. Is there anything else I need to know?"

"The living dead are biting people in the Office of the Dead, but the police are chopping all their heads off. Blunt is dealing with the bear, and the Devil is here."

"Bear, police, Blunt, and the Devil?"

"Yeah, the actual Devil."

Neat's right eye twitched. "I see, and the bear?"

"Teddington Rex, off the telly, he's alive."

"He's filming it live?"

"No, he's literally alive, as in not really dead."

"I see. Well then, shall we get to work?"

THE EASY WAY

When the elevator doors opened Blunt stepped out into the lobby before he had time to process the scene in front of him. As the doors rattled closed behind him he stepped backwards, desperately pressing the call button so the doors would reopen. A mound of thirty heads in a pyramid shape filled the centre of the lobby, as if Blunt had walked in on a new supermarket readying its displays for the day. Some looked in his direction. Standing at the top of the pyramid was a stuffed lion. In its paws it was holding a walking stick, a cane. The cane had a head for a pommel, and it was talking.

"-and lo, the living rose to cast aside the dead. Such things must happen, but the end is still to come. Nation will rise against nation, and kingdom against kingdom. There will be famines and earthquakes in various places. All these are the beginning of birth pains."

"Oh… bollocks," Blunt said, "this looks bad."

"Does it?" the Grim Reaper said, "could you perhaps describe it? It might be helpful."

"Uh. There are about a hundred people milling round. Some of them are eating other people. There's a gigantic pile of decapitated heads, and there are a couple of police officers who are hacking off the heads of the people who are eating them. Then there's a woman's head on a stick shouting."

"New testament, Matthew 24, I can hear, I can't see," the Grim Reaper said.

"Does it help?"

"Religion is a complicated subject. Some people find solace in their faith, it can do great things, but then there are others who twist the intent of such things."

"I wasn't asking if religion helps. I meant, does it help us get out of here?"

The sound of flesh being torn and chewed, the snapping of bones, and the indistinct murmur of unintelligible moaning faded. All eyes that could move turned to Blunt.

"Sorry," Blunt said to the room, "got off on the wrong floor," he shrugged as the elevator behind him rang a bell signalling its arrival.

"Heathen!" Molly screamed, "where is the Grim Reaper?"

"Grim Reaper? Never heard of him, the Happy Reaper is a restaurant mascot, I've met him, nice bloke." Blunt said, stepping backwards as the doors opened.

"Get him," the head on the stick shouted while the toy holding her in the air thrust her toward Blunt.

Inside the lift Blunt pressed the door closed button while watching the decrepit figures lurching towards him. Some of them, dressed in the familiar grey of the Gloomwood police, moved faster than others.

"Blunt," one of them said, "you're a bastard."

"I know," Blunt shouted back at the man who was holding a serrated bread knife in one hand, "everyone bloody knows."

"It's just a little bite," another said, "don't even hurt. Then you're alive!"

"Are you? That's nice."

"Don't run away, you coward. We're going to the mortal realm."

"Why don't you piss off to it and leave me alone?" Blunt said as the doors started to close. They stopped midway to closing and Blunt hammered the button. "Bloody doors."

"There's a stairwell to the right," Death said as quietly as he could manage.

From her position, behind the protective screen of the reception desk, Morgarth the Destroyer watched.

MINIONS

"Clive, Vellmar, Garglemier, Dysentrous, Trevor, Bilious Fogg, I thought of that one myself it's a Jules Verne riff, brilliant, Agonisious, Killy, Severnicus, Kyderican, Lafrayer, and Arazaiphi… eal.. o.. mus. Yes? These are the twelve apostles, or they were, but that whole thing seems to have gone down the pan. Demons, meet Twist Lenworth, she is not to be disembowelled, dismembered, or discorporated in any way unless I say so. She's on team Beelzebub."

The twelve soft toys nodded, at least the ones that could, did.

Twist nodded with them. "This is the elite demonic guard?"

"Don't let their appearance fool you, Miss Lenworth, they're more than a match for anyone in this miserable little afterlife."

"Some of them are stronger than they seem," Twist said.

Beelzebub raised one perfectly shaped eyebrow, "You mean the big blue one?"

"Yes, he was strong, faster than I expected."

"There are some exceptions. Come along now demons, today's the day the Teddy Bears have a picnic!"

RUN

Some people run like they are born to it. The practised gait, the smooth action. There are natural runners, natural fighters, natural dancers. There was nothing natural about the way Augustan Blunt ran. He ran like every step was a guess. He'd been told the best and fairest description was flailing and failing. With the nuanced misstep of a man who lived life on the edge of total collapse, he careened around corners.

He heaved, huffed and puffed, with the desperate breathing of someone who was moments from hyperventilating into a paper bag, All of this was in despite of repeating, in his head like the deranged mantra of a diver suffering from nitrogen narcosis, 'I don't need to breathe'.

He was correct. The reason blood was a luxury item for the dead was because respiration was unnecessary. The energy that was used to propel the body wasn't any kind of cellular metabolism. Cells, in the afterlife, were rooms with bars on the windows. Haemoglobin was only a word used for pretentious band names. Despite all this, despite the abandonment of the Krebs cycle, the worthlessness of diffusion across alveoli, Blunt continued to huff and puff.

Death isn't a problem. Death is nothing at all. The problem is letting go of life. Like an addict who cannot put down their drug of choice, life holds on. Habits are hard to kick.

In Gloomwood there is a football league. It's highly competitive and extremely lucrative, and the best players are not the fittest, strongest, or tallest. They are the deadest. The more dead you are, the less you need to concern yourself with fitness, it is willpower that determines physical ability.

Blunt was familiar with will power. It wasn't a friend of his. As shown by his inability to stop drinking, smoking, and being self-destructive. He was also, in Gloomwood terms, fresh.

Over his right shoulder, gripped in one hand, held like that one shopping bag carried even though it's too heavy, overloaded, and has a handle that might snap, was the black bag. The cheap bag that still had embossed on one side of it the name of a gym that had shut down a decade ago on one side. The same bag that contained the only living person in the city of Gloomwood. The same person who was a thieving little bastard. The black bag that also contained Death himself.

"Ouch," the Grim Reaper said.

"Shut up," Blunt shouted between ragged breaths. With his free hand, he shoved his hat on to his head once again. There was a rhythm to it. Every three steps, mush hat. Stride, stride, mush, stride, stride, mush, his feet carried him towards the emergency exit. Dodging wayward arms and legs that attempted to slow him, grab him, and convert him to the cause.

"How... did.. the... police... not... beat... these... idiots?" He wheezed.

"In the thick of battle identifying friend and foe becomes difficult, then the fog descends and," Death said.

"Stop talking. They're after you more than me."

"Could you run a little smoother," Ted's voice came from the bag, "this chafes."

"Chafes?" Blunt said as he kicked the metal bar across the emergency exit. The green sign above it had a flickering light. "You're chafing? Do I strike you as someone who likes a run, did you think, ooh, nice running gear when you saw what I'm wearing? My inner thighs feel like I'm holding a cheese grater between them and don't get me started on..."

TEAM MEETING

The second lift arrived with a trill of its bell. When the doors opened Beelzebub stepped out followed closely by Twist Lenworth and twelve stuffed toys.

"Hello Molly," Beelzebub said, giving the head on a stick a wave, "And hello living dead!" Beelzebub put his hands behind his back and beamed that wide jagged grin.

Those who had not given chase to Detective Blunt, because they were still aware enough to realise they had no hope of catching him, eyed the Devil.

"Ah, I see your great leader failed to mention that it was I, Beelzebub, who brought you all here, and brought you to life."

"De-vil?" A woman in police uniform with a pair of broken legs, they were hers, said.

"Yes," Beelzebub clapped his hands, "well done. I am the reason you have all come back to life. Now, all we have to do is find the Grim Reaper, and the teddy bear. When we've got them we kill the teddy bear, because he's alive too, and then the gateway to the mortal realm will tear through space and time and we all scuttle in there wreaking havoc all in time for the end of days! Yay us!"

"Teddy bear?" Molly asked.

"Ah, yes Molly, sacrifices must be made."

"What teddy bear?"

"Oh, he's quite famous, I understand. On the television, some kind of spurious talk show?"

"I don't watch television."

"No, of course you don't," Beelzebub said, "so, I don't suppose the Grim Reaper has come through this way?"

The furry lion holding Molly's head turned the cane, so she shook her head.

"Stop doing that," Molly said, "but no, we haven't. The only person who came through was a man in a hat and coat who ran away."

"The detective," Twist said with a sneer, "he left when I arrived."

"Ah, so nobody for a good hour?" Beelzebub said.

"No," Molly said, "it was two minutes ago. He was carrying a bag, and he ran off up the stairs."

"Leggit," a constable slurred.

Beelzebub frowned and turned to look at Twist. "He was here before you?"

"Yes, I told you, he delivered the bear to the Grim Reaper."

"I need to make a call," Beelzebub said, pulling his phone from his pocket.

💀 STAIRWAY TO BARBARA 💀

"Fourth floor?" Blunt said.

"Are they still chasing us?" Ted asked from within the bag.

"Yes, of course they're still chasing us. They're zombies."

"They're not," said the Grim Reaper.

"Why not? Seems to fit the definition to me," Ted said.

"Please," Blunt said between breaths, "just stop talking." He pushed open the door to the fourth floor and stepped through it into a cavernous office space. Row upon row of depressing grey cubicles filled the area. "Right. Get out of the bag," Blunt said. He unzipped it and tipped it upside down so that the contents spilled out onto the near-black carpet tiles. "We need an alternative plan."

Ted sat up when he rolled out of the bag as he scattered metatarsals and other small bones. "Where are we?"

"The fourth floor. I already told you."

The Grim Reaper's bones began pulling themselves together, and with growing momentum, he took form. "Robe," his voice came from a whirlwind of skeletal parts, "robe, now!"

Blunt grabbed the black cloth and held it out. A skeletal hand reached out from the spinning hurricane and snatched the cloth away. When the spinning stopped the Grim Reaper stood looming. "You didn't see anything, did you?"

"Just a load of bones," Blunt said.

"What else is there to see?" Ted asked.

"I don't want you to see me naked, it's unbecoming."

"I've been in a bag with you for over an hour, wasn't that unbecoming?" The bear asked as it looked up at the Grim Reaper through one button eye.

"Possibly," Grim said.

The door behind Blunt clicked shut, punctuating the silence of the office space. The cubicles were near identical. Even the attempts to personalise the space by adding individual flourishes were near uniform. A quirky figurine, a photo of a loved one, a handmade cushion on a standard issue black wheeled chair, a calendar of Burke and Hare's best bits showcasing top end custom bodies that only the richest could afford, then the cycle would repeat. A doll, a photo, a mug that says, 'don't talk to me until I've had this coffee', a calendar, a cushion. "Is this Hell?" Ted asked.

"No," Grim replied, "you will beg to be somewhere like this when you get to Hell."

"I'm... I'm definitely going then?" Ted said.

"No," Grim said as he started walking between the cubicles, "nothing is written in stone."

"Except stone carvings," Blunt said.

"Yes, the detective is correct, some things are written in stone, or carved in stone, perhaps it's engraved, anyway, some things are, but not you going to Hell."

Ted scurried after the Grim Reaper. Blunt hesitated, looked at the door they had just walked through, then shoved a chair under the handle. "That should keep them out for... that will not keep them out. Where are we going?" He shouted after Ted and the Grim Reaper who were halfway across the room.

"But I stole that time, and then..."

"I don't believe time stealing is a factor. Not that it wasn't evil, it was evil, very evil, but you were already dead and so it shouldn't really count. What you have done since stealing it will be taken into consideration, and what you did before you died... the first time. Unless," Grim stopped and tapped a finger against his chin. "Judgement took place once so we may have a case of double jeopardy."

"Double jeopardy?" Ted said.

Blunt tripped on a chair and shoved it to one side. "This is fascinating, really, but where are you going? There's a horde of zombies in your lobby and you're talking to the only living person in this city. Don't you think you need to fix it?"

"We have discussed this, Detective. I am neutral. Anyway, why do you care?"

Blunt sighed, "I don't want them to eat me alive."

"Good. There's no chance of that happening. They might eat you dead, though. Ah, here we are."

They stopped in front of an office door. On the door was a plastic plaque. The type that came with a strip of paper on the back that you peeled off to reveal a sticky layer of glue. The cheap kind. On it was one word, Barbara.

"Who's Barbara?" Blunt asked.

The Grim Reaper turned to look at Blunt, "Barbara is the operating system."

"Ah, so it's a clever acronym that spells Barbara?" Ted asked.

"No," Grim said, reaching out to the silver doorknob, "her name is Barbara," the Grim Reaper gripped the knob with one hand but hesitated to turn it. "Barbara can be a bit... antisocial and this isn't just her office, it's her home, so be polite."

"Polite," Blunt said, "I can be polite."

"Can you?" Ted asked.

A buzzing sound interrupted their conversation, and the Grim Reaper reached inside his robes. He pulled out the phone and sighed as he looked at the display, "It's the Devil again."

"Isn't that only supposed to happen when we speak about him?" Blunt asked.

"Does anyone else ever call you?" Ted asked.

"No," the Grim Reaper replied, "to both of you." He tapped the front of the screen several times, with increasing intensity, until it responded then placed the phone at the side of his head. "What is it, Beezy?"

"Ah, Grim, you finally answered."

"Where are you?"

"In the Office of the Dead building, where are you?"

"In my office," Grim said.

"No, I've been there. It was nice to see Eric again though, it's been a while."

"What do you want?"

"I want the bear."

"If I let you have the bear, you'll kill it and then this afterlife will collapse on itself removing these souls."

"Don't worry, I'll offer them a place with me."

"In Hell?"

"Obviously."

"I don't think they'll like it."

"That won't really change anything, Grim. Come on now, it's over."

"No, I'm taking the bear out of the city."

"Oh? Interesting... so the boat is here."

"No, it isn't."

"It is."

"It's not. I'm going to leave through the Deathport."

"Grim, you're a terrible liar."

"I don't know what you're talking about," Grim said, then he prodded at the phone screen several times.

"Are you trying to hang up on me?" Beelzebub asked on the other side of the phone.

"Stop talking, it ruins the effect."

"There's one of those little blue stickers you used to wear inside the phone case for the touchscreen."

"Really? That's very thoughtful of you... Thank you. Now goodbye, you source of all that is evil."

"Ciao for now."

Death hit the screen a few more times, then turned to Blunt. "Could you press the red hang up icon? I'm not very good with touchscreens, no skin you see."

WAIT

"You want us to wait here?" Molly asked.

"Yes, exactly. Meanwhile, I, my elite guard, and Miss Lenworth will prevent their escape," Beelzebub said walking towards the rotating doors.

"But why are you leaving then?"

"Because you are the deterrent. They will not come back down, but now I know where they're going."

"So you're just abandoning us here?"

The Devil grinned. "Have some faith, Molly. When I have the bear in my possession, I will return and open the path to the mortal realm by cutting its furry little throat. Releasing a living soul here will cause huge rips in the veil's fabric, and we'll all step through back to the land of the living."

"So we wait?"

"Correct."

DEADER

Johnson stood with Ralph Mortimer, third assistant to the Manager of the Office of the Dead. A stalwart champion of all things Gloomwood. Mortimer was the man who collected every stamp on his free cup of coffee card and then kept it in his wallet for a rainy day rather than spend it. The person who knew exactly how much change was in the space by the handbrake of his car. Mortimer was the ideal bureaucrat. The ultimate in mundane, unobtrusive, head down, work before play, professionalism.

"This is a disaster," Johnson said.

"Yes, well, mustn't grumble."

"Why?"

"It's… inefficient? I suppose, maybe? But then complaining builds camaraderie and team spirit… so yes, this is quite terrible. I agree," Mortimer said. He had his hands in his pockets and was turning from side to side as he spoke, as if with a little more momentum he would spin around. "So tell me again about the living dead."

"I only know that they bite someone else and then that person goes crazy. They all say, 'I'm so hungry' and 'I'm alive' then they bite other people. I can't see how biting anyone has anything to do with being alive, but then I wasn't ever a person. Did you bite many people when you were alive?"

"I… oh, no, not really. People frown on biting others. I would never bite someone. Though I suppose if they bit me I wouldn't have a choice."

Johnson nodded, "it looked that way," he was holding a truncheon in one hand and a cleaver he had picked up from Patrick's Curry House, courtesy of Ahmed, in the other. Ready for the impending onslaught of the living dead if the police failed in their attempt to contain the problem. That was the phrase Sowercat had told them to use.

'The police are working on containing the problem. They will ensure that it does not progress any further. We are to keep a safe perimeter around the building until we are told otherwise. Anyone who gets closer will put themselves at risk, and they cannot hold us responsible for what might happen. For that reason we may legally hurt you if you try to walk past us.' Sowercat had made them repeat it, like school children rote learning, at least that's what Sowercat had said it was like. Neither Petal nor Johnson had ever been to school.

"Is that them?" Mortimer said, "they don't look that bad. Do their bodies change that much."

"No, that's not them," Johnson said as he watched the figures marching towards them. Twelve stuffed toys, the man in the suit, and the woman who had decapitated Petal. "They might be worse. Clear a path," he shouted to the crowd of people around him.

"Allow me," Mortimer said, "according to article 472 addendum 3b you are to vacate the central column of the surrounding area to ensure a lack of impediments for journeys considered essential during times of emergency. Should you wish not to move, please complete form 473 addendum 6e and post it to the Office of the Dead permissions department." When Mortimer finished, he gave a small smile and nodded. The queuing employees shifted immediately. The void that remained was littered with confused members of the public and rogue reporters who, seeing their cover blown, jumped out of the limelight immediately.

"That was impressive," Johnson said.

"Thank you, but I'm only doing my job."

The two men turned to watch the Devil and his entourage approach.

"So kind of you to clear a path," Beelzebub said as he drew closer. "Should I introduce myself or will you be sensible and keep out of the way?"

"No," Johnson said. "There is still law here."

Beelzebub smiled, that grin that stretched too far, too long, that threatened to see the top of his head topple off. Then he snapped his fingers and John Jacob Jeremiah Johnson melted.

He didn't scream or thrash. Panic flashed across his face for a moment but, mercifully, it was quick. With a glance down at his feet, he knew he saw his doom. His boots, and feet inside them, sizzled then evaporated as if the cobblestones he stood upon had been super-heated. He turned to Ralph Mortimer and spoke his last words in Death, "tell Petal to stay calm."

Then there was nothing but steam.

Beelzebub smirked as he walked past Ralph Mortimer, who had no words to say.

"Shame about that," a woman with a scythe said.

BARBARA

The Grim Reaper opened the door, then poked his skull inside the darkened room. "Barbara? It's me, Death, are you in?"

Blunt stood on his toes, trying to peer into the darkness beyond the doorway, but the Grim Reaper was too tall.

After waiting a moment the Grim Reaper turned to face the detective and the bear, he kept his skeletal grip on the door handle. "Hm, she may be in a mood, or amid a pan-dimensional way, she's not of this universe."

"Actually," a voice came from within the room and a pressure like force threw Blunt and Ted across the room. Blunt landed on a desk with a shout of pain, scattering sticky notes and a computer monitor onto the floor. "I was in the middle of a team assault. My clan will not be happy."

"You have a clan?" Grim asked.

"It's in a game. Why are you here? You're supposed to knock."

"I was wondering if you could point the way out of the building that doesn't involve the ground floor."

"That would be a window," the voice from within said.

Blunt was crawling behind a row of desks, trying to find his hat. He spotted it underneath the next desk along.

"Yes," Grim said, "but it's quite a long drop from here."

"Did you really open the door to the eternal abyss just to ask me which window to climb out of?" The voice asked.

The voice of whoever was beyond the doorway was a screeching sound like fingernails down a blackboard and with every word spoken he winced as he inched towards his hat. Just as his fingertips grazed the edge of the brim something lifted it to reveal a pair of blue fluffy dinosaur feet. "Shh," Morgarth said, "just put me in the bag."

The Grim Reaper was leaning against his scythe, his head tilted to one side. "There's no need to get cranky, Barbara. I have a bit of a situation here and I just thought I'd pop my head in to see if you might help."

"Because?"

"It's your building."

"No, it isn't. I gave it to you."

"Barbara. I'm only asking-"

"Grim, I have been AFK for several minutes and Jethro in Connecticut gets all stroppy if we drop out during a mission."

"Jethro?"

"If I get kicked out of the clan, I will destroy the multiverse and start again."

"You can't just... Fine Barbara, but I'll remember this."

"Ugh, the window on the west side of the building by that busy-body Carol's office is at the same height as the restaurant roof next door. You can climb out there, walk across the roof, and then drop through the doughnut shop."

"You mean the cafe?"

"It's a doughnut shop, everyone knows it's a doughnut shop," the door slammed shut, pulling the Grim Reaper's hand off.

Death pulled his own hand off the door and reattached it at the wrist while Blunt joined him. "Well," the detective asked, "who the hell is Barbara?"

"Barbara is a trans-dimensional being who... sort of came with the building. I was hoping she'd just sort magic us out of here, to be honest."

"Just sort of magic us? Are you being serious?"

"Oh yes, I never joke about things I don't understand. Where's the bear?"

"Ur?" A voice said behind Blunt.

The detective turned to find himself face to face with a woman who seemed like she might have had better days. "Zombie!" Grim shouted before instinctively throwing a wild fist in her direction.

The Grim Reaper's hand caught his wrist.

"Good morning Carol, you're in early."

"Ugh, morning sir, I fell asleep at my desk, woke up as the reconfiguration was happening. Shan't complain though, it looks like my office only moved a few feet. Who's this? Was he going to punch me? Did you call me a zombie?"

"Long story Carol," Grim said, "he's a bit out of sorts. I wonder if you could show me your office, and specifically, the window."

"Alright then, did Barbara call me a busy-body again?" The disheveled looking Carol asked as they followed her between desks. As they did, a sheepish-looking Ted ran up behind Blunt and tugged on his ankle. Blunt grabbed the bear and shoved him into his pocket behind Carol's back. As he zipped it up, a squawk of fright came from within it along with a scuffle. He slapped at the back and held it tight against his body with his right arm.

Carol turned to stare at Blunt.

"Sorry," Blunt patted his chest, "indigestion."

"Here is the window," not sure why it's so fascinating.

"Thank you. I would suggest you knock on Barbara's door and tell her I asked her to hide you."

"Hide me?"

"Mhm, for the best, I think. The building is under attack."

"From who?"

"Very unpleasant people. I'm sure Barbara won't mind."

"She's a weirdo, you know. Keeps her room in complete darkness and never leaves. I'm sure she's doing something strange in there."

"Yes, I'm quite sure she is, but as a being who doesn't exist in this dimension, she probably has a very different understanding of social norms compared to us."

"Yeah," Carol shrugged, "I mean, who am I to judge?"

"Quite," Death said as he opened the window.

DRUMS

Beelzebub was humming. Twist didn't recognise the song, but he was humming. A strange tune that had a rhythm to it that was almost infectious.

"What is that song?"

"Hm," Beelzebub said, "oh, I forgot you were there. An old song. Come along, we must hurry. The walking dead thing is petering out. If they set sail, then you can't have your time back."

"What's in this for you?" Twist asked.

"Me? It's just a job. Destroying this place. I will harvest the souls and, as they have defied being pigeon-holed into any religion, I'll keep them for myself."

"So you're doing this for the souls? Because you seemed pretty upset when that skeleton's head fell off."

"Mind your own business reaper. I wanted to see the look on Grim's face when he lost all of this to me."

"His face?"

"Don't do that. He hates it when people do that."

"The Grim Reaper?"

Beelzebub stopped and looked at her. Taking in the long coat, the vicious but elegant scythe, the way she held herself. "You look like a singer, do you sing?"

"Changing the subject."

"I understand you fought the blue Demi-god."

"I did."

"And you're still here. That's impressive. You may need to do that again."

"You've got these demons."

"They won't fight him."

"They won't? Don't they do as you command?"

"I won't fight him either. You can, though. There's nothing in the rules about you fighting him. Come along now and be ready."

The twelve demons trapped in the bodies of soft toys followed behind them in a line. Twist could hear them talking to each other in low voices. Snickering and snarling, their eyes glowed red, and she felt their aggression when they looked in her direction. Like they were hungry. Like she was food.

They neared the wall, and what she saw in the distance intrigued her.

SWEET ENOUGH

Blunt exited the cafe, or doughnut shop depending on who you spoke to, covered from head to toe in powdered sugar. Over one shoulder he carried the bag once again containing the body of the Grim Reaper and now two sentient stuffed toys.

"I don't see why you couldn't have waited until after we'd walked across the roof and fallen into a tonne of powdered sugar to get into the bag."

"Because the Grim Reaper creeping across a rooftop in the early hours of the morning fleeing a dramatic hostage situation might have raised questions. Also, I'm sweet enough already. Are you sure you're a detective?" Grim said.

"There's no need to be rude," Blunt said.

"There was also no need to refuse to grab me a doughnut on our way out, either, Detective, but that didn't stop you."

He shouldered the bag, a little more roughly than he needed to, and started jogging. There are positives to a city full of the weird and macabre. A man running through the streets covered in powdered sugar didn't raise many eyebrows. The back door of the cafe had led them to an alleyway beyond the barriers and lines of waiting Office of the Dead employees, but he caught the tail end of an orderly queue talking as he slowed.

"Demonstrative terrorism."

"Nah, I heard it was demotivational terrorism."

"It's the Manager of the Office of the Dead up there, he's not going to make a mistake. Keeps waving about his umbrella."

"I believe the official term is bumbershoot."

"There's an official term?"

The detective quickened his pace once again. Mumbling under his breath, to the tune of 'remember you're a womble', "remember you were murdered." It wasn't inventive, but it seemed to help him quell the instinctive need he had to gasp for air.

"Beelzebub has removed Johnson from the game," Grim said.

"What does that even mean?" Blunt said. He was slowing down, the pace too much for him. He slowed to a stop and put his hand against a lamppost.

"It means John Jacob Jeremiah Johnson isn't here anymore."

"He was never here," Ted said, "he was back at the Office of the Dead."

"That's not what I was saying," Grim said.

"He's... he's Ableforthed Johnson?" Blunt said between breaths.

"What?" Ted said, "but Jayjay was a good guy. He was the good guy. Jayjay and Petal helped me, even when there was nothing in it for them. They're my friends."

Blunt coughed, a long hacking disgusting cough. He wiped his mouth on the sleeve of his coat and stood up. "You haven't got friends, you are a thieving little bastard."

"I've more friends than you," Ted snapped back.

"How far, Detective?" Grim asked.

"Just around the corner... um... we might have a problem," Blunt was looking down the street towards the wall that marked the edge of the city. Lined up atop the wall, and milling around the base, were toys. All different shapes and sizes.

SOWERCAT'S STAND

Chief Sowercat of the Gloomwood police had waved away the citizens he had escorted out of the building and turned around. He was confident they would do what they needed, but his goal had only been to get them out of the building. He tied the dish towel he had taken from the kitchen around his face like a bandana covering the mess of his nose, then walked to the front of the restaurant.

He'd hammered on the door until, after a stream of obscenities that had neighbours leaning out of windows to heckle him, Ahmed had opened the door.

"You again?"

"Me again," Sowercat said to the confused chef, "I'm going to need two of your biggest knives."

Nobody thought the Gloomwood police had principles. Sowercat was their captain for a lot of reasons. He was a liar, a thief, a charlatan, a thug, and worse, but above all of them he was the Chief of police and he would be damned if he was going to walk out while the rest of the city's police eaten by a horde of decomposing brain-washed bitey dullards. There was only one kind of numbskull who got to strut around the city delivering unprovoked violence, and that was the police.

"You want me to barricade the door?" Ahmed asked.

"Unless you're cooking people, then nobody in there is going to be good for business."

"I thought you were a food inspector."

"You didn't really think that, did you?"

Ahmed shook his head, "it's easier not to argue."

"Barricade the door. Whatever you hear, whatever anybody says, this door stays shut, forever, understood?" Sowercat said as he hefted the two knives, "are these sharp?"

The chef rolled his eyes, "yes they're sharp. I don't suppose I'll get them back?"

Sowercat shook his head. "It's not likely, but, for both our sakes, I hope so."

"They're only knives," Ahmed shrugged, "it's not that big a deal."

"I'm being heroic."

"By stealing my knives?"

"No, by, forget it. Do me a favour and don't tell anyone you saw me. I'd rather not spoil my image."

"That's pretty funny for a man with your face."

"Hah, hilarious. I call for a little encouragement and you give me that."

"I've been robbed a few times, but this is probably the weirdest. Who asks for encouragement for stealing knives?"

"I'm about to embark on a quest to rescue every officer in the Gloomwood police, putting my very existence on the line, shut up about the knives."

"Okay, if you say so, I'm going to get back to making bread. I have a death to make, you know? I'll wait half an hour before calling the police. They rarely turn up until lunchtime anyway, and then they steal half my bhajis."

"I... right. Bye then."

"Shove off."

WAR

Mortimer was on his knees. His hands pulling at the clothes that lay there. The heavy wool coat had seen better days. A wallet that was threadbare and empty. Inside it was Johnson's driving license and a picture of Petal.

"No, this doesn't make sense," Mortimer was muttering, rambling, "can't just do that. Why? Who would do that?"

"What's going on?"

Mortimer fell to one side as he turned to address the person who spoke. "You can't be here, this is an official barricade."

"I know. Crispin Neat sent me to tell you that this is a thirty… thirty-seven…"

"A thirty-seven G, yes thank you. You are?"

"Petal."

"Oh," Mortimer couldn't stop the tremor in his voice as he looked up, "I see. This. A man came out of the building with a woman, and toys."

"Is Johnson following them? What's with the clothes."

"The clothes…"

"Is that… why do you have Jay's wallet?"

"He. He said to tell you to stay calm. So, um, 'stay calm'."

"Jay said that? Where is he?"

"He was right here. Then that man came out of the building. He was wearing a suit, and he was red. Was it the Devil? Maybe the Devil could do this."

"Where is he?"

"I don't know. The Devil did something and then he just melted and I'm so sorry, I'm so, so sorry."

"Melted… you mean this. No, that's ridiculous. Jay can take care of himself."

"I was standing right next to him."

"No."

"I just."

"No."

"…"

"NO."

Mortimer scuttled backwards on his hands and knees. His eyes locked on the big blue man.

"NOT JAY, NO, NO, NO," Petal shouted. The streetlight closest to them shattered, spraying the crowd with glass. His hands curled into fists. The wound around his neck seemed to glow, then vanished. With a cry of anguish he smashed his fist into the cobblestones, pounding a hole through the stone. His eyes were alight with flickering blue flames that came from somewhere within. "This shall not stand," he said, his voice deep, resonant.

Something inside him broke. A torrent of repressed memories flooded forward. What poor barricade had blocked out those things that had come before, shattered. The dam that built in terror and held together by love, burst.

Petal Stormbreaker was the name he had taken for himself. A name plucked from the air without thought or consideration, but he'd liked it. The days since he had strode across the fields of battle stoking fires of violence and laying waste to all and sundry had passed, but they would return.

"P-Petal, are you, can I get you something?" Mortimer asked, being sure to keep a safe distance between himself and the seemingly unstable figure who was staring at the hole he had smashed into the very ground they stood upon.

"Petal," he didn't lift his head, "was the man who loved John Jacob Jeremiah Johnson, but there is no longer a man of that name. Petal too must die. Look upon me now, little man. Strange little man with your suits and ties, your polished shoes, and your bumbershoot."

"I... you don't sound okay."

"Look upon me and remember that stirring inside. That furious rage and tempestuous thirst for battle,"

"You sound a little funny. Maybe a cup of tea? A cup of tea usually helps."

"I am War, hoarse man of the apocalypse, and I bring the bass."

"What? Now you're not even making sense. Horseman?"

Petal stood up, "I said, hoarse man, and I bring the bass."

TOY ARMY

Blunt was not a warrior. He believed in right and wrong and he would stand up for others, but the only fight Blunt wanted to be in was the kind where everyone either shook hands at the end, or that left the other side with a good kicking. His natural gifts lay in taking a beating and scaring the crap out of people without ever hurting anyone. Blunt was the threat of violence encapsulated in the body of a man who might end up winning a fight through sheer bloody-mindedness, but definitely not skill.

"Any of you bastard toys gets in my way and I will rip out your guts and fold you inside out," he bellowed, "that sounds a lot scarier when you're not already a toy."

"Whatever," a rag doll said, tossing her woollen braids over one shoulder. "Just get on with whatever you're doing. We're waiting for someone."

"Oh, fair enough," Blunt said, "um, who are you waiting for?"

"Death or the Devil, whoever comes first, that alright with you?"

Blunt nodded. "Yup, sorry, just asking. Bit of an unusual group, that's all. Anyway, coming through, coming through." He waded through the toys feeling like Gulliver in Lilliput muttering pleasantries the whole way, "Morning, nice hat, you alright there? Yup, morning, morning, hiya, how are you doing?"

A giggle came from the bag, and Blunt froze, but none of the toys seemed to notice. It turned to a guffaw and a unicorn with a rainbow embroidered across its stomach looked up at him. "Is your bag laughing?"

"Radio," Blunt said, must've forgotten to turn it off.

"That tickles," Ted's voice came from the bag.

"That's not the radio," the unicorn said, "what's in the bag?"

"Who are you? Bloody Starbrite the bag police?"

"I'm Yargval the Mildewy."

"Mildewy?"

"I'm a demon, we're all demons," the unicorn said. It was white with pink hair and a rainbow horn.

"A demon... of mildew?"

"Well nobody likes mildew, do they?" The unicorn said. Others around it were paying attention. "We can't all be demons of violence and terror, you know."

"It's just I hadn't really thought of it before. I didn't think demons were in Gloomwood."

"We're new," another demon said, "just transferred in."

"Oh... so is this like some kind of refugee thing?" Blunt asked, looking around.

"Could say that, yeah. We're fleeing persecution."

"That seems reasonable. Are you all from Hell then?"

A cough came from the bag, "Let me out Blunt," Morgarth said.

"See, it's not a radio!" Yargval the mildewy said.

Blunt placed the bag on the concrete pavement and carefully unzipped it just enough to pull Morgarth out. The other demons fell silent as Blunt placed the dinosaur on the floor.

"Morgarth?" Yargval the mildewy said.

"Yes, it's me. Morgarth the Destroyer, leader of the Elite."

"Oh, wow, can I get your autograph?"

"No, I struggle to hold a pen with these little arms," Morgarth said. "demons, what is this talk of fleeing?"

The sound of a hundred soft toys gasping sounds almost the same as the sound of a pillow dropping onto a stack of more pillows.

"We didn't mean it Morgarth. It was a demonic ruse. We were lulling this man into a false sense of security," Yargval said, "tell her Hellvar of the broken biscuits," the unicorn said, shoving a stuffed chicken toy forward.

"Uh... cluck?" the chicken said.

"Oh, that's a shame," Morgarth said, "because I really am defecting to this afterlife and if you're not... then I guess you're going to stop me?"

"You're going to defect?" A demonic pink hippopotamus said.

"Yes, my fellow Hellspawn. I've had enough of being in servitude to the Devil. Even if I'm stuck in this body, at least I'll be able to have a mundane, boring, peaceful death. I just want to sit in front of the television without having to peel the skin off a screaming mortal. Or enjoy a cup of hot chocolate without the stench of excrement. Don't you ever wonder what it's like to get dressed in the morning without the smell of burning hair and flesh lingering on your clothes? I just want to shower without wondering if it's my nipple that just fell to the floor or one of my victims," Morgarth said.

The demons were nodding with her. Blunt knelt beside Morgarth. "I'm not sure what this is, but I'm going to carry on. You, uh, have fun? It was nice meeting you." He stood up, looked around, and began stepping over the heads of the toys once again on his way to the wall.

"If we stay here, there are jobs for us. Look around this place. Can't you see how these people are? I've even seen some of them smile. Actual smiles not forced rictus grins, it's amazing. I want to smile one day. Just once. I'm only a demon, just like you, but I believe in a brighter future. A future where little demon toys can walk beside dead mortals, forgotten hopes, lost dreams, even dead gods, as equals rather than as torturers. If the Devil stands in my way, then I say bring it on. I will fight for my right to stay here. This isn't Beelzebub's afterlife. It's the Grim Reaper's. I've met Death, and he offered me cake! Cake!"

"I'd like cake," the hippopotamus said.

"Me too Vargon of the 'bought the wrong size batteries' and we can have it because we're already here, and we shall not be moved!"

TUNE

The spotlights were bright and when they were on it was impossible to see anything beyond the edge of the raised stage.

"What's next?" Pestilence asked.

"Are you drunk?" Famine snapped, "it's the same order as last week in the third level."

"I thought this was the third level," Pestilence muttered while looking down at the effects pedals on the stage floor. He hefted the Fender Stratocaster to one side as he stepped forward.

The Grim Reaper held the microphone stand. His skeletal fingers curled around it as he walked away from it so it was on a slant towards him. "We love you fifth level!"

A roar came from beyond the edge of light. The sound terrifying and enthusiastic in equal measure. The wails of suffering once-mortal souls drowned out by the cries of adoration from demons and divine beings, the immortals who existed without a need for mortal belief, the eternals.

"Are you ready?" Death asked.

The Devil stepped forward towards another microphone stand, a guitar in the shape of flames hanging from a leather strap across his shirtless muscled torso. " We said, are you READY?!" The roar washed over them, doubled in strength.

Behind them, the drums kicked in. That driving thunder delivering War's characteristic rhythmic beat. Pestilence on rhythm guitar, Famine on the bass, Beelzebub on lead guitar and backing vocals, with the one and only Grim Reaper as front man. They were unstoppable. The greatest band to grace the immortal realms, a new sound that nobody could get enough of.

"We are the Hoarse men! And we bring you, Armageddon!"

DEMONIC PROTEST

"What is that?" Beelzebub said.

"It looks like some kind of protest for demon rights," Twist said, unable to hide the smirk on her face.

"Demon rights... I hate this place. Demon Elite," Beelzebub said, "remind these demons where they come from."

The twelve demon toys at Beelzebub's back leapt forward. Moving at a speed that should not have been possible they scurried up the street bouncing from wall to wall, over vehicles, shoving people out of the way as if their size bore no relation to their strength or mass.

Beelzebub's grin reappeared, creeping across his face as if it was being sliced open, until a small blue dinosaur toy stepped forward from the mass of toys. The twelve bounding towards the dinosaur slowed and Beelzebub heard the voice of Morgarth. "Lord Beelzebub, this is our official notice of resignation."

The Devil's smile vanished. The horns on his head, subtle and unnoticed, grew more pronounced, taller, curved, more lethal. "Official notice of resignation," the Devil said his voice was only loud enough for Twist to hear but she backed away as Beelzebub walked forwards.

He pushed his arms out, lifting cars into the air through force of will. They smashed against the rows of terraced houses in one of the poorest parts of the city. A boom of thunder rumbled and roared echoing off the walls drowning out any screams.

Beelzebub strode forward, the heat around him turning the rain to steam before it was within inches of landing upon his suit. A heat haze refracted the light, causing an aura of power to form around the Devil. His steps echoed, as if cloven hooves were stepping upon polished marble, even though he wore shoes on tarmac.

"Your official notice of resignation," Beelzebub said. His voice carried clear down the street two hundred meters, which were fast disappearing as he walked forwards. He didn't rush, the Devil walks, he never runs. As he grew closer, the toys behind Morgarth shuffled backwards, but the little blue dinosaur held her ground. Beelzebub grew closer, "is rejected."

The twelve demons of Beelzebub's elite guard formed a semi-circle, as if following instructions that nobody else could hear. They faced Morgarth, who remained stoic, unflinching, though her tail was no longer wagging.

"You will find," a woman ran across the road and he clicked his fingers. Her flesh vanished, melting to nothingness as Johnson's had while she screamed. "That you are contractually obliged to continue working until I find a replacement. Which, in case you're wondering, will take forever." Beelzebub reached into his coat and brought out the cigarette packet. "I realise this may be difficult to understand."

"I quit," Morgarth said, "you don't own me."

"Yes, Morgarth you poor stupid feckless little dinosaur, I do. You're a demon, not a person. You're not damned to Hell, you are of Hell, you don't go somewhere else. You don't die. It's just an endless loop for you."

Morgarth stepped forward. "You don't get to decide."

"Of course I do," Beelzebub said. The grin appeared but there was no humour behind it, "you are nothing unless I say you are."

"This," Morgarth waved a small arm around, "isn't yours. You brought us out of Hell and put us in these bodies, but they aren't yours. If the Grim Reaper says we can stay, then we stay."

Beelzebub looked around. Demons looked back at him. Their glowing red pupils on oversized eyes, stitched on to the bodies of pastel coloured cuddly animals, looked back at him. "You wish to stay here?" He said looking back at Morgarth. "Trapped forever in these cutesy little vessels as if these people will accept you, demons?"

"We'll find out."

"I am going to destroy this world. It is an abomination. A false afterlife that shouldn't exist. If you want to stay, so be it,"

Beelzebub said, "it's not like there isn't plenty more of you to go around." He clicked his fingers as he walked through the arc of elite demons. They shuffled to stand either side of Beelzebub and the crowd of toys parted.

"I thought you'd be angrier," Morgarth said.

"Oh, I was, but then I realised you're giving in to temptation. Who am I to deny that?, I am the lord of free will. It would be more than a little hypocritical of me to lose my temper because you revolted. Let's not forget how the story goes, hmm, on that note. Should you stay, and this applies to all of you, you'll be fallen demons, are we clear?"

Morgarth nodded. "Yes, your lordship."

"Well, at least you're polite, Morgarth. Are you all coming?" He looked from side to side at the demons marching. "You don't have to."

The demons shuffled, three of them moved to join the crowd of toys.

"I see, well at least you're still here Vellmar, and you Araza... actually you can go, I really don't mind. No? Fine, come on then. Let's destroy this afterlife. Get it over with."

💀 <u>BRAVERY</u> 💀

He stood with his hands balled into fists at either side. "No," his voice shook. "You have not completed form 137 dash b and so you shall not pass... on this occasion. Please return to the back of the queue and start again," Ralph Mortimer said.

Mortimer was a brave man. He had proven it many times but were you to ask him he would shake his head, "Bravery isn't a real thing," he would say. When Mortimer watched Johnson melting, shock had gripped him. He had not frozen, but tried to see if there was anything he could do. As Petal had broken before his eyes, a violent torrent of emotion bursting free of whatever restraints had been there, Mortimer had not cowered. Well, not much when you realise how close he was to being clobbered by what might be War himself. No, Mortimer had offered him a nice cup of tea.

Bravery is a lie. In Mortimer's world, everything is a balance book. Risk and reward. People often had the values wrong. People, truth, justice, were much more valuable than other things like power, or money, it just happened that many people were stupid. So, when Mortimer was standing in front of a paper towel barrier which had collapsed beneath the rain, he had done what any soft spoken, polite bureaucrat would do. He arranged a queue and a careful system of applications for the asking of questions or walking over the barrier. This was bravery. Staunch dedication to the magic of paperwork to slow down any situation.

He turned to look across to the other side of the road, where in the distance Crispin Neat had arranged a line of bicycles to replace his own collapsed barrier.

Across from the cobblestones of Dead Square, the building they all awaited entry towered like a solemn guardian over the city. Or that one teacher on playground duty that no student ever wants to engage in conversation. Mister Office of the Dead kept a watchful, stern eye on things. The central door turned and someone in the Gloomwood Grey of the police stumbled out. Dragging one foot and using some kind of walking stick, the man held a head under one arm. A bandana obscured his face. He drew closer to the barricades and looked from left to right.

Mortimer approached him from one side. From the other came Crispin Neat.

"Chief Sowercat," Neat said, "is the building secure?"

Sowercat nodded. "As far as I can tell, there is not a single person in that building with their head attached to their body."

"I see," said Neat, "that's good to hear."

"Why?" Asked Mortimer, "why is that good?"

"Because they were zombies, obviously," Sowercat said, "every one of them, thanks to this muppet."

"The resurrection continues," Molly Gormley, leader of the resurrection, and erstwhile head on a stick, now just head, said.

"This needs further analysis," Crispin Neat said. As he finished the sentence a white van appeared slowly forcing its way through the lines, over the cobblestones. Whoever was driving pounded the horn, making it impossible to ignore. "Speak of the scientists," Neat said.

TIME'S UP

"Who are you?" The woman asked. She was short, stout, and would win any audition for a 'little teapot'.

"What?" Blunt said, "who the hell are you?" He was stepping down from the narrow platform that projected out into the sea from the wall on to what some might call a boat. He stumbled as he tried to keep his footing on the platform. A wooden jetty that some maniac in the Office of the Dead had designated a port.

They do not prohibit sailing in Gloomwood, it's just pointless. The only vessels that traverse the purple roiling currents with any success are repair ships built like oversized dodgem cars. Meters of protective rubber rings surround them, allowing them to survive being smashed against the cliff edges and preventing them from being pulled into the depths by creatures below, or at least, bobbing back up to the surface when it happened. Repair work was a job only taken by the most desperate. Few people returned from more than a handful of trips in the bouncing boats, and those that did, well, they didn't call it being rattled for nothing.

"Who am I?" the woman asked as she held an oar in one hand, "You're on my sodding boat."

"Your boat, this is the Grim Reaper's boat."

"Who told you that?" She had a voice that spoke of a career spent screaming into storms. "This is my boat."

"Open the bag," the Grim Reaper said.

Blunt placed the black bag on the deck of the boat. Flecks of paint scattered as it hit the wooden boards, and the vessel groaned beneath his feet. The woman eyed him with her fingers tight on the oar, but she waited as Blunt pulled the zip. Ted leapt out onto the deck.

"Demon!" The woman shouted as she swung the oar at Ted. Before it made contact, a skeletal hand snapped out of the bag and caught it mid swing. The bones of the arm rose out of the bag, followed by the Grim Reaper dressed in his black robe, which billowed in the gale.

"Hello Sharon," Grim said.

"Hello Sharon? That's what you say after leaving me here. It's been months."

"I said you didn't have to stay."

"You knew I would. You owe me two coins."

"Ah yes, about that," the Grim Reaper said while patting himself down, "I'm a little short right now."

"Nobody skips paying the ferry."

"The ferry," Blunt interrupted, "wait, is this the actual ferry? As in the ferryman?"

"Ferrywoman," Sharon said.

"Charon... is Sharon?"

"Blunt," Grim said, "you have read a book?"

"Don't include me in this nonsense," Blunt snapped, "you're here. The bear is here. I guess that's job done," he said.

The Grim Reaper leaned forward just enough to make Blunt wonder if he was nodding or swaying in the wind. "Yes, Detective, thank you, and good luck."

"Good luck? Why are you telling me good luck? I've done my bit."

"Well yes, but now I have to take Jeremy, or Ted, across the Styx, to the mortal realm, and ensure he dies to restore balance to things. You still have to deal with Beelzebub."

"I, what? Why aren't you dealing with him? This is your mess."

The Grim Reaper turned to Blunt and shook his head. "I am neutral in all things Detective."

"I'm not responsible for dealing with this. I don't care."

"Then this will be the end of Gloomwood."

"Good. Then that's it. Finally," Blunt said.

"Yes. All those people," the Grim Reaper pointed towards the city, "people like Leighton Hughes, Sarah Von Faber, Ralph Mortimer, Helga from the coffee shop who serves you even though you're rude to all her customers, oh, I know exactly what you mean. Much easier to not care about any of them."

Blunt frowned. His hat rose, threatening to escape in the wind, and he slapped it down, holding it in place with one hand. "You've stitched me up," he muttered, "everyone hates me and I just wanted to be alone."

"Hm, well then this is convenient. Just do nothing. It has nothing to do with me. Good luck with… nothing."

The detective scowled, then snatched up the bag from the floor of the boat. "I'm keeping this."

"Oh, well, okay then. I shall play the world's smallest violin for you while you complain that, 'nobody likes me,'" Grim said.

Blunt's eyebrows shot up. "That… what did you just say?"

"Goodbye, Detective. Oh, don't tell anyone I've gone that could cause problems."

"Gone? You can't just go. This is your afterlife."

Blunt stepped off the boat despite his own protests.

"No, Detective. It's an afterlife I made for people like you. I'm not dead, I am Death, there's a difference. I'm not abandoning you. I'll drop you a line."

The ferrywoman bustled forward, pulling up the gangplank. "Stop nattering on like a pair of fishwives and help me raise the anchor. Wind's picking up, we're in for a doozy. This is four coins you'll owe me."

"No problem," the Grim Reaper said, "I left my wallet on the other side."

Their voices faded as Blunt watched the boat move away from the jetty.

"Okay, Blunt… you've been in crap situations before. This is nothing new. Just got to make a deal with the Devil. The actual bloody Devil."

STREETS OF RAGE

War does not happen by itself. It requires instability and disquiet. A political jigsaw of pieces all falling into place at just the right time. Prodded and pulled by the manipulators of economics and thirst for resources or power. In contrast to this, rage fueled War as a person.

He strode through the streets of Gloomwood, clearing a path before him with a contempt for the souls nearby. Petal was no more. He delivered destruction without deliberation or distinction between people or inanimate objects. The squeal of metal against metal was as meaningless as the screams of agony. The low thrum of a bass line drove through everything else. A relentless beat that came from somewhere deep. Each step was in rhythm to the sound but this was no dance, it was a march.

People shrank away from the sound before they even knew where it was coming from, which is very difficult to do because shrinking away requires direction. They watched crouched in doorways or peering out of windows while twitching the curtains like every neighbourhood gossip who hasn't discovered reality television. This beat, this volume, this cursed sound, was the sound of war.

There was no need for a guide. Conflict drew him towards it with magnetic precision. In the city of Gloomwood there was conflict everywhere, but none of it compared to the Devil himself.

"Petal," a voice shouted, a child, or at least a person who wanted to remain one, "you selling again yet? Petal, oi I'm talking to you."

War stopped and turned, his eyes now dark except for the blue flames that escaped from behind them and flickered against the black marble-like sclera. He didn't speak. A low rumble in his chest reverberated along the street. A tremor passed through the buildings. Windows rattled and a crow, so seldom seen far from the Office of the Dead, let out a solemn caw.

"Never mind. I thought, well, I'd better be off."

His head turned to one side as if listening to a whisper on the wind. Then he was moving again. Striding to that rhythm.

When he rounded a corner to find vehicles strewn on either side of the road, like they were little more than playthings, he knew he was close. His pace quickened. The destruction was impressive if needlessly elegant.

Ahead was a small regiment of demonic soldiers. Something happened to his face. It was neither a smile nor snarl; it was something in between. Involuntary joy brought on by impending violence.

The demons parted. He could see them as they were, and as they should have been. "Demons?" He asked, his voice challenged the growing wind.

"Petal?" A dinosaur asked, "it's Morgarth. We're fallen demons now, um, defectors, refugees. Where's Johnson?"

Pain. There was pain. The demon had attacked him without him realising. A trick, a ploy to distract him while they stabbed him in the back. He turned. Nothing there. The pain was internal. Why was there pain?

BAD TIMING

"Detective Blunt," Twist Lenworth said. The smile she gave epitomised smug in a way that made Blunt want to wipe it off her face. She was standing next to the Devil.

"Twist," Blunt said, "and you must be the Devil. Pleasure to meet you."

The man with the horns smiled. He was smoking a cigarette and for a moment Blunt thought about asking for one.

"Please," the Devil said, taking the cigarette case out of his jacket pocket. He pressed the side of it and it clicked open, "help yourself."

"I don't smoke."

The Devil let out a chuckle. "Everybody smokes Detective, provided you burn them the right way."

Blunt shrugged. "I'm okay for a cigarette."

"No? Sensible. I would have pretended we had struck a bargain, then made the price completely unreasonable. You would have felt honour bound to keep your side of the bargain or fear losing your soul and then the irony of it all would be that you would carry out the thing I requested and lose your soul because of those actions."

"That's very specific," Blunt said.

"It wouldn't be the first time. Where's the Grim Reaper and the bear?"

Blunt took the hat off his head. The wind was strong and holding it in place was getting tiresome. He didn't have enough hair to care about that being blown in all directions. With one hand, he squashed the hat in half and shoved it in his inside coat pocket.

The Devil watched and shook his head. "Why bother having a hat at all if you're going to treat it like that? Disgraceful. If you'd care to answer the question, you'd save us all a lot of time."

"He's gone," Blunt said. There was no way he could get past them. The wooden jetty was too narrow and as the wind picked up, it lurched from side to side, threatening to collapse at any moment. Twist and the Devil didn't seem perturbed, but Blunt couldn't help glancing down to the waters below. They looked angry. It hadn't been that long ago that he would've jumped in, but other people's deaths hung in the balance. "What do you want?"

"Ah, I need to remove the living thing from the afterlife. It is like a cancerous cell ready to divide, growing into a tumour before it spreads further. Tiny lives floating among the other afterlives, infecting them all. I'm just cleaning up. Being the Devil comes with a reputation that is quite unfounded. I may enjoy making people suffer, but it isn't my raison d'être. Everything needs to be in balance. I agreed to come here to balance things out. Life belongs on the other side."

Blunt knelt. People didn't expect you to kneel or take a seat in tense standoffs. It catches them by surprise. You can't have a standoff unless everyone is standing. There's no such thing as a standy-sitty off either. If you sit down, or kneel, it's no longer a standoff. "So, you just came here for the bear?"

"Mostly," Beelzebub said.

"That's why she came," Blunt pointed to Twist, "why did you come here?"

"Oh, investigating, are we? Death's really gone, hasn't he?" Beelzebub said.

"He's taking the bear to the mortal realm to make sure he dies properly."

"My time," Twist said, "he's taking my time."

"He's gone… wait, did he go with Sharon?"

"Uh, yeah, actually, he did."

"Wonderful. There's not a lot to do now other than destroy this pathetic place. Don't worry, Detective. As the last person standing who might have some idea of why this is happening, I'll leave you until the end. He just had to pick up the phone. Some people."

Beelzebub turned just as the jetty moved. It lurched violently to one side. There was a sound like the beating of a drum that Blunt could hear despite the wind.

"Ah, big blue has arrived. A little early. I'd rather not be on this bridge," the Devil turned to look at Twist, "well you fought him before. Off you go."

"Petal?" Twist said.

The rain and spray from the Styx seas below combined with a mist that rolled across the city. All that Blunt could see were two blue flames moving towards them.

"That's not Petal," Blunt said.

"Not anymore, no, that's our old friend War."

SAIL AWAY

"Did you really just send that man back there to save your whole made up city?" Sharon said as she gripped the ship's wheel. It wasn't a big boat, a 22ft sloop with two sails and a small interior area where Sharon lived. Ted has already found a space inside.

"It's called Gloomwood, Sharon, you've been here long enough to give it a name," Grim said. He was standing behind her, looking over her shoulder and casting glances back towards the city. "I'm doing the important bit."

"Killing a teddy bear?"

"Yes. You make it sound so… minor."

"Why didn't you just kill him back there."

"Really? You've been the ferrywoman for millennia, and how many people have you carried who I killed? Well?"

"I don't know. I don't speak to them. They're always all, 'woe is me, I can't believe I'm dead, do you think the cat will eat my dead body?' It's painful enough to listen to without engaging in conversation." She did something that the Grim Reaper didn't understand to some kind of device he also didn't understand and tutted.

"Ah, I see."

"Don't do that thing where you pretend you understand how to navigate the Styx. If you did, you wouldn't need me. Also, no changing the subject. What's going on?"

"Beezy."

"Beezy? This is all because of Beelzebub? I thought you weren't talking to him anymore."

"I'm not! Actually, I think that might be the problem."

She grabbed a towel and wiped her face before reaching behind her with one hand. Grim grabbed the towel out of her hand and swept it across his skeletal brow.

"I know it's none of my business but is this all about… you know that thing."

"What thing?"

"That video. On Bitter."

"I don't know what you're talking about."

"Yes, you do. You know it's not really a thing anymore, don't you?"

"It's not?"

"No. Just a shame about the hoarse men. They were pretty popular."

"I know, but I embarrassed them and... I'm neutral. Oh, I've an idea, may I borrow your phone?

She narrowed her eyes. "Why?"

"Just let me borrow it."

"For a call?"

"A text message."

"...fine."

TWIST AND...

Her scythe cut through the howling wind coming off the purple oceans with a piercing whistle that caused the demons dressed as toys to turn in her direction. The huge blue man facing her looked up, and she felt something she hadn't the last time they had met. Fear.

"Petal," she said, "I suppose it's time for our rematch?"

The demons scattered, leaving a path between them. She could sense they weren't doing it out of deference to her. "I see you've made friends with the demons, nice bunch I've heard, though the Devil doesn't seem too pleased."

"Beelzebub?" The being that had been Petal said in a voice that drowned out the wind. "Where is he?"

"Well, if you beat me I suppose you'll find out, won't you?" She said.

The smile that grew on the blue man's face was unnatural and Twist realised that whatever this person was, he wasn't the same man she had walked through the city with. She gripped the scythe a little more tightly.

Twist Lenworth had walked through the valley of death countless times. She had sent demons and wraiths back to where they came from. Guided humanity's worst to the gates of Hell and watched friends' souls snatched unwillingly by the things that stalk the netherworld. Through all of it, she had gripped her scythe and stood, confident in her will. Until now.

War walked towards her with purpose in every step. A deep throbbing sound filled the air, and she felt fear as it silenced every thought, until there was only the scream of terror behind her eyes. As he drew within striking distance, she realised she couldn't move. Not even to release a whimper of panic.

He reached out with one hand and gently pushed her to one side. Before stepping beyond her.

"Well, that's disappointing," Beelzebub's voice came from behind her, but she couldn't turn to look.

SPEAK OF...

"War! I thought it was you. You know, I considered not trying to wake you up, but it was so touching seeing you and that, what was he, a Hope? Well, anyway, here you are now."

"Beelzebub," War said from where he was on the edge of the seawall, "why did you do that?"

"You look annoyed, angry even, so I'll keep it simple and see if you calm down. This place," he waved his hands, "is not supposed to exist. You've been missing for a long time and Grim, well, between you and me I think he may have had some kind of breakdown."

War curled his hands into fists and took a step onto the platform.

"Oh, I wouldn't do that," Beelzebub smiled, "it's really not very safe. Now, I can see you want to blame me for this War, but when have I ever let you down? I didn't create this place, and I didn't start letting Hopes and Dreams, and other nonsense like that turn into individuals. What you should be angry at, is this city, don't you think? I mean, if this place didn't exist then you wouldn't be feeling the way you do, would you?"

"Shut up," War said, "you always do this. Turn things around with your words. You will suffer-"

"Me? What did I do?"

"You killed him-"

"Uh, I don't think so, old buddy, he was dead already and technically wasn't even a thing. All I did was apply a little reality."

"Bring him back."

"That would be pointless. You aren't the same person you were before. Look at you. All rippling with muscular fury, practically salivating at the prospect of destruction. How long have you been building walls to bury your true nature? Petal? What was that about?"

War rubbed at his head. "I wanted to be him-"

"But you're not him, are you? Even if you were him, you're not anymore. If one little thing can trigger-"

"He was a person, not a little thing, not an insignificant thing."

"Hah!" Beelzebub looked up into the rain, "a person is an insignificant thing. What has happened to you? Come on, we're going to have some fun tearing Grim's playground apart, oh, and I've got a few new songs to play you."

"I'm going to destroy you."

"Yes, yes, not the first time you've said that, but celestial beings don't go around destroying each other over mere mortals. Oh sorry, he wasn't even a mortal. How does this even work, you need to explain it to me and then, if I'm wrong, well I suppose you'll destroy me?"

"I'm War, not some mortal for you to play mind games on Beelzebub. I will destroy you, now."

"Ah, it really must wait, I'm afraid. If it were up to me we'd do it, but it isn't. I'm here on actual netherworld business, you see. There really has been an almighty cock up, whoops, when I say almighty I mean Grim, so maybe just a little mighty, wouldn't want to upset you know who. Anyway, what was I saying?" Beelzebub strode forward off the jetty and put an arm around War's shoulders. "Oh yes, we can work out some of this tension that you're carrying, oh my, feel that, right across your shoulders, you need a good bit of destruction. How about we knock down Grim's little tower of office workers? Give you something to do while you calm down and apply some logic."

"I will destroy you."

"I heard you the first time. Come on."

BITTER

The jetty shook beneath him and he collapsed, from kneeling to lying down. He had watched Twist, and then the Devil himself, turn and walk away from him, content knowing he was no threat to either of them. As he lay with his face pressed against the wooden platform, he couldn't even summon the energy to scream in rage. He was just done.

Then the music started. A tinny, muffled, familiar tune. He remembered it from the radio. It was a song he'd never heard before coming to Gloomwood. It was the elevator music in the Office of the Dead, the background noise in Helga's cafe, the more it played the more places he remembered hearing it. He lifted his face off the wooden planks with a sucking noise and then he remembered the bag, and the Grim Reaper's phone.

He scrambled backwards on his hands and knees. The wind and rain whipping across his face, blurring his vision as he desperately unzipped the bag and pulled out the glassy rectangular phone.

Blunt jabbed at the screen. Dots of moisture appearing on its surface from the spray and rain. This was all he had left. Everything else would crumble and burn thanks to the Devil if there wasn't something here.

He wasn't technologically savvy. This kind of thing had confused him when he was alive, and now it eluded him. What he knew was people, and the Devil acted like a person.

'Blunt, if you can see this, the answer is Bitter, and the phone is unlocked.' The message had said followed by several cartoon skulls, a crown, and a thumbs up after the text.

Bitter. What the hell was bitter? He swiped the screen. There were pages and pages of icons. Abstract shapes, or pictures of things that meant nothing to Blunt. There was an envelope, a tiny house, different coloured circles. It was alien to him, like looking at hieroglyphics. Then he saw it, a lemon with wings, an even smaller exclamation mark was on top of the icon. "Bitter... lemons, makes sense," he stabbed the icon with his stubby index finger and the screen changed.

It was a confusing mass of messages. Most of them referenced things Blunt didn't understand. This, he knew, wasn't the important bit. Another little circle with an exclamation mark in it. He pressed this one, and then it all made sense.

Underneath the video were three icons; a pitchfork, a rotating arrow, and a speech bubble. All of them had numbers with an 'M' next to them. Blunt surmised this to be millions, but it was the video that answered the question. Someone with the name 'Him had posted it' but it was Beelzebub in the picture. "You bastard," Blunt muttered.

The video was of the Grim Reaper. His skill was covered in glitter and he was singing. It was difficult to make out where he was singing, but if Blunt had to guess, it was a karaoke bar and the Grim Reaper was not sober. Judging by the slurring of words, which until that moment Blunt had assumed was impossible with the way the skeleton projected his voice, and the occasional stagger backwards or forwards, sober was a vague memory.

"Sing it again Grim, you're killing it," said the person holding the camera. There was no mistaking that voice. It didn't sound sober, but it was still imperious, commanding, dripping in contempt for everyone and everything.

"You better not share this," the Grim Reaper said, "I've got ones of you too," then the singing started again.

Blunt scrolled through the comments, expecting the horrific abuse that was coming, but they surprised him. They seemed in order of popularity. The days didn't make much sense to Blunt, presumably because they were in some kind of demonic calendar. According to the phone, the date was 67892, but the most recent comment was from 59363. The most popular one, and the most recent, was short, "The Grim Reaper was a brilliant singer. This video ruined the #hoarsemen." It had 867 million likes.

It didn't matter if people liked the video or not, Blunt realised, it would still embarrass Grim. Humiliating. If Beelzebub had posted this, then Grim was probably pretty angry, but he was neutral in all things, the bastard. Which meant... which meant that he probably tried to be the bigger person by just walking away. "It can't be that simple," Blunt said.

The answer was in front of him; he knew it, but he couldn't access it. Sitting on the jetty, he slipped the phone into his inside pocket and pulled the hat out from the other side. Punching it into shape, he forced it down onto his head, "Morgarth," he said.

REPENT

"I don't want to die," Ted said.

Inside the small cabin, the Grim Reaper was crouching with a cup in his hands that had steam coming from the tea on its surface. "It's not that bad, you've already done it once."

"I can't go back to the reapers. They'll destroy me," the bear was sitting on top of a crate in a darkened corner of the cabin.

"That won't happen," Grim said, "you'll go somewhere else this time."

"But-"

"There is hope," Grim said, "there is always hope. Perhaps you could repent?"

"Does that work?"

"I don't know. I've never been alive. People think I know these things. There's always so many questions, but I'm not the arbiter of who goes where. I'm the guide."

"Then you must know where I'm going to go."

"Sorry," Death reached across the cabin towards a tiny kitchenette. On top of the surface, next to the kettle, was a biscuit tin, "would you like a biscuit? Ooh, chocolate bourbons, my favourite."

"I hope, I hope, I hope," Ted said under his breath.

☠ MESSAGES FROM BEYOND ☠

"What now?" A demon asked Morgarth.

She shrugged, a strange gesture in her body but the meaning was clear. "I guess we see what happens."

Muttering broke out from the rear of the demon horde and she turned to see Detective Blunt stumbling down from the seawall with the bag on his back. "Blunt, is he still in the bag?"

"Morgarth, uh, no."

"It's just you?"

"Just me," Blunt said as he made his way through the crowd of pint-sized demon toys, "you could be a little less disappointed to see me. I did just come face to face with the Devil after carrying the Grim Reaper on my back."

"What now?" She asked.

"Yes," Twist Lenworth, who had been sitting on the floor staring into space, said.

"You," Blunt looked at her, "did you come through the Deathport?"

"Yes."

"So you Ableforthed the woman on the entry desk?"

"I... yes."

"But it got covered up?"

"The Deathport is technically not in Gloomwood. So the police didn't have any jurisdiction."

"The Grim Reaper knew you were here?"

"No, maybe, I'm not sure."

"But the police?"

"Clueless, frightened, I'm not sure which."

"And it was all for nothing," Blunt said.

She nodded, her eyes glazed over and she stared into space once more.

Blunt looked around at the demons and then down at Morgarth. "Can you stop him?"

"Me? Stop the Devil and War?"

"There are loads of you. You're an army of demons. Can't you just pull out some kind of demon magic and," he waved his fingers.

Morgarth looked at him with her oversized eyes. "No."

"Right then," Blunt looked around, "then maybe you can help me with something. We could do with being somewhere more private."

"Can I help too?" Twist asked.

"You?" Blunt and Morgarth said in unison.

Blunt turned, so he was facing Twist and then stopped to look back at Morgarth. "Wait a minute, the Grim Reaper and War. As in War the horseman of the apocalypse?"

"That's the one," Morgarth said.

"When did War get here?" Blunt said.

"He caught up with us after I chopped off his head," Twist said.

Blunt turned back to her, "you did what?"

"That's not right," Morgarth interrupted, "he wasn't War then."

"Right," Blunt snapped, "if the world's about to end, I want to know what the hell has been going on, and I want a coffee. Come on."

DEMOLITION

"I intend to rip out your spine with your head attached, then whirl it around until your head pops off," War said.

"You used to be much more... succinct in your threats. You need some practice. Oh, that music, it's kind of-"

They walked along the streets towards the Office of the Dead.

"I don't care about the music. I left that all behind."

"I know, and it's the perfect time for the comeback tour. We can do The Devil and the hoarse men ride again."

"We can't, Grim would never come back."

"Aha, so you are thinking about it."

"No. I'm just explaining how you ruined something great because you're an egotistical maniac who couldn't stand not having all the attention on himself," War said as he stopped in the middle of the street. "Then you come here and you take away the only other good thing I've ever had."

"That's not true," Beelzebub said, "you're not being very fair at all. I'm not that egotistical... but I was the frontman of the band-"

"Did you hear what I just said?" War roared, windows and streetlights exploded.

"There's no need to shout. Yes, I heard you but really," the Devil's phone buzzed, "ah, this will be Grim begging us not to destroy his city."

"There's no us," War snapped.

THE DEVIL'S PHONE

"So this is all about a band?"

"Not a band," Morgarth said, "the band. They traversed genres, people were crazy about them."

"I'm not really into music," Twist said.

"Thanks for the input," Blunt said, "why don't you keep polishing that scythe until you come up with something that might be helpful."

Twist gave Blunt a look that would have frozen his blood cold, if he'd had more than a thimbleful in his body.

"So this band all fell apart because of some video posted on the nether web? Which is demon speak for the internet?"

"Well, there are a lot of conspiracy theories and things, but yeah. Beelzebub posted a video of the Grim Reaper with his head covered in Glitter. He was drunk, and it was embarrassing and… well, the Grim Reaper just walked away and the band collapsed."

"Are you pulling my chain?"

"I… don't know what that means?" Morgarth said.

Twist leant forward over the coffee table. The staff in the tiny coffee shop didn't expect anybody to sit down for coffee in the morning rush. People milled around queuing while two impossibly perky baristas shouted out names and took orders. "It means are you being serious?" She gave Blunt a smug head tilt and picked up her coffee.

"Helpful," Blunt muttered.

"Yes. I'm not sure why I wouldn't be serious. Five of the most powerful immortal beings in the universe were in a band together and then one of them got humiliated online, in front of everyone, so he packed up and left," Morgarth had to use two hands to pick up a biscuit and dunk it into the cup in front of her, "like this?" she asked.

"Yeah, that's called dunking, you've nailed it. So," Blunt reached into his coat and pulled out the phone, "this video you're talking about," he put the phone on the table and flicked through the screens until he found what he was looking for, "is it this one?"

"Yes, you have Bitter here?"

"This is the Grim Reaper's phone."

"I know, I gave it to him, but it's not locked. That's quite dangerous. There's lots of personal information on a phone. It's very important that-"

"He unlocked it on purpose and said this had the answer, but I don't understand what he means."

"Oh," Morgarth said.

"Oh?" Blunt replied, "just, 'oh', not, 'yes, this is it' and some air punching?"

"Well... Beelzebub is pretty big on social media."

"I don't know what that is."

"It's, well it's... I don't suppose it's actually that important, but the Grim Reaper said in the video that he had ones of Beelzebub so..."

"So we can blackmail the Devil into leaving." Twist said.

"Oh," Blunt and Morgarth said in unison.

SEASICK

"I don't feel well."

"Sneezing will have no effect on me or Sharon," the Grim Reaper said.

"I didn't do that on purpose."

"No, sneezing on command is difficult, unless you're allergic. Spicy food makes me sneeze. Not that I have it often."

"At least you'll be guiding me."

"Me? Oh no, I'm only here because Sharon wouldn't take you unless I came along too."

"But you're the Grim Reaper, you're Death-"

"I'm retired."

"Then what's going to happen? A reaper can't collect me, they all hate me."

"Oh yes, that would be terrible."

UNSOLICITED MESSAGES

"Just hold on a minute War," Beelzebub said.

"Hold on? You said I could destroy something," War kicked the wall of a building, sending it tumbling to the ground. Inside, a man sitting in his underwear on a sofa stared out as dust tumbled down onto him.

Beelzebub's eyes were locked to his phone.

-Hello.

-Grim! Finally using your phone.

-Remember this?

-Hah, yes, good times. I didn't realise you had that.

-I'm going to post it to my feed.

-You wouldn't do that, Grim. You're far too kind.

-This isn't Grim.

-You're not funny, Grim. Look, I'm sorry about the whole afterlife city but I've already destroyed it so we might as well let bygones be bygones.

-This isn't Grim. You can leave and nothing will happen, but I'm posting this in sixty seconds.

-Who is this?

-ROFL

-You don't ROFL at the DEVIL who is this?

-LMAO

-Morgarth? Morgarth is this you?

-Guess again, thirty seconds.

-Blunt! You miserable, pathetic specimen of a mortal. How dare you! I am the Devil and I will destroy you.

-Tick, tock. Oh, Morgarth says I can screen shoot this.

-You don't scare me, I'm the Devil, fear is what I do.

-I mean screenshot

-Blunt?

-Blunt? Are you there?

-Don't you dare.

-Fine. I'm going, but this isn't over.

Beelzebub slid the phone back into his inside jacket pocket. There was no way to tell anything was there once he had put it away. No outline, no bulge spoiling the line of his suit. He reached into his coat pocket and snapped open the silver cigarette case. Flicking one up and catching it in the air with his forked tongue. His horns were growing, and he seethed.

"Why do you look like that?" War asked.

"I'm angry."

"You're angry? I was a perfectly content former demigod before you-"

"Oh, will you shut up with your fake story? It was a fantasy. Get over it. Eventually it was all going to come out and you know it"

"Maybe at the apocalypse, but that's probably never going to happen."

"I have to go, it's an emergency."

"What? You don't awaken War, then vanish. We have things to deal with."

"If I don't go…"

"What?"

"Everyone on the nethernet is going to be laughing at a video of me singing while wearing a tutu riding an inflatable unicorn. I have to go."

"Go?" War snatched Beelzebub up by his throat. "Go?"

"Fine, you can come with."

From inside his house, sitting in his underwear, Archie Bragg watched as the Devil and War vanished. His only thought was, "What they hell do I tell the insurance people?"

EASY

Blunt looked at the phone and then up at Morgarth and Twist. "That's it then?"

Morgarth's head bobbed up and down in agreement while Twist continued to scowl.

"Fate of the afterlife saved by threatening to post a silly video onto some stupid social media site-"

"Platform," Morgarth interrupted.

"Right, social media platform, because that was the important bit," he picked up his cup and winced as he tasted unpleasant, and now cold, coffee. Then he put it down again. "I suppose I'll go home then," he said.

"What?" Twist asked, "what are we supposed to do?"

"I don't know. What's it got to do with me?"

"But the Grim Reaper isn't here either," Morgarth said, "and we know nothing about this place."

"That's not my problem. You're a bloody demon."

"Fine," Twist said, "demons aside, you're not just going to abandon a lady in trouble, are you?"

"What was the first thing you did when you arrived in Gloomwood again? Oh yeah, I remember now, you cut a woman's skull in half like a watermelon. Right, try to make me out to be the bad guy here," Blunt said, snatching his hat off the tabletop. He put the hat on and tugged at the brim.

Twist and Morgarth stared at the hat and Blunt scowled at them, "What? Something on my hat?"

"I think you'll find I'm the bad guy here, Detective Blunt," Beelzebub said from behind Blunt.

"Jesus!" Blunt said as he leapt out of his chair and rolled away on the floor.

"That sort of thing is really not going to help," The Devil said as he watched Blunt scrambling away. "You can either give me the phone or my big blue friend here will take it."

"No, I won't," War said, "I'm not your bloody servant. Sort your own mess out and when you're done, I'll decide what to do about you."

"Now isn't the time to bicker about the fact that you can't hurt me anyway," Beelzebub said.

"Oh, we'll see," War said before looking around the shop at the gawking customers and bellowing, "out!" They scattered like crows from a gunshot.

"Blunt, you're a remarkably stupid individual, even for a mortal. The phone, or you will suffer-"

Blunt stood up and flicked the collar of his coat up. "No."

"No? Well then, I guess we'll do this the hard way, Morgarth, get the phone."

Morgarth was still sitting at the table. Her enormous eyes blinked as she looked backwards and forwards from Blunt to the Devil. "No," she said.

"No? You are the head of the Demon elite. You will obey," Beelzebub snapped his fingers at her.

"No, I'm not. You said we could stay here. You gave us the choice and we have free will here so, no. You can stick it up your big red-"

"Fine, you, reaper woman, I can still save your soul. You get the phone," Beelzebub barked at Twist.

"Can you?"

"Of course I can, I'm the Devil."

Blunt looked at Twist, who took a sip of her coffee and placed it on the table. "Don't listen to him Twist, he said it himself, he's the Devil."

She stood up and took hold of her scythe. "I've no reason to believe he can do anything, but I've no reason not to give him a chance. I mean, as you said, the first thing I did here was, how did you put it again? Oh yes, chop open someone's skull like it was a watermelon."

Blunt inched towards the counter where, crouched down on the floor, were the two suspiciously happy baristas. They weren't so happy now.

"Is there a back door?" Blunt asked.

"We can all hear you," Twist said from across the room.

"Yes," a four-armed barista said, pointing with two of her arms to a door on the other side of the counter.

"Blunt, give me the phone, and then at least something good might come of this. Oh, and I won't have to cut your head in half," Twist said, standing up.

He dove across the counter, and she launched herself across the room.

Blunt scattered cups and coffee as he fell across the coffee bar and landed on his side with a thud. Something internal crunched, but he kept moving towards the door and burst out of it into the street. His coat caught on something and he realised it was his own rib that was poking out of his chest as he stumbled forward. It hurt, but through gritted teeth he told himself, "you're dead, don't need lungs when you're dead," before breaking into a stumbling run.

Twist appeared at the door as he turned out of the alleyway into the street.

Beelzebub stood behind her. "Run after him then."

"I don't run after people. I'm a reaper," Twist said.

"A woman after my own heart," Beelzebub said with a grin, "not literally of course. If you were after my heart you'd have a hard time finding it. Do you know where he's going?"

"Back to the seawall and the jetty."

"Why would he go there?" Beelzebub asked.

"He thinks the demons will help him."

"Ridiculous. Though it makes for a more dramatic last stand. I will give him that."

DYING

"Is this it?"

"Yes. Now normally I would appear and make a dramatic entrance. Lots of fog and mist, I like to go 'wooo' as well but it seems pointless as I've been here all the time. Would you like me to wooo?"

Ted was curled up in a ball on the floor of the cabin. "Don't I get to see the mortal world one last time?"

"Oh no, you'll be dead long before we get there. You're a teddy bear. Physically I'm surprised you made it this close. We just need to cross the veil. I could do a countdown."

"I hate you," Ted whimpered.

Then he sneezed.

The Grim Reaper stepped forward and drew from his robes a cylinder. It was a little narrower than the tube that sits inside a kitchen roll, but otherwise suspiciously similar. He looked through one end of it and then placed it against the single button eye of the Teddy Bear. "Walk into the light Jeremy."

The door opened with a bang and the howling storm from outside made itself known. Sharon stood in the doorway in her bright yellow cagoule which flapped in the wind. "Oh, bad time?"

"Not for me."

"So he's dead then?"

"Yes, all dead."

"Is that a toilet roll?"

"Don't be ridiculous, it's a kitchen roll. Ugh, if you're using this for loo roll I don't want to know what you've been eating."

"So am I going all the way to the mortal realm or are you going to go back and save the day at the last minute?"

The Grim Reaper picked up the teddy bear and slipped it inside his robe, then he took a seat on the crate Ted had been perched upon. "You mean ride in on chariots of fire to save everyone like a hero?"

"Well, that would be the dramatic thing to do."

"It's not very neutral though."

"This again. If you're neutral, and Gloomwood is the afterlife you built, then isn't saving it still neutral, anything you do there is neutral by definition. It's in a bubble of neutrality."

The Grim Reaper clicked a finger against his teeth. "They'll be fine."

"Will they?"

LAST STAND

War watched Blunt run by the front of the coffee shop where he was leaning against a wall waiting for things to be over and smirked. He remembered everything from his time in Gloomwood. A few hundred years seemed like a lot when it was everything but he was War, eternal and everlasting, and he knew in a few weeks it would feel like a ten-day beach break at an all-inclusive that he got on a cheap last-minute deal. Still, he had enjoyed being Petal. Especially in the more recent times where violence was more something he could do if he wanted, rather than the terrible addiction he couldn't escape.

He pushed off from the wall and followed Blunt, slowing to a quick walk when he realised he was in danger of overtaking the detective and then stopping as they reached the seawall and the crowd of toys. He could hear Blunt shouting at them.

"You've got to make a stand or we'll all be cast into oblivion," he shouted at them.

A small grey rabbit in a tuxedo looked up at the panting detective. "You realise we've all just come from Hell? Being cast into oblivion isn't that scary for us, in fact, given the choice of Hell or the abyss most of us would probably pick the abyss."

"But you don't need to. You have this place. The Grim Reaper will welcome you and you'll be able to be dead like the rest of us."

"No offence meant, but you don't seem that happy. Maybe oblivion wouldn't be too bad for you either?" The rabbit asked.

"It's not about me. What about all those other people?"

"You mean all those complete strangers."

"Those people who are good and bad. The people who haven't run over here to set fire to you all with pitchforks-"

"Oh, is there gardening," the rabbit asked.

"Uh, no, everything's dead, that's not the point."

"Yeah, listen, we'd help, but the truth is we can't do anything. This," the rabbit used its paws to wave up and down its tuxedo, "is what you get now. What's a fluffy bunny going to do to help?"

"Demon magic?" Blunt said, his voice reaching a pitch that he wasn't in control of.

"Ooh, that would be amazing. We could shoot balls of fire, or dark matter, from our furry backsides and send Beelzebub back to Hell."

"Could you? You can't, can you?" Blunt said.

"No, we can't," the rabbit said, turning to the other toys, "come on, we've gotta get out of here. This idiot has brought Beelzebub back, and he's going to be even more annoyed than last time. I don't know about you, but getting smote doesn't float my boat! Hah, I should write that down... can't hold a bloody pen though, can I?" The rabbit walked away talking and laughing with the other toys around it.

"You should just give the phone back and use the time left to say goodbye," War said.

Blunt turned around and put his hands in his coat pockets. "Petal, how could you turn on us all?"

"I'm not Petal," War said in a low rumble, "when the Devil took away Johnson he broke the man you call Petal. He'd been strong for so long, so very long, but nothing lasts forever."

"When you say War, do you mean the horseman of the apocalypse?"

"Yes, you've heard of me then?"

"I've... yes, I've heard of you. So, are you here to take the phone from me?" Blunt asked.

"Nah, this is pretty amusing, and this place was pretty good to me."

"Are you going to stop Beelzebub?"

War rubbed a hand across his clean shaven head and sighed for a moment, looking as he had just a few hours ago. "I'd love to tear that pointed headed tool apart, I really would, but there are rules and if I break them, then there's a lot more than this tin-pot afterlife that would be in danger. Beelzebub's a nasty piece of work but he is doing his job."

"Destroying this afterlife is his job?" Blunt asked.

"Well," War shrugged, "I think the Teddy Bear thing was the job, but really, this place shouldn't be here. Grim, that's Death, he was bending the rules making it. I mean it could exist but,"

"Stop talking War," Beelzebub's voice carried from further up the road, "it doesn't matter now. I'm far too angry to consider what you're thinking. And Grim had his chance. He gave his phone to this mortal, and now he's threatening me. Threatening me, the Devil."

Blunt pulled the phone from his pocket and held it up. "Take another step and I'll press send."

Twist was standing at the Devil's side with a small smile on her face. "If you send it, then it's over for you," she said. "You'll have played your card so we'll just destroy you all."

The Devil nodded. "She's right, it's not the bargaining chip you think it is. True, you'll embarrass me, humiliate me, but that's hardly going to help you, is it?"

"I think I'll keep it then," Blunt said, "we're at a stalemate."

The Devil laughed. It was a sound that sent shivers up Blunt's spine.

"You'll keep it?" Beelzebub said, still laughing, "Twist, take the phone, please."

Twist leapt forward, covering the distance between Blunt and her before the detective knew what was happening. Her scythe swung and then stopped, the end of it slicing into Blunt's cheek but moving no further.

Blunt had his eyes closed and as he opened them he saw War's hand holding the Scythe. The big blue figure lifted it with Twist still attached.

STORMY WATERS

"We could go to a karaoke bar. It's been so long since I've done karaoke," The Grim Reaper said.

"I hate karaoke," Sharon replied, "do you really have my coins?"

"No. I gave the last coin away."

"What? One of my coins?"

"It was an emergency."

"You didn't give it to the bear, did you? He doesn't deserve that."

"No, no, I gave it to someone worthy."

"Can we please turn around?"

"Fine."

A WATERY DEATH

"You better run," Twist said through gritted teeth as War lifted her up into the air. She hung on to the scythe as the big man chuckled.

"You change sides too often. Is that why they call you Twist?" War asked.

Blunt didn't have time to wait; he turned and leapt up on to the wall while Beelzebub approached.

"I do so hate getting my hands dirty Detective, but at this point I've little choice. Give me the phone."

"I won't," Blunt said, "one more step and I'll jump."

"How will that help anyone?" The Devil asked.

"I'm pretty sure the phone is waterproof. So I'll be at the bottom of the Styx, ready to press send at any moment. Are you much of a swimmer?"

The Devil scowled, then his hand was around Blunt's throat.

Blunt felt himself lifted off the ground before he even knew the Devil had moved. He could smell the flesh around his neck burning. "You don't threaten the Devil, mortal."

Music played, and the Devil frowned. With his free hand, he reached into his pocket and retrieved his phone from his jacket pocket. "Beelzebub speaking, I'm in the middle of something right now."

"I know," Twist said.

Beelzebub turned to see War and Twist standing on the edge of the seawall.

"What are you doing?" He shouted, his horns growing larger and his flesh flickering with flames.

"She's calling you," War's voice boomed, "now Beezy, listen carefully. If anything happens to these people, I'll be posting that message and a lot more."

"You can't stand up to me. You're a horseman and I'm the Devil. There are rules."

War smiled. "Call me Petal," he said as he took the phone off Twist and placed her on the ground. Then he turned and dove over the seawall, disappearing into the purple roiling waves far below.

☠ THE RETURN OF DEATH ☠

Grim stepped off the boat and walked up the jetty to find Blunt on his knees. Standing by his side was Morgarth and Twist Lenworth.

"Fear not," Grim said, "I have returned to save the day."

"You bony bastard," Blunt said, his voice a hoarse whisper.

"Well, that's not the greeting I expected, but this is a stressful time. I have a plan, but it's going to take all of us working together. First, did you get my message? And have you used my phone to call in the cavalry like I suggested?"

"What cavalry?" Twist asked.

"Gabriel, of course. He owes me a favour and hates Beelzebub. Didn't you read the messages on Bitter? Why else would I give you my phone?"

"It wasn't because of the videos on Bitter?" Morgarth asked.

"What? How would that help? Where's Beelzebub?"

"He's gone," Blunt said, standing up, "it's over. While you were hiding on your boat. Where's Ted?"

"Over? What do you mean it's over? I've come back to save you all and pose heroically."

"Where's Ted?" Twist asked.

"Ah, Ted is Dead, hah, I'm a poet, and I didn't even know it. He's here," The Grim Reaper withdrew a cardboard tube from his pocket and handed it to Twist. You know what to do with that, I presume."

"I... my time?"

"Some of it is still there. Not all of it I'm afraid, but at least you can go back, if you want to. You can't stay here though. You don't belong."

"I'd say I can't think of anything worse, but I can. This place is still pretty crap though. No offence," she said, directing the last to Blunt.

"None taken," he said with a croak.

"So, it's all over then?" Grim asked, "Why's Morgarth still here?"

"Detective Blunt said that you said we could stay."

"Oh... right then. This will be interesting. Ah, is Petal around?"

"You mean War?" Blunt said, shoving his hat onto his head once again and staring out to the sea.

"Oh, cat's out of the bag then, yes, is he around?"

"No. He..." Blunt stopped as he stared out into the sea.

"He what?" Grim asked.

"He jumped into the ocean to save everyone."

"What? Why did he do that? Oh, this is just perfect. And I used my last coin for this. Detective Blunt, I'm afraid you're a terrible disappointment."

JOHNSON

John Jacob Jeremiah Johnson stood in a small room dazed and confused. He was dressed exactly as he had been when he had stood by Ralph Mortimer as they had watched the group approach them from the Office of the Dead. The man with the smile had approached, and then all he remembered was falling.

Now he was here, holding the coin the Grim Reaper had taken from a box of cereal. Staring at four white walls. The ceiling was white. The floor was white, and time had even less meaning than usual.

A door appeared. It was green. It opened and a stout woman in a yellow plastic raincoat appeared. "You Johnson?" She asked.

"Yes, that's me."

"John Jacob Jeremiah Johnson, the hope that whatever sporting team you support won't suffer a humiliating defeat?"

"I prefer to keep that to myself."

"Do you have a coin?"

"Yes?" He said.

"Well, hand it over," the woman held out a hand.

He shrugged and put the coin in her hand.

"Right. Welcome back to Gloomwood and tell the Grim Reaper that he now owes me three coins. Walk through that door."

"I... okay?"

"Don't forget, three coins."

"Who shall I tell him-"

"Sharon, but he'll know. Right then. Bye," she said before walking through the green door and then it vanished.

A yellow door opened on the opposite side of the otherwise barren white walled room.

DEAD HEADS

"Well?" Crispin Neat asked. Standing over a pyramid of confused heads, Sarah Von Faber held a clipboard. Her own head had vanished, as it often did, so the pencil she was chewing on seemed to disintegrate in thin air. Standing at her shoulders were her assistants, Jean and Paddy.

"She can't answer until her head comes back," Jean said.

Paddy nodded. "Yeah, you just have to wait then when she pops back in again, she says something clever like, 'Eureka' or 'put the kettle on'."

Only someone paying attention, the special attention that requires slow-motion video capture and sensitive equipment, would have noticed Crispin Neat's eyebrow quiver.

"Perhaps one of you would care to offer an opinion."

"Oh, they're dead," Jean said, "don't you think?"

"Definitely dead," Paddy said with a confident nod.

"Good. Grab a wheelbarrow then and we'll give the support group organisers a call. They're going to like this."

ARRIVALS

"It's opening, it's opening, everyone in position," Tomb Mandrake shouted as his team of secret police operatives took positions around the terminal of the Deathport. The veil, the long curtains behind the luggage carousel, twitched and then a figure stepped through.

"Don't take another step," Mandrake said.

"Okay," John Jacob Jeremiah Johnson said, "why not?"

"Where did you come from?" Mandrake asked as figures in black appeared from hidden positions to stand at his side.

"Near the Office of the Dead. What happened?"

"You're from Gloomwood?"

"Aren't you?"

"What do you know about the door?"

Johnson turned around to look back at the door he had stepped through. "It's yellow?"

That's it.

You're still here then?

Fine, we'll return to Gloomwood soon.

Stick the kettle on.

There are many people to thank.

Please imagine me looking meaningfully into your eyes and slowly saying, "Thank you."

More from Ross Young can be found at rossyoung.ink, including comics, games, and more from the Gloomwood universe. Sign up for the newsletter for free Gloomwood stories.

Printed in Great Britain
by Amazon

21789413R00196